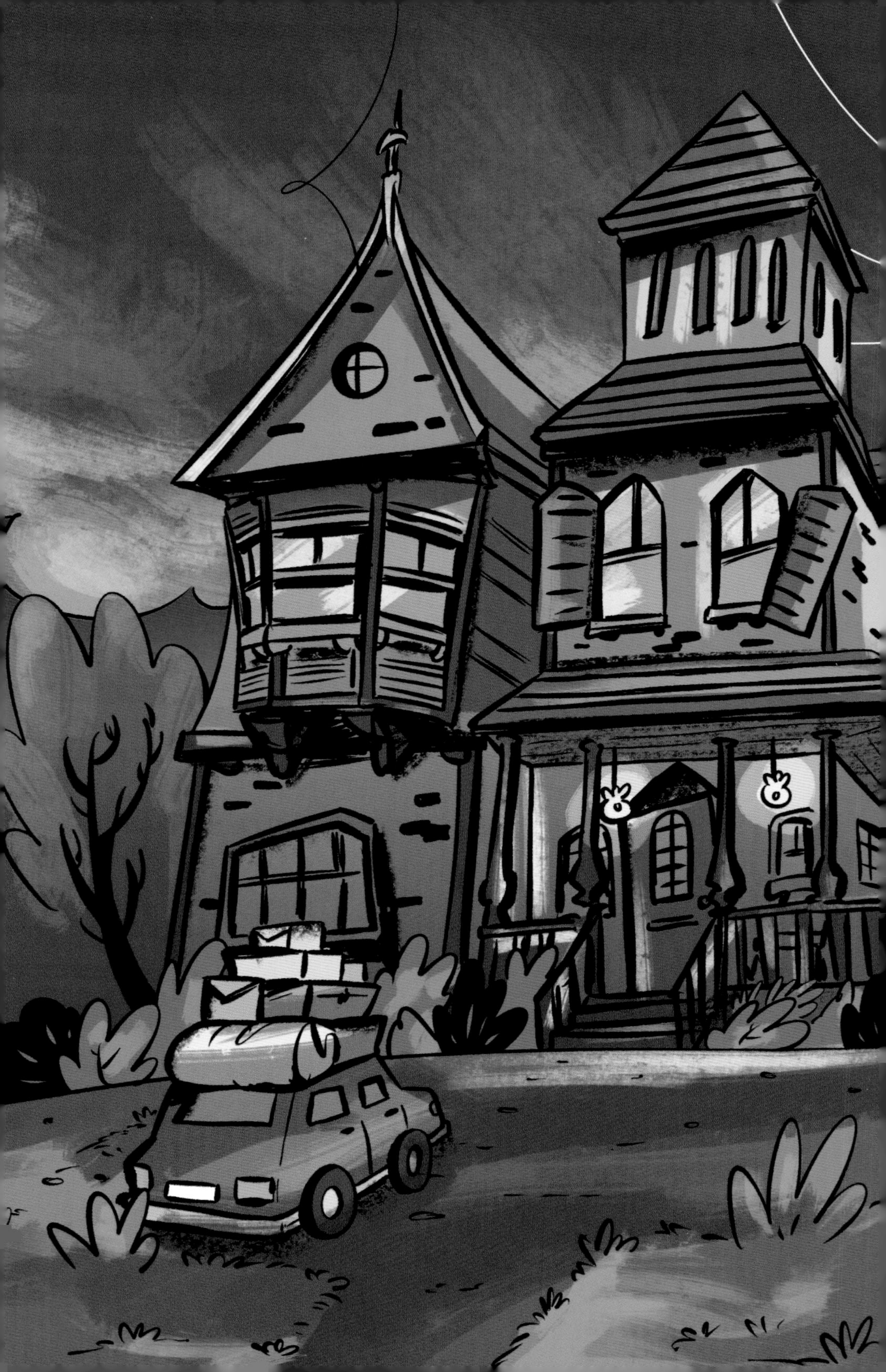

Graphic Novel

Spirited

DAY OF THE LIVING LIV

By Liv Livingston

Illustrated by Anna Volcan at Glass House Graphics

LITTLE SIMON
New York   London   Toronto   Sydney   New Delhi

LITTLE SIMON
An imprint of Simon & Schuster Children's Publishing Division
1230 Avenue of the Americas, New York, New York 10020
First Little Simon edition January 2024
Copyright © 2024 by Simon & Schuster, Inc.
All rights reserved, including the right of reproduction in whole or in part in any form.
LITTLE SIMON is a registered trademark of Simon & Schuster, Inc., and associated colophon
is a trademark of Simon & Schuster, Inc.
Simon & Schuster: Celebrating 100 Years of Publishing in 2024
For information about special discounts for bulk purchases, please contact Simon & Schuster Special
Sales at 1-866-506-1949 or business@simonandschuster.com. The Simon & Schuster Speakers Bureau
can bring authors to your live event. For more information or to book an event, contact the
Simon & Schuster Speakers Bureau at 1-866-248-3049 or visit our website at www.simonspeakers.com.
Designed by Brittany Fetcho • Cover by Manuel Preitano. Illustrated by Anna Volcan at Glass House
Graphics. Assistant on layouts Giulia Balsamo and Roberta Papalia. Colors by Giorgio Antonio
Pluchino, Antonino Ulizzi and Vanessa Costanzo. Lettering by Giovanni Spadaro/Grafimated Cartoon.
Supervision by Salvatore Di Marco/Grafimated Cartoon. • Manufactured in China 0923 SCP
2 4 6 8 10 9 7 5 3 1
Library of Congress Cataloging-in-Publication Data
Names: Livingston, Liv, author, artist. | Glass House Graphics, illustrator.
Title: Day of the Living Liv / by Liv Livingston ; illustrated by Glass House Graphics.
Description: First Little Simon edition. | New York : Little Simon, 2024. |
Series: Spirited ; 1 | Audience: Ages 5–9
Summary: Eight-year-old Olivia "Liv" Livingston loves her town Pleasant Place, but when her family
moves to spooky Gloomsdale, she must learn to adjust to this ghost town where its residents are
all from various decades and centuries, the hall monitors are bats, and some students have fangs.
Identifiers: LCCN 2023004066 (print) | LCCN 2023004067 (ebook)
ISBN 9781665942270 (paperback) | ISBN 9781665942287 (hardcover)
ISBN 9781665942294 (ebook)
Subjects: CYAC: Graphic novels. | Supernatural—Fiction. | Schools—Fiction. | LCGFT: Paranormal
comics. | Graphic novels. Classification: LCC PZ7.7.L596 Day 2024 (print) | LCC PZ7.7.L596 (ebook) |
DDC 741.5/973—dc23/eng/20230705
LC record available at https://lccn.loc.gov/2023004066
LC ebook record available at https://lccn.loc.gov/2023004067

Contents

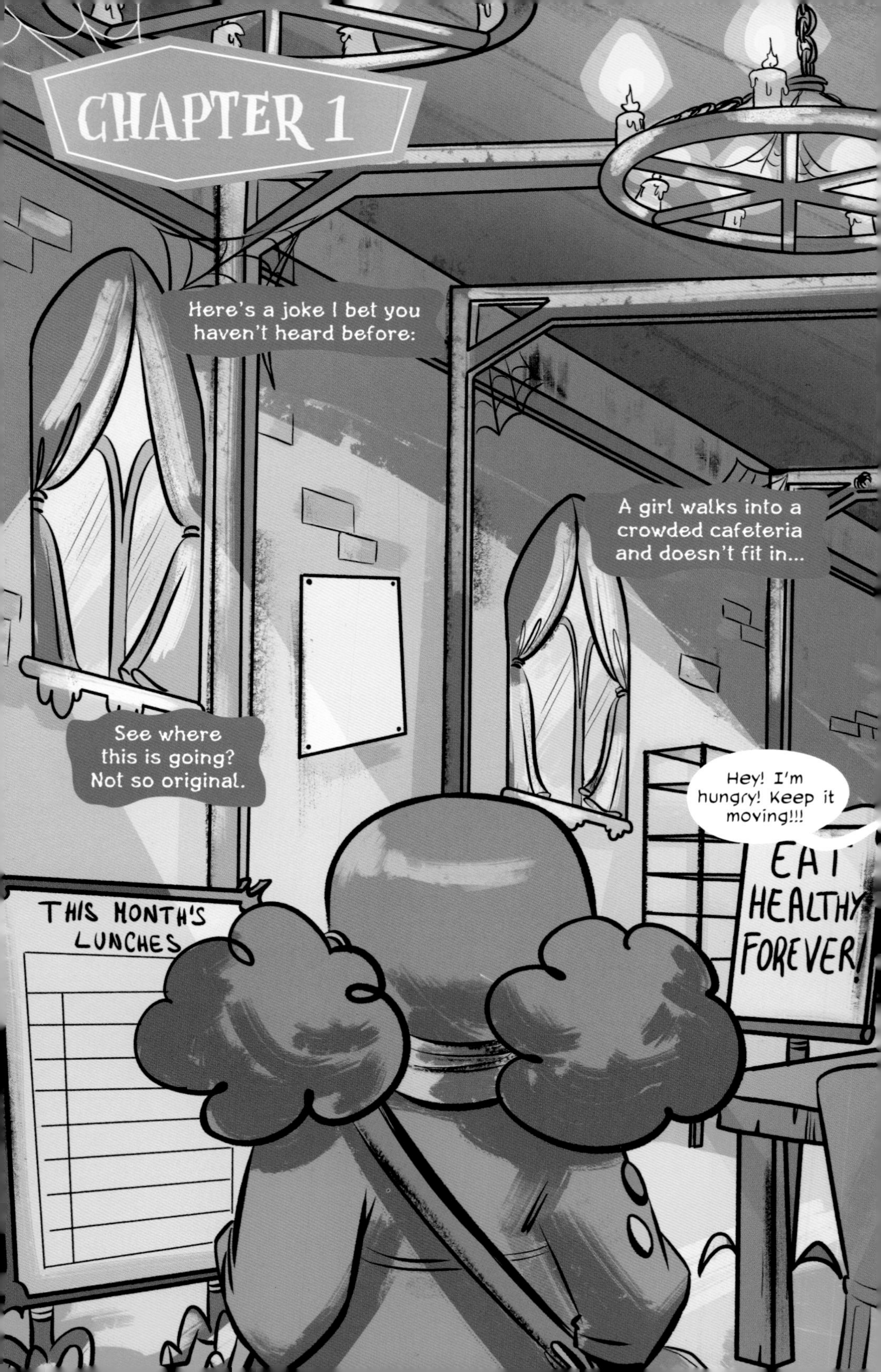
CHAPTER 1
Here's a joke I bet you haven't heard before:
A girl walks into a crowded cafeteria and doesn't fit in...
See where this is going? Not so original.
Hey! I'm hungry! Keep it moving!!!
THIS MONTH'S LUNCHES
EAT HEALTHY FOREVER!

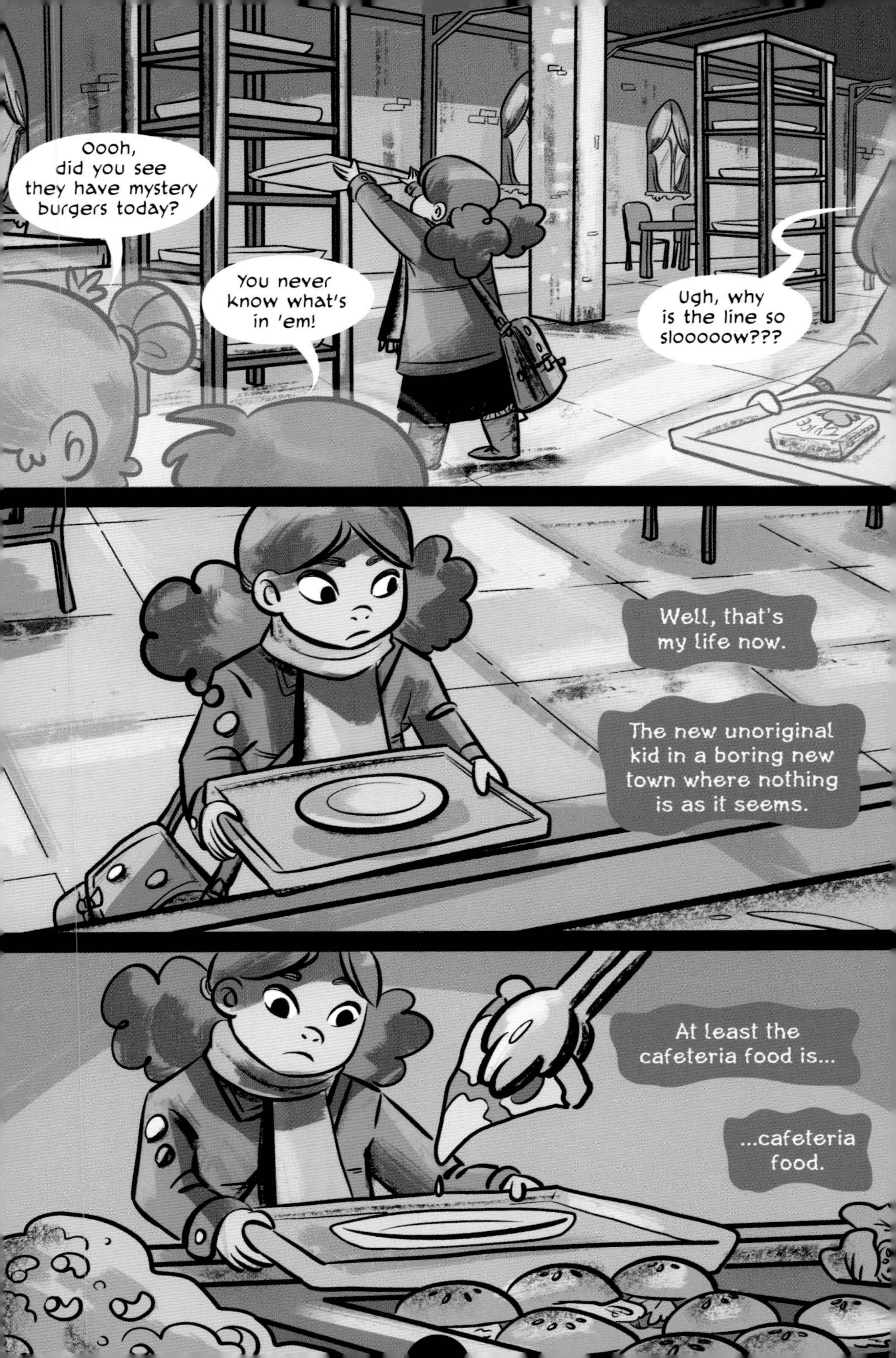
Oooh, did you see they have mystery burgers today?
You never know what's in 'em!
Ugh, why is the line so slooooow???
JUICE
Well, that's my life now.
The new unoriginal kid in a boring new town where nothing is as it seems.
At least the cafeteria food is...
...cafeteria food.

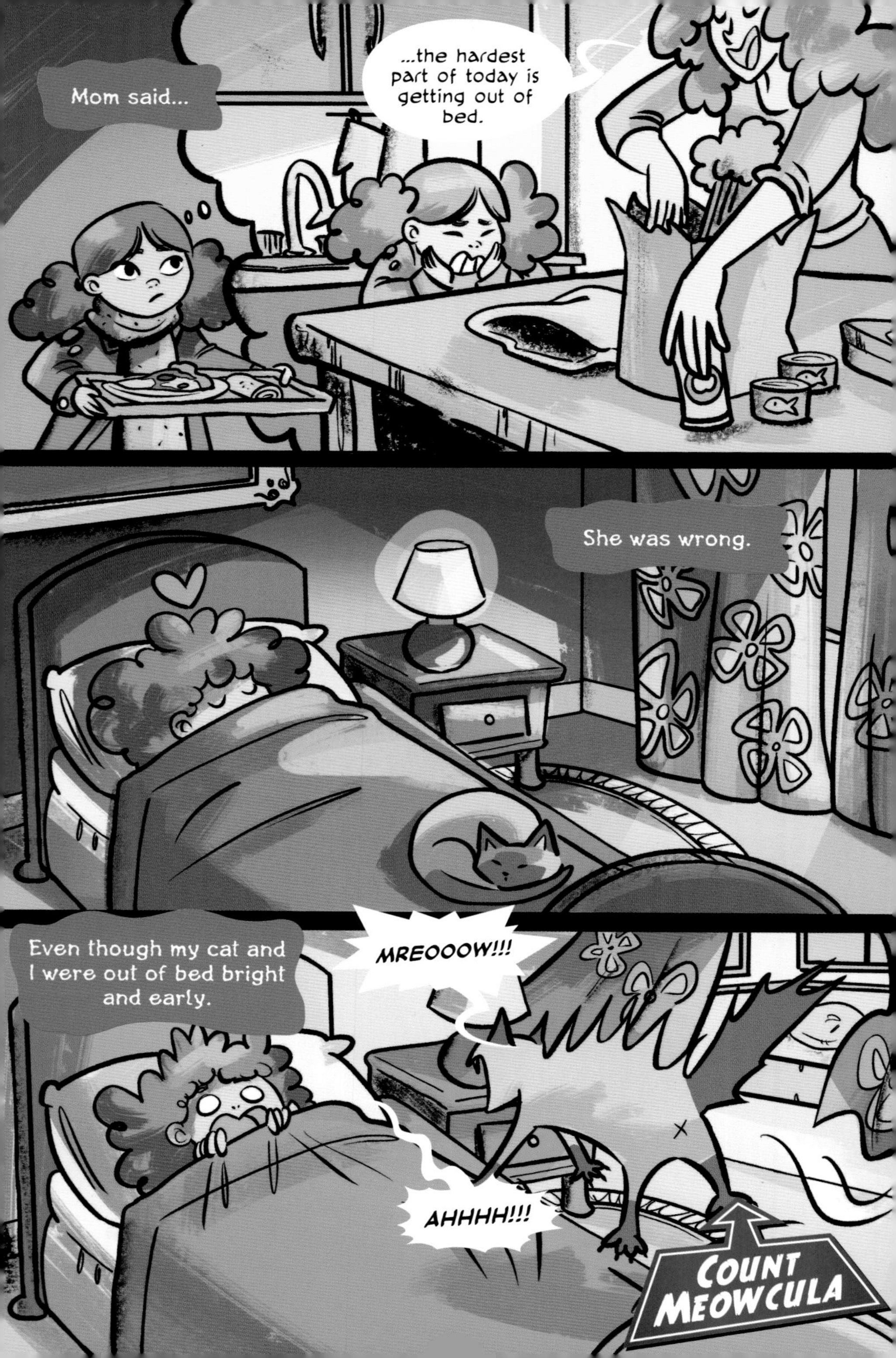
Mom said...
...the hardest part of today is getting out of bed.
She was wrong.
Even though my cat and I were out of bed bright and early.
MREOOOW!!!
AHHHH!!!
COUNT MEOWCULA

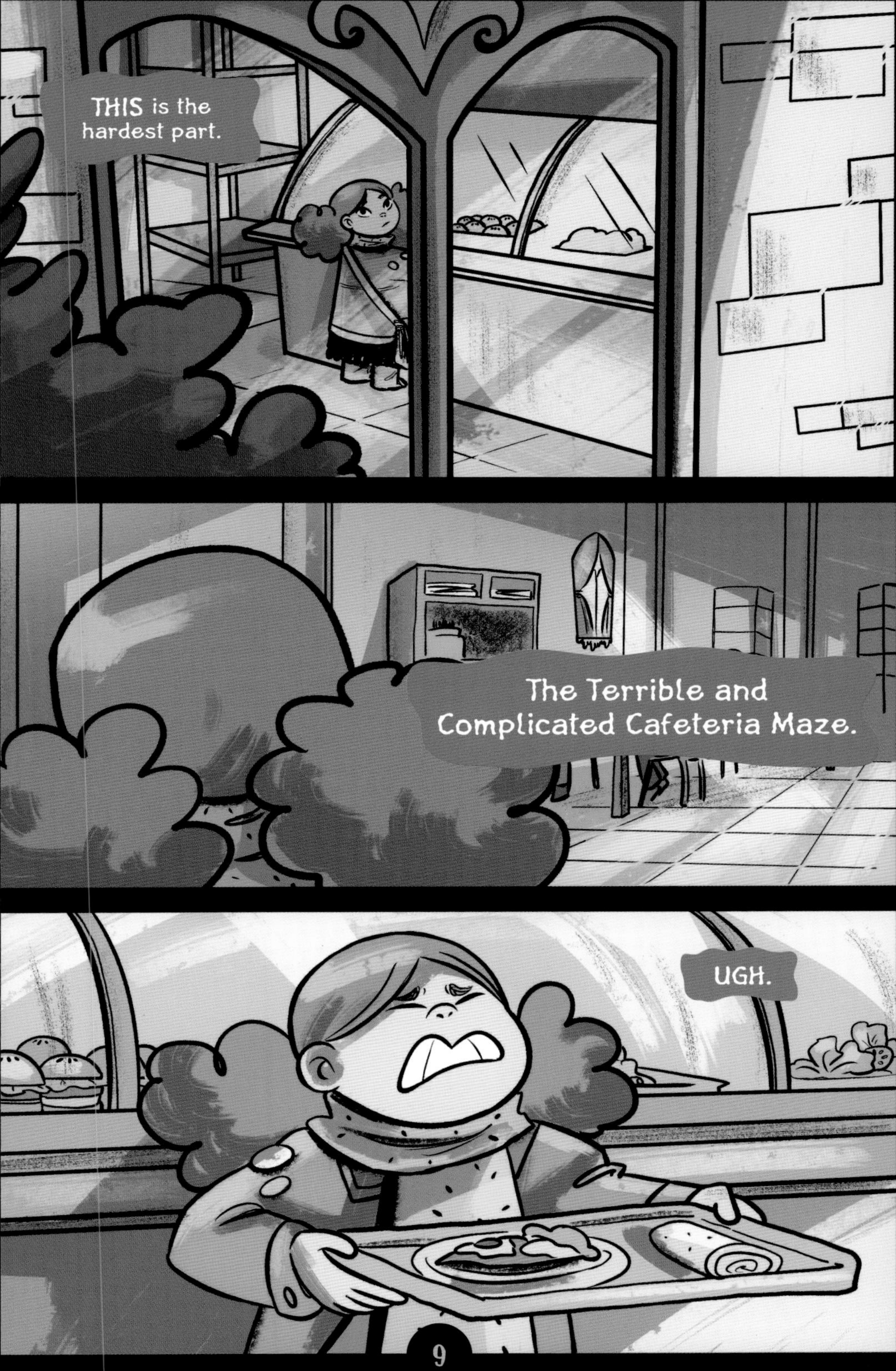
THIS is the hardest part.
The Terrible and Complicated Cafeteria Maze.
UGH.

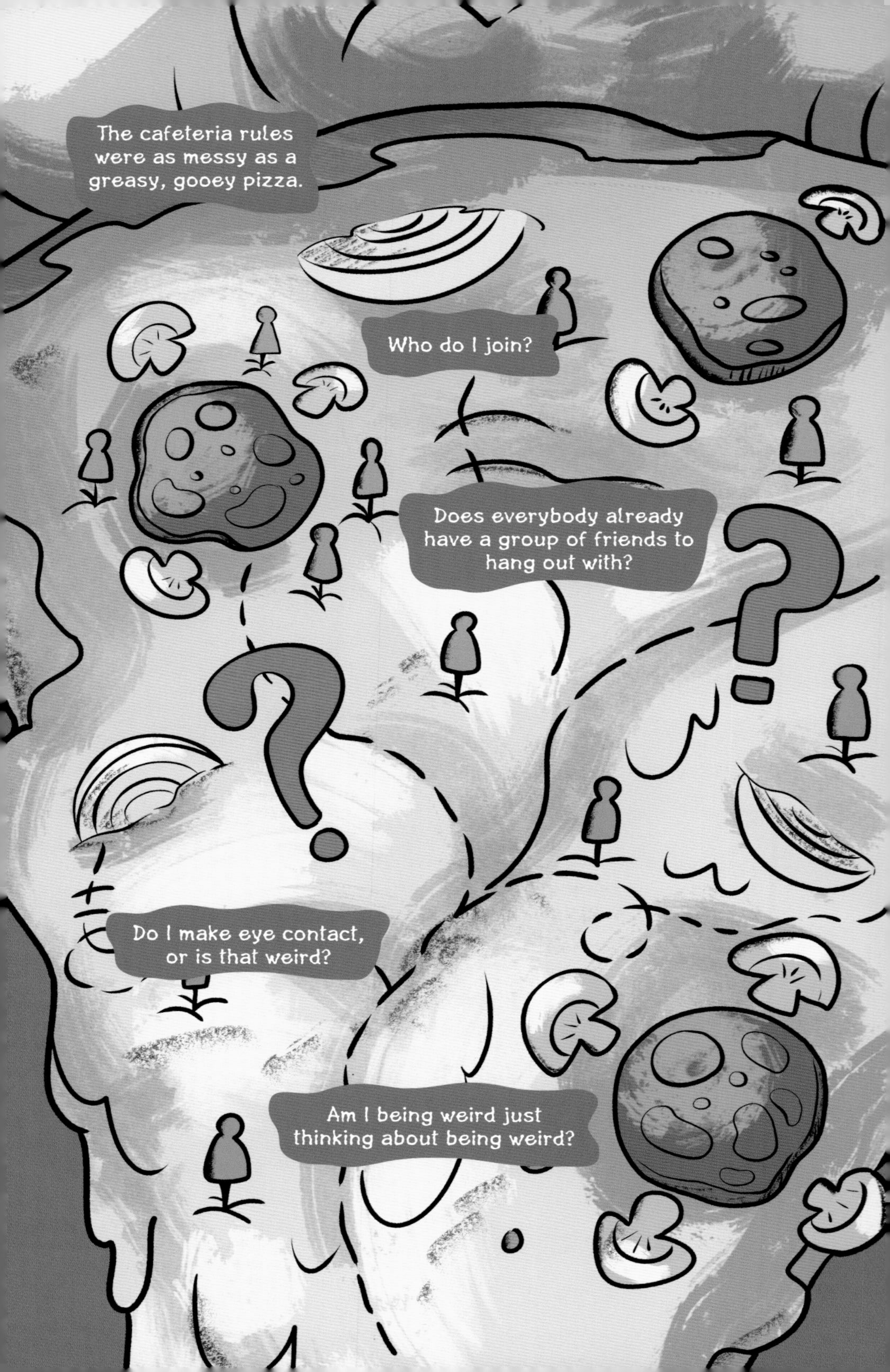
The cafeteria rules were as messy as a greasy, gooey pizza.
Who do I join?
Does everybody already have a group of friends to hang out with?
Do I make eye contact, or is that weird?
Am I being weird just thinking about being weird?

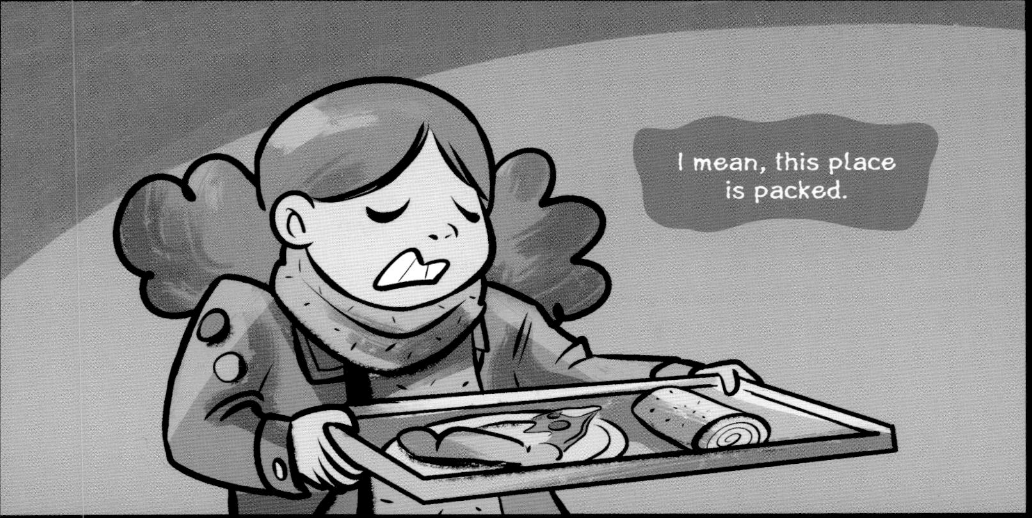
I mean, this place
is packed.

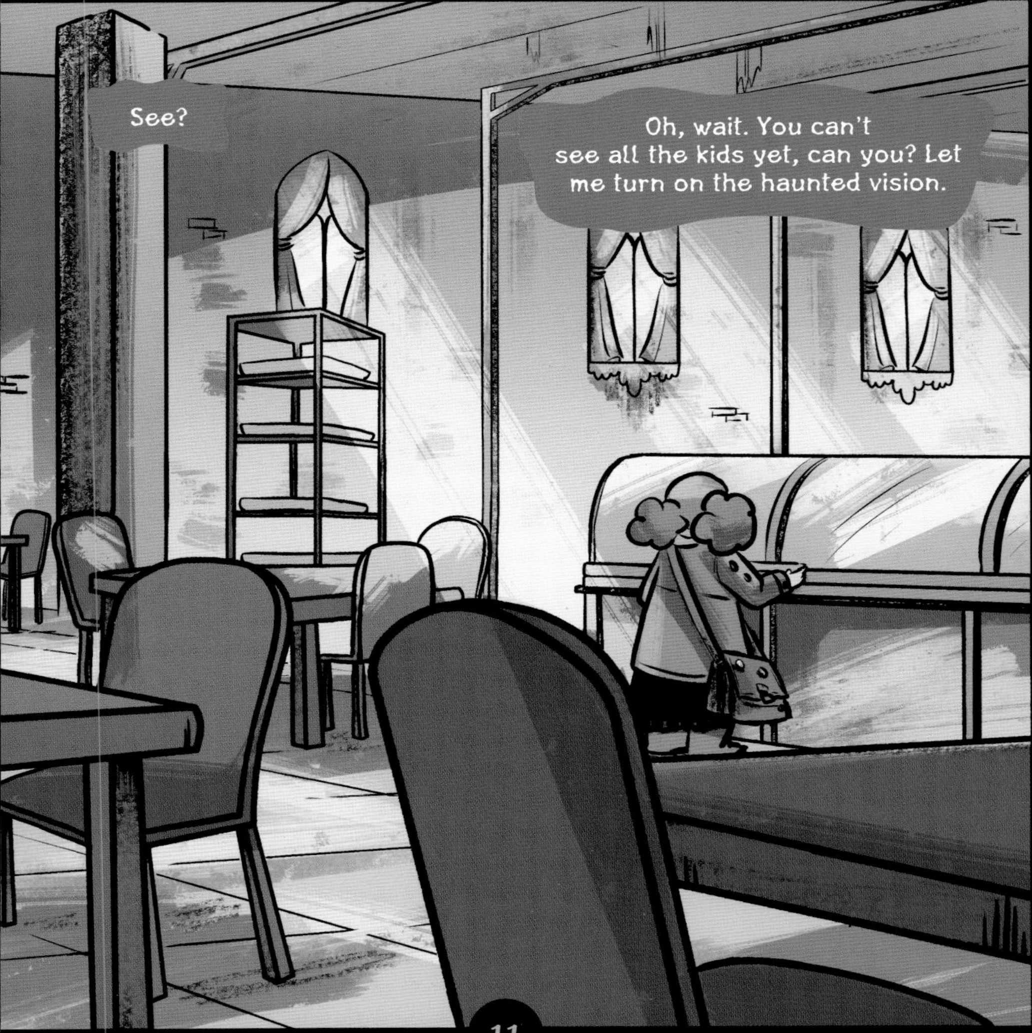
See?
Oh, wait. You can't
see all the kids yet, can you? Let
me turn on the haunted vision.

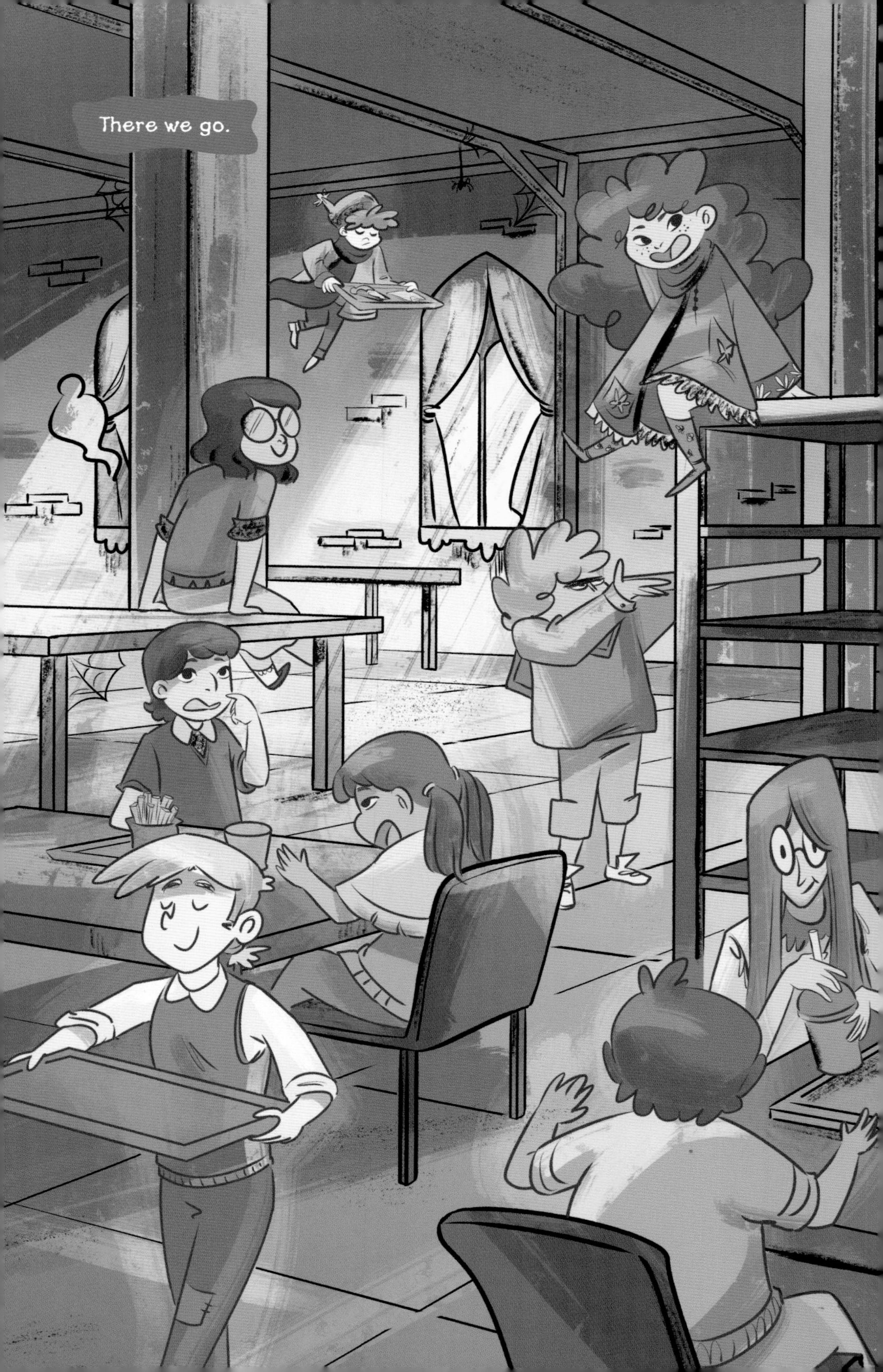
There we go.

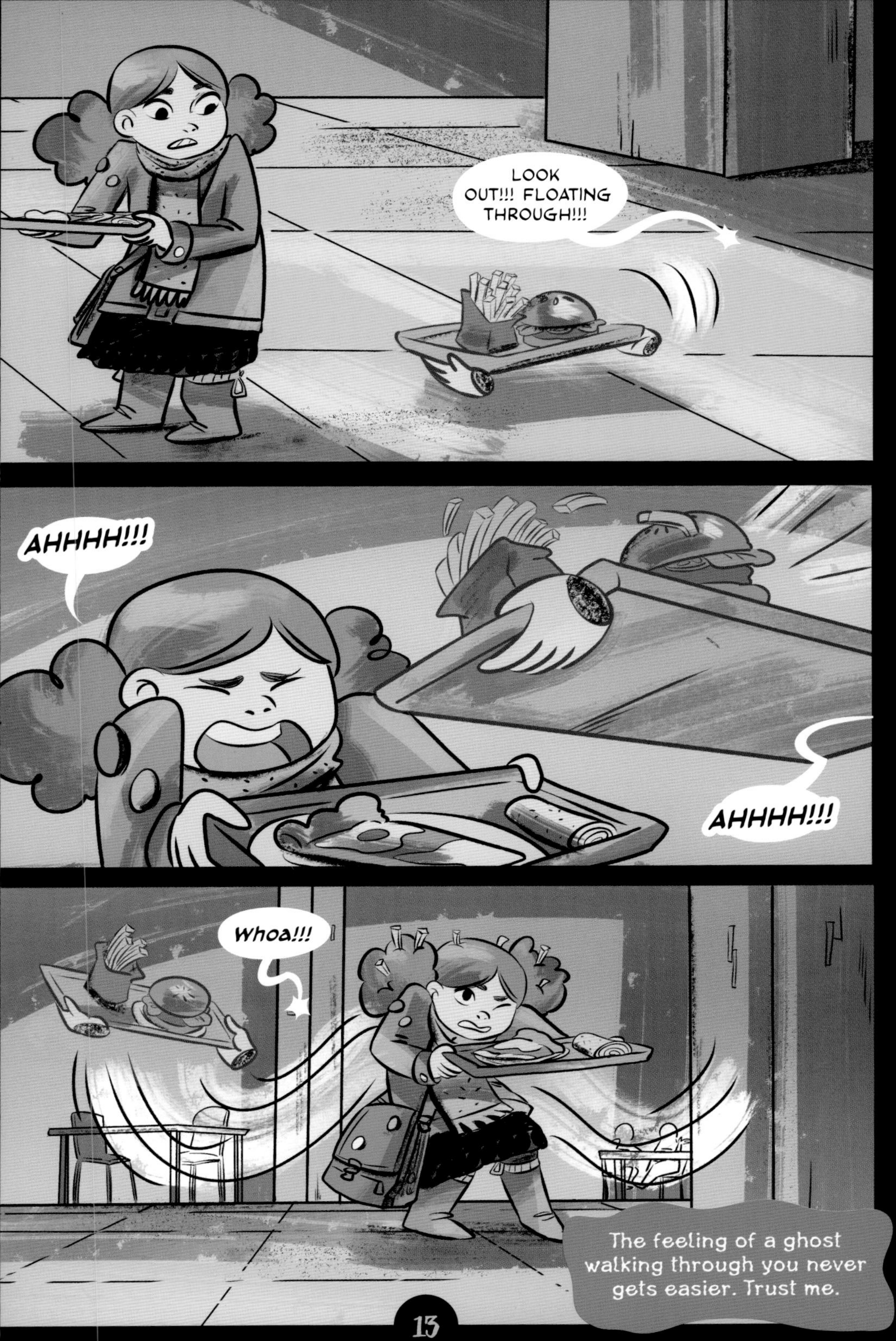
LOOK OUT!!! FLOATING THROUGH!!!
AHHHH!!!
AHHHH!!!
Whoa!!!
The feeling of a ghost walking through you never gets easier. Trust me.

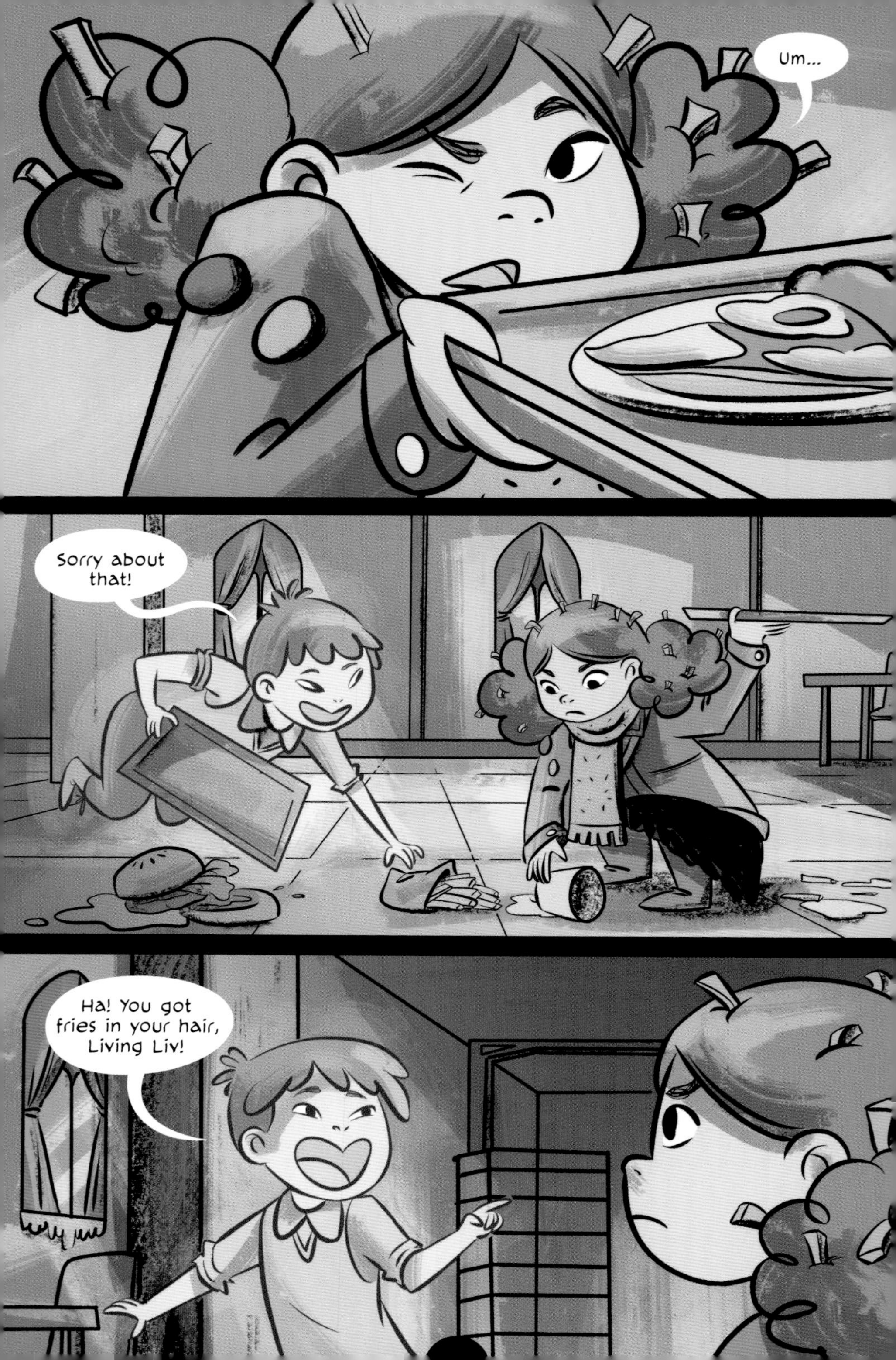
Um...
Sorry about that!
Ha! You got fries in your hair, Living Liv!

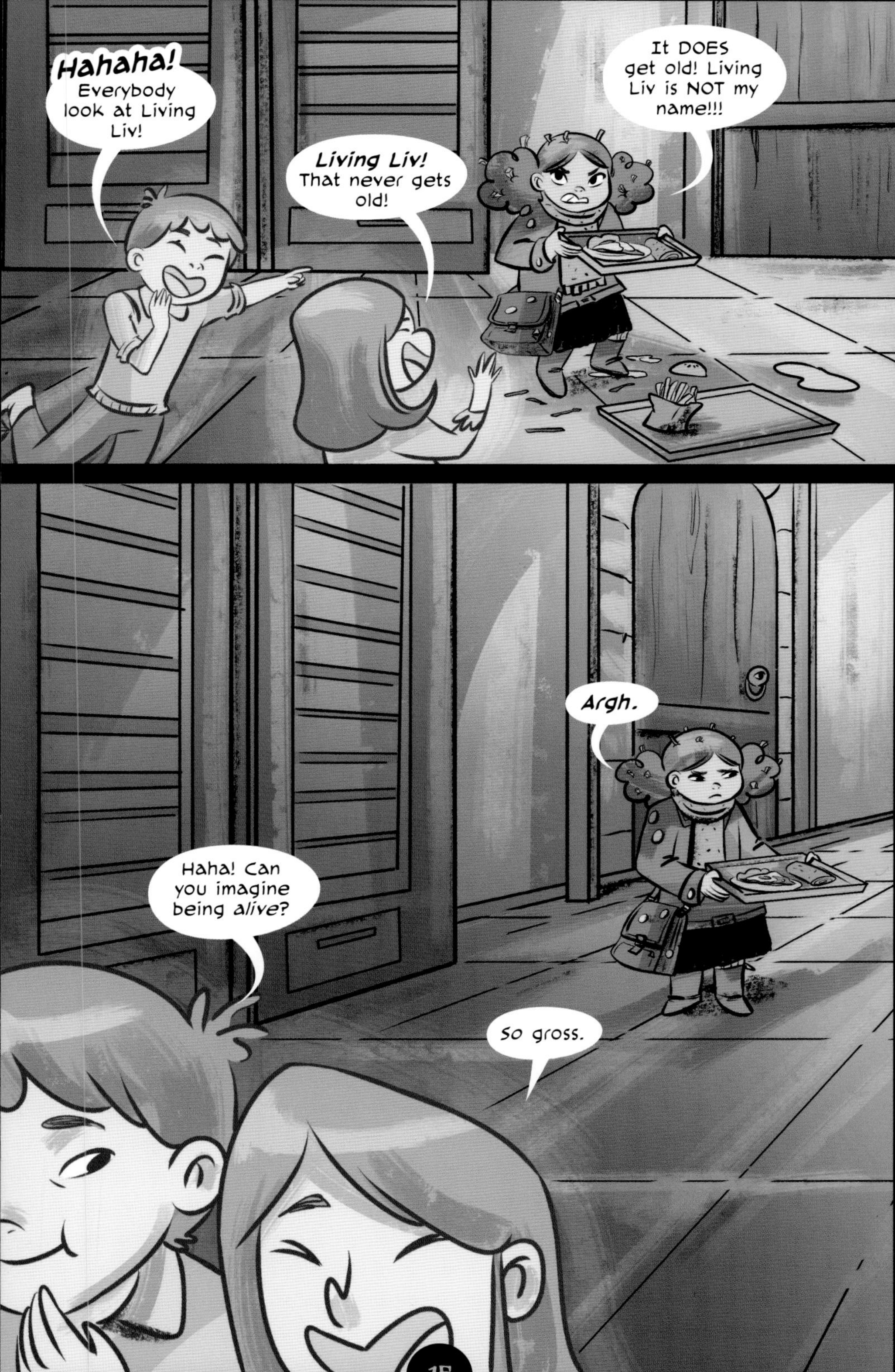
Hahaha! Everybody look at Living Liv!
Living Liv! That never gets old!
It DOES get old! Living Liv is NOT my name!!!
Argh.
Haha! Can you imagine being alive?
So gross.

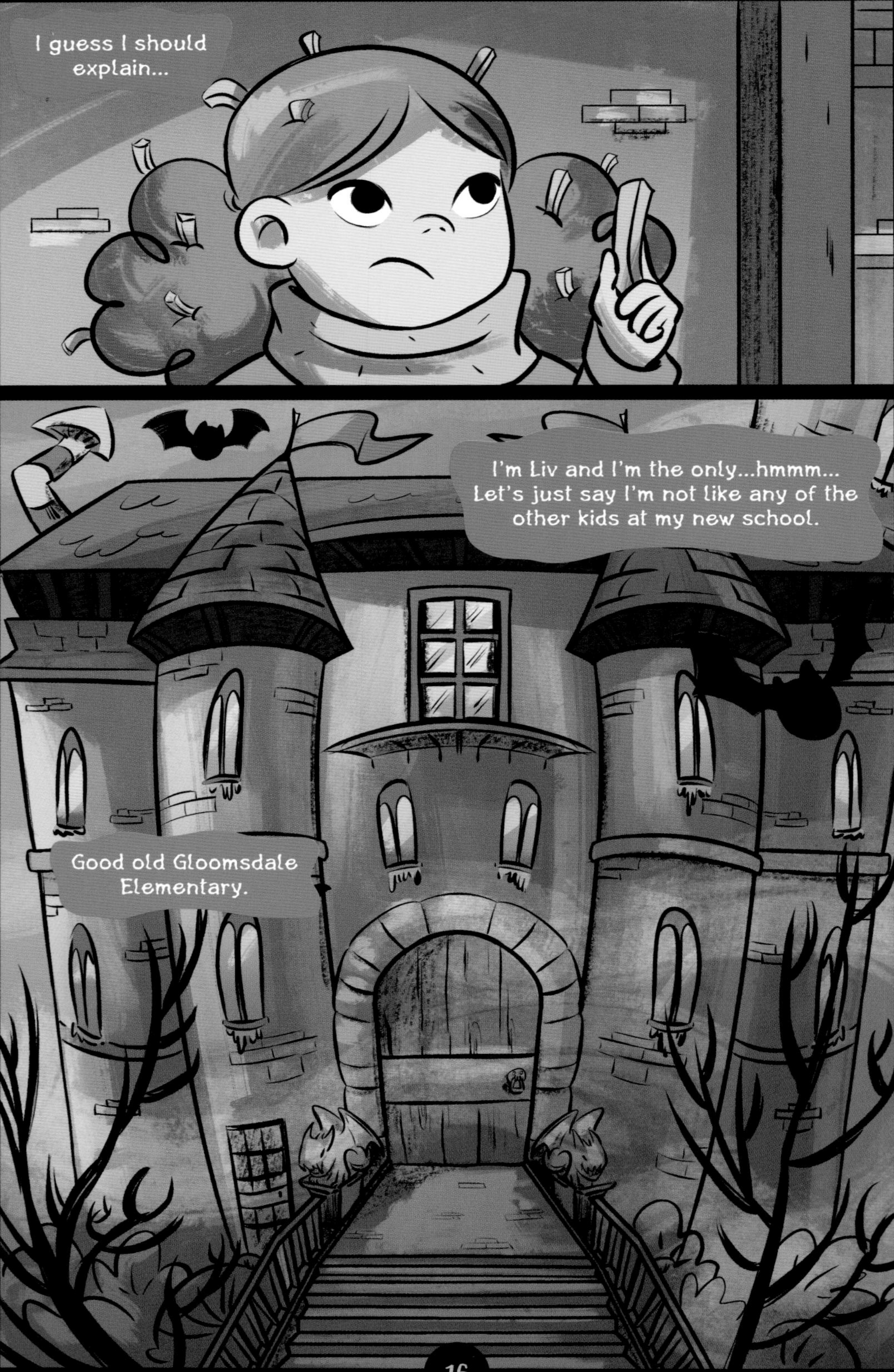
I guess I should explain...
I'm Liv and I'm the only...hmmm... Let's just say I'm not like any of the other kids at my new school.
Good old Gloomsdale Elementary.

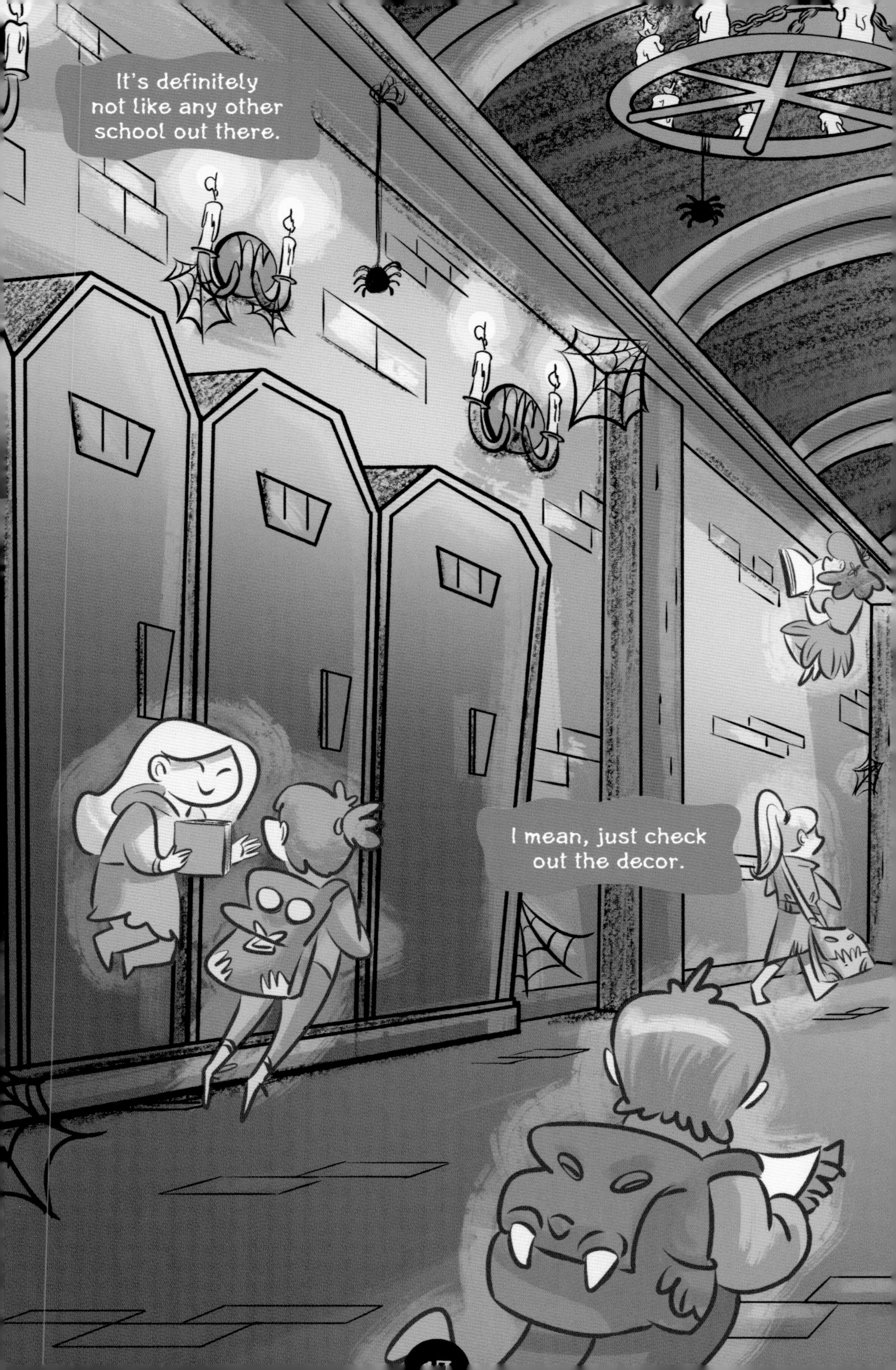
It's definitely not like any other school out there.
I mean, just check out the decor.

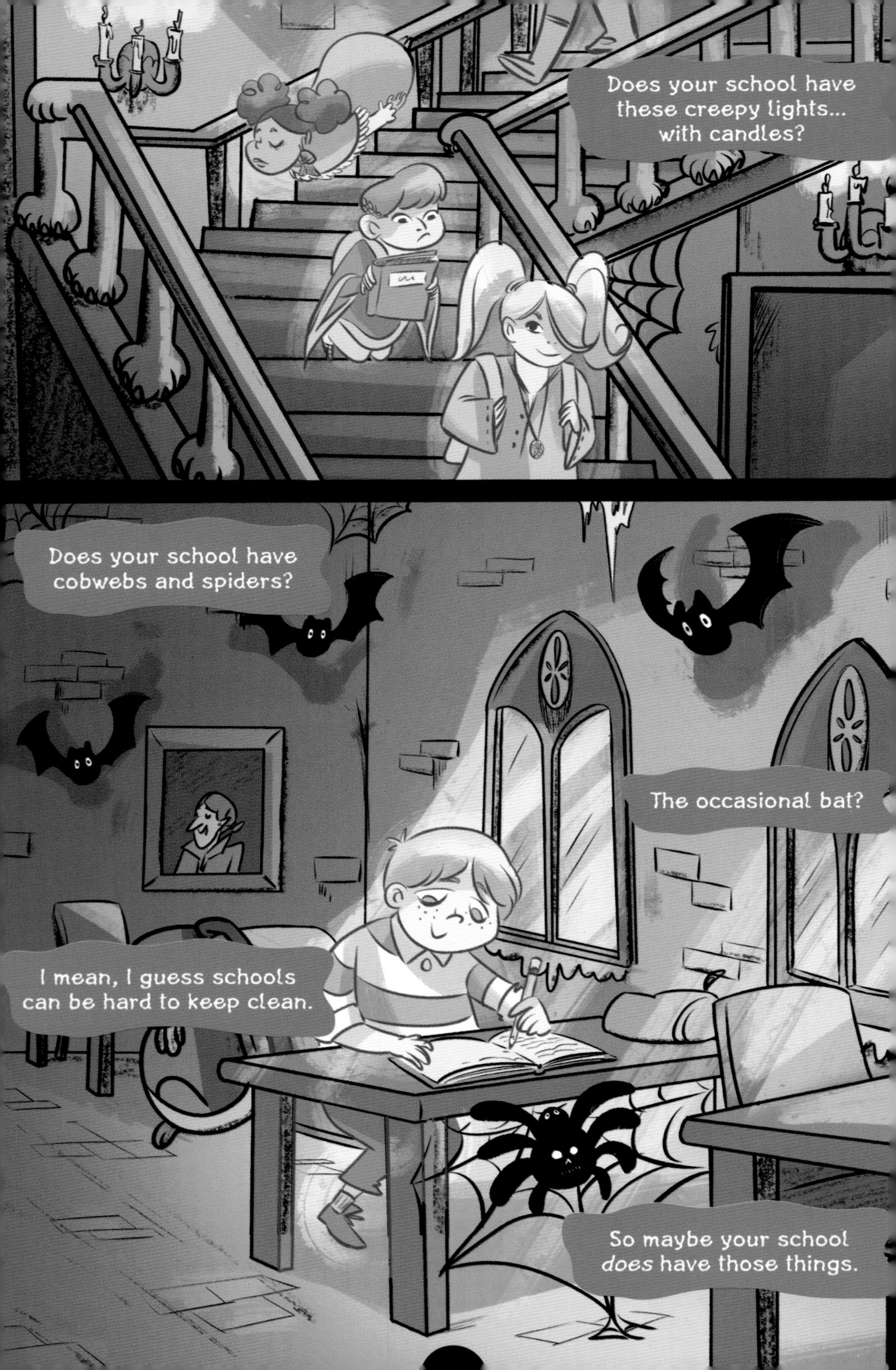
Does your school have these creepy lights... with candles?
Does your school have cobwebs and spiders?
The occasional bat?
I mean, I guess schools can be hard to keep clean.
So maybe your school *does* have those things.

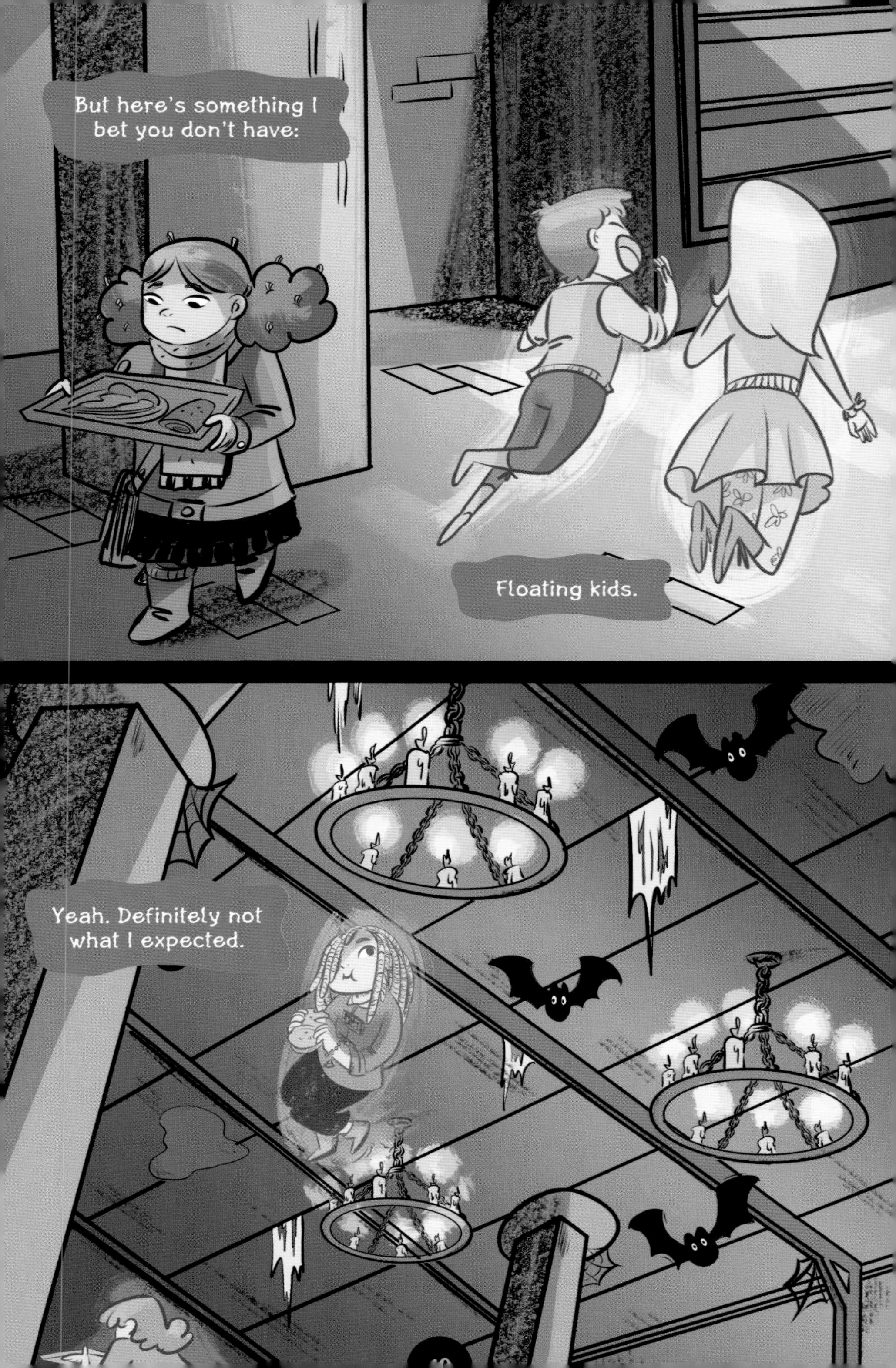
But here's something I bet you don't have:
Floating kids.
Yeah. Definitely not what I expected.

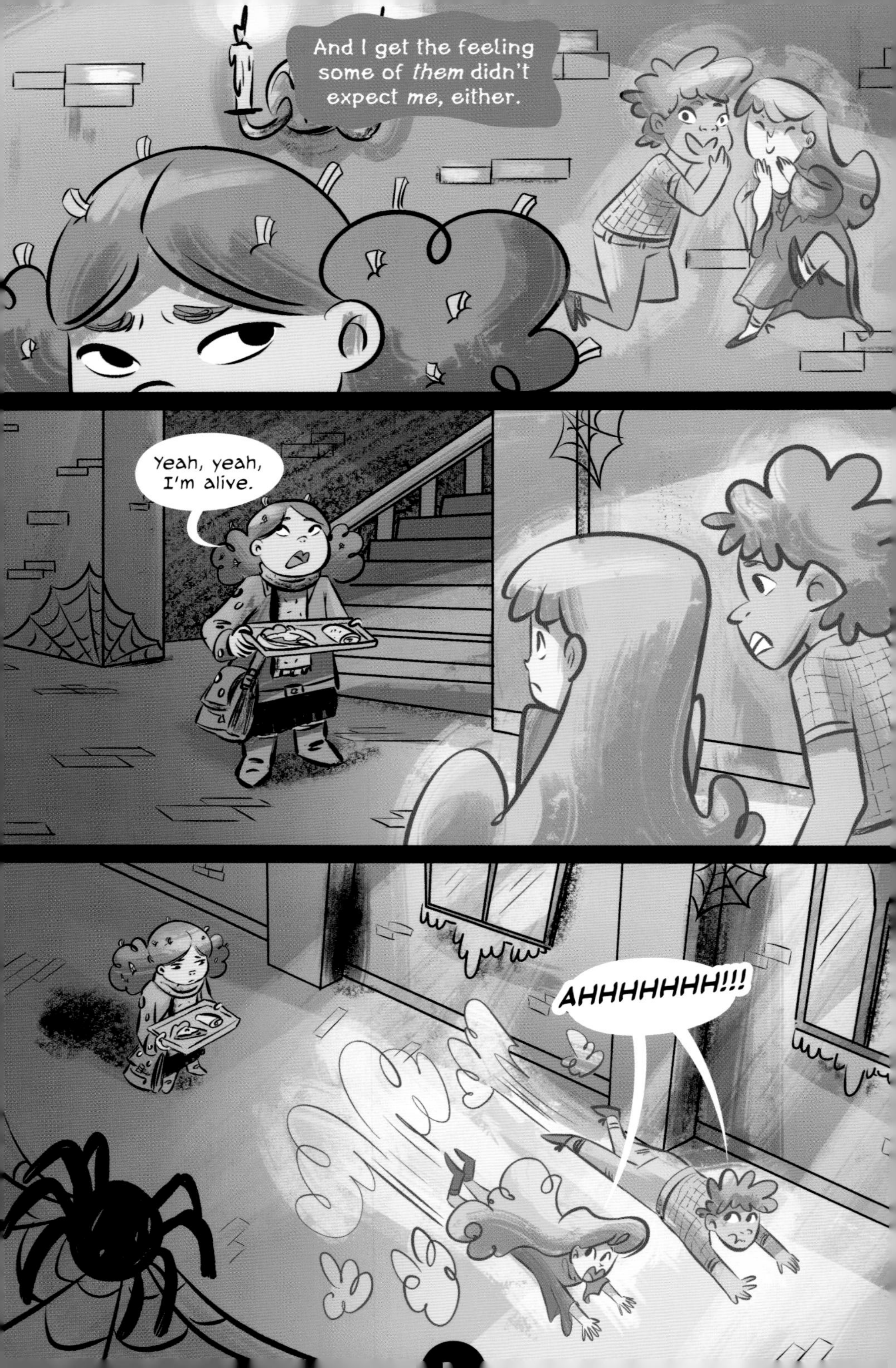
And I get the feeling some of *them* didn't expect *me*, either.
Yeah, yeah, I'm alive.
AHHHHHHH!!!

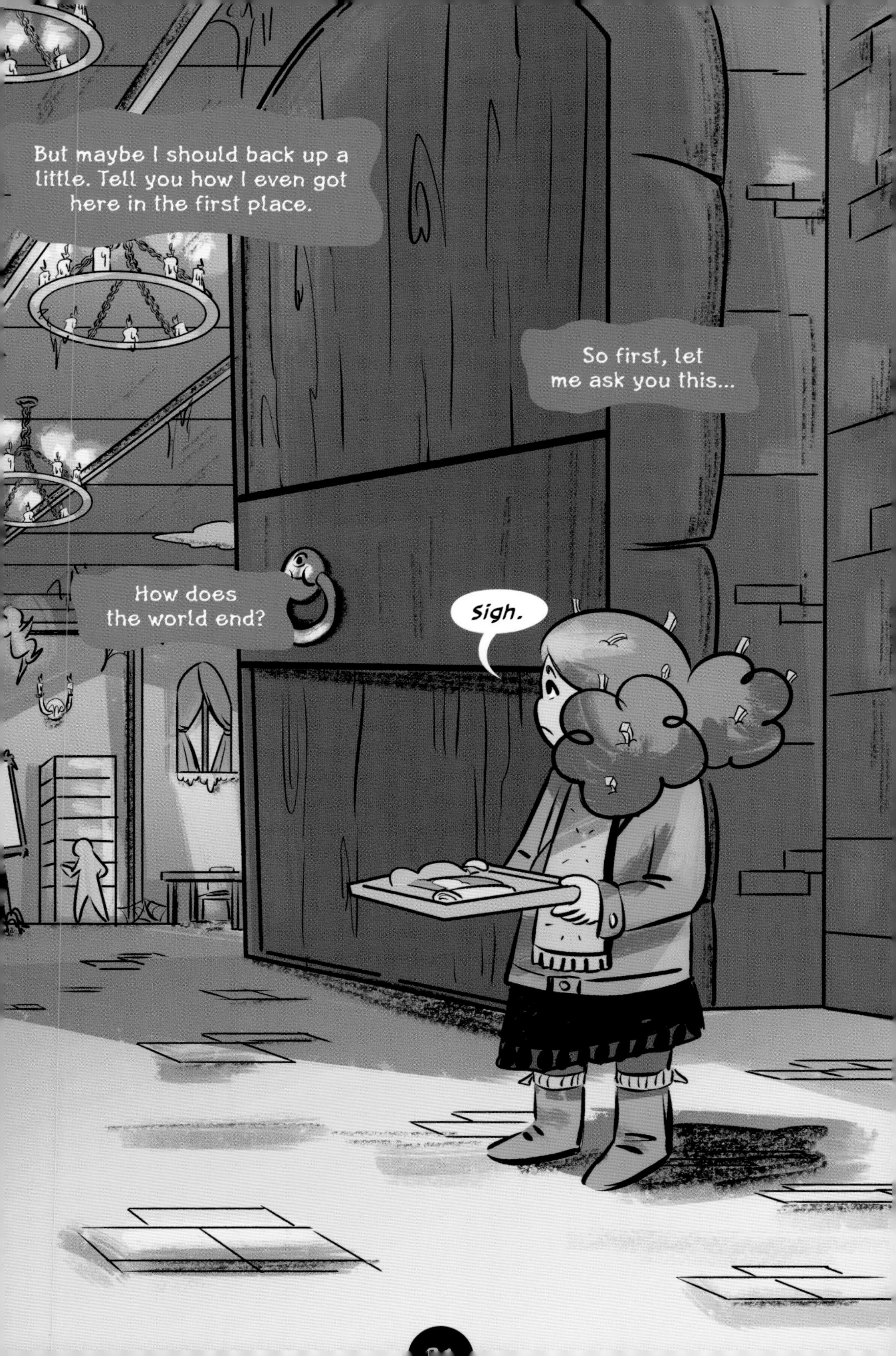

But maybe I should back up a little. Tell you how I even got here in the first place.
So first, let me ask you this...
How does the world end?
Sigh.

CHAPTER 2

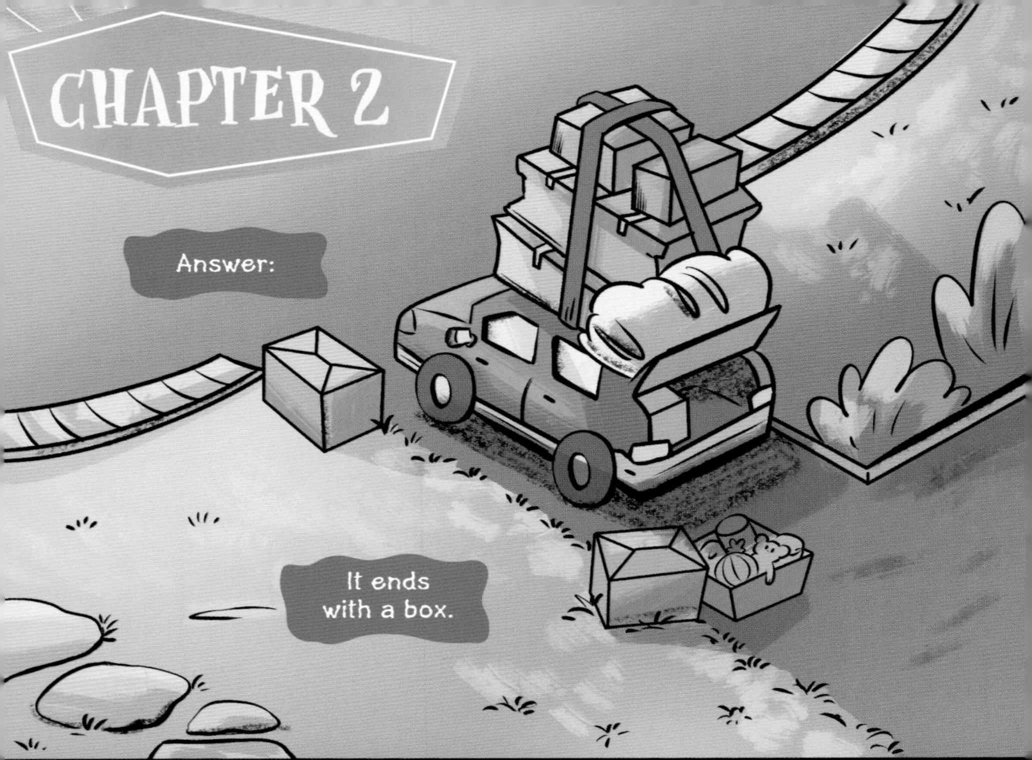
Answer:
It ends with a box.

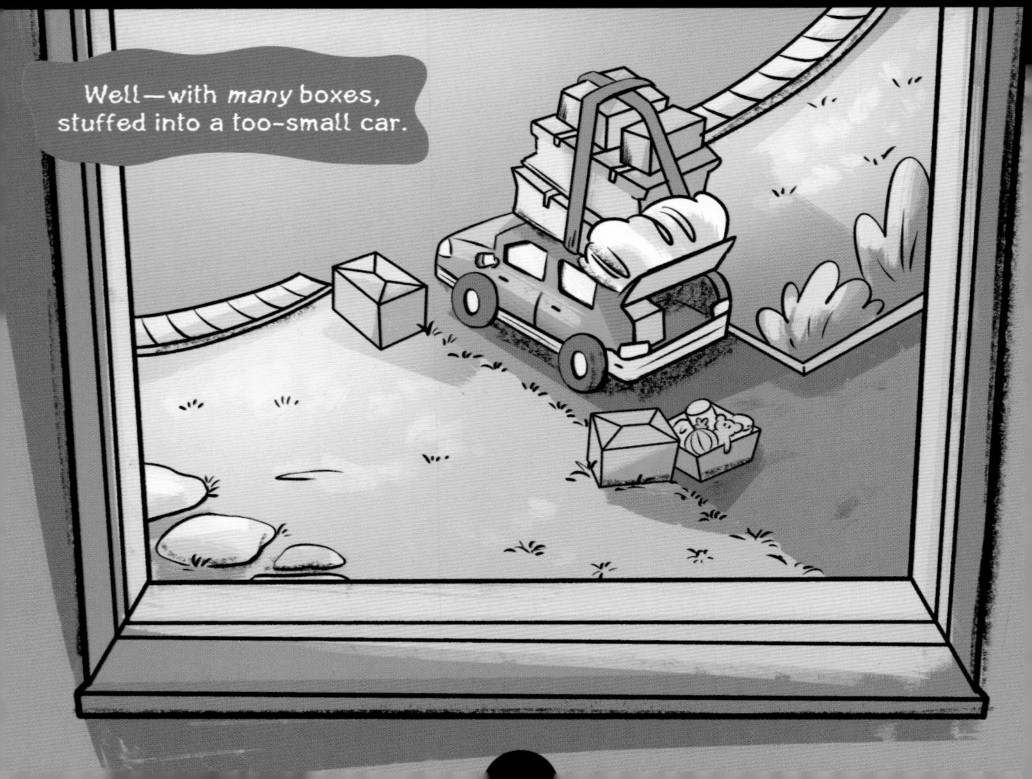
Well—with *many* boxes, stuffed into a too-small car.

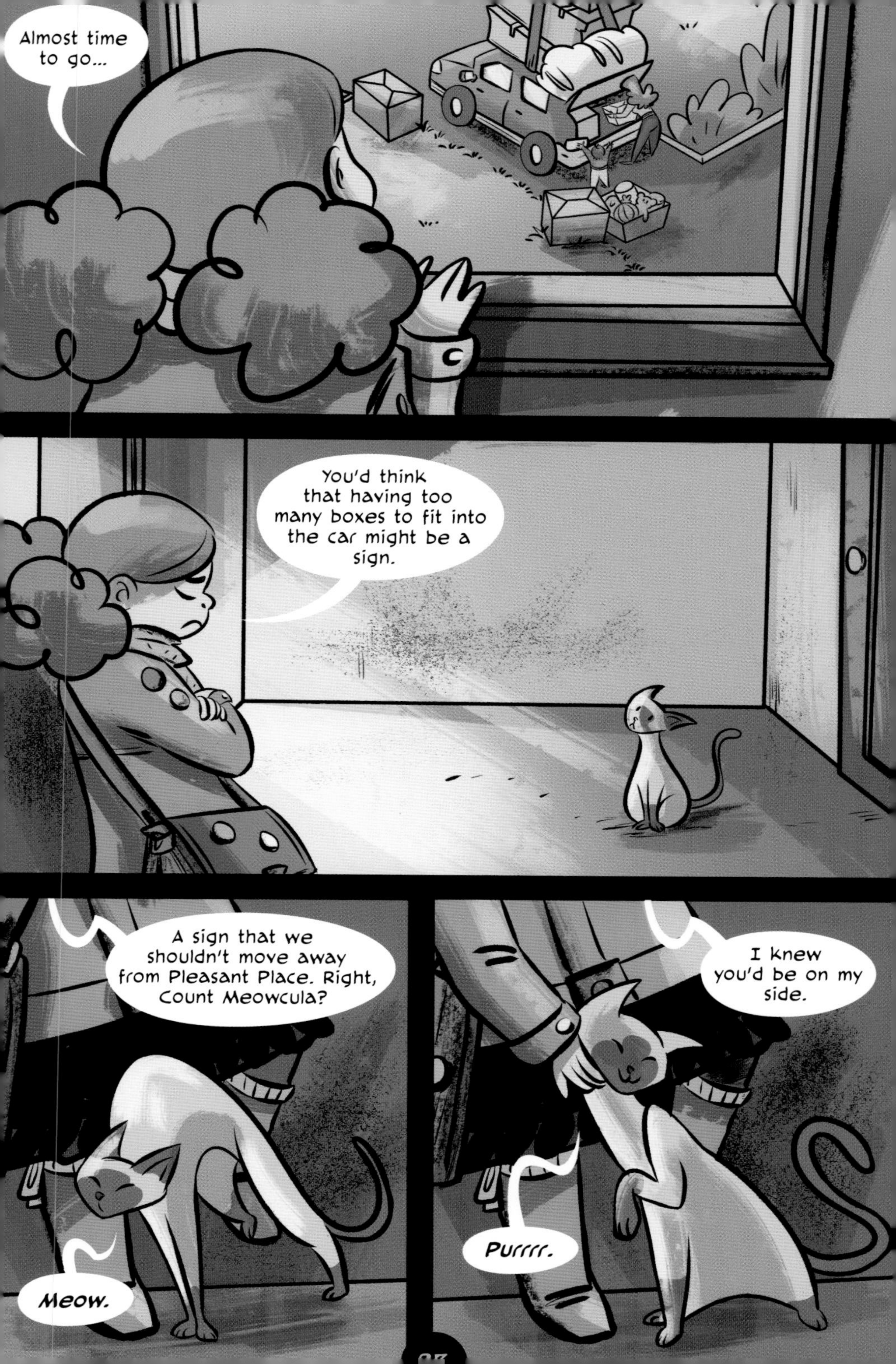
Almost time to go...
You'd think that having too many boxes to fit into the car might be a sign.
A sign that we shouldn't move away from Pleasant Place. Right, Count Meowcula?
Meow.
I knew you'd be on my side.
Purrrr.

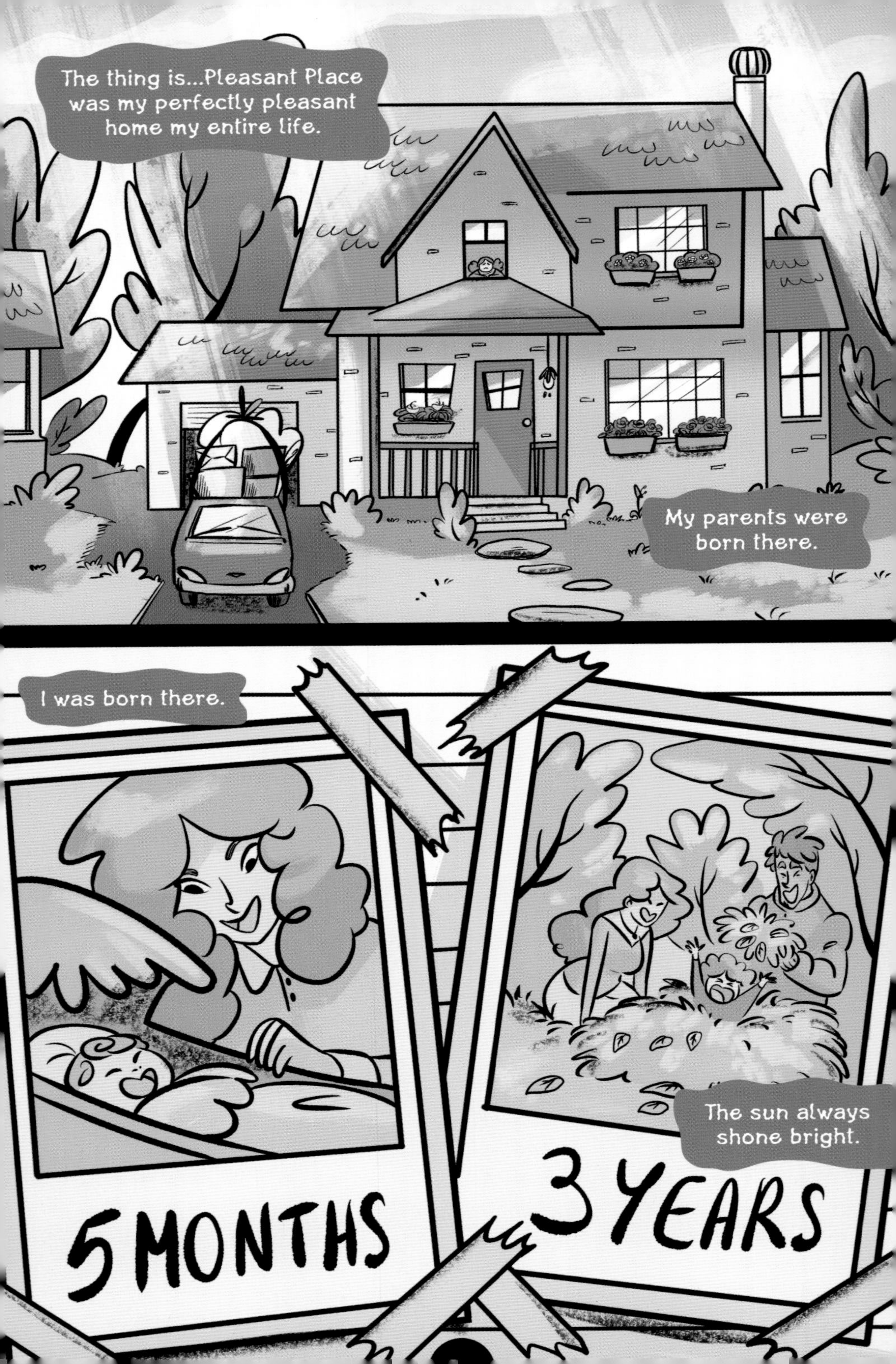
The thing is...Pleasant Place was my perfectly pleasant home my entire life.
My parents were born there.
I was born there.
5 MONTHS
3 YEARS
The sun always shone bright.

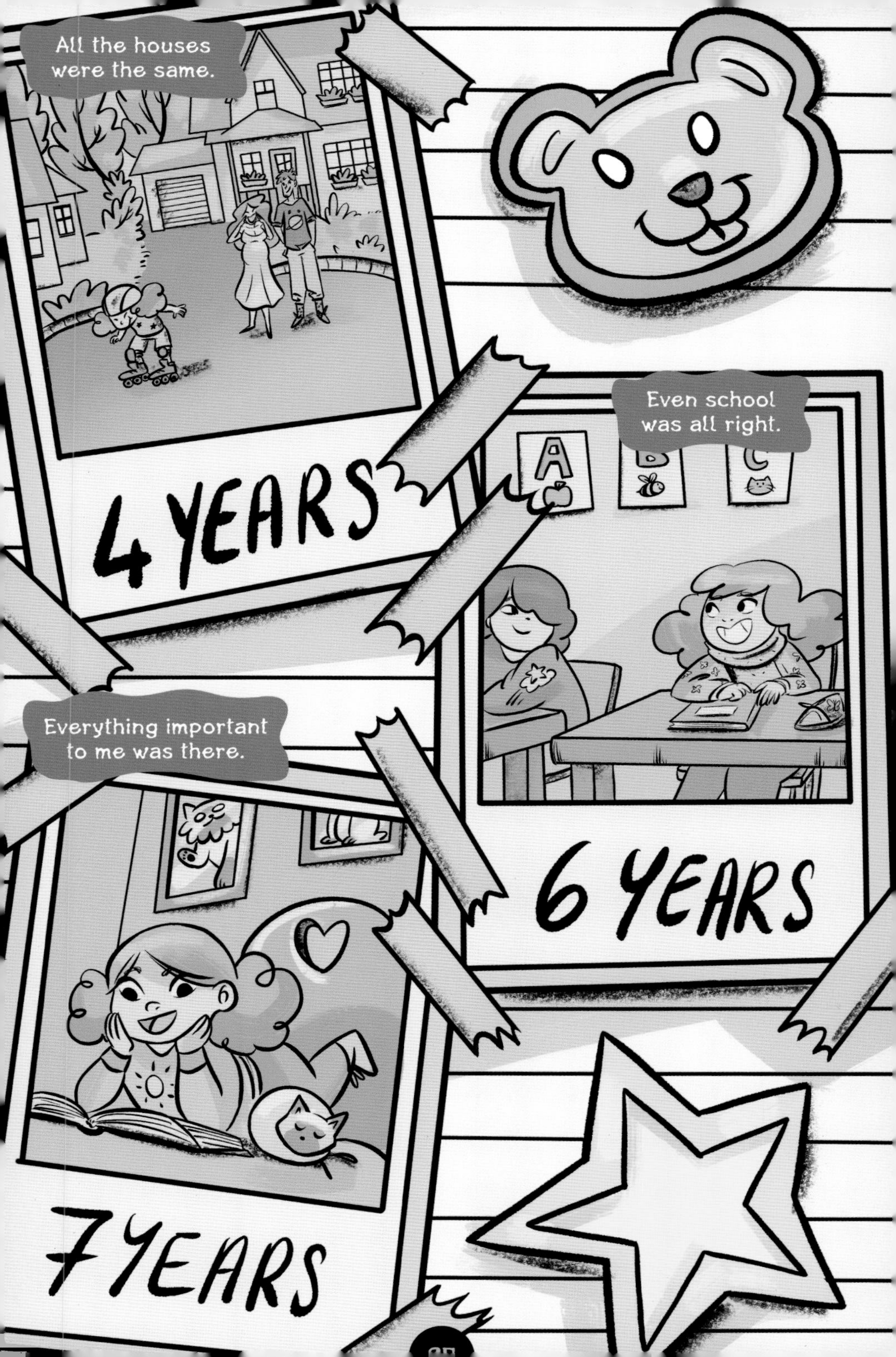
All the houses were the same.
4 YEARS
Even school was all right.
A
B
C
6 YEARS
Everything important to me was there.
7 YEARS

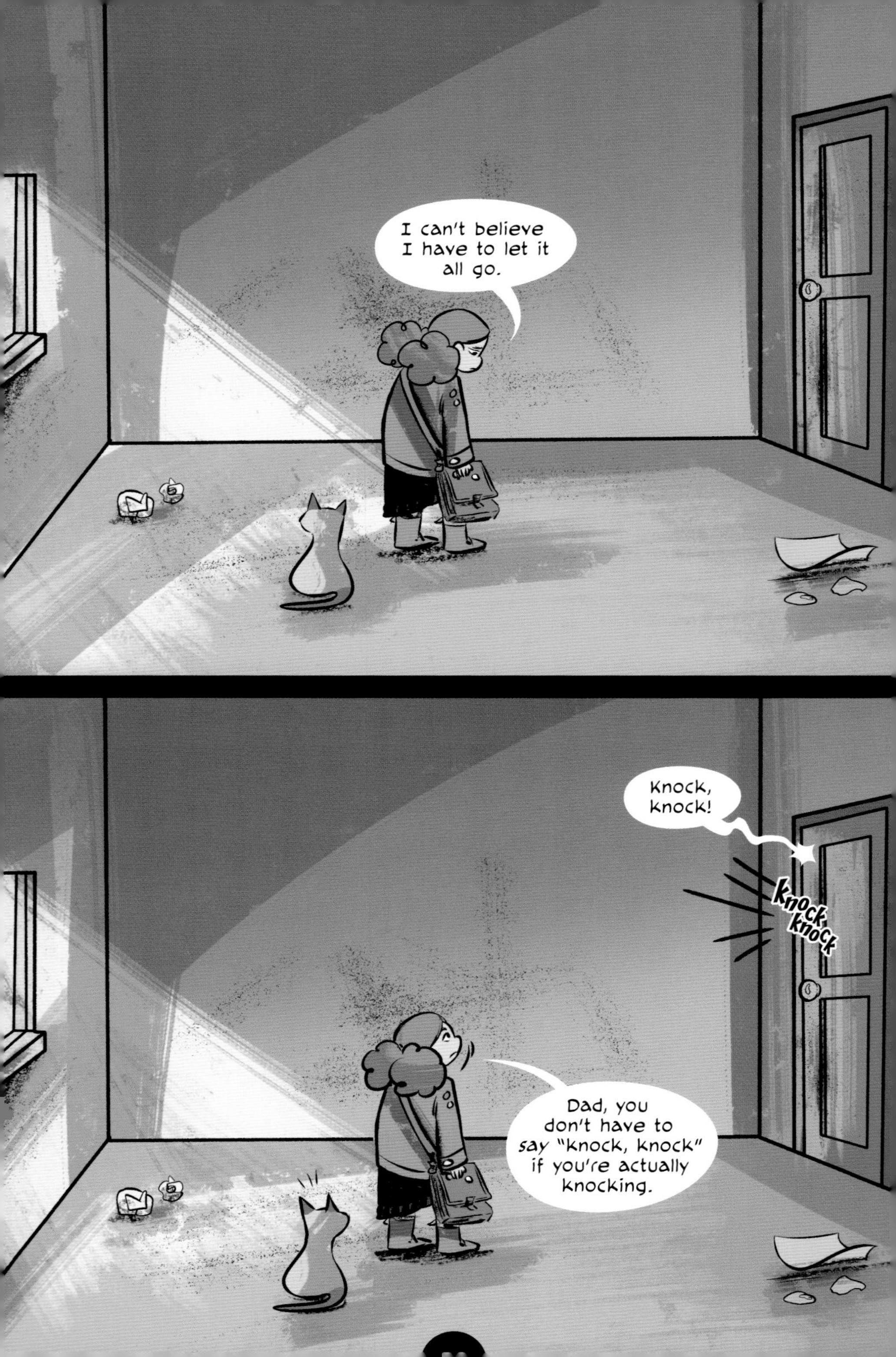
I can't believe I have to let it all go.
Knock, knock!
Knock knock
Dad, you don't have to say "knock, knock" if you're actually knocking.

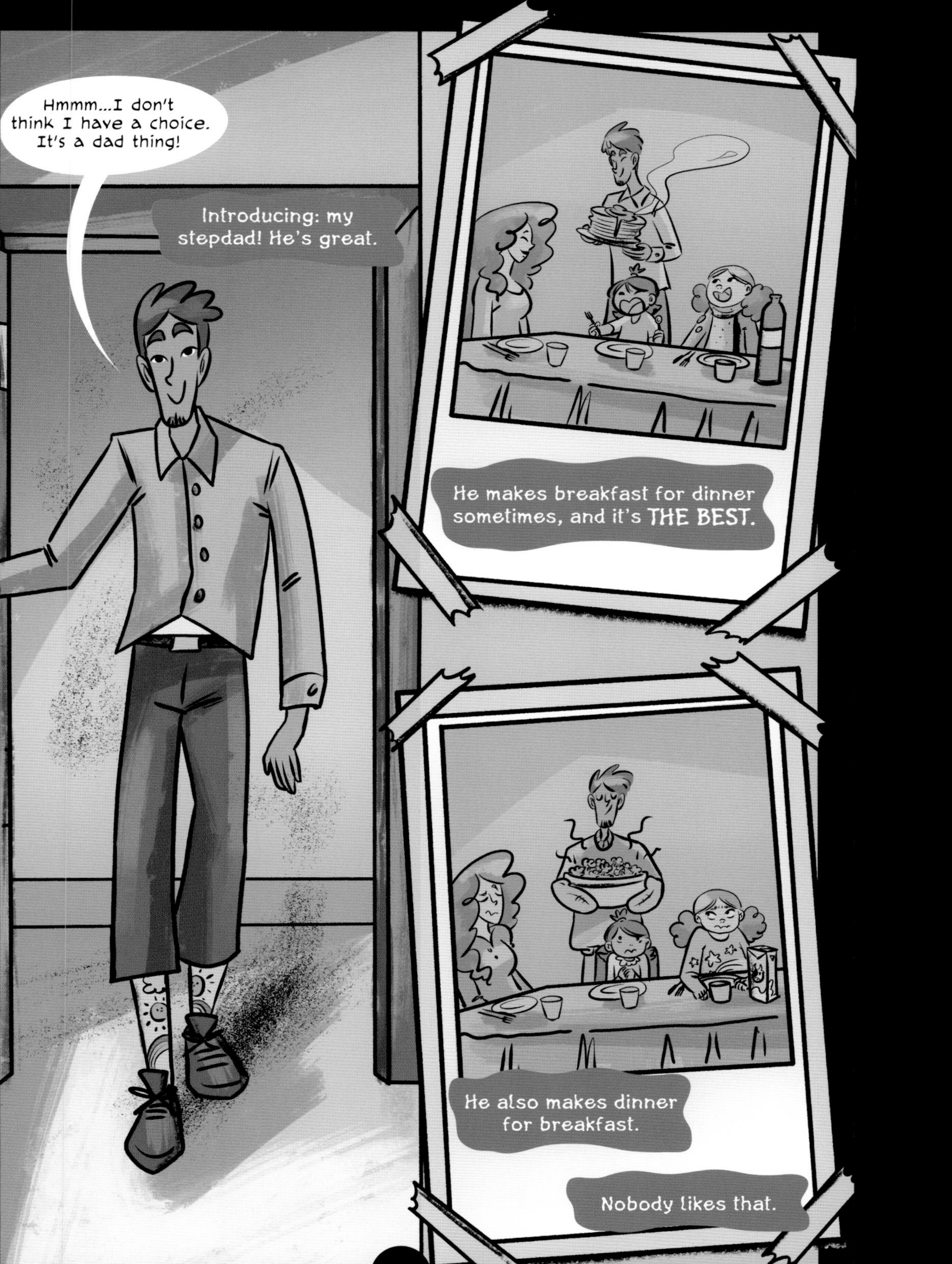

Hmmm...I don't think I have a choice. It's a dad thing!
Introducing: my stepdad! He's great.
He makes breakfast for dinner sometimes, and it's THE BEST.
He also makes dinner for breakfast.
Nobody likes that.

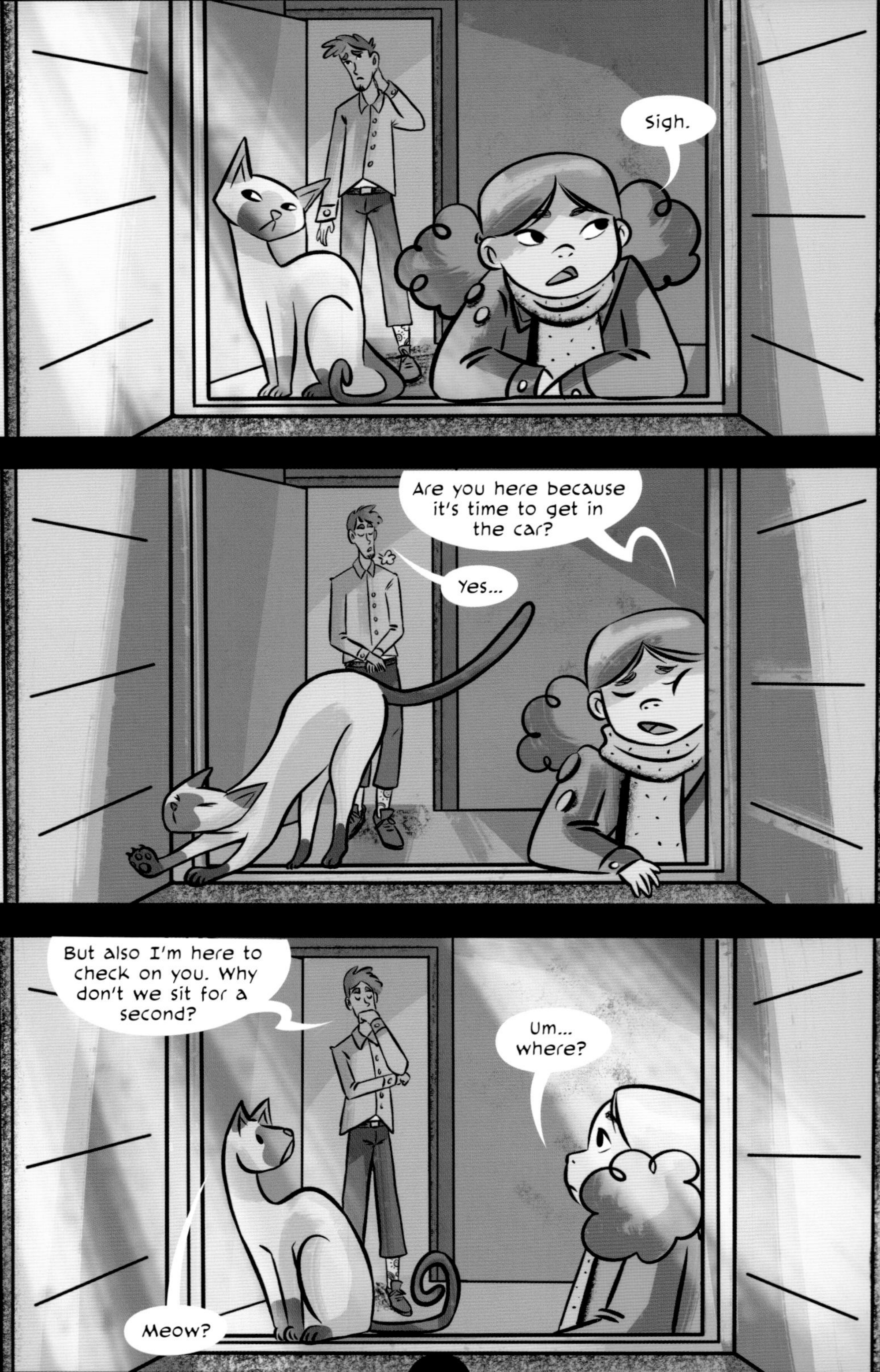
Sigh.
Are you here because it's time to get in the car?
Yes...
But also I'm here to check on you. Why don't we sit for a second?
Um... where?
Meow?

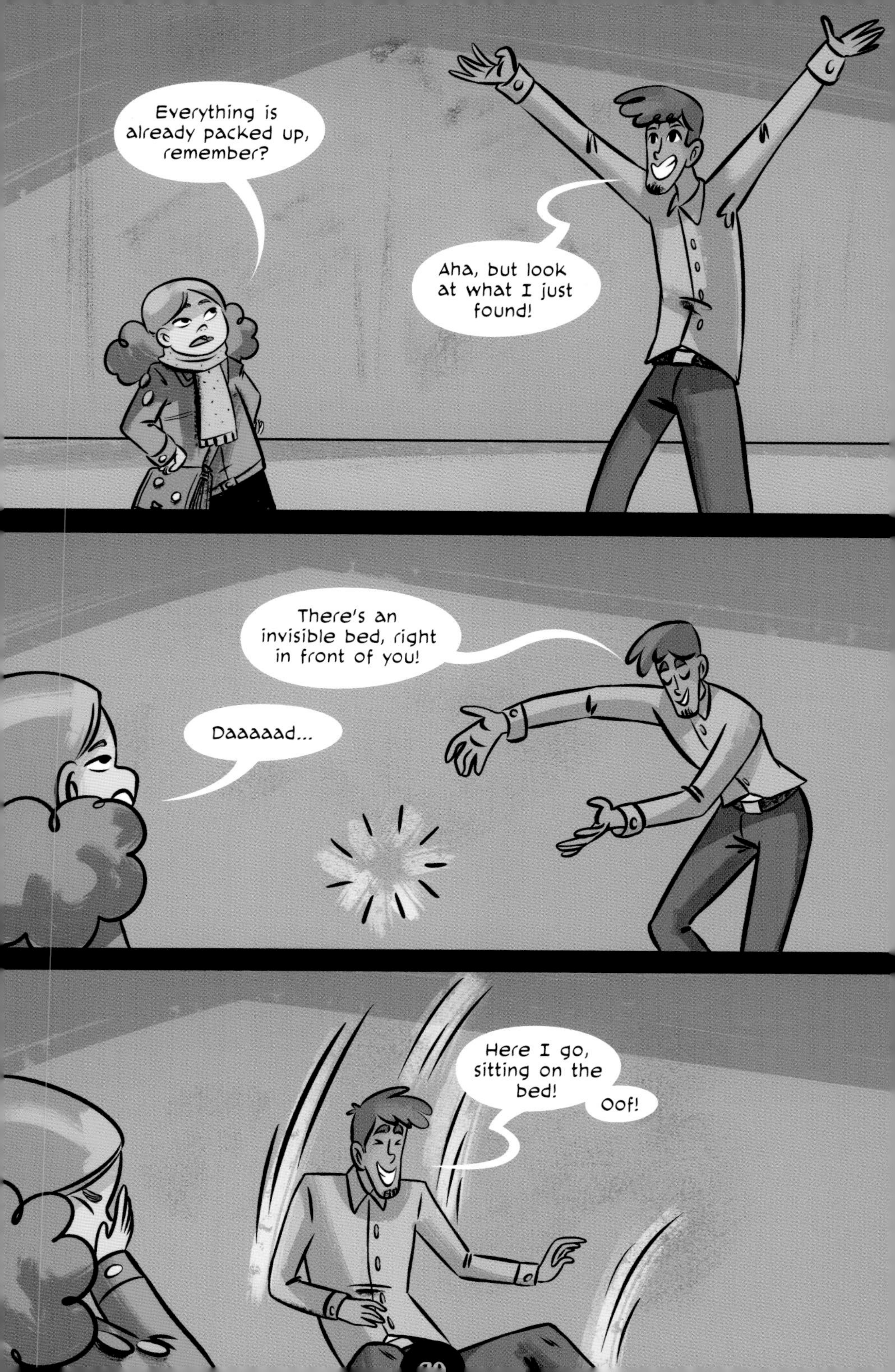
Everything is already packed up, remember?
Aha, but look at what I just found!
There's an invisible bed, right in front of you!
Daaaaad...
Here I go, sitting on the bed!
Oof!

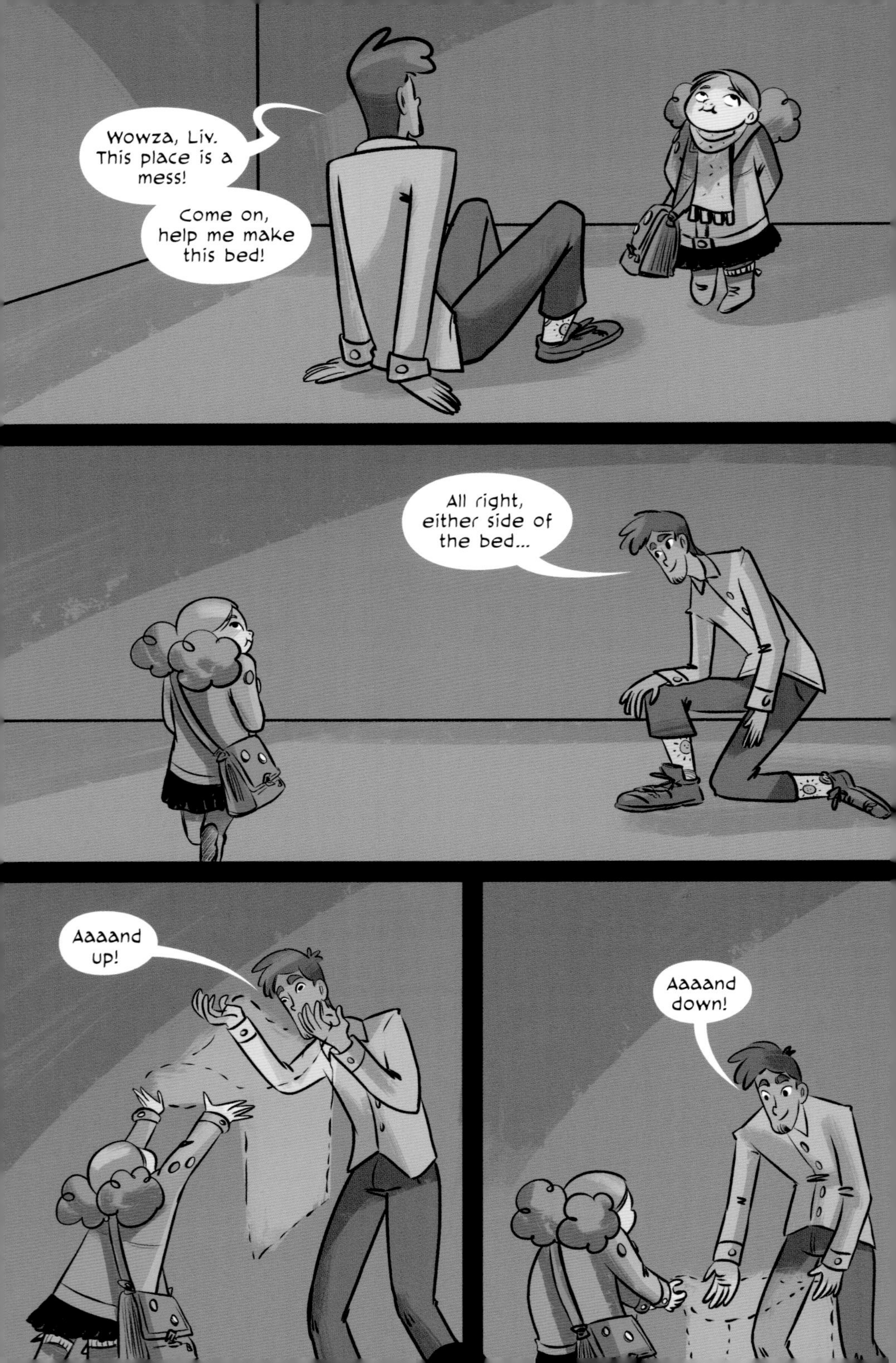
Wowza, Liv. This place is a mess!
Come on, help me make this bed!
All right, either side of the bed...
Aaaand up!
Aaaand down!

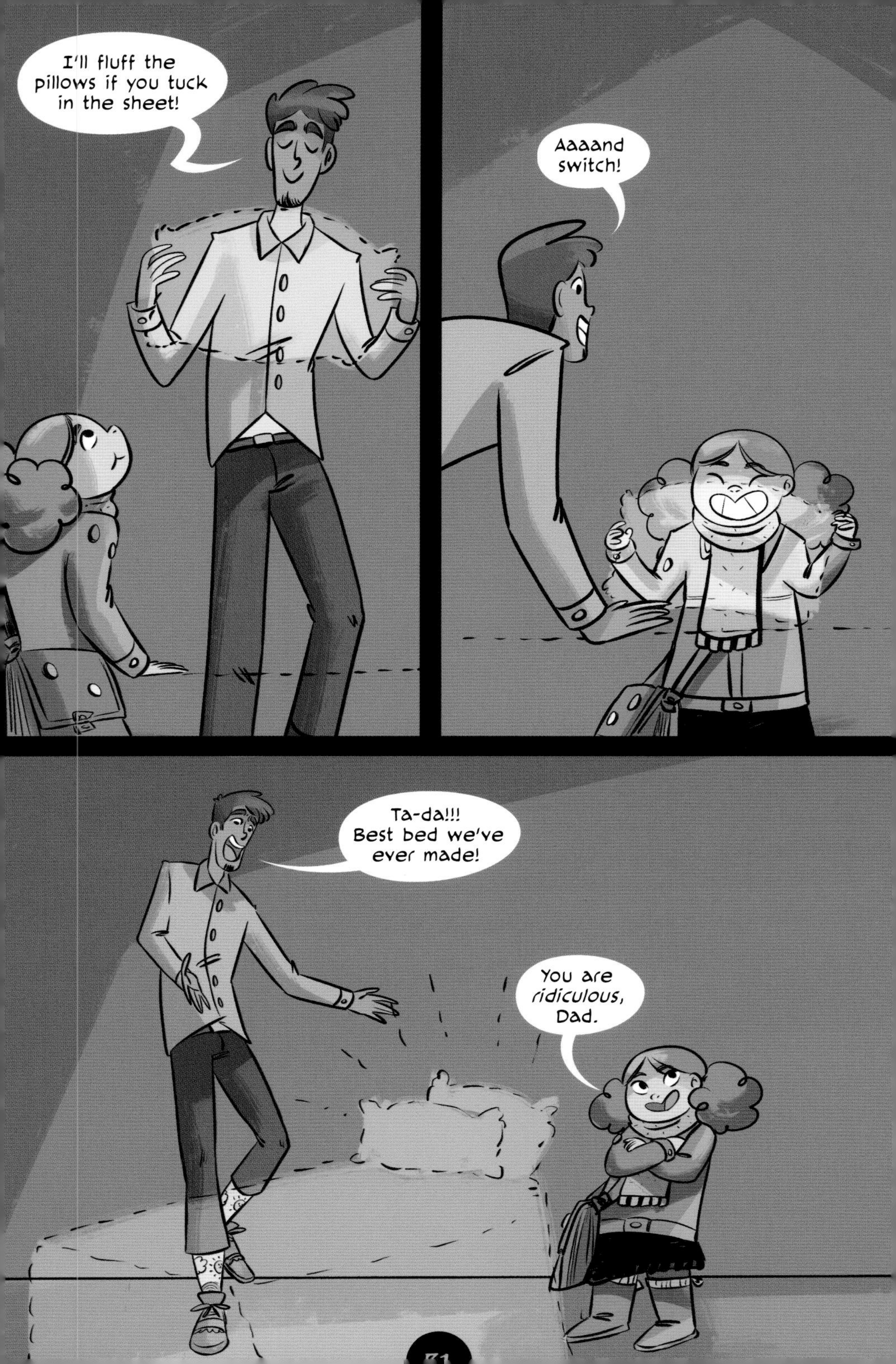
I'll fluff the pillows if you tuck in the sheet!
Aaaand switch!
Ta-da!!! Best bed we've ever made!
You are *ridiculous*, Dad.

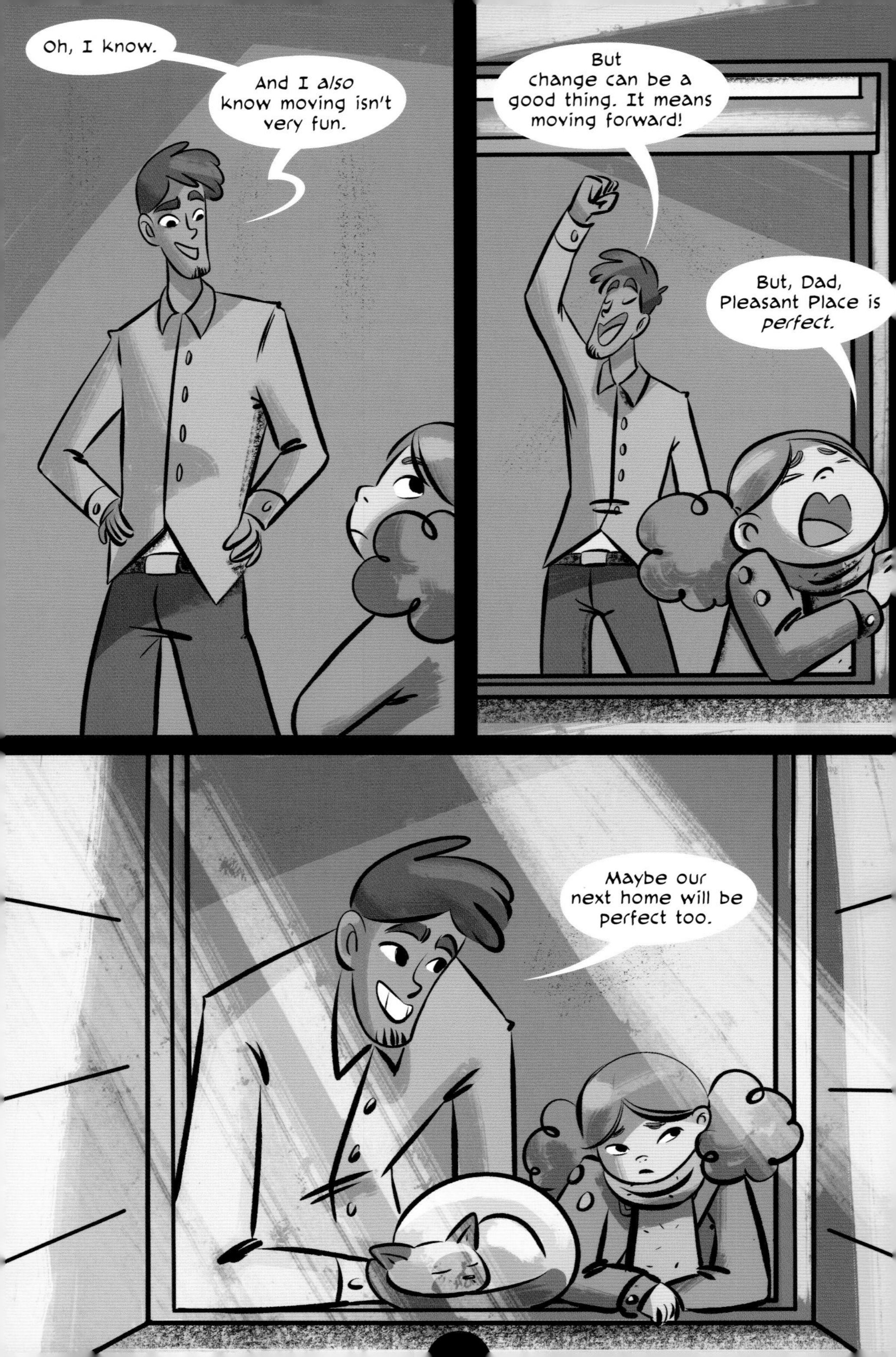
Oh, I know.
And I *also* know moving isn't very fun.
But change can be a good thing. It means moving forward!
But, Dad, Pleasant Place is *perfect.*
Maybe our next home will be perfect too.

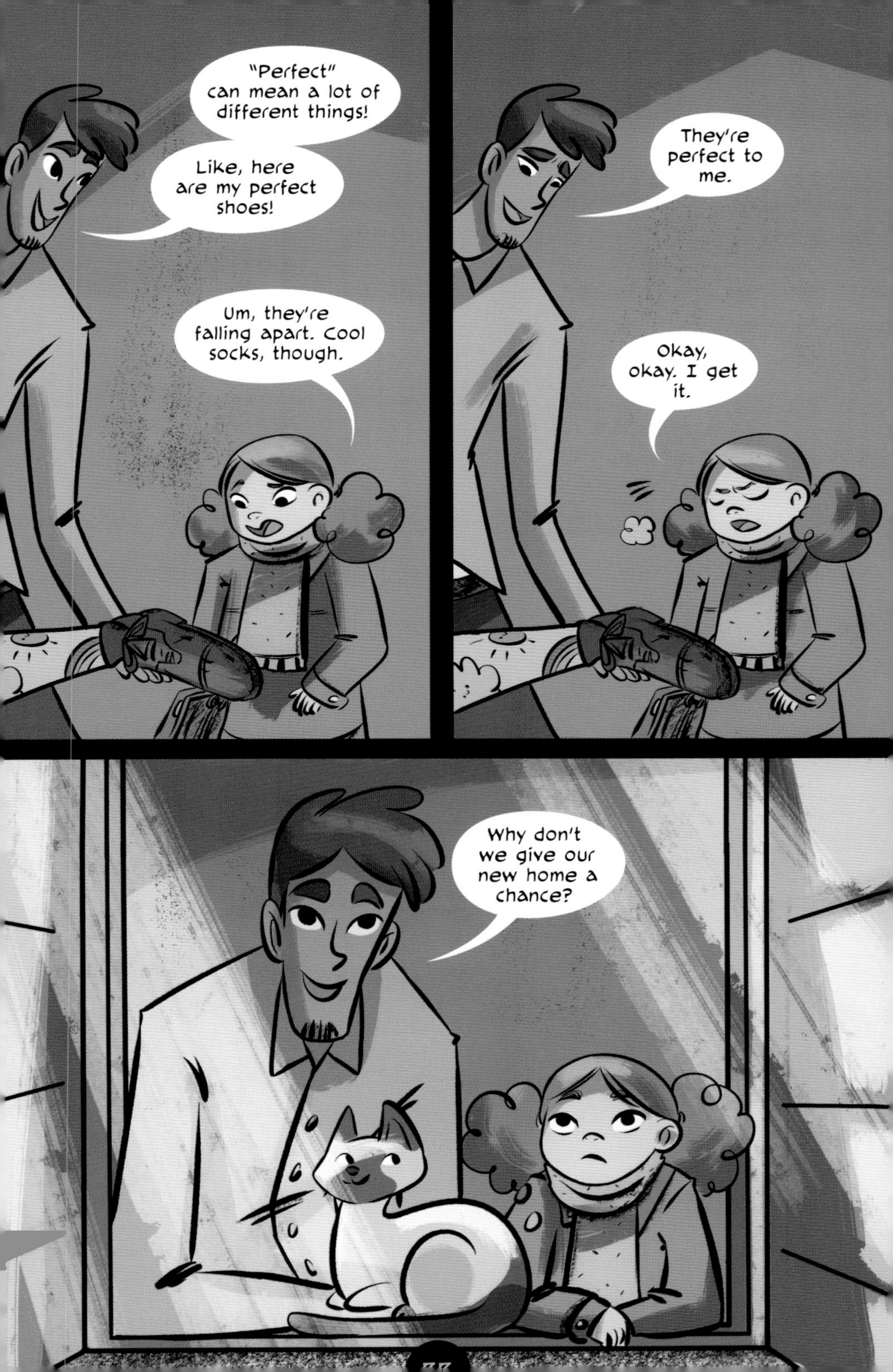
"Perfect" can mean a lot of different things!
Like, here are my perfect shoes!
Um, they're falling apart. Cool socks, though.
They're perfect to me.
Okay, okay. I get it.
Why don't we give our new home a chance?

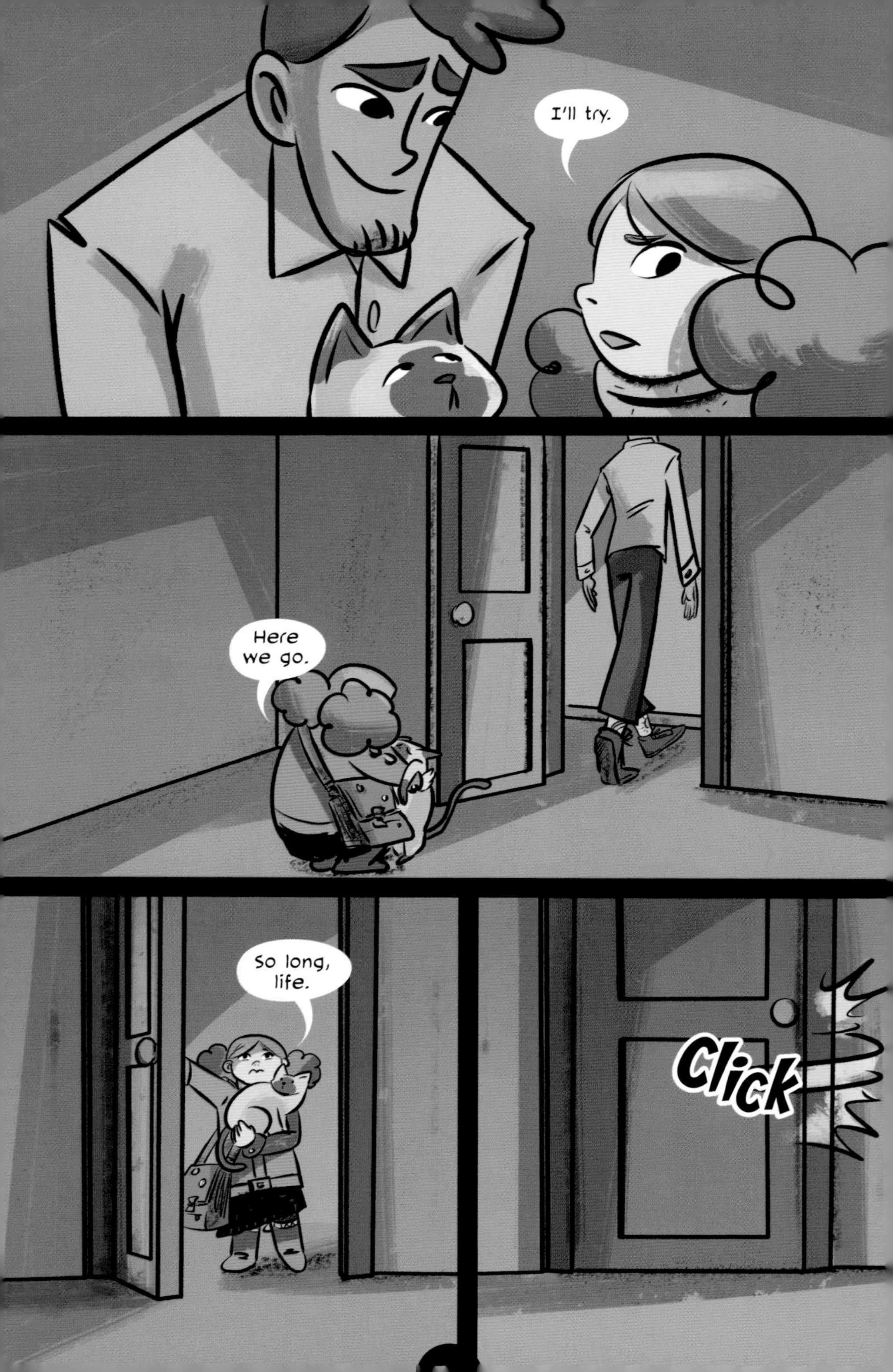
I'll try.
Here we go.
So long, life.
Click

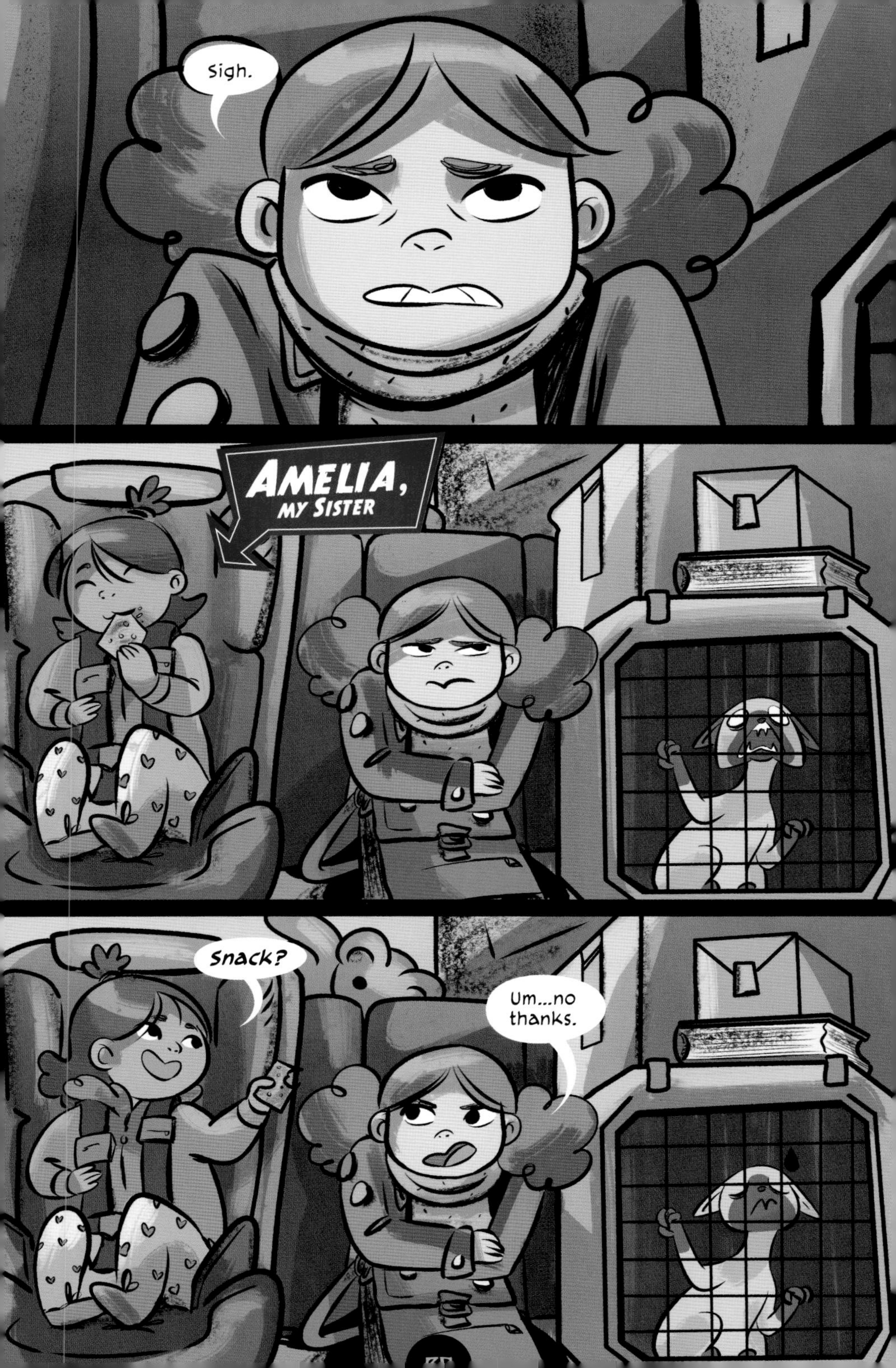
Sigh.
AMELIA, MY SISTER
Snack?
Um...no thanks.

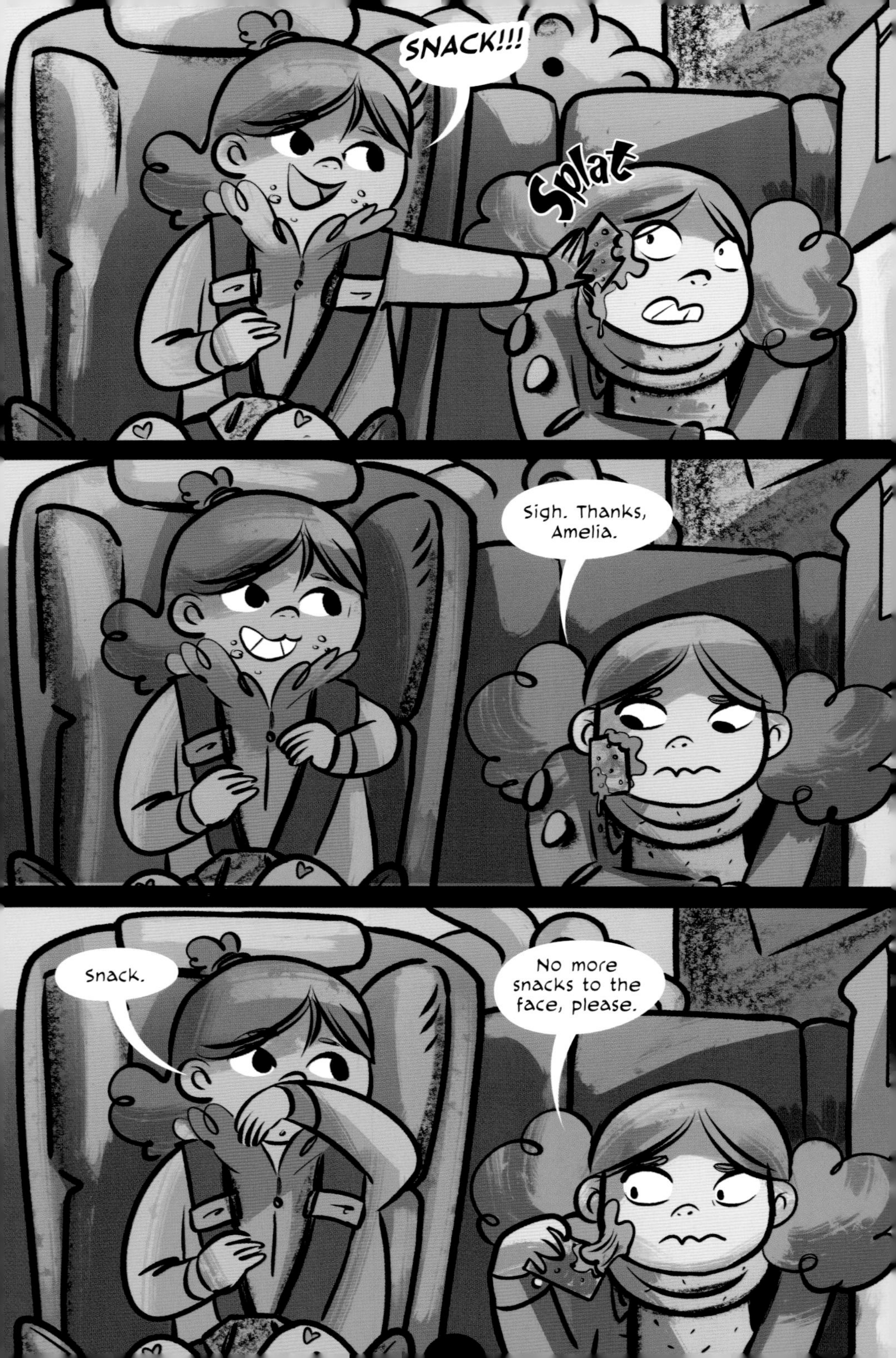
SNACK!!!
Splat
Sigh. Thanks, Amelia.
Snack.
No more snacks to the face, please.

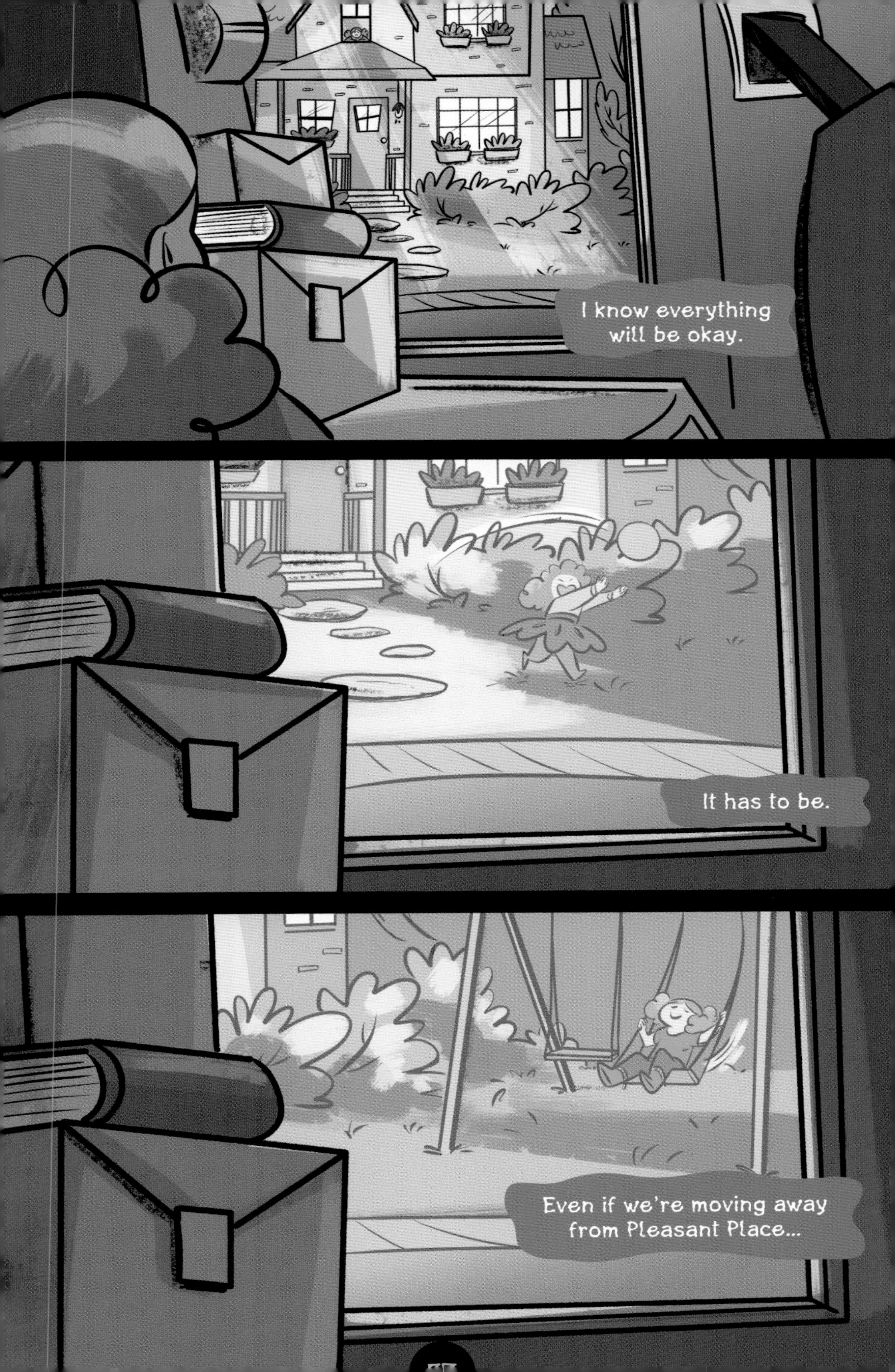
I know everything will be okay.
It has to be.
Even if we're moving away from Pleasant Place...

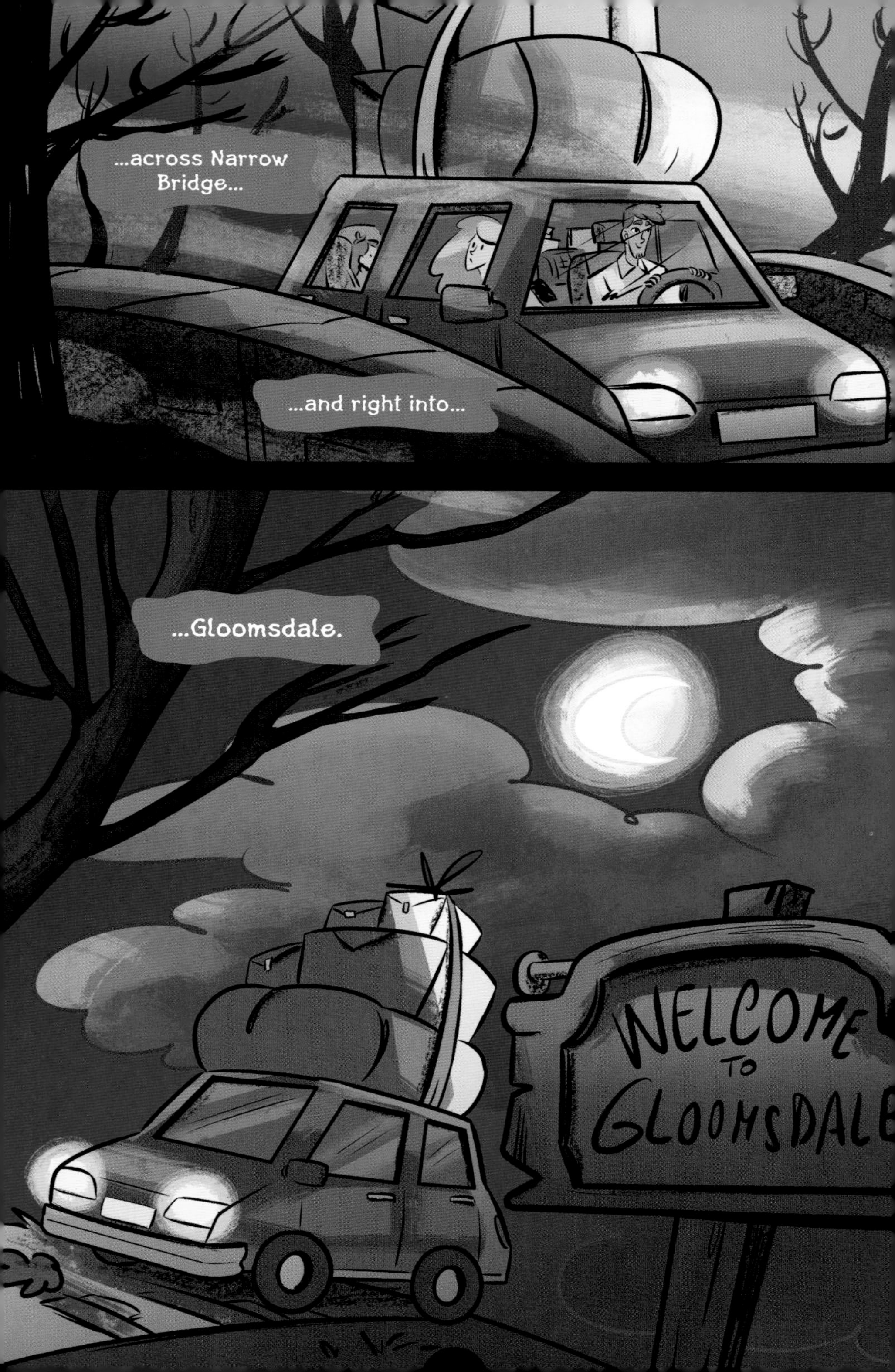
...across Narrow Bridge...
...and right into...
...Gloomsdale.
WELCOME TO GLOOMSDALE

CHAPTER 3

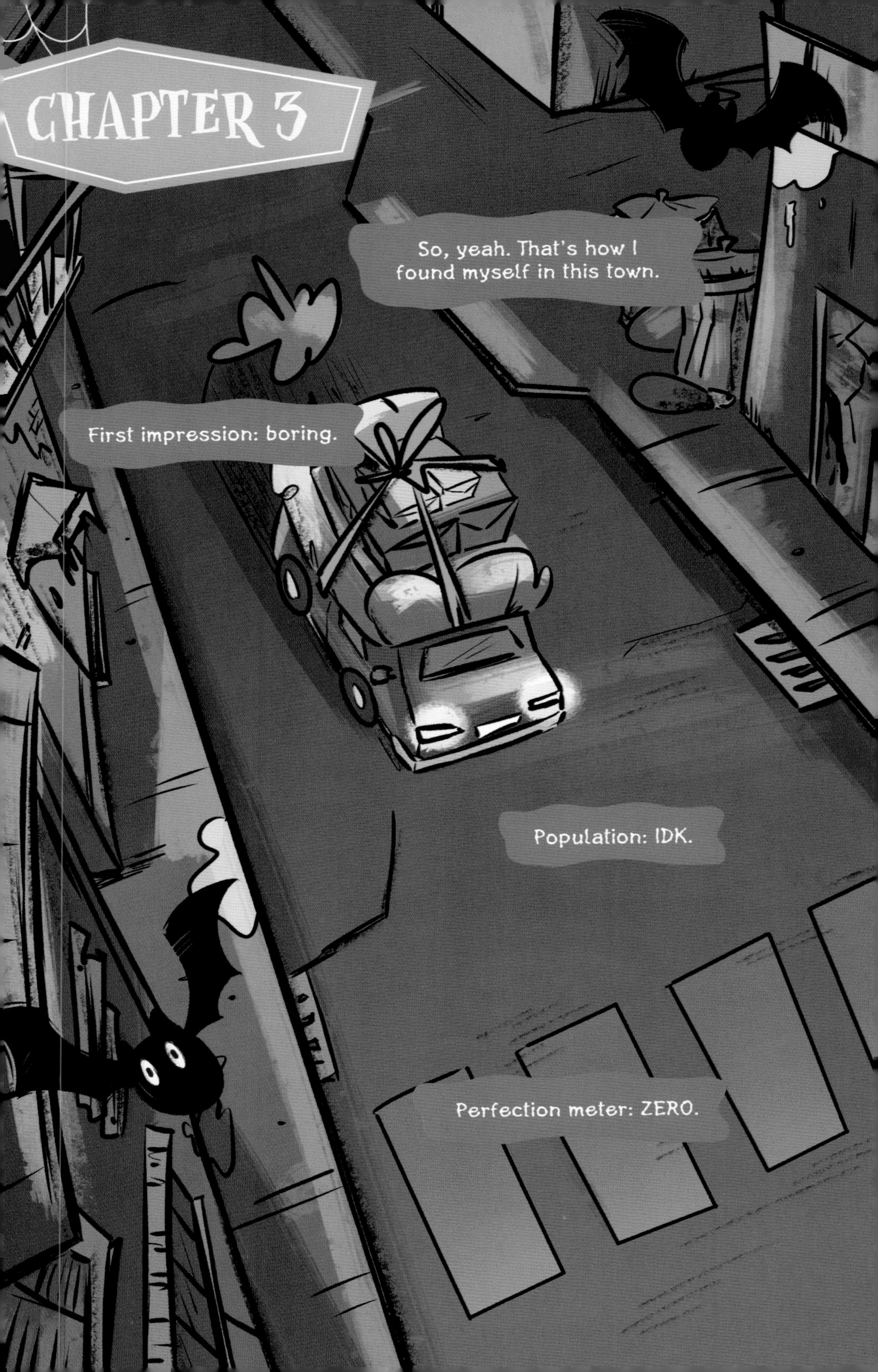
So, yeah. That's how I found myself in this town.
First impression: boring.
Population: IDK.
Perfection meter: ZERO.

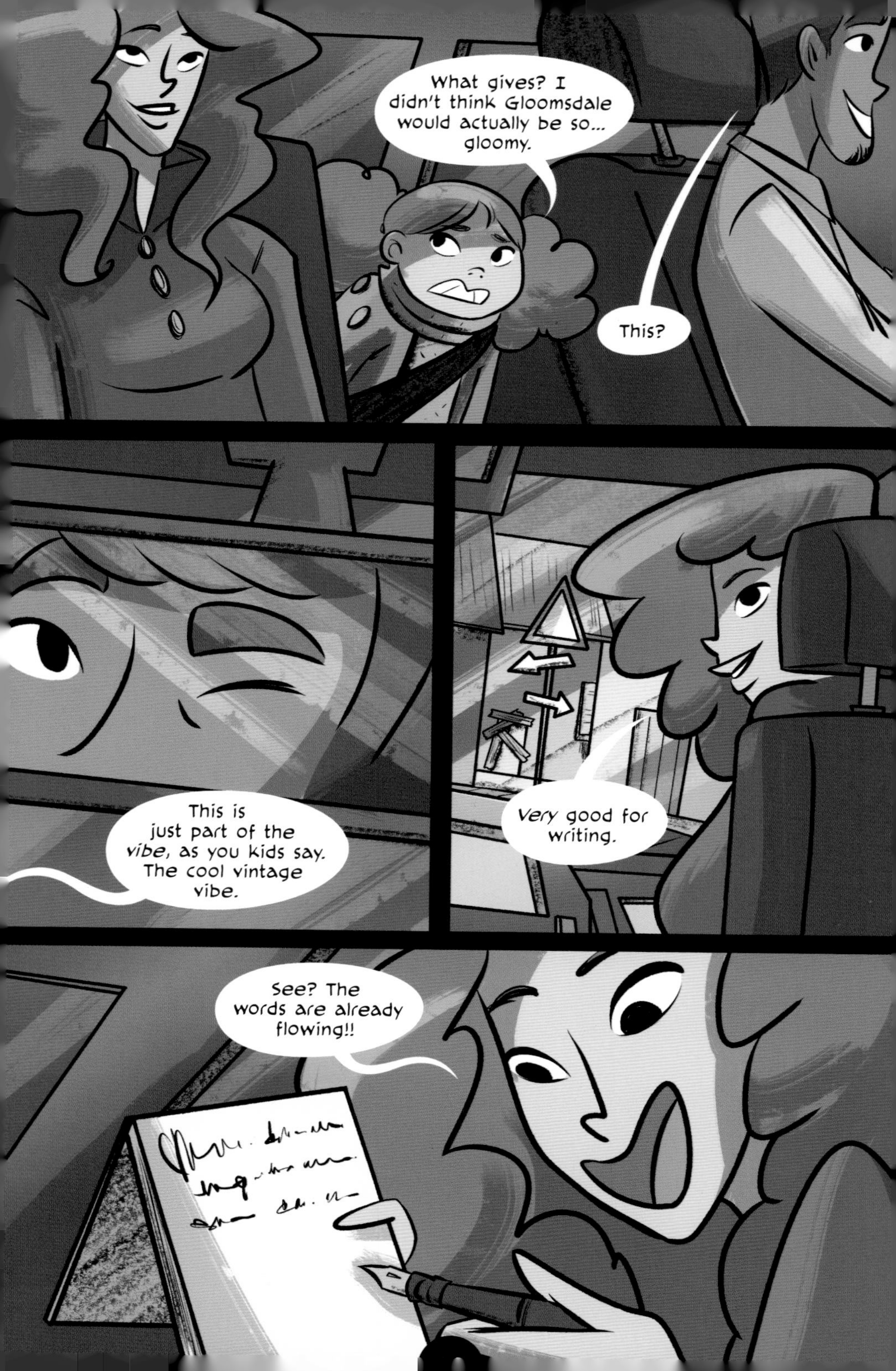
What gives? I didn't think Gloomsdale would actually be so... gloomy.
This?
This is just part of the *vibe*, as you kids say. The cool vintage vibe.
Very good for writing.
See? The words are already flowing!!

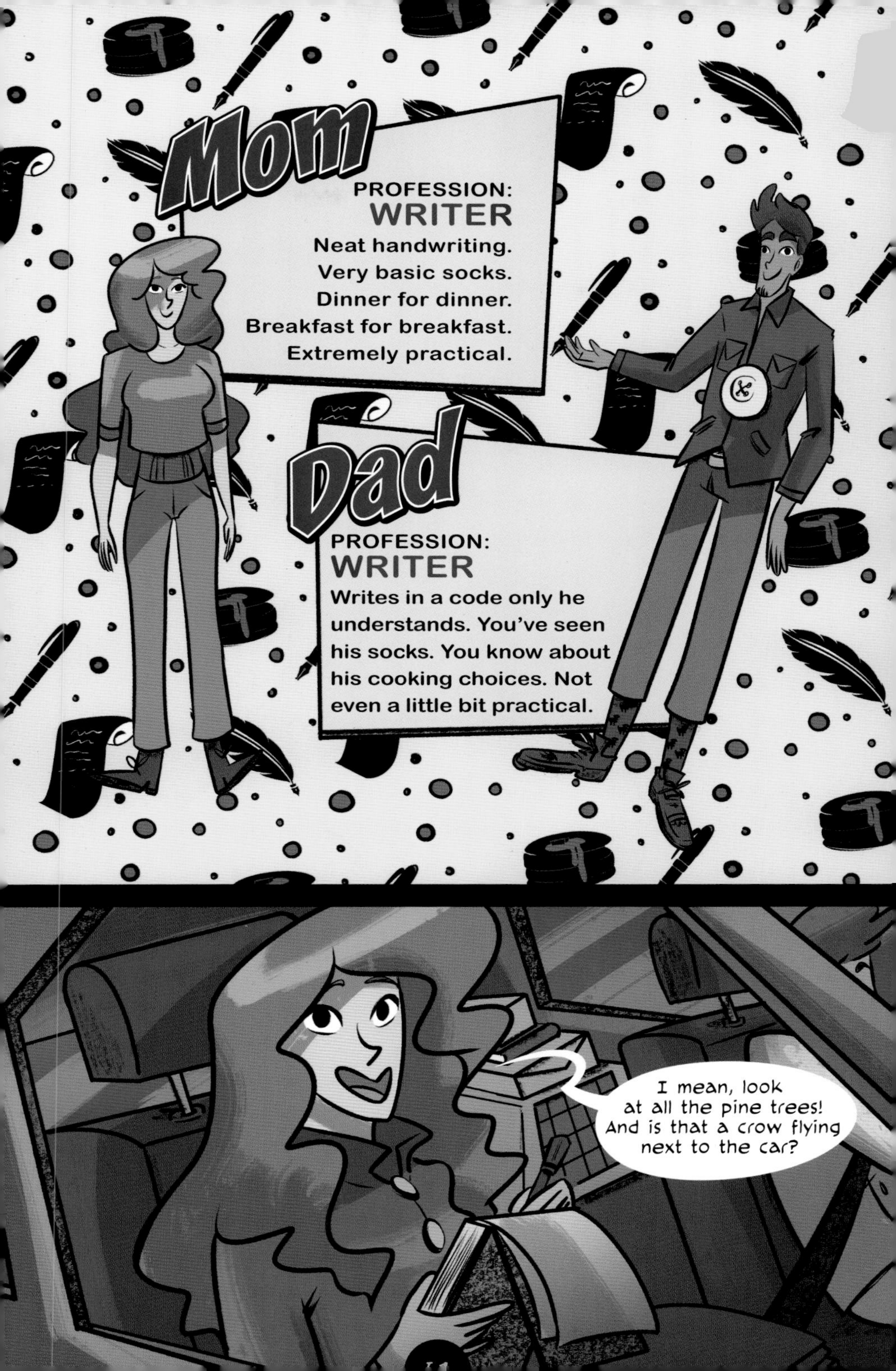
Mom
PROFESSION:
WRITER
Neat handwriting.
Very basic socks.
Dinner for dinner.
Breakfast for breakfast.
Extremely practical.
Dad
PROFESSION:
WRITER
Writes in a code only he understands. You've seen his socks. You know about his cooking choices. Not even a little bit practical.
I mean, look at all the pine trees! And is that a crow flying next to the car?

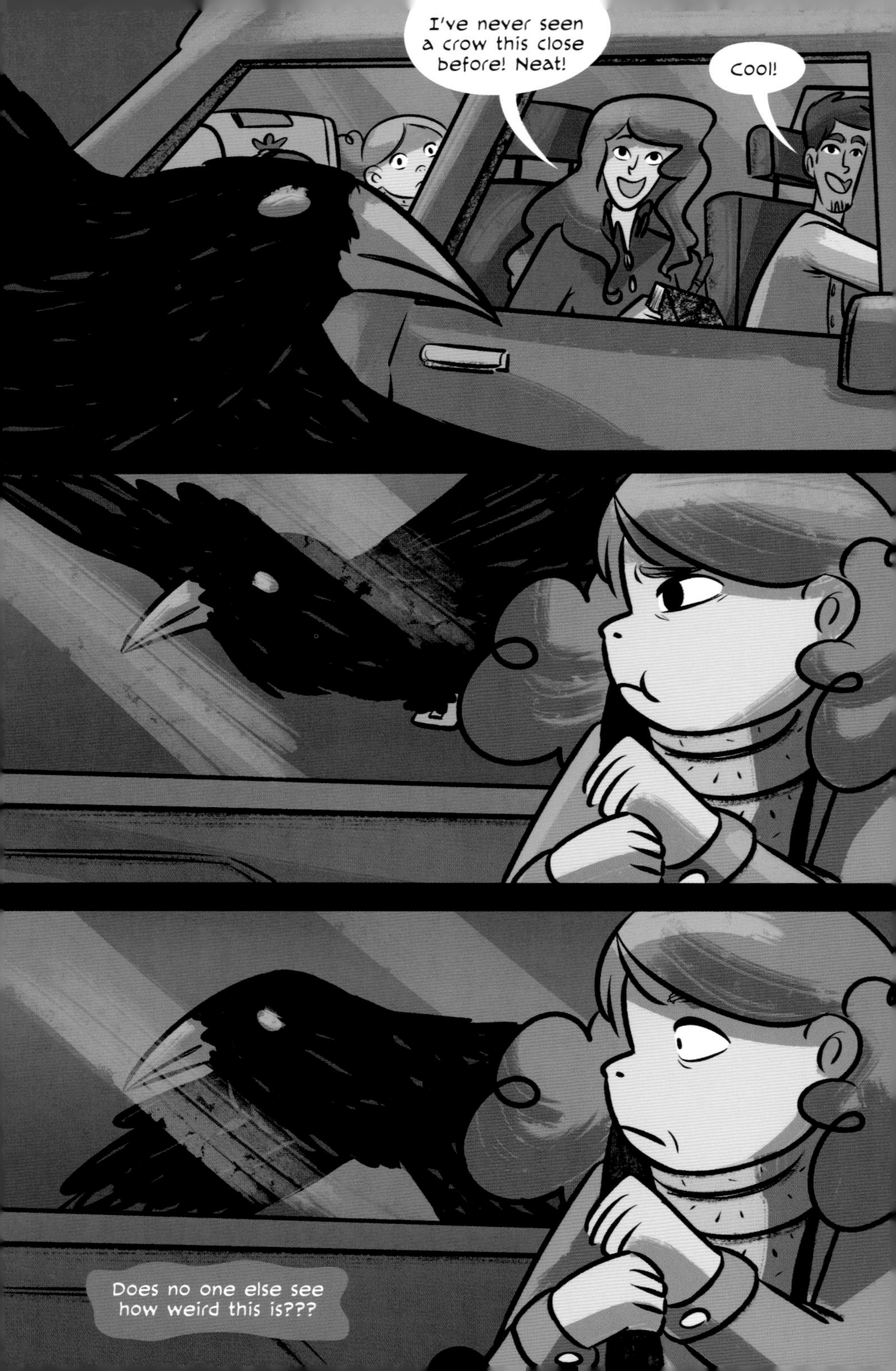
I've never seen a crow this close before! Neat!
Cool!
Does no one else see how weird this is???

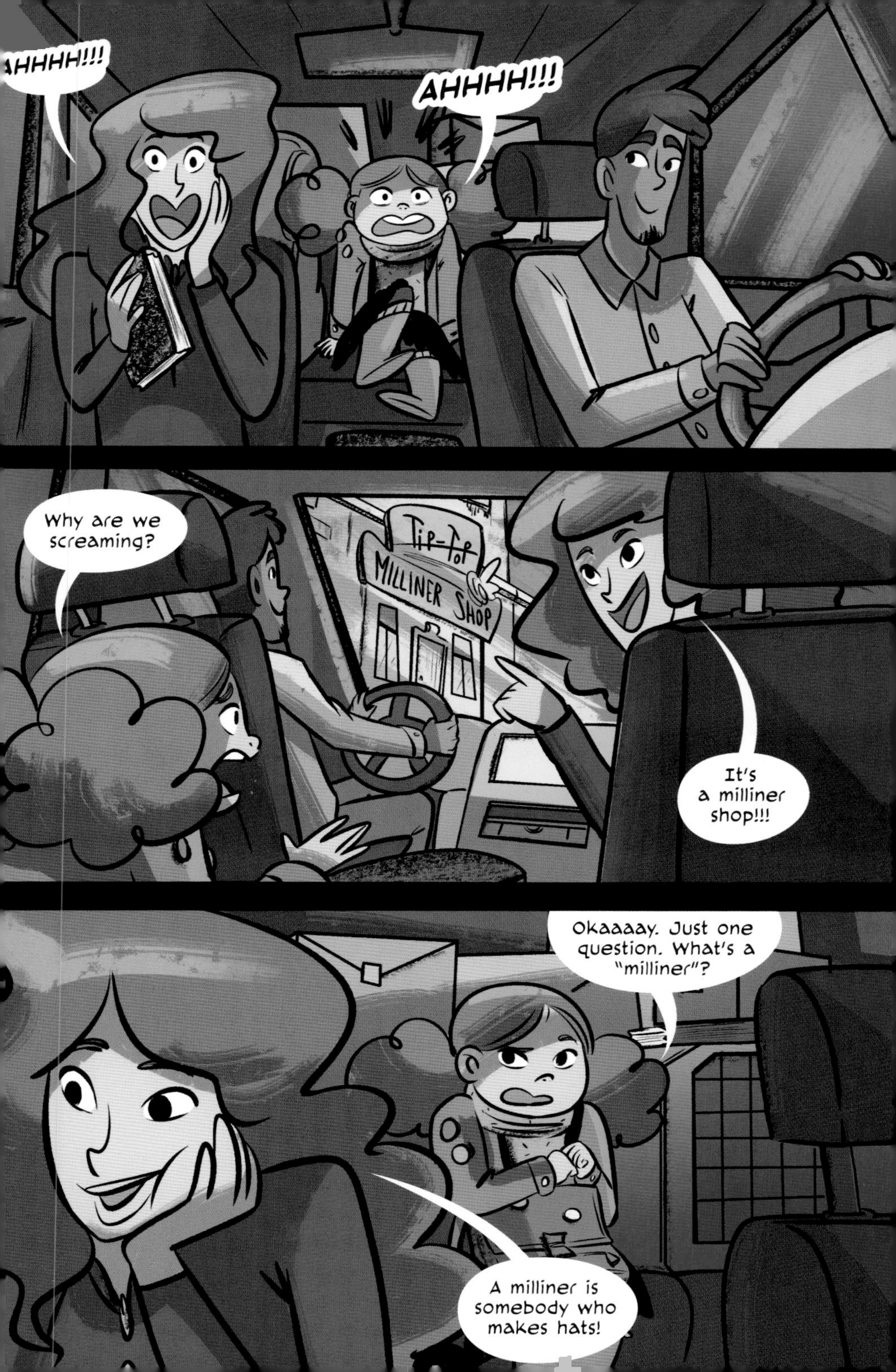
AHHHH!!!
AHHHH!!!
Why are we screaming?
Tip-Top
MILLINER SHOP
It's a milliner shop!!!
Okaaaay. Just one question. What's a "milliner"?
A milliner is somebody who makes hats!

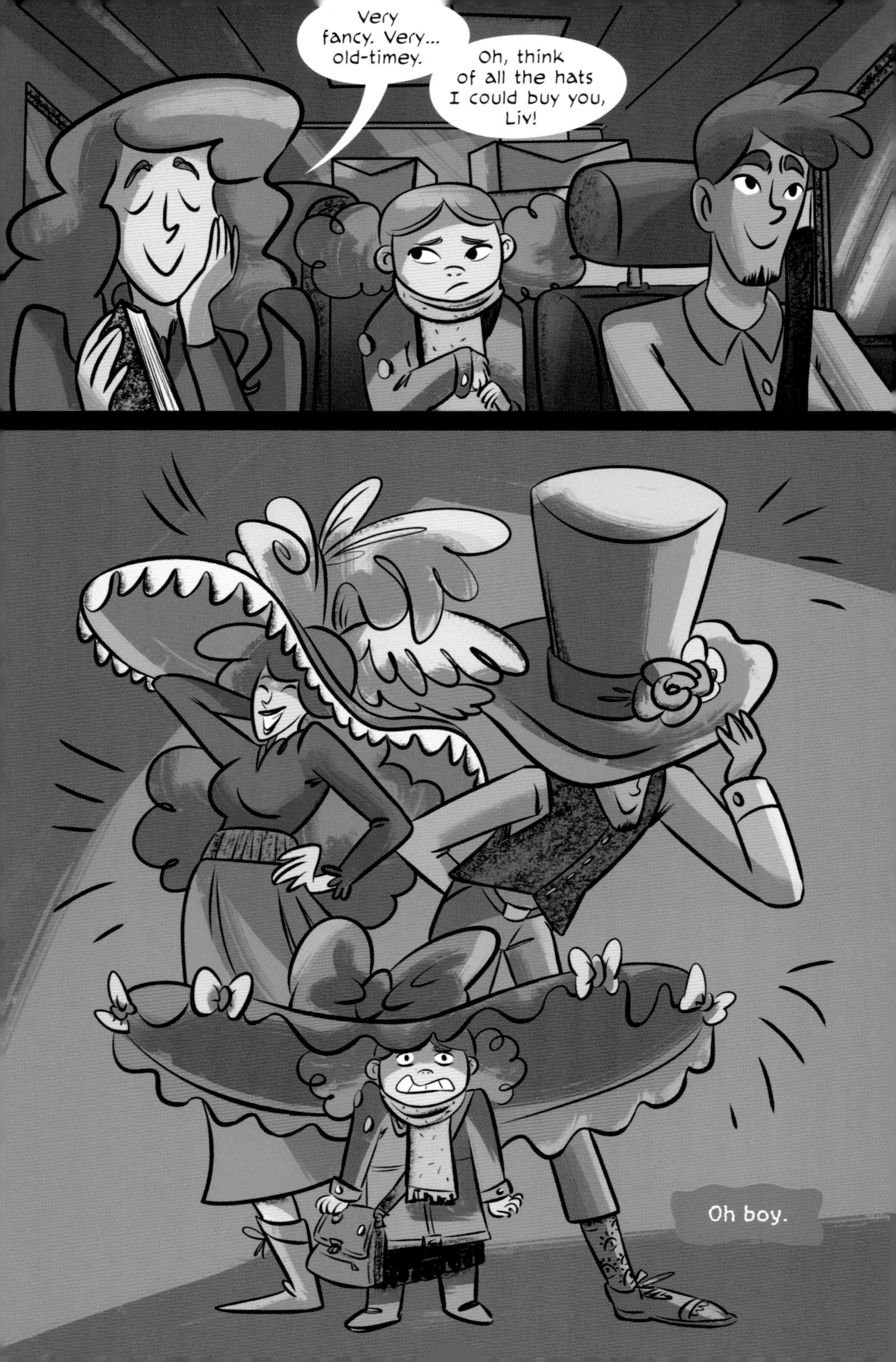
Very fancy. Very... old-timey.
Oh, think of all the hats I could buy you, Liv!
Oh boy.

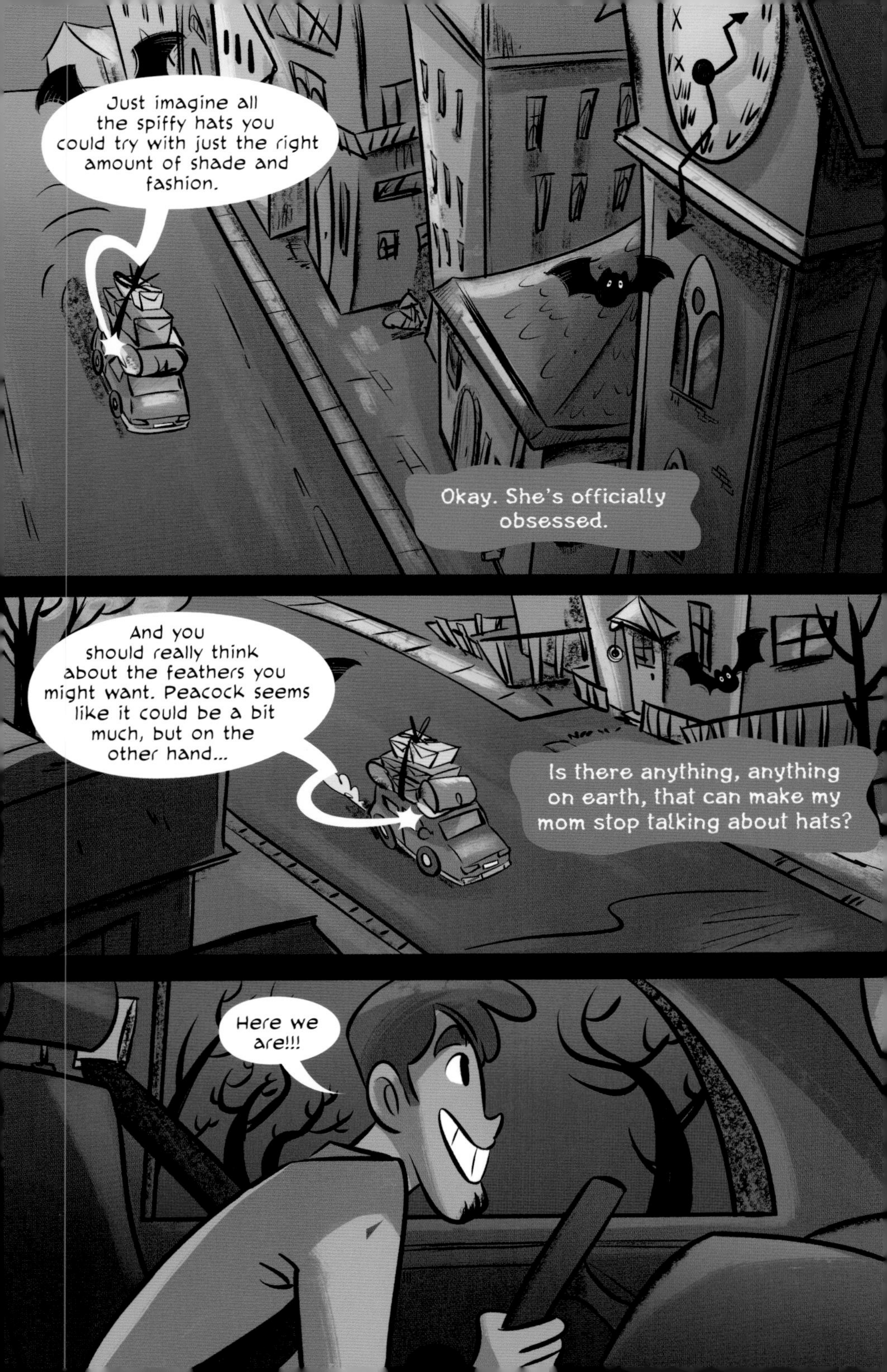
Just imagine all the spiffy hats you could try with just the right amount of shade and fashion.
Okay. She's officially obsessed.
And you should really think about the feathers you might want. Peacock seems like it could be a bit much, but on the other hand...
Is there anything, anything on earth, that can make my mom stop talking about hats?
Here we are!!!

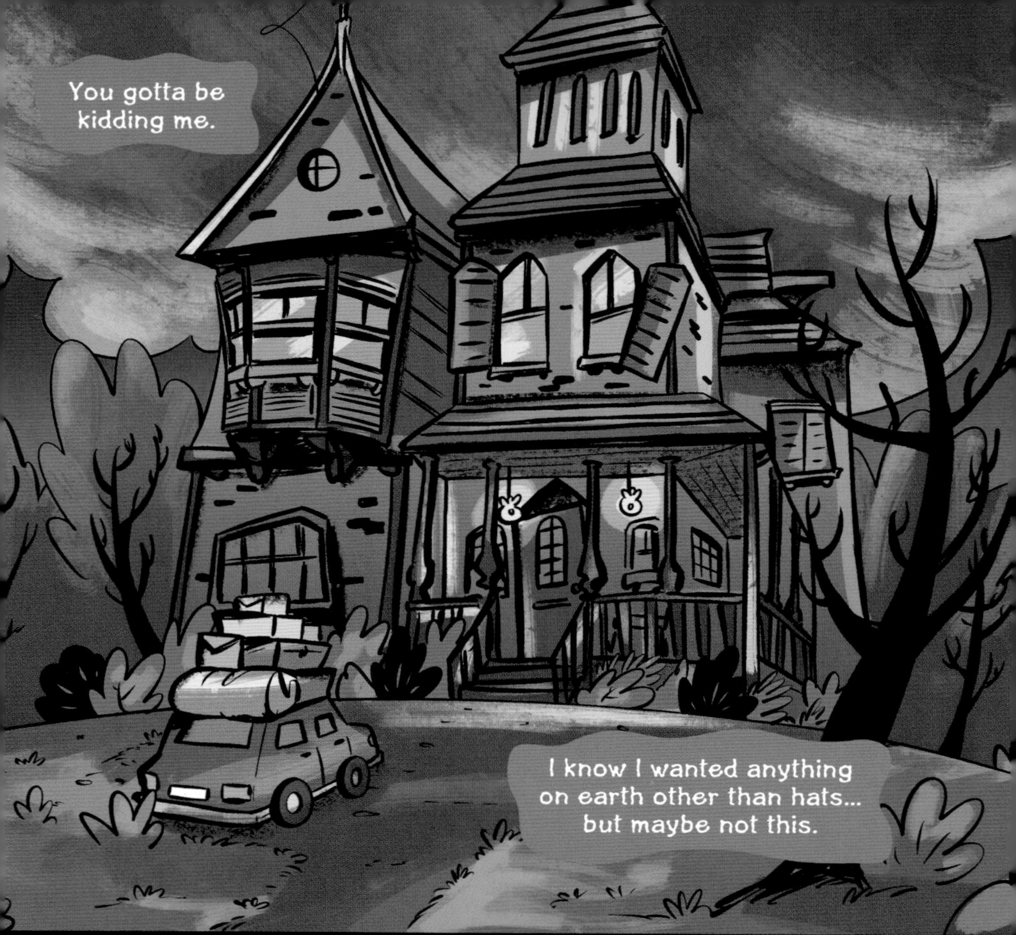
You gotta be kidding me.
I know I wanted anything on earth other than hats... but maybe not this.

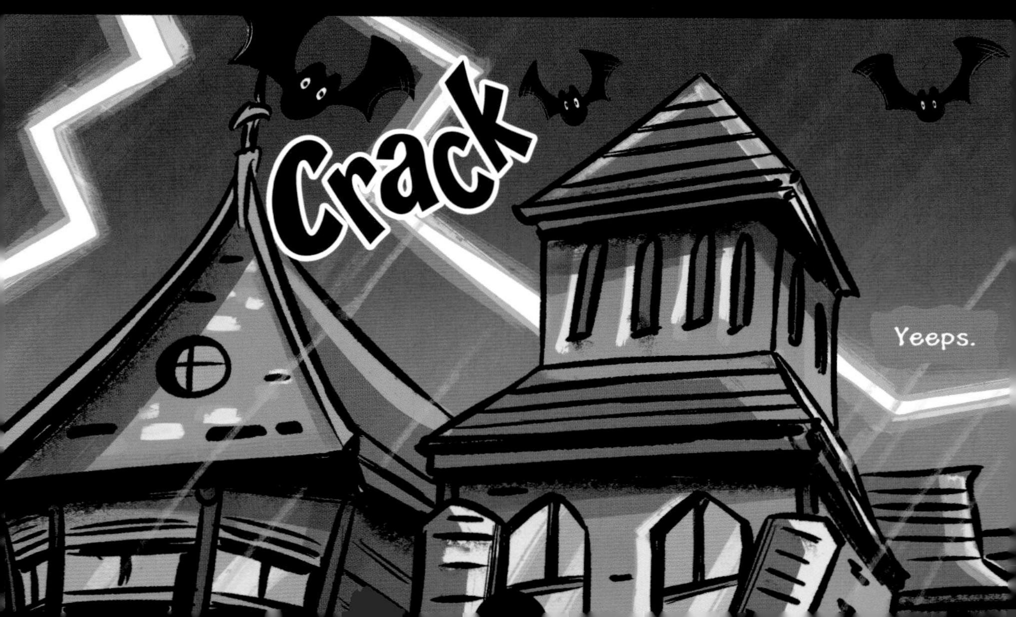
Crack
Yeeps.

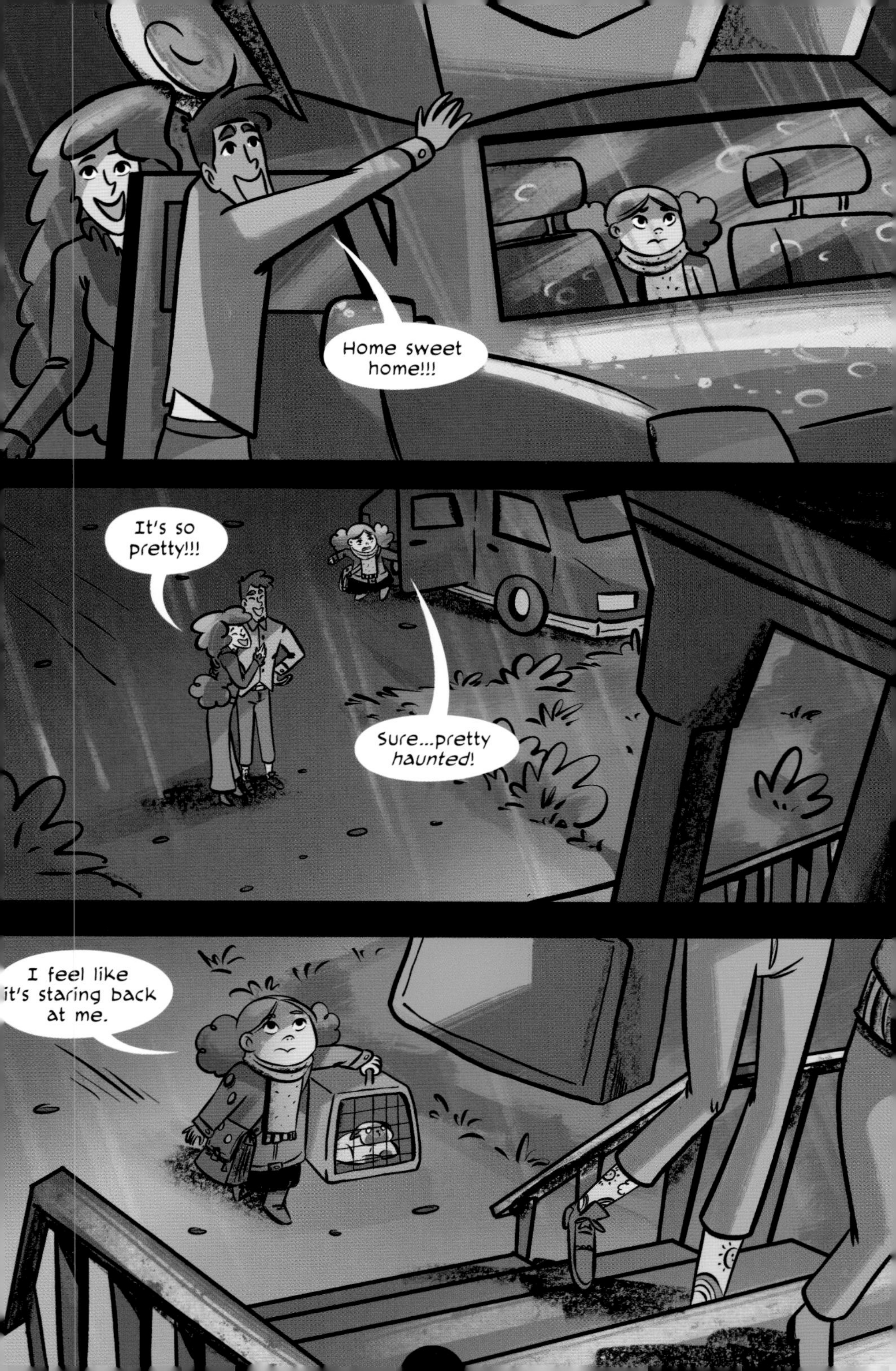
Home sweet home!!!
It's so pretty!!!
Sure...pretty *haunted*!
I feel like it's staring back at me.

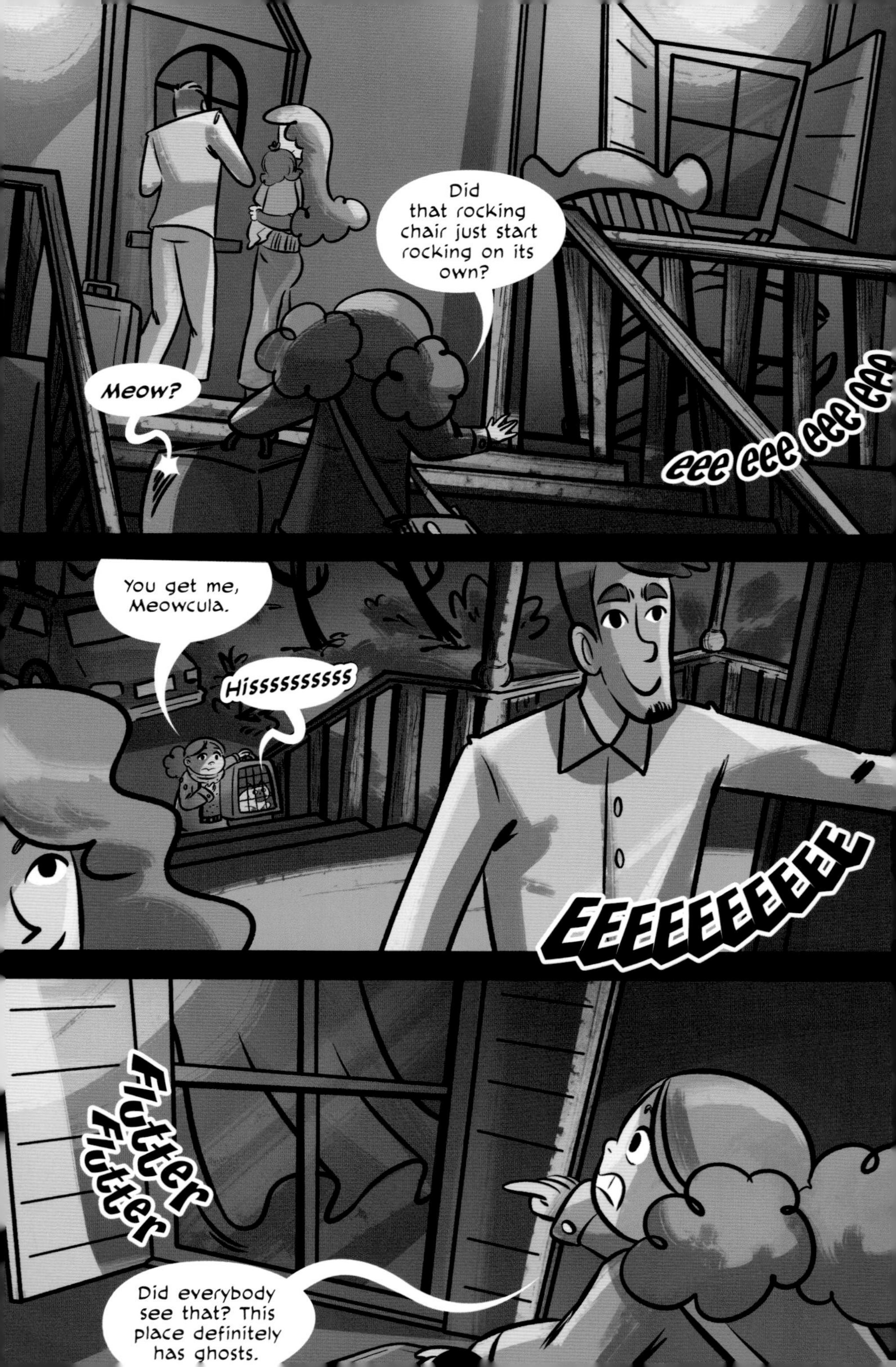
Did that rocking chair just start rocking on its own?
Meow?
eee eee eee eee
You get me, Meowcula.
Hissssssssss
EEEEEEEEEE
Flutter Flutter
Did everybody see that? This place definitely has ghosts.

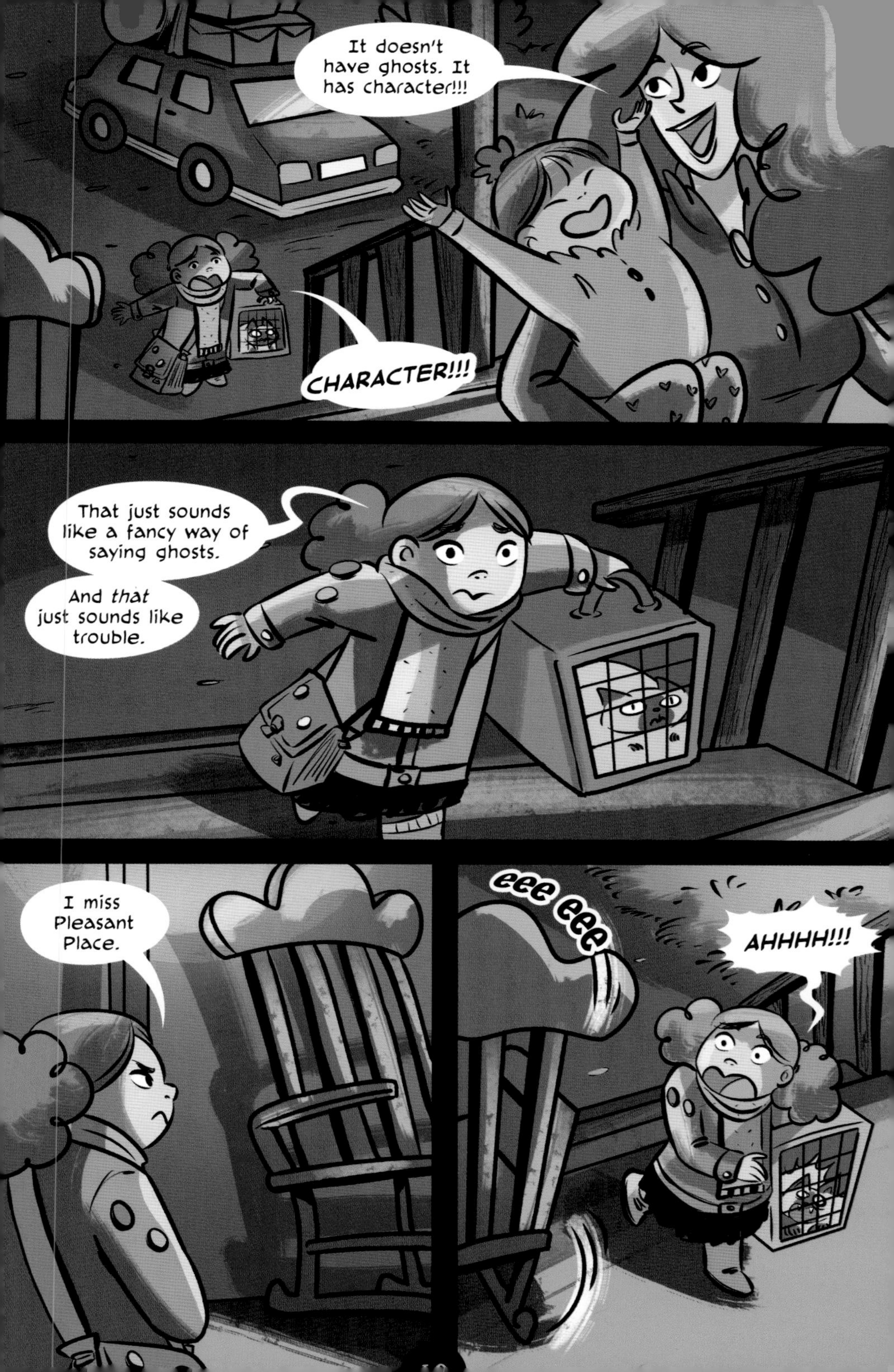
It doesn't have ghosts. It has character!!!
CHARACTER!!!
That just sounds like a fancy way of saying ghosts.
And *that* just sounds like trouble.
I miss Pleasant Place.
eee eee
AHHHH!!!

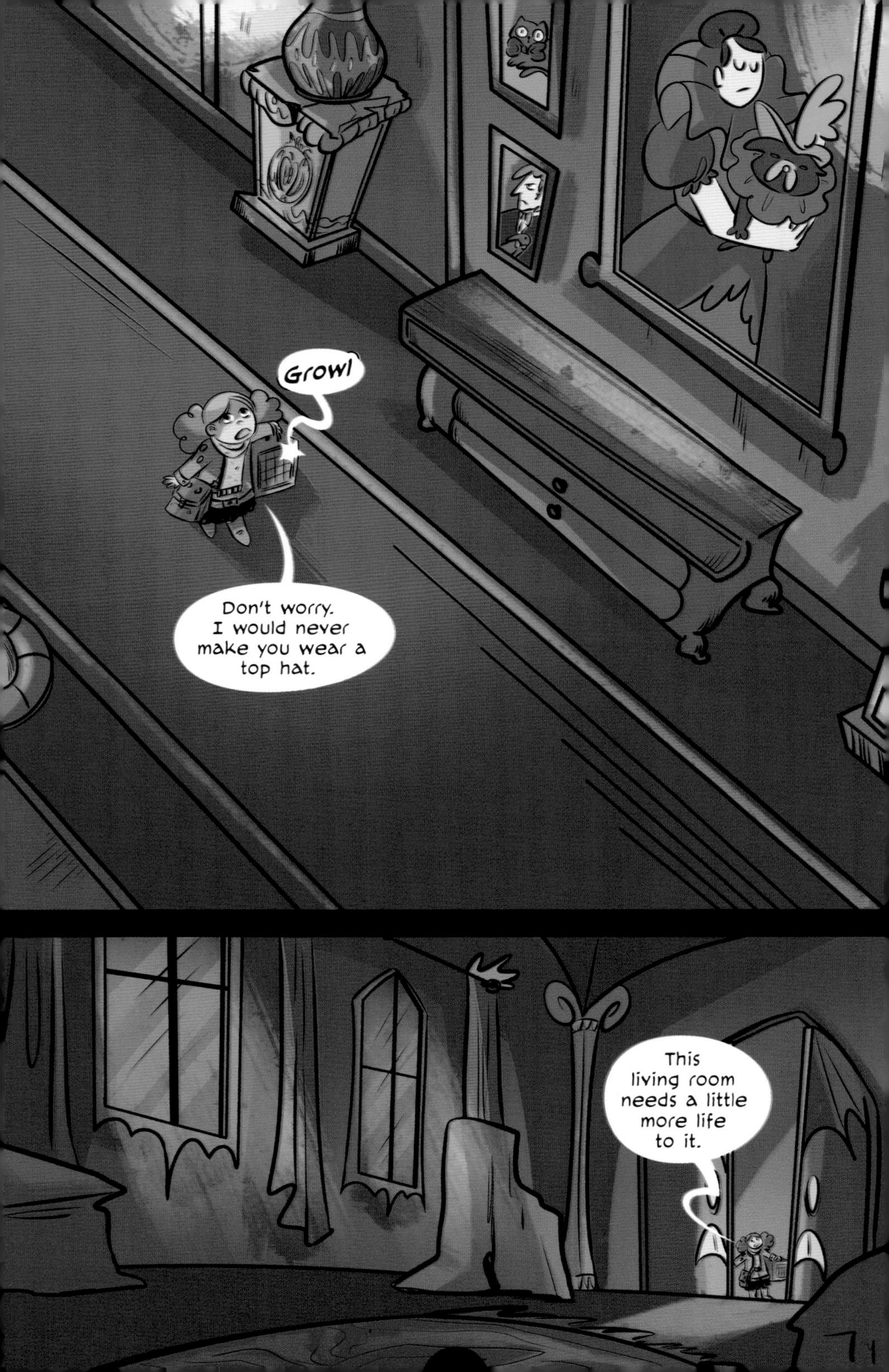
Growl
Don't worry. I would never make you wear a top hat.
This living room needs a little more life to it.

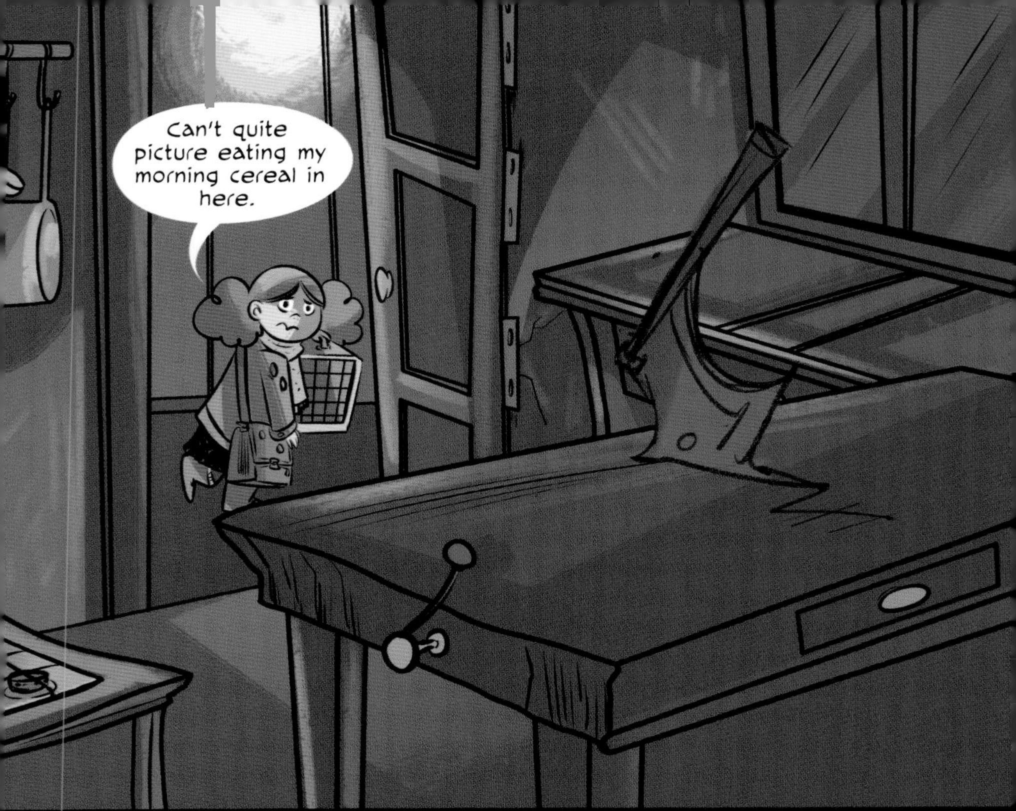
Can't quite picture eating my morning cereal in here.

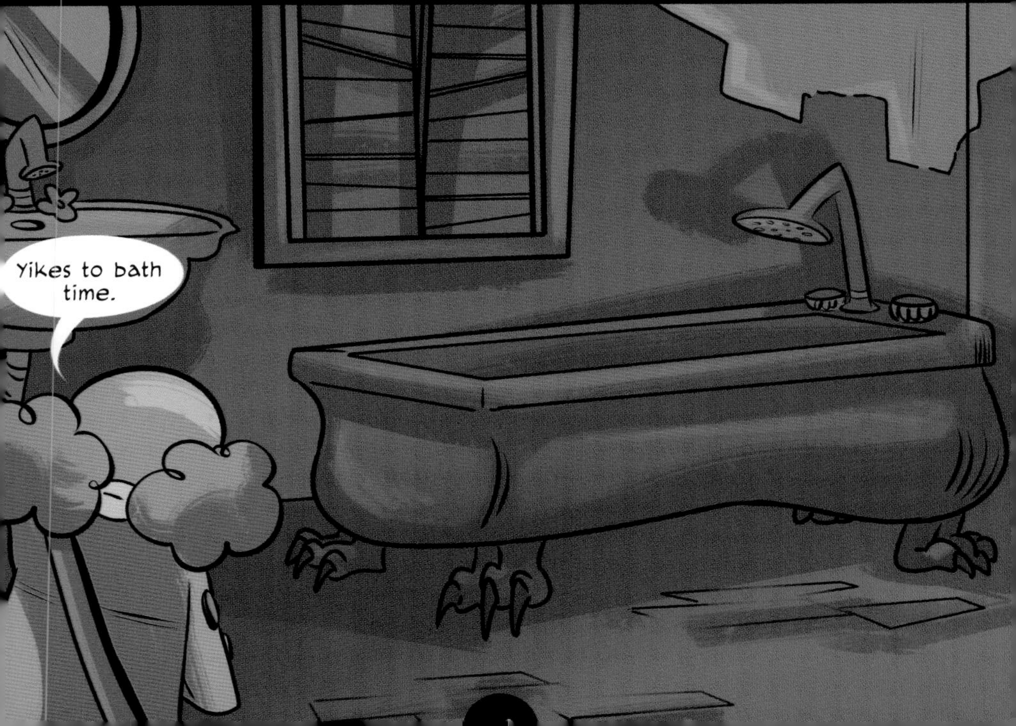
Yikes to bath time.

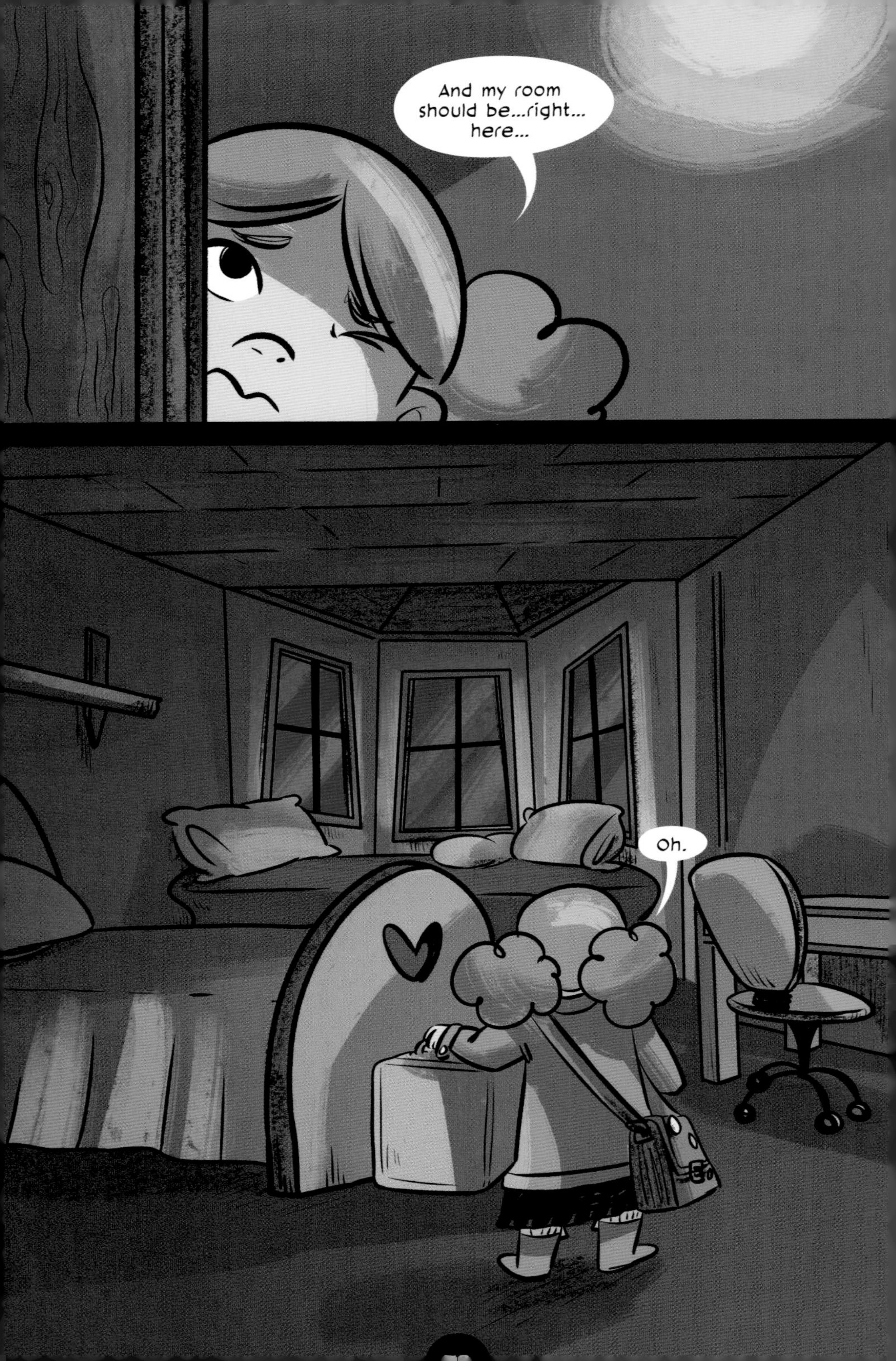
And my room should be...right... here...
Oh.

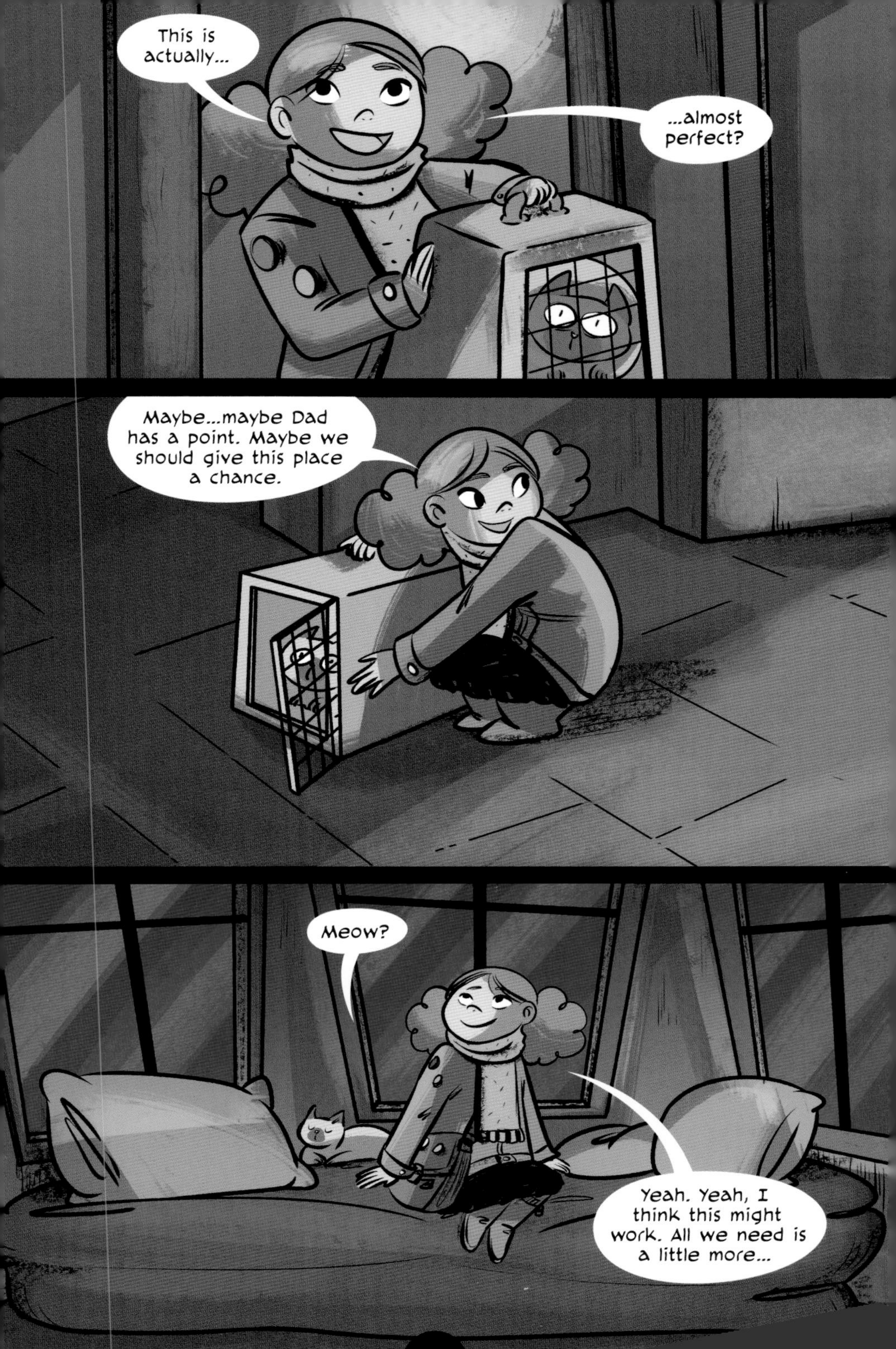
This is actually...
...almost perfect?
Maybe...maybe Dad has a point. Maybe we should give this place a chance.
Meow?
Yeah. Yeah, I think this might work. All we need is a little more...

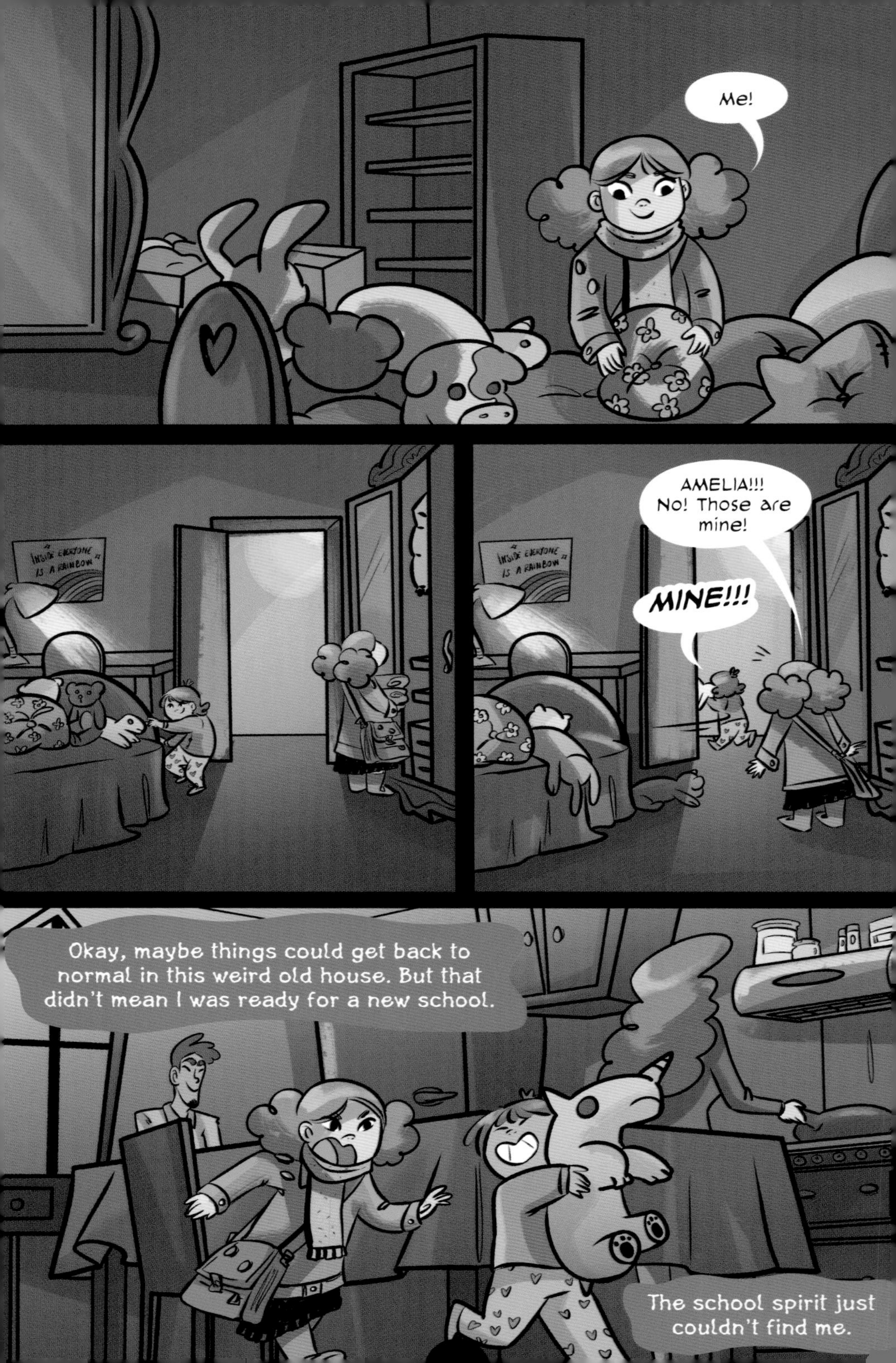
Me!
INSIDE EVERYONE IS A RAINBOW
INSIDE EVERYONE IS A RAINBOW
AMELIA!!! No! Those are mine!
MINE!!!
Okay, maybe things could get back to normal in this weird old house. But that didn't mean I was ready for a new school.
The school spirit just couldn't find me.

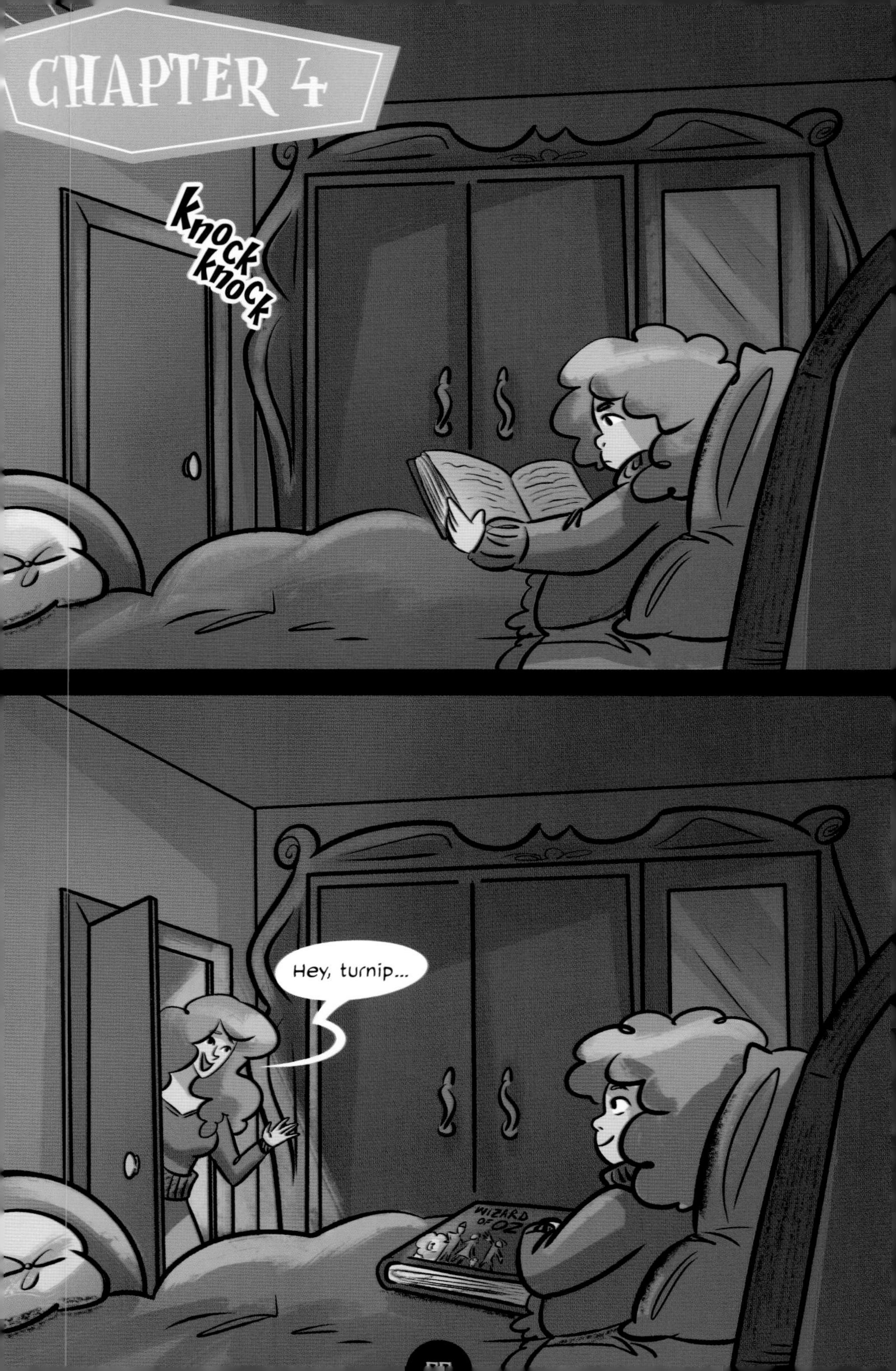
CHAPTER 4
knock knock
Hey, turnip...
WIZARD OF OZ

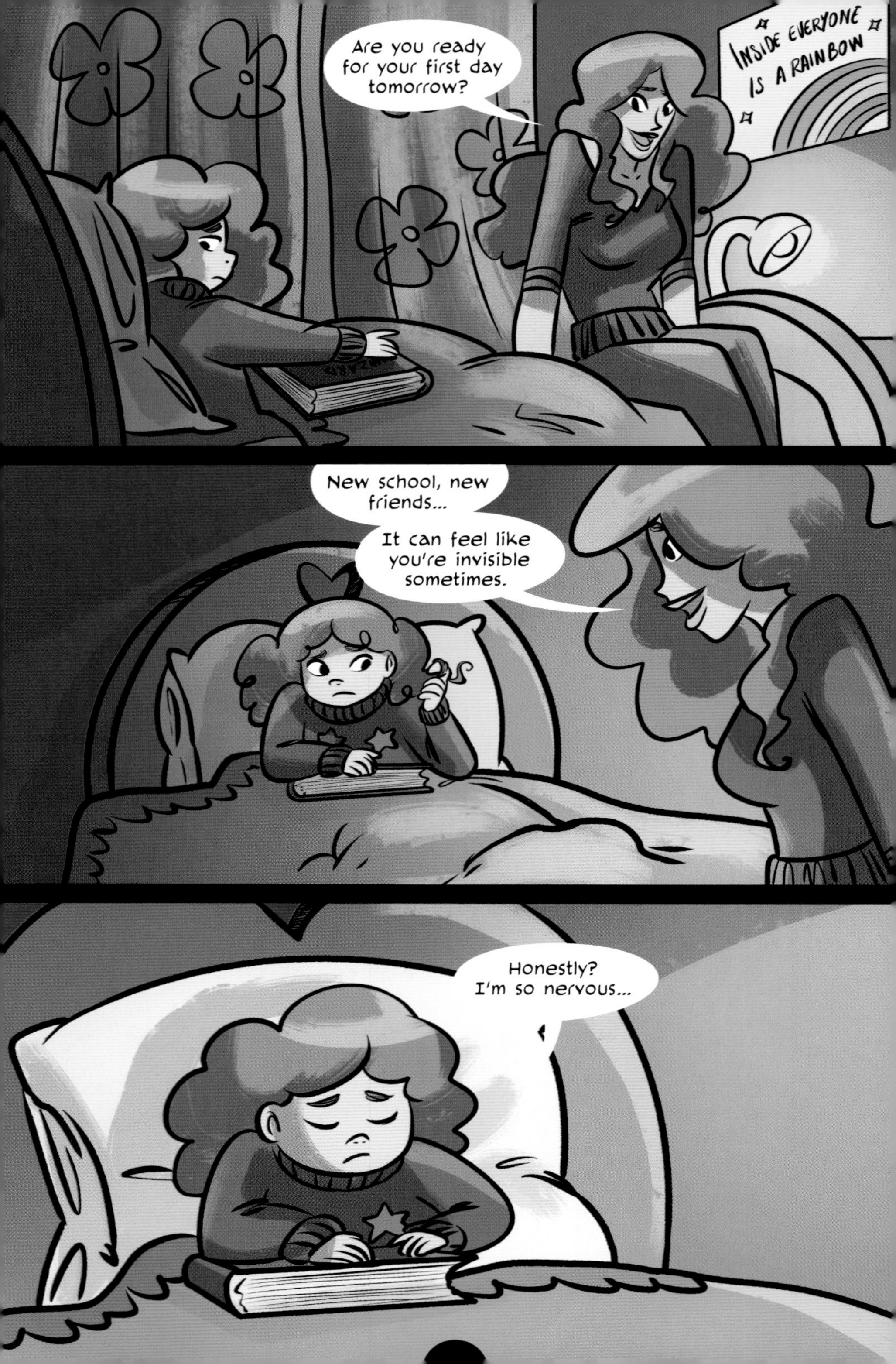

INSIDE EVERYONE IS A RAINBOW
Are you ready for your first day tomorrow?
New school, new friends...
It can feel like you're invisible sometimes.
Honestly? I'm so nervous...

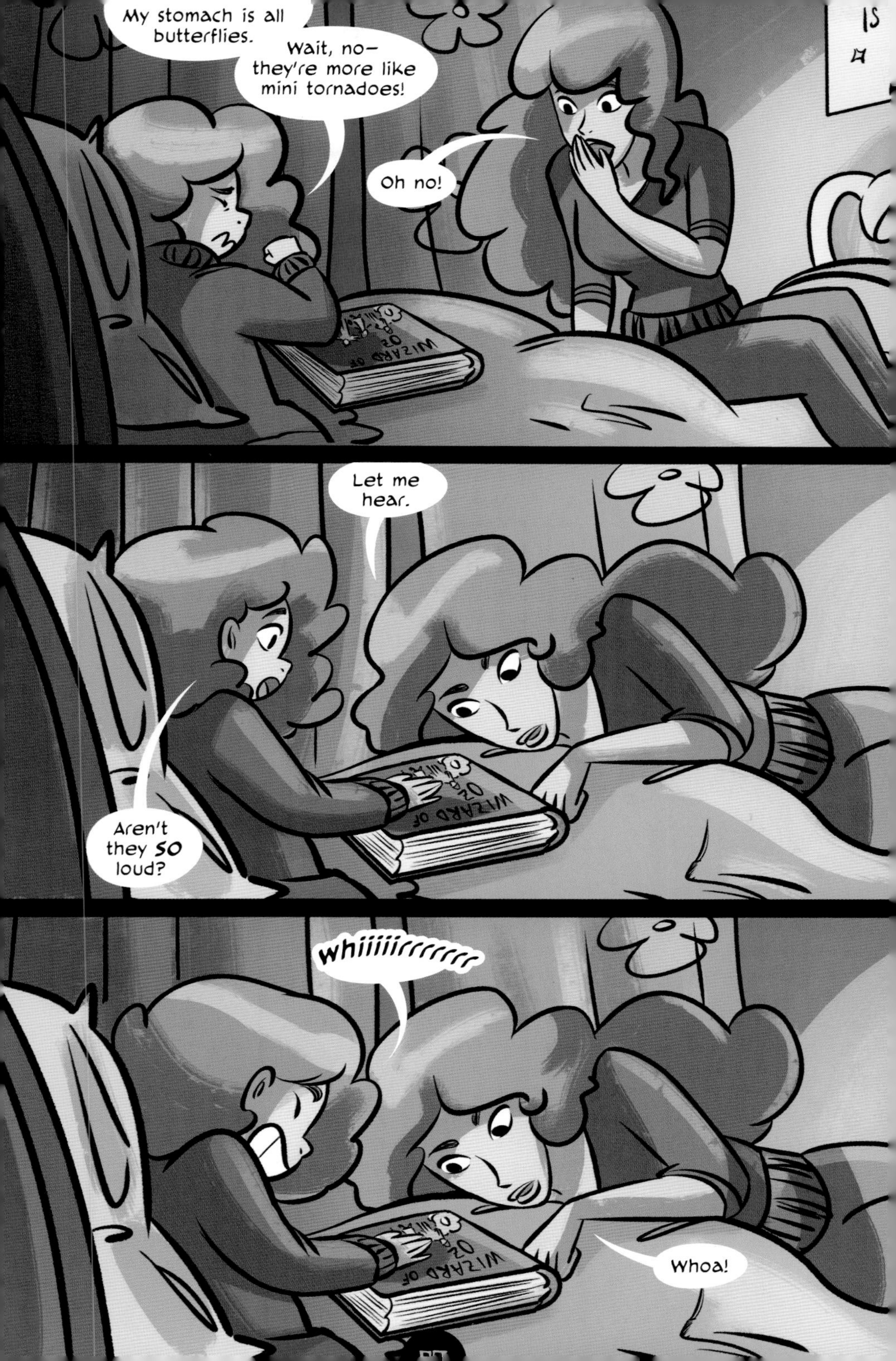

My stomach is all butterflies.
Wait, no—they're more like mini tornadoes!
Oh no!
WIZARD OF OZ
Let me hear.
Aren't they **SO** loud?
WIZARD OF OZ
Whiiiiiirrrrrrr
Whoa!
WIZARD OF OZ

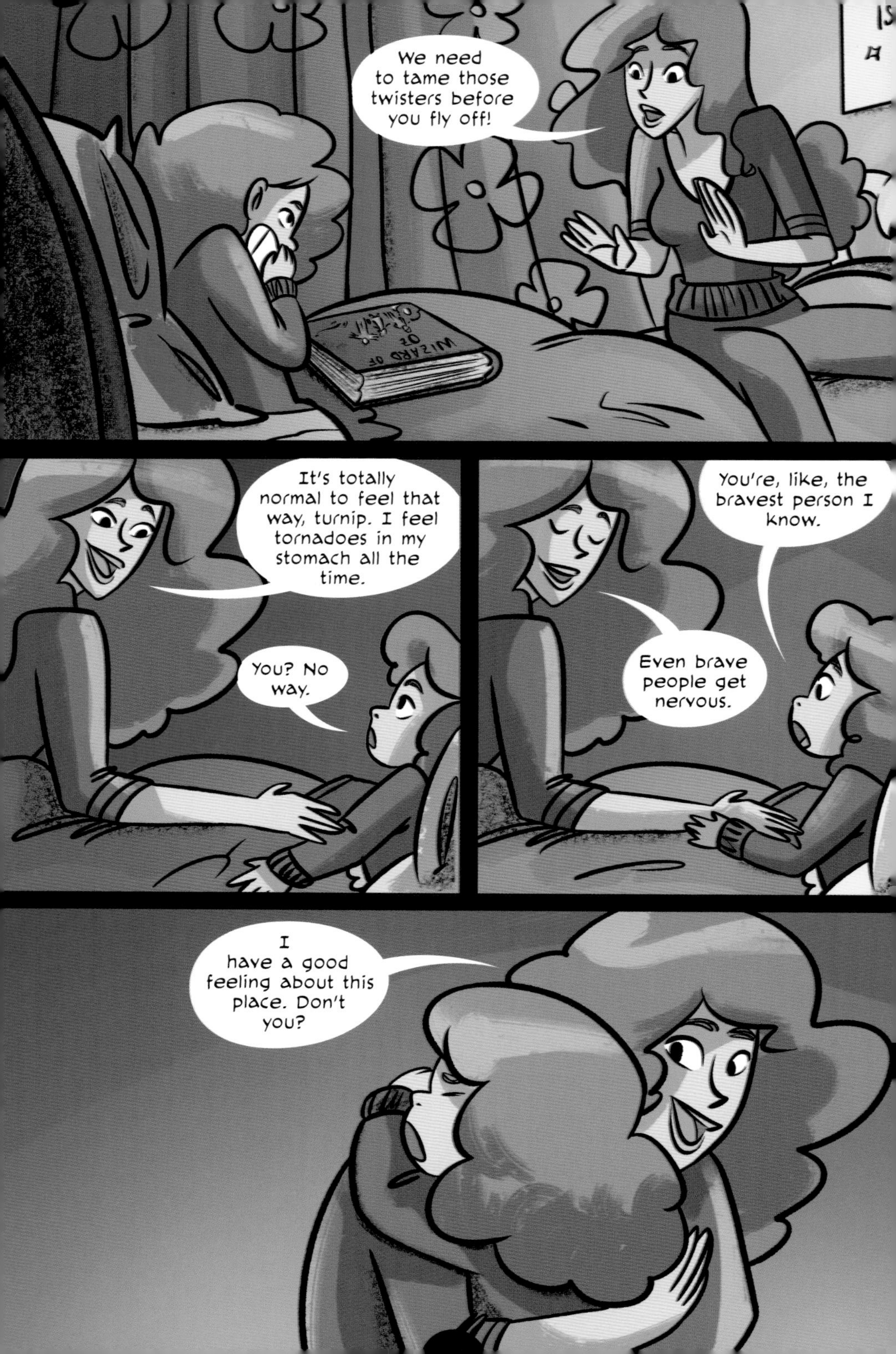
We need to tame those twisters before you fly off!
WIZARD OF OZ
It's totally normal to feel that way, turnip. I feel tornadoes in my stomach all the time.
You? No way.
You're, like, the bravest person I know.
Even brave people get nervous.
I have a good feeling about this place. Don't you?

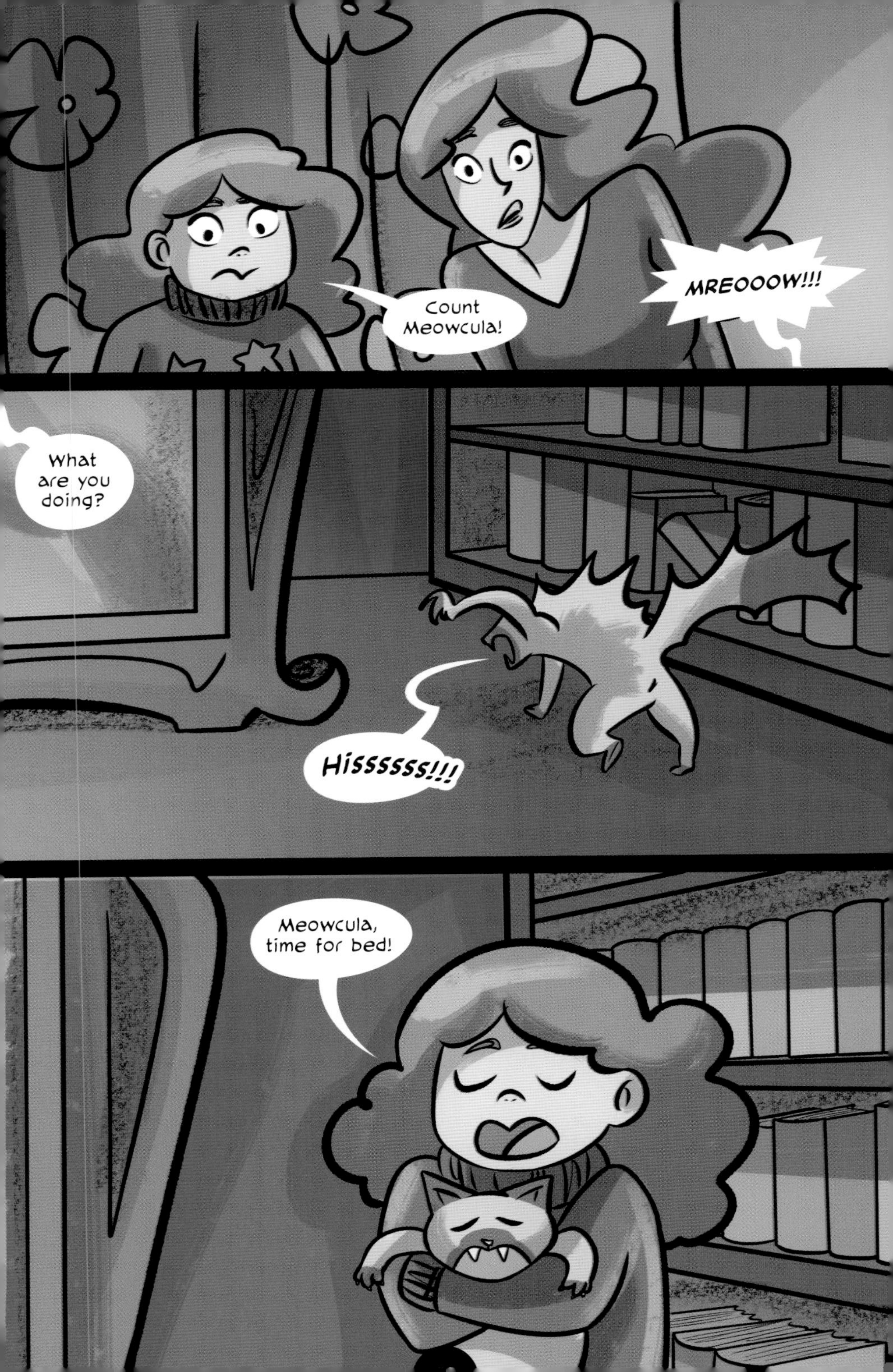

Count Meowcula!
MREOOOW!!!
What are you doing?
Hissssss!!!
Meowcula, time for bed!

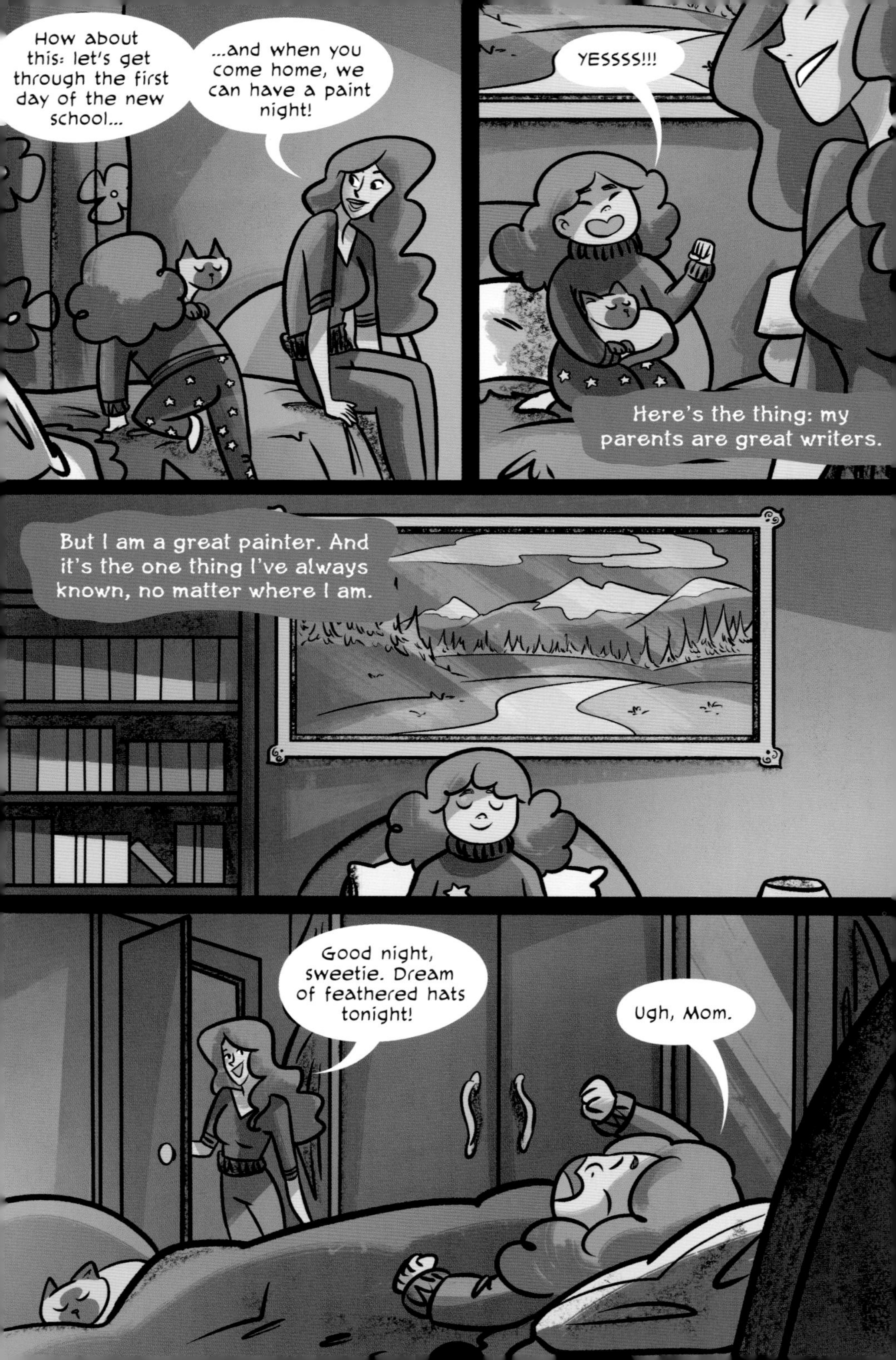
How about this: let's get through the first day of the new school...
...and when you come home, we can have a paint night!
YESSSS!!!
Here's the thing: my parents are great writers.
But I am a great painter. And it's the one thing I've always known, no matter where I am.
Good night, sweetie. Dream of feathered hats tonight!
Ugh, Mom.

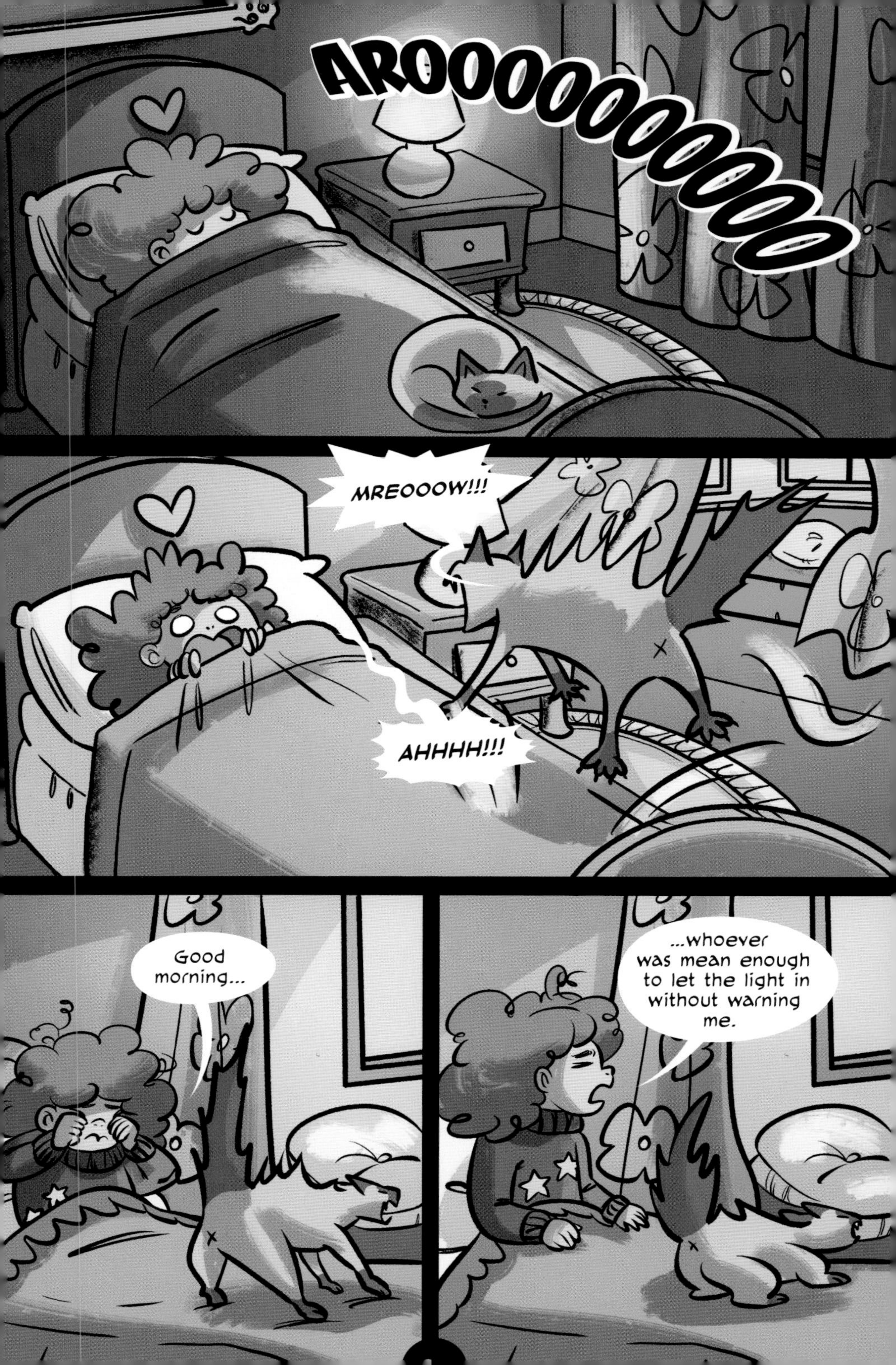
AROOOOOOOOOOO
MREOOOW!!!
AHHHH!!!
Good morning...
...whoever was mean enough to let the light in without warning me.

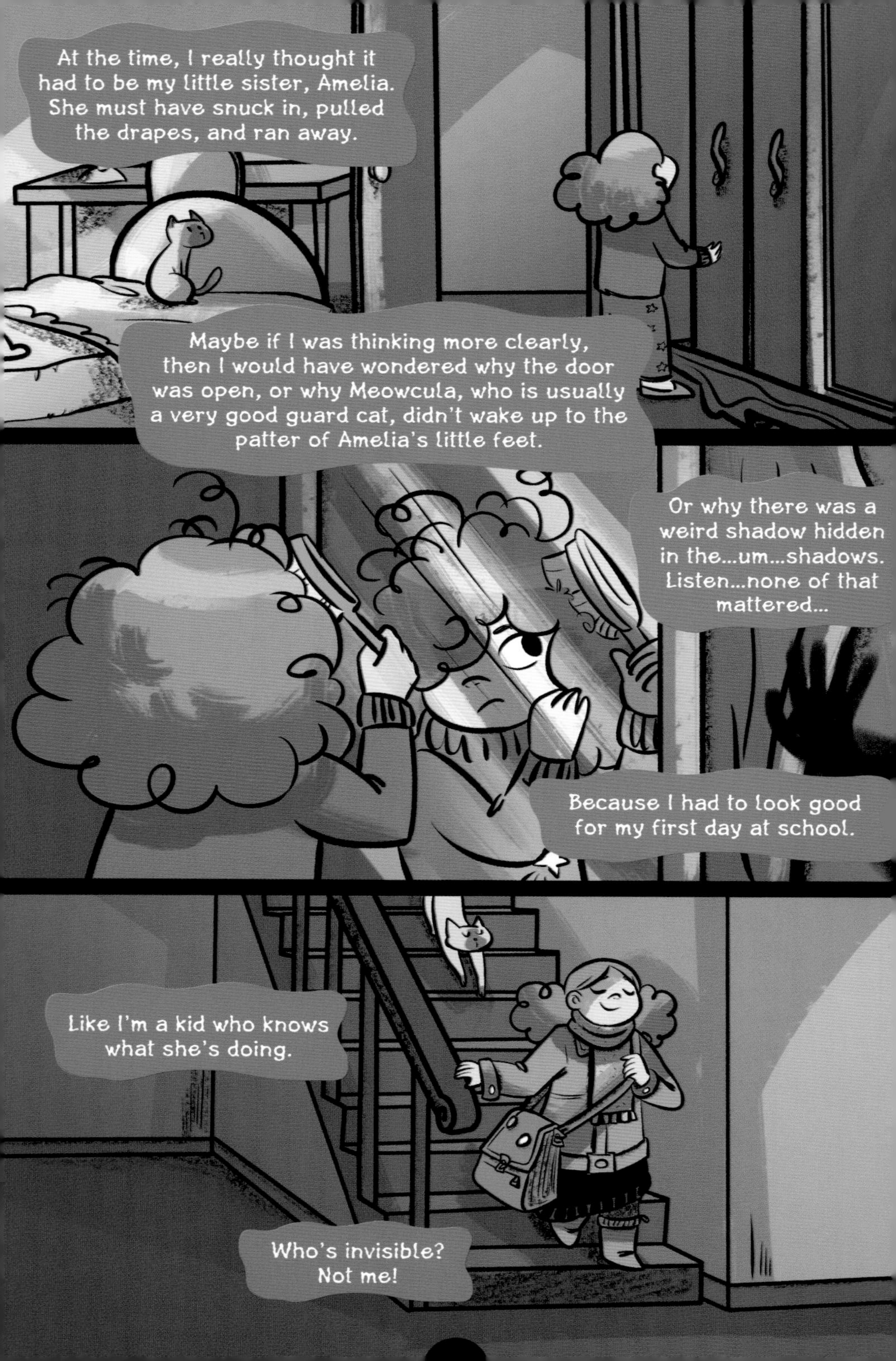
At the time, I really thought it had to be my little sister, Amelia. She must have snuck in, pulled the drapes, and ran away.
Maybe if I was thinking more clearly, then I would have wondered why the door was open, or why Meowcula, who is usually a very good guard cat, didn't wake up to the patter of Amelia's little feet.
Or why there was a weird shadow hidden in the...um...shadows. Listen...none of that mattered...
Because I had to look good for my first day at school.
Like I'm a kid who knows what she's doing.
Who's invisible? Not me!

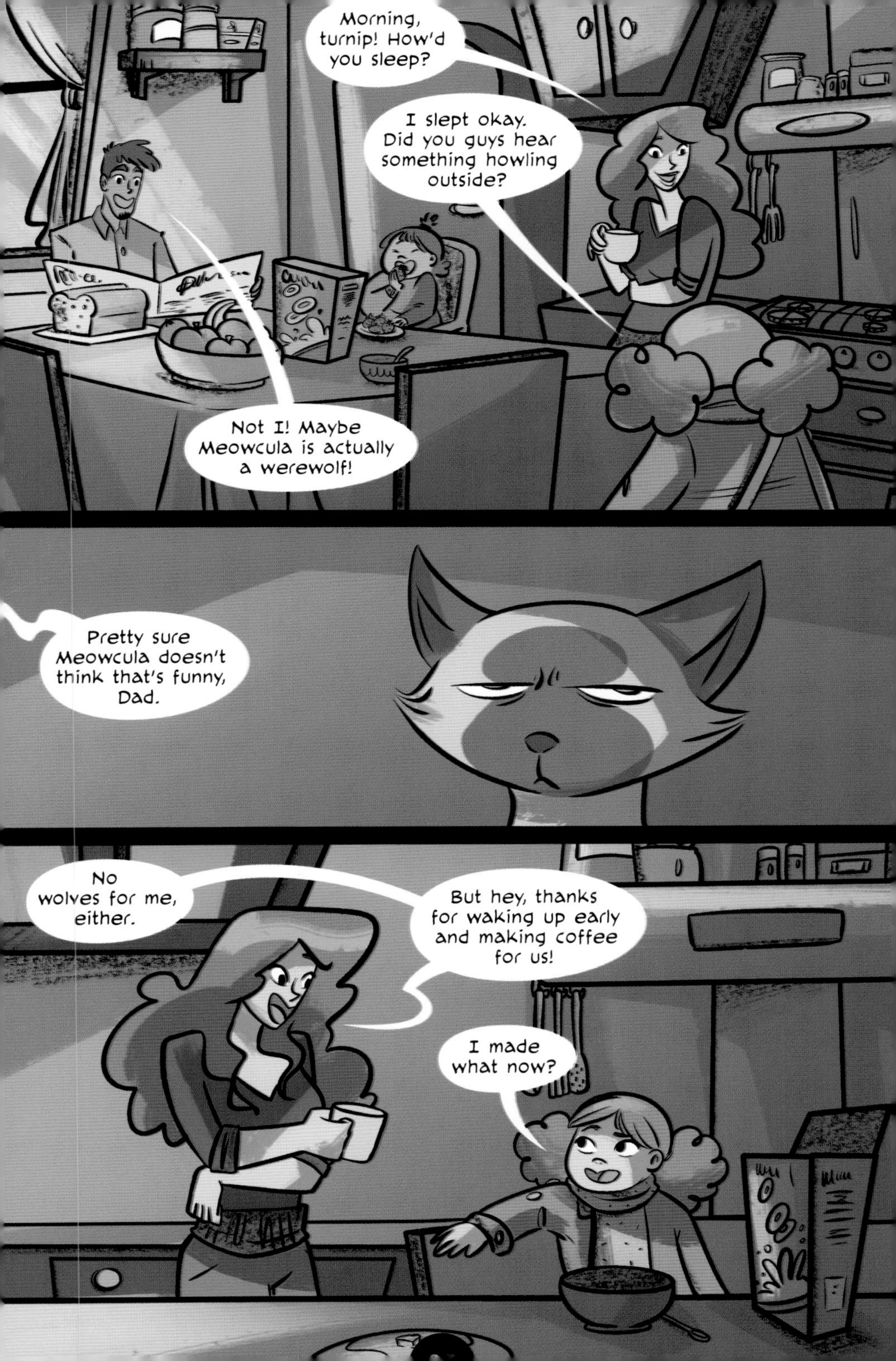
Morning, turnip! How'd you sleep?
I slept okay. Did you guys hear something howling outside?
Not I! Maybe Meowcula is actually a werewolf!
Pretty sure Meowcula doesn't think that's funny, Dad.
No wolves for me, either.
But hey, thanks for waking up early and making coffee for us!
I made what now?

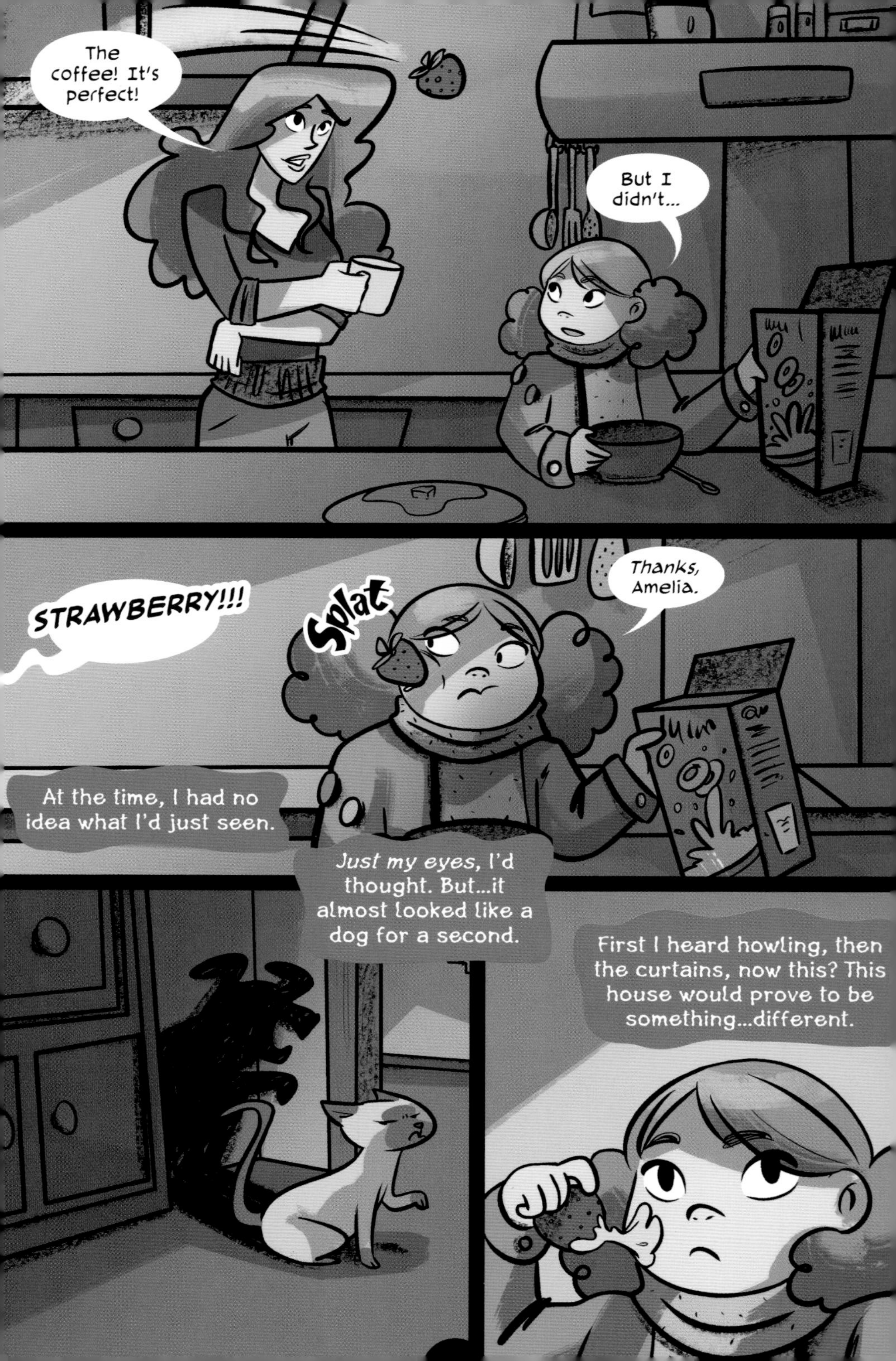

The coffee! It's perfect!
But I didn't...
STRAWBERRY!!!
Splat
Thanks, Amelia.
At the time, I had no idea what I'd just seen.
Just my eyes, I'd thought. But...it almost looked like a dog for a second.
First I heard howling, then the curtains, now this? This house would prove to be something...different.

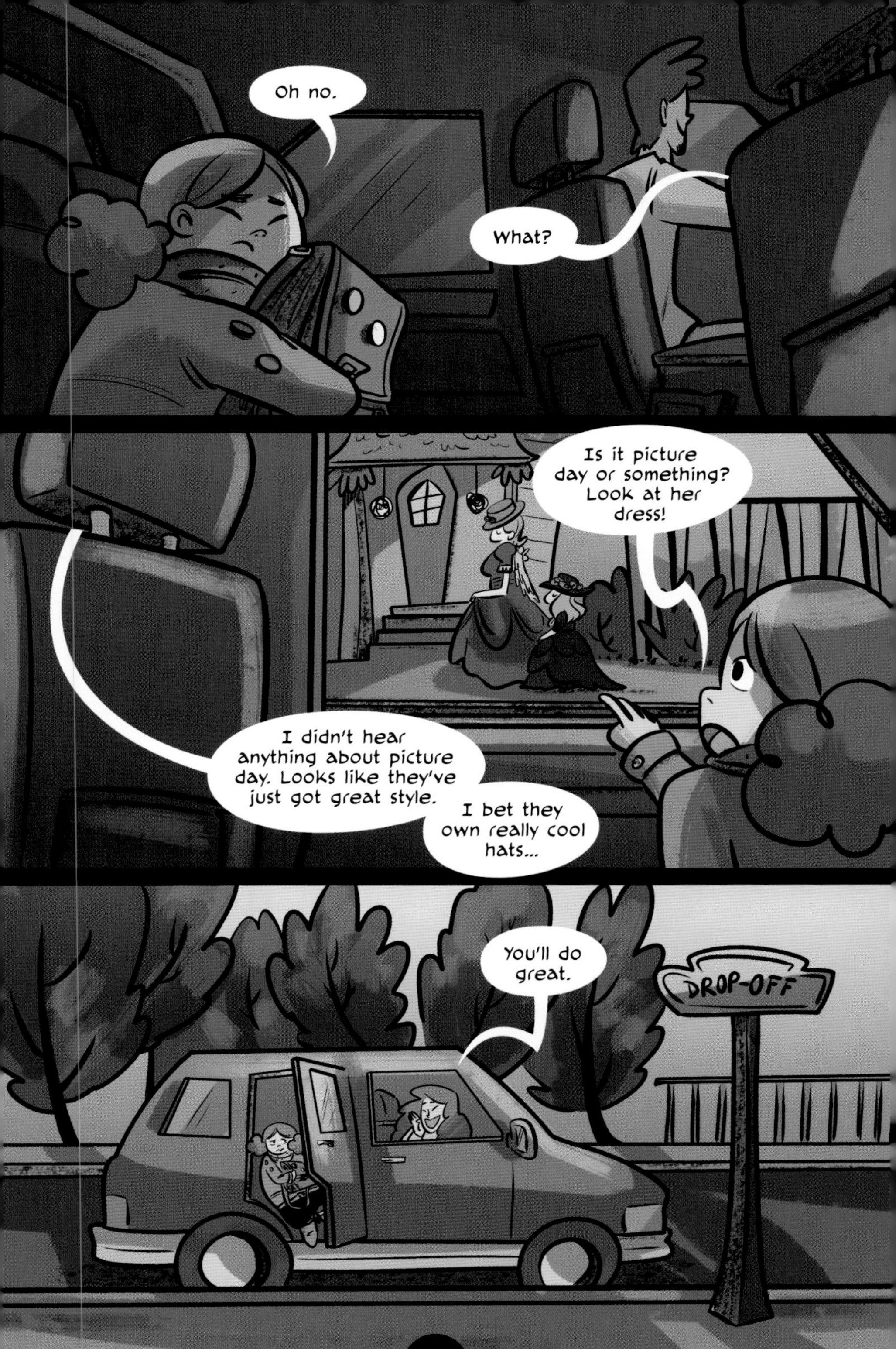
Oh no.
What?
Is it picture day or something? Look at her dress!
I didn't hear anything about picture day. Looks like they've just got great style.
I bet they own really cool hats...
You'll do great.
DROP-OFF

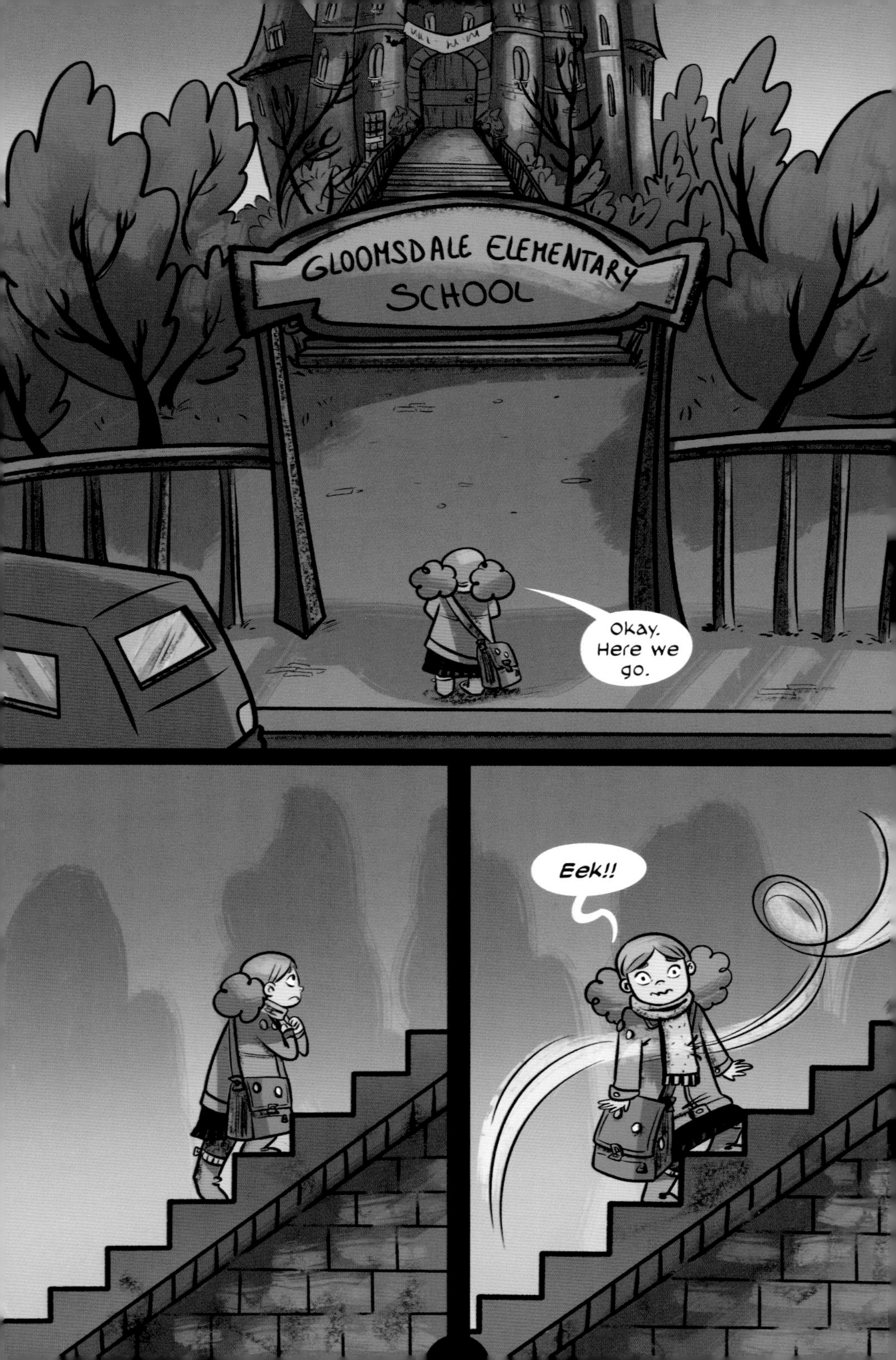
GLOOMSDALE ELEMENTARY SCHOOL
Okay. Here we go.
Eek!!

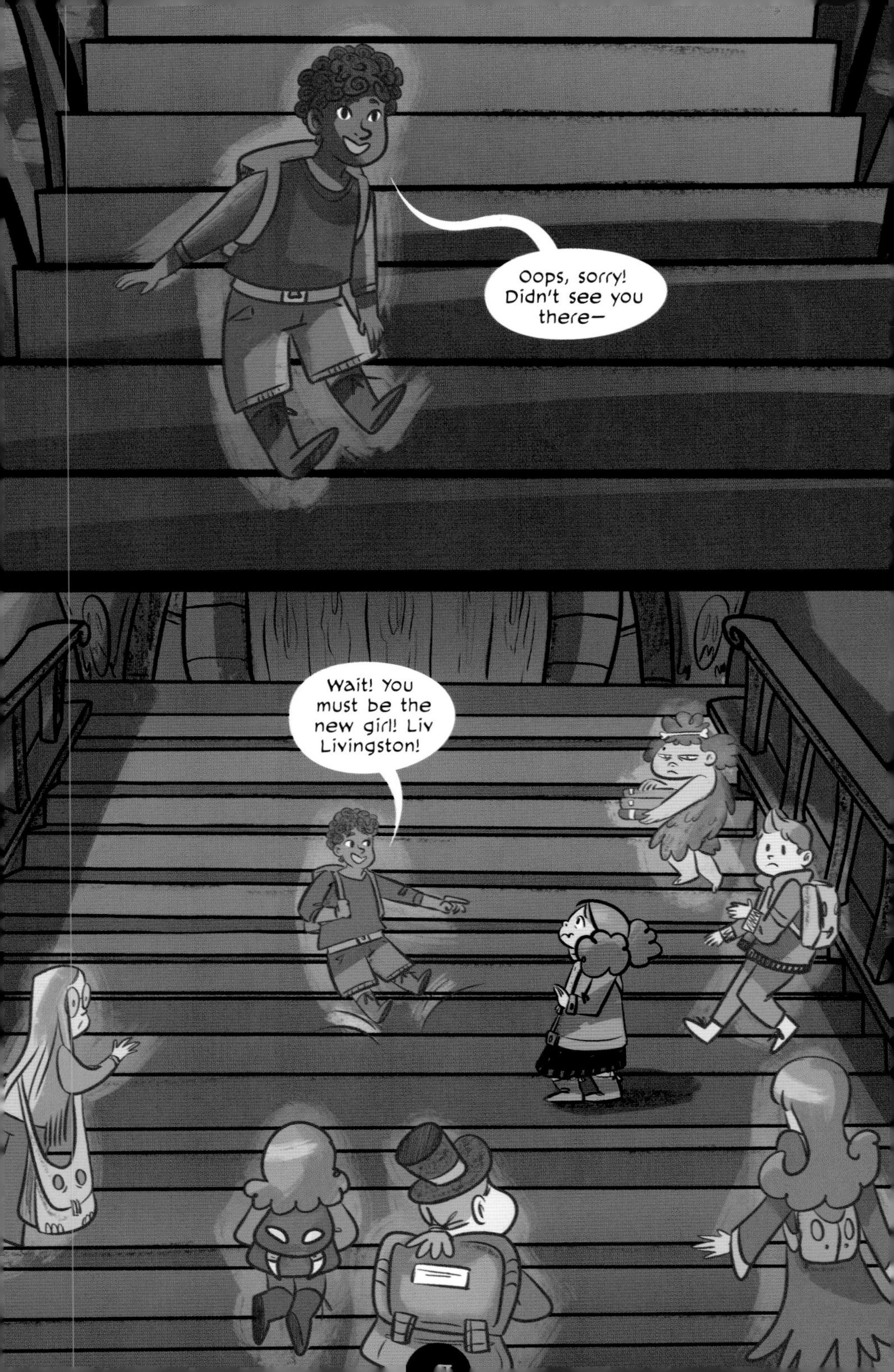
Oops, sorry! Didn't see you there—
Wait! You must be the new girl! Liv Livingston!

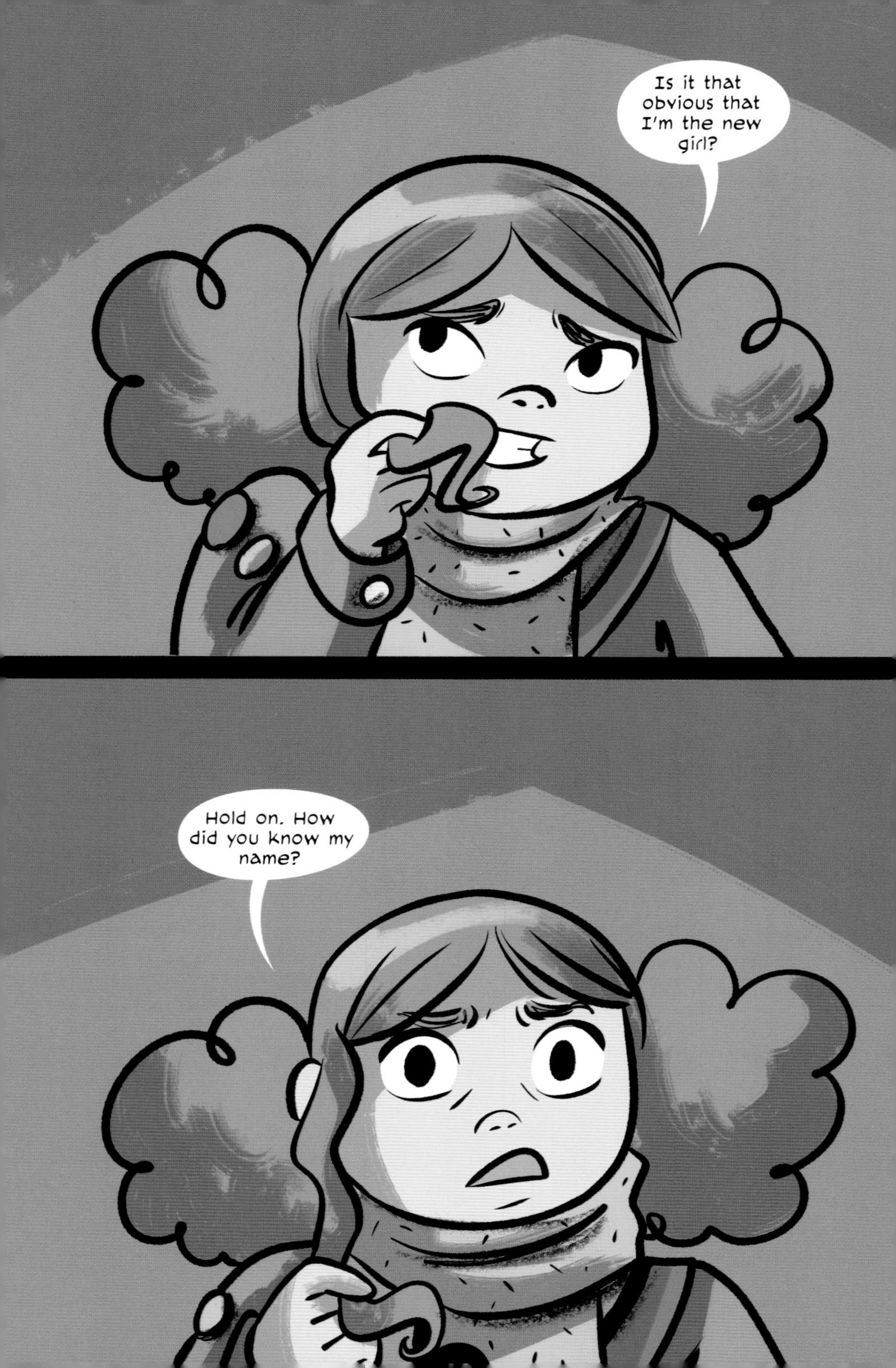
Is it that obvious that I'm the new girl?
Hold on. How did you know my name?

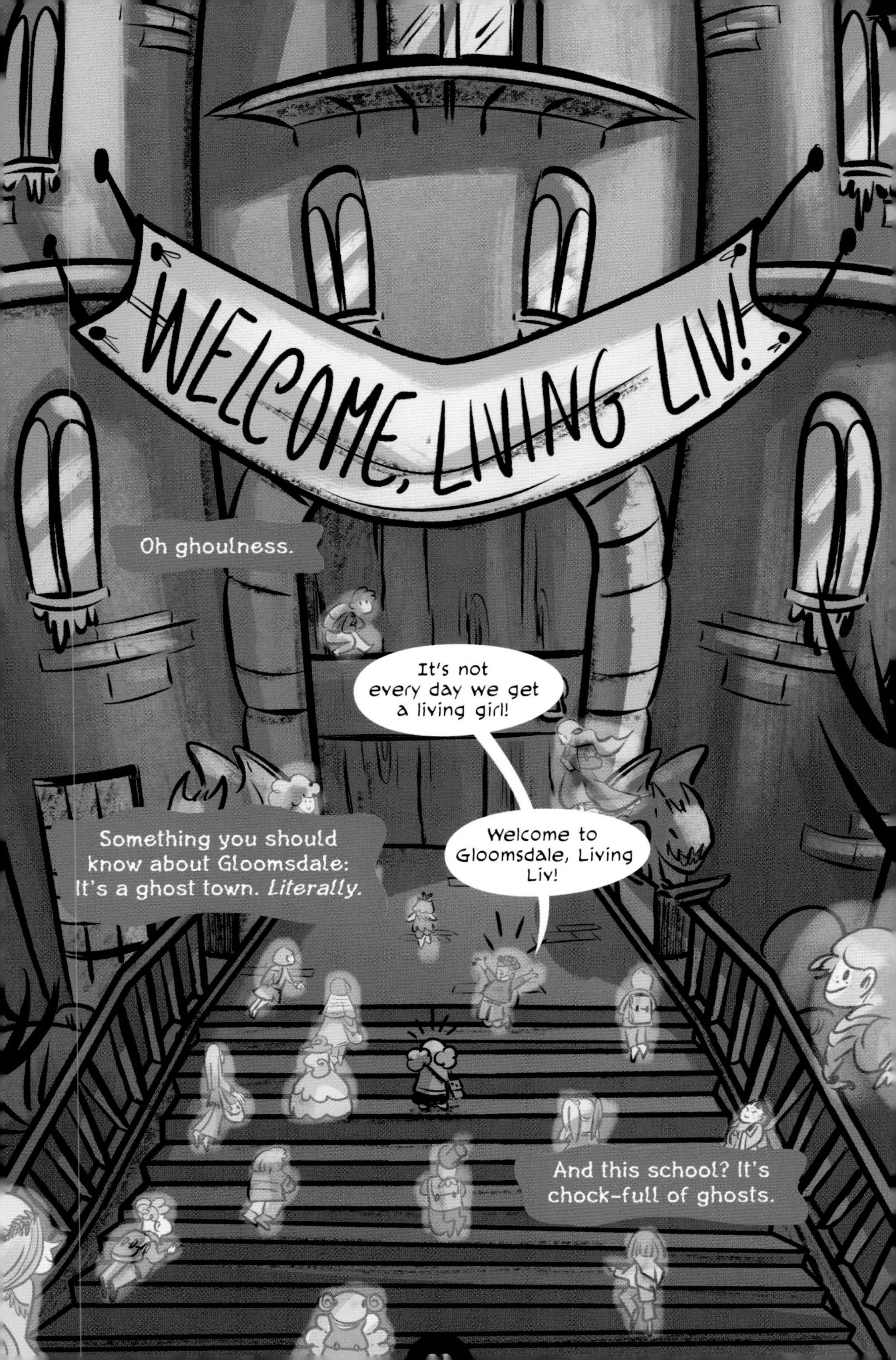
WELCOME, LIVING LIV!
Oh ghoulness.
It's not every day we get a living girl!
Welcome to Gloomsdale, Living Liv!
Something you should know about Gloomsdale: It's a ghost town. *Literally.*
And this school? It's chock-full of ghosts.

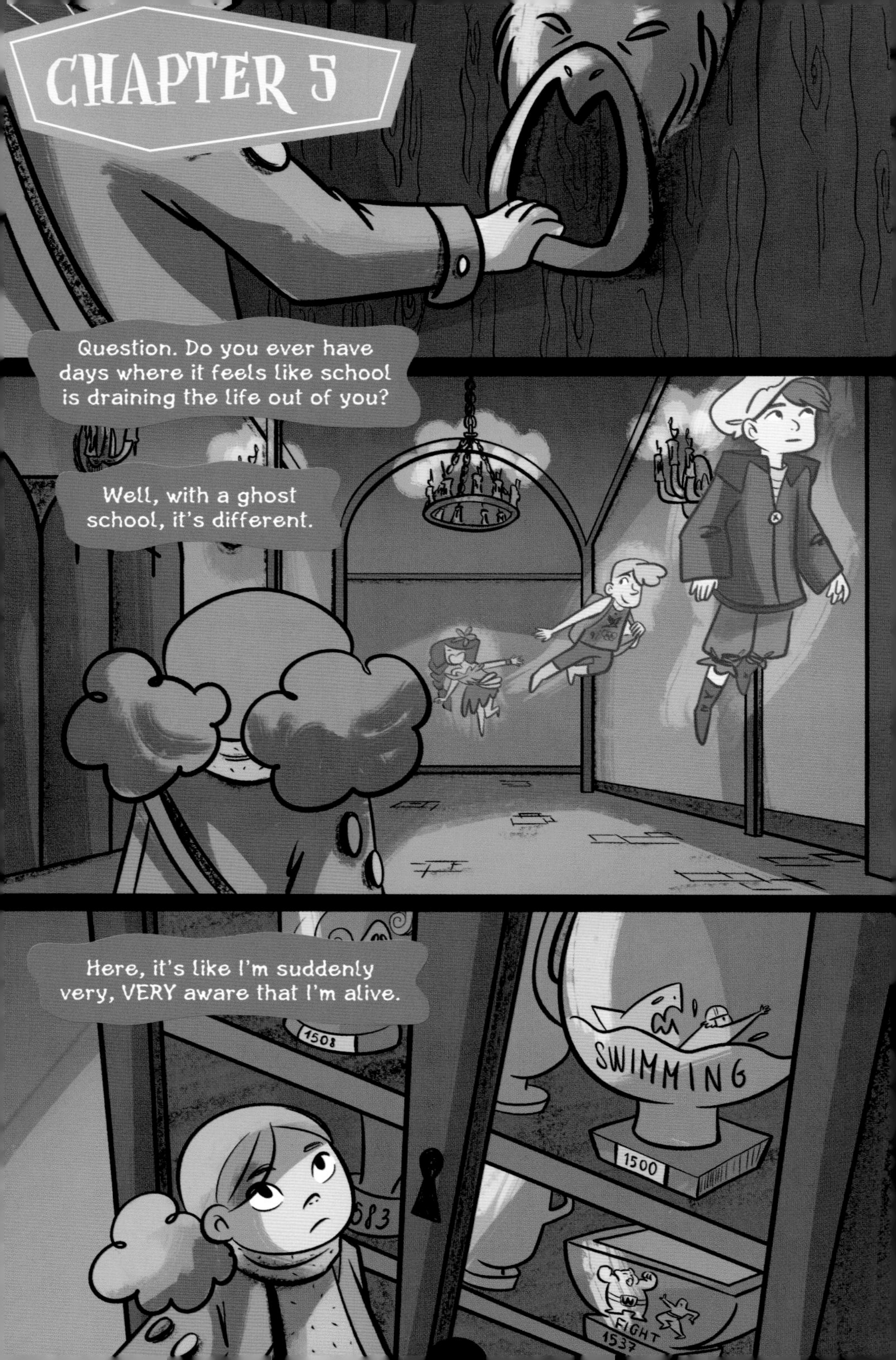
CHAPTER 5
Question. Do you ever have days where it feels like school is draining the life out of you?
Well, with a ghost school, it's different.
Here, it's like I'm suddenly very, VERY aware that I'm alive.
1508
SWIMMING
1500
583
FIGHT
1537

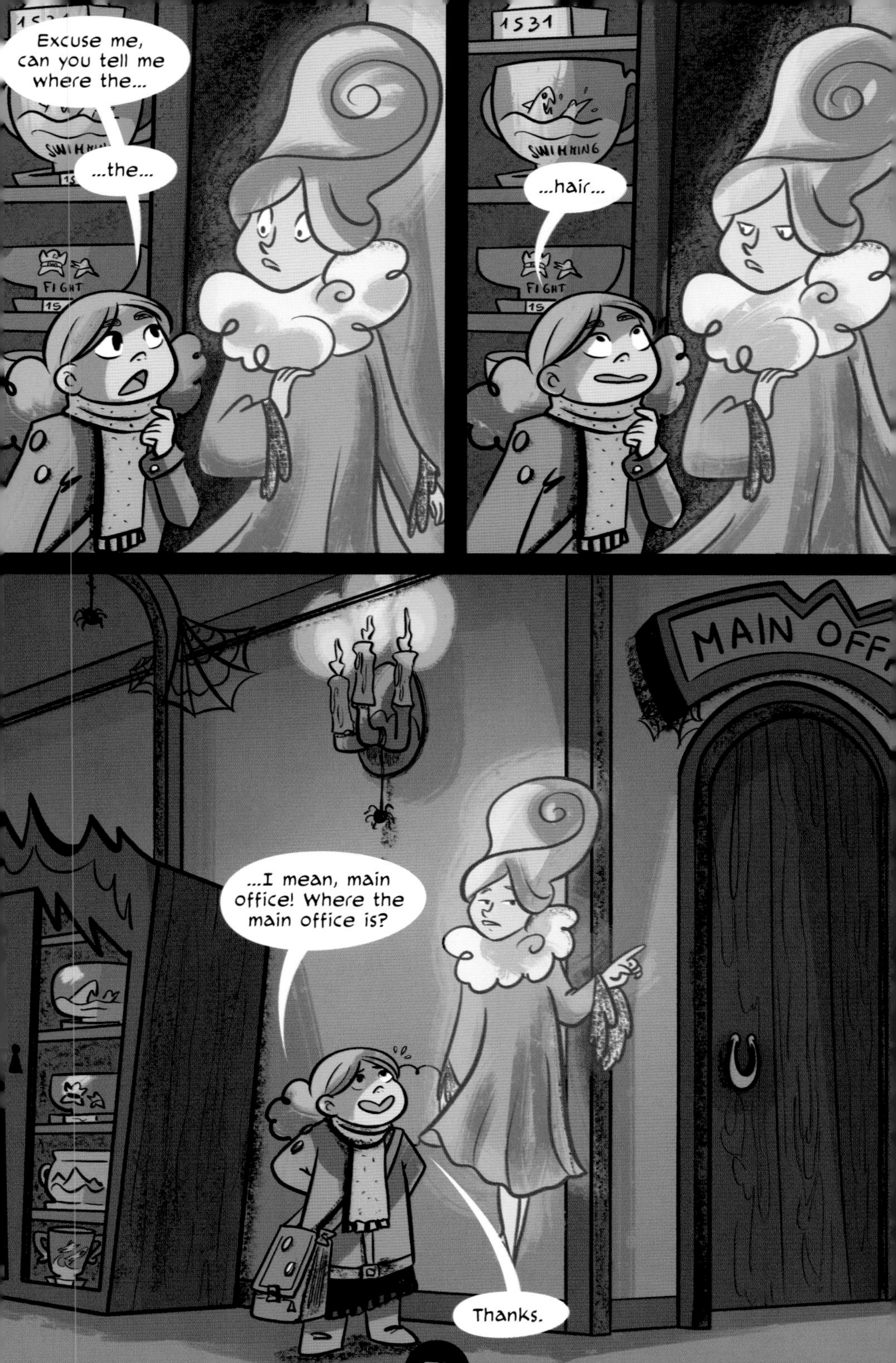
1531
SWIMMING
FIGHT
Excuse me, can you tell me where the...
...the...
...hair...
MAIN OFF
...I mean, main office! Where the main office is?
Thanks.

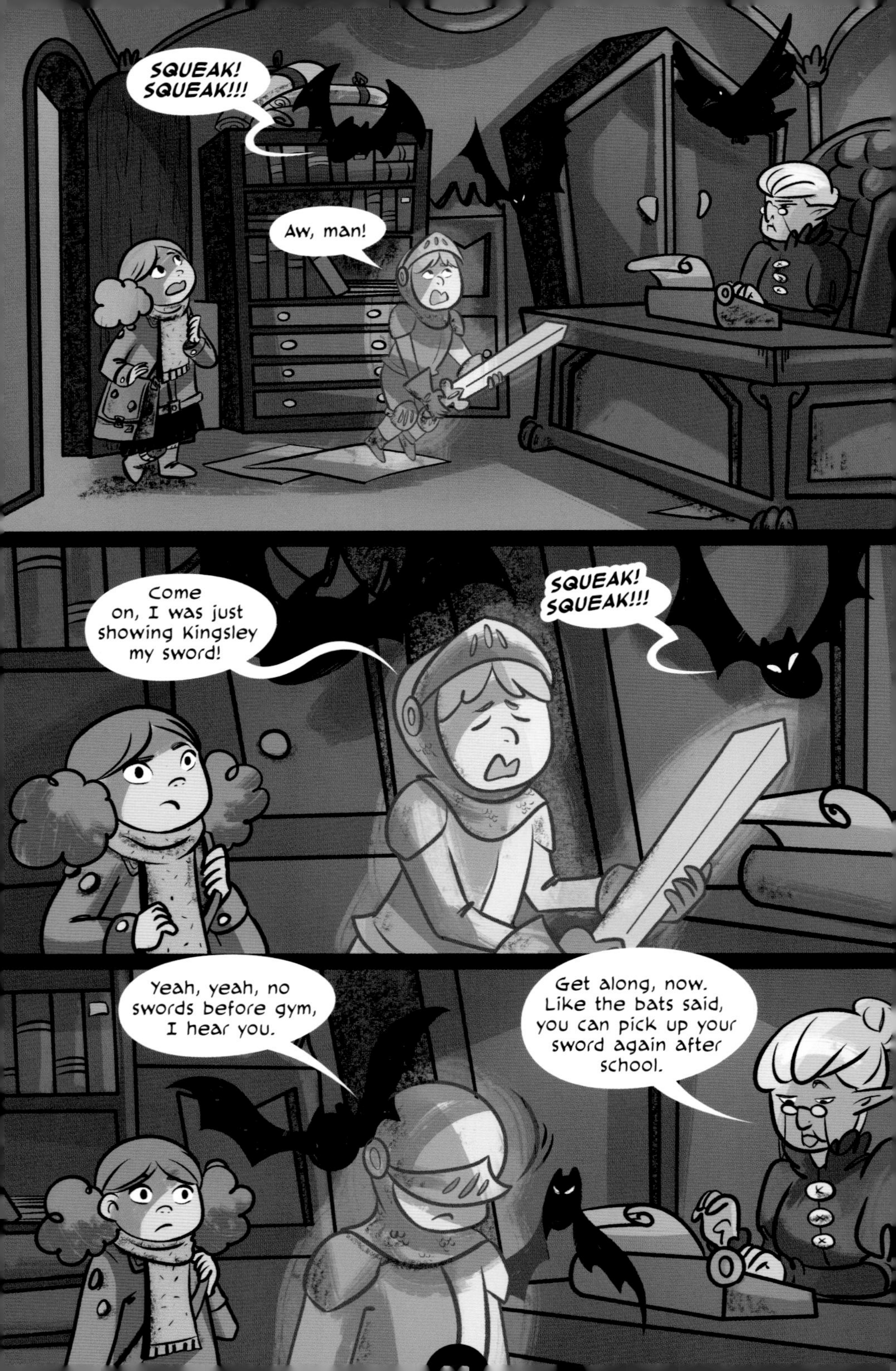
SQUEAK! SQUEAK!!!
Aw, man!
Come on, I was just showing Kingsley my sword!
SQUEAK! SQUEAK!!!
Yeah, yeah, no swords before gym, I hear you.
Get along, now. Like the bats said, you can pick up your sword again after school.

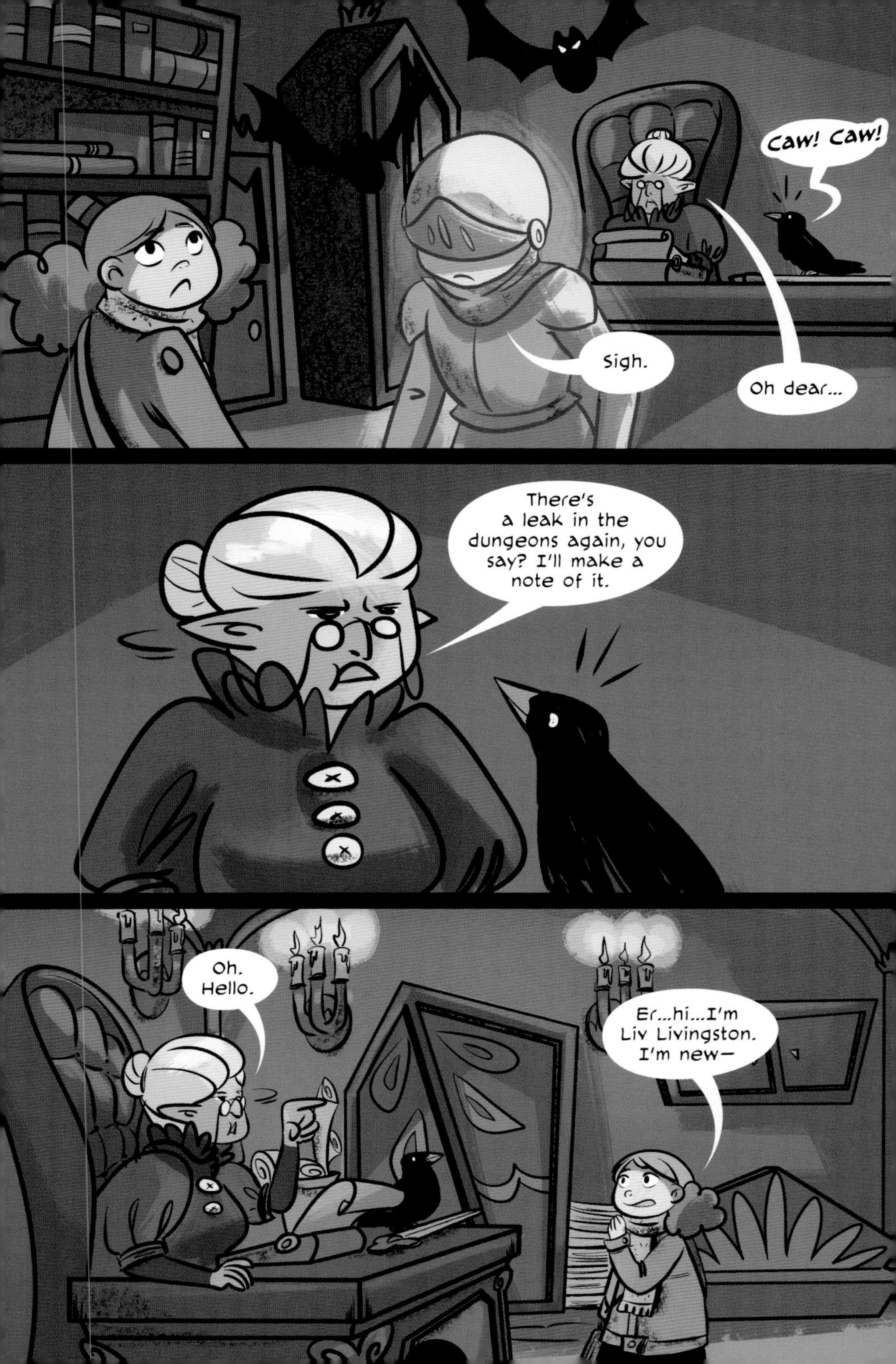
Caw! Caw!
Sigh.
Oh dear...
There's a leak in the dungeons again, you say? I'll make a note of it.
Oh. Hello.
Er...hi...I'm Liv Livingston. I'm new—

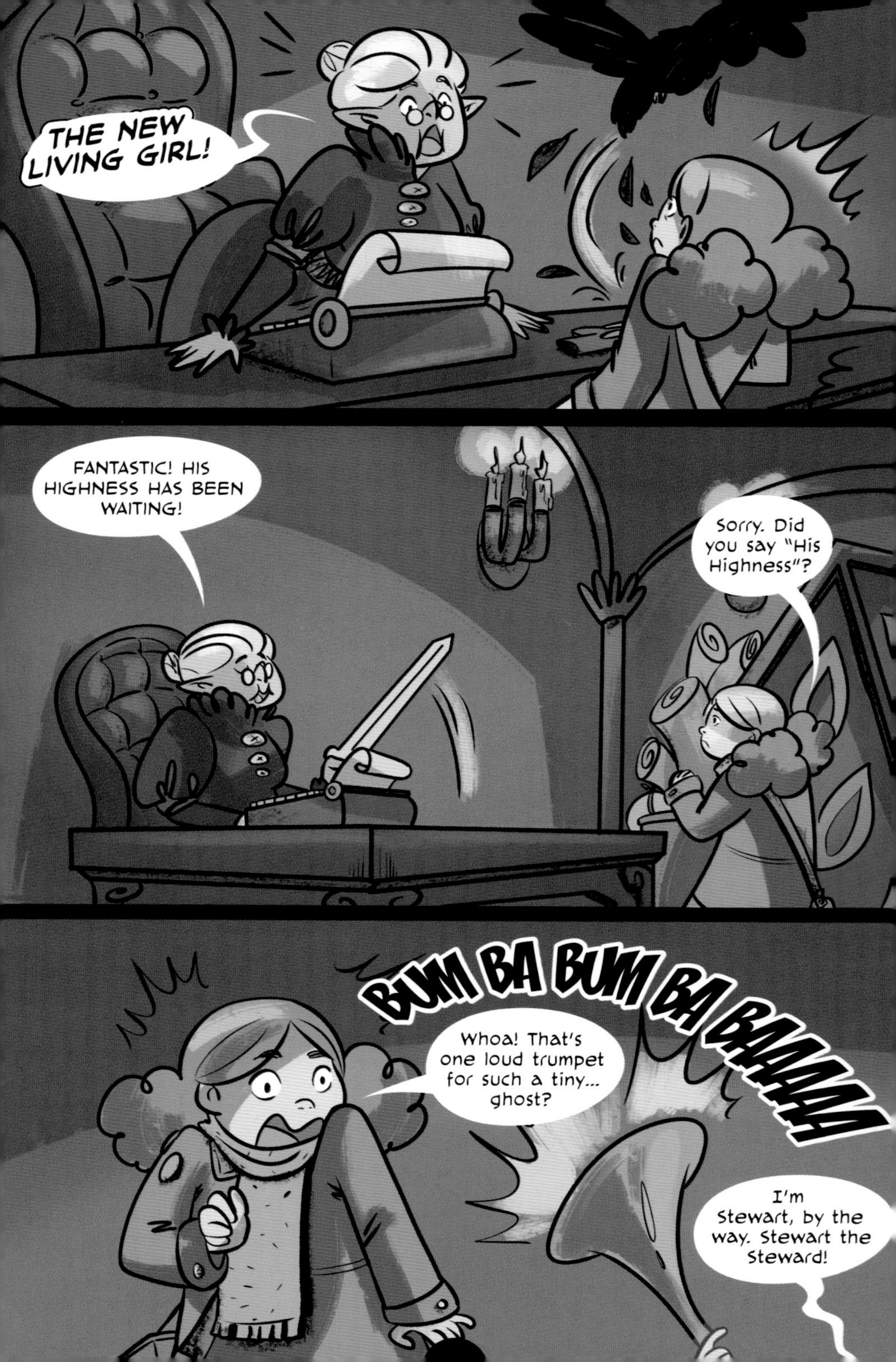
THE NEW LIVING GIRL!
FANTASTIC! HIS HIGHNESS HAS BEEN WAITING!
Sorry. Did you say "His Highness"?
BUM BA BUM BA BAAAAA
Whoa! That's one loud trumpet for such a tiny... ghost?
I'm Stewart, by the way. Stewart the Steward!

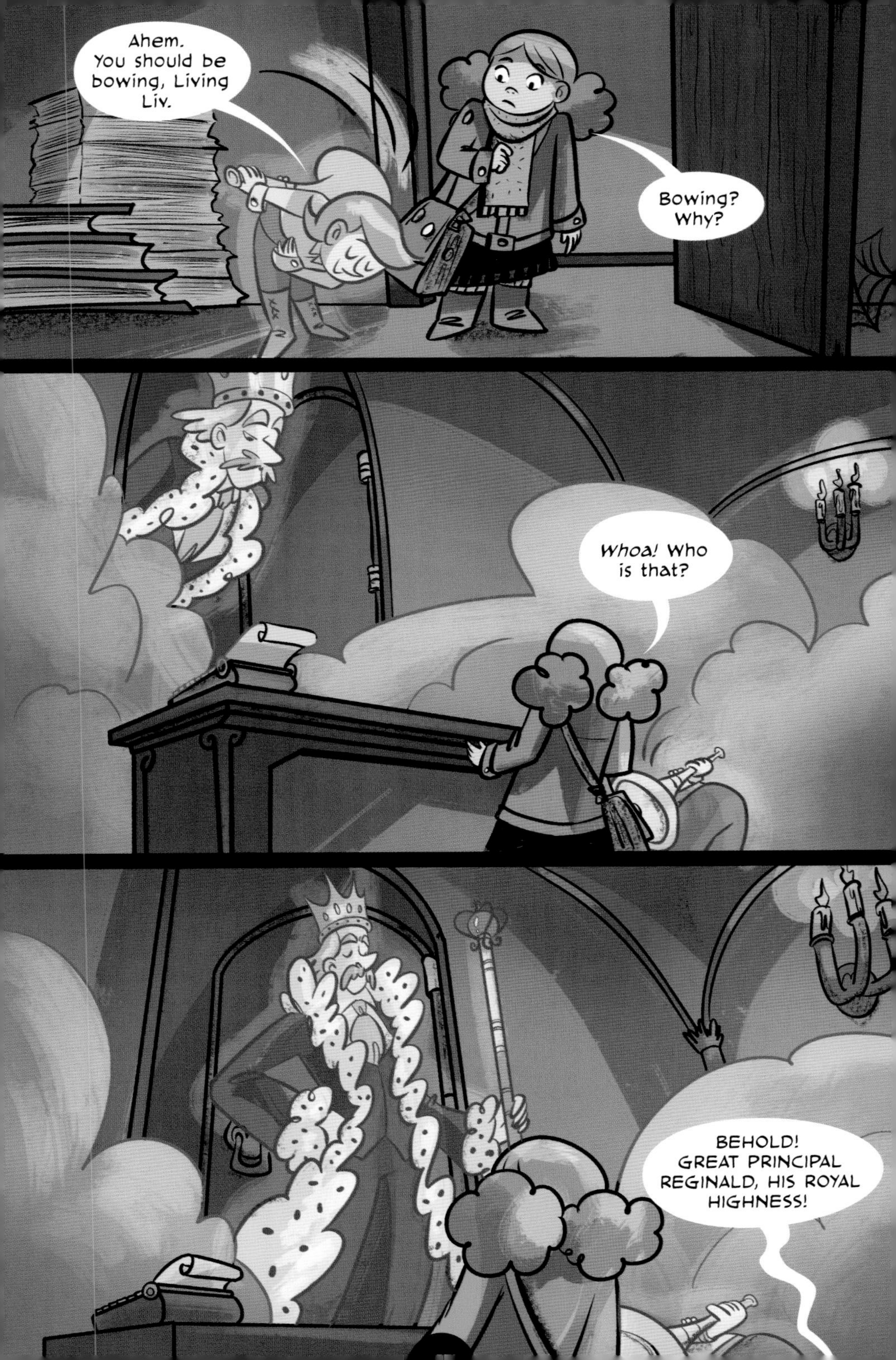

Ahem. You should be bowing, Living Liv.
Bowing? Why?
Whoa! Who is that?
BEHOLD! GREAT PRINCIPAL REGINALD, HIS ROYAL HIGHNESS!

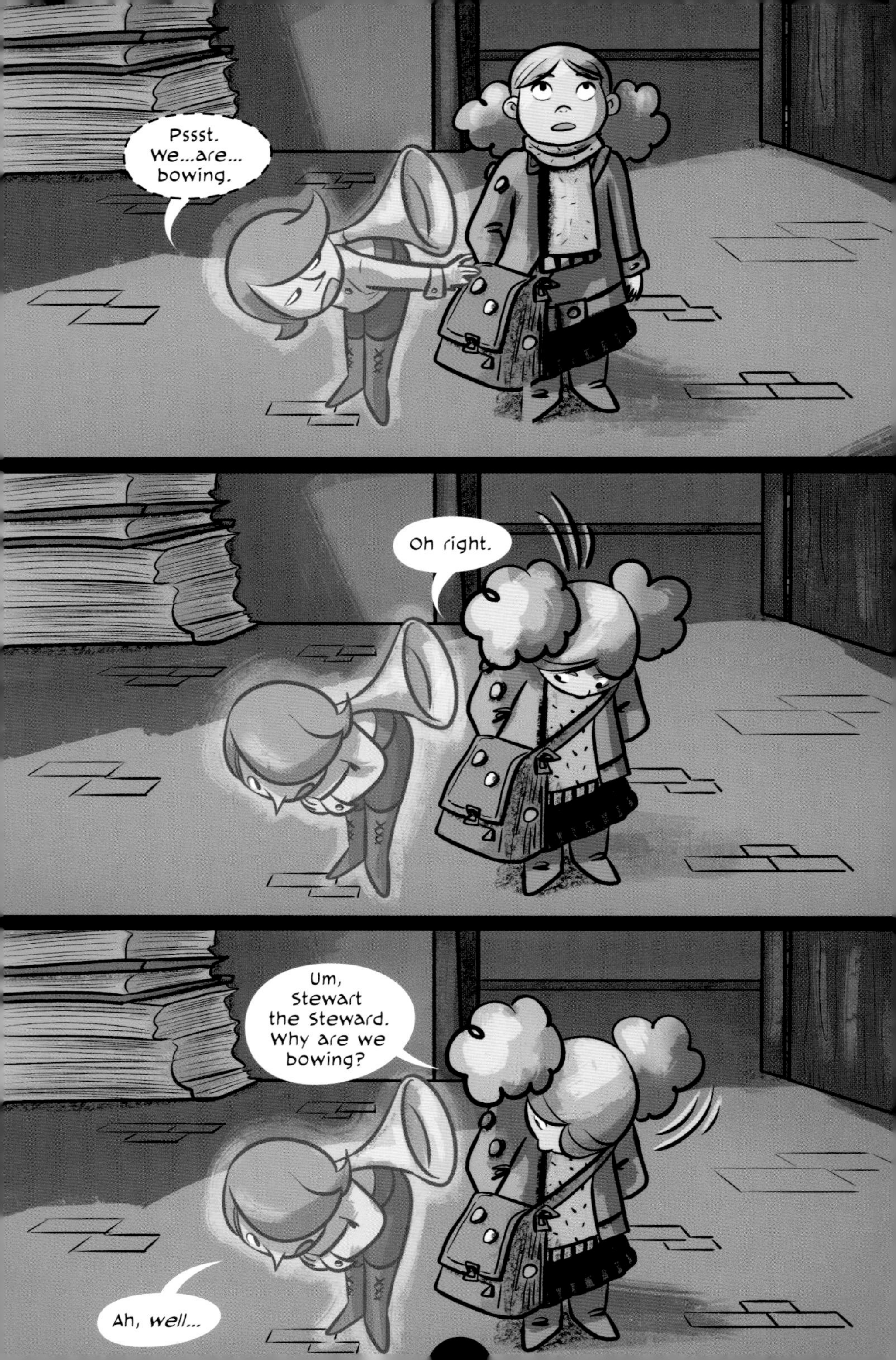
Pssst. We...are... bowing.
Oh right.
Um, Stewart the Steward. Why are we bowing?
Ah, well...

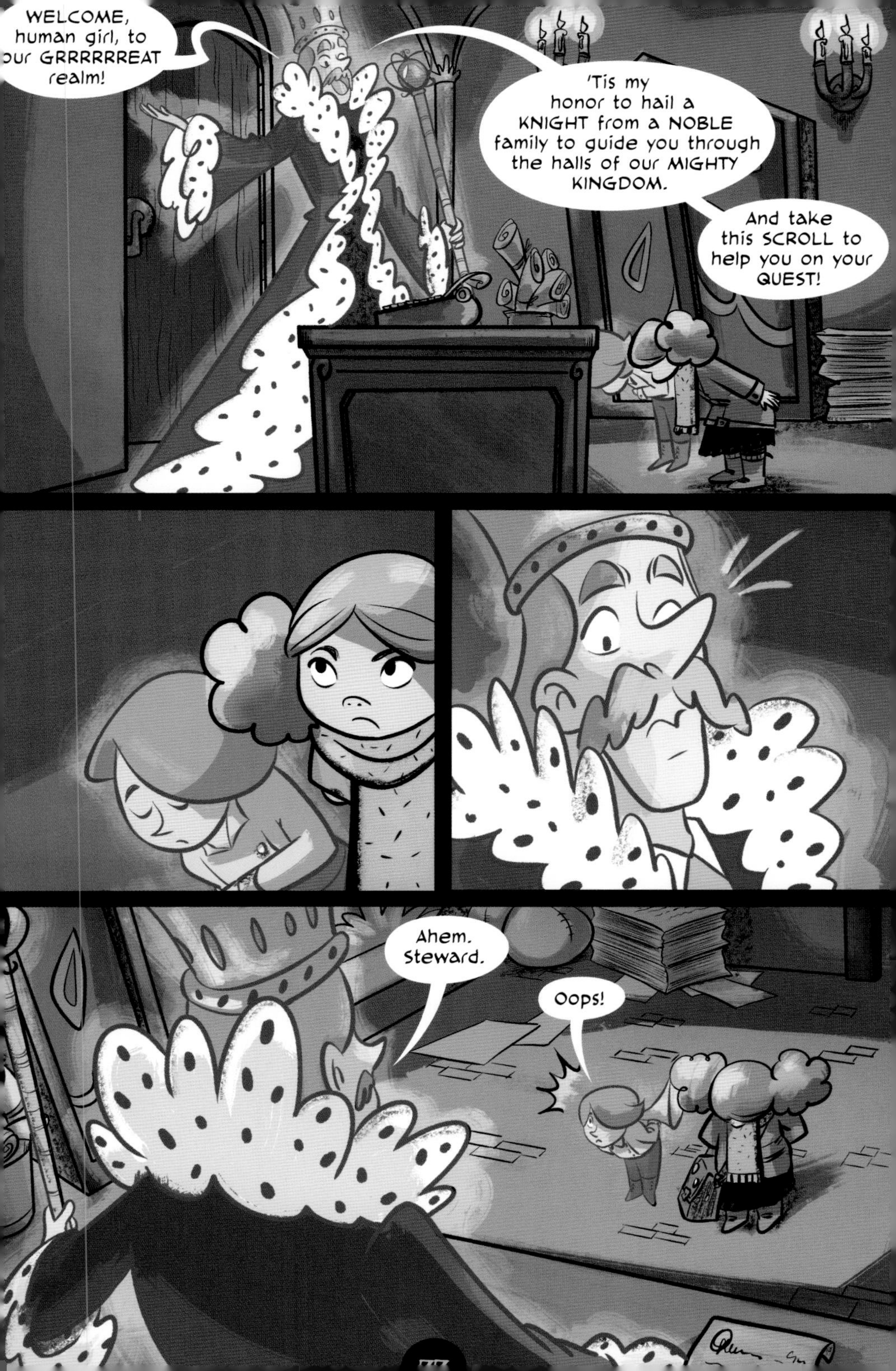

WELCOME, human girl, to our GRRRRRREAT realm!
'Tis my honor to hail a KNIGHT from a NOBLE family to guide you through the halls of our MIGHTY KINGDOM.
And take this SCROLL to help you on your QUEST!
Ahem. Steward.
Oops!

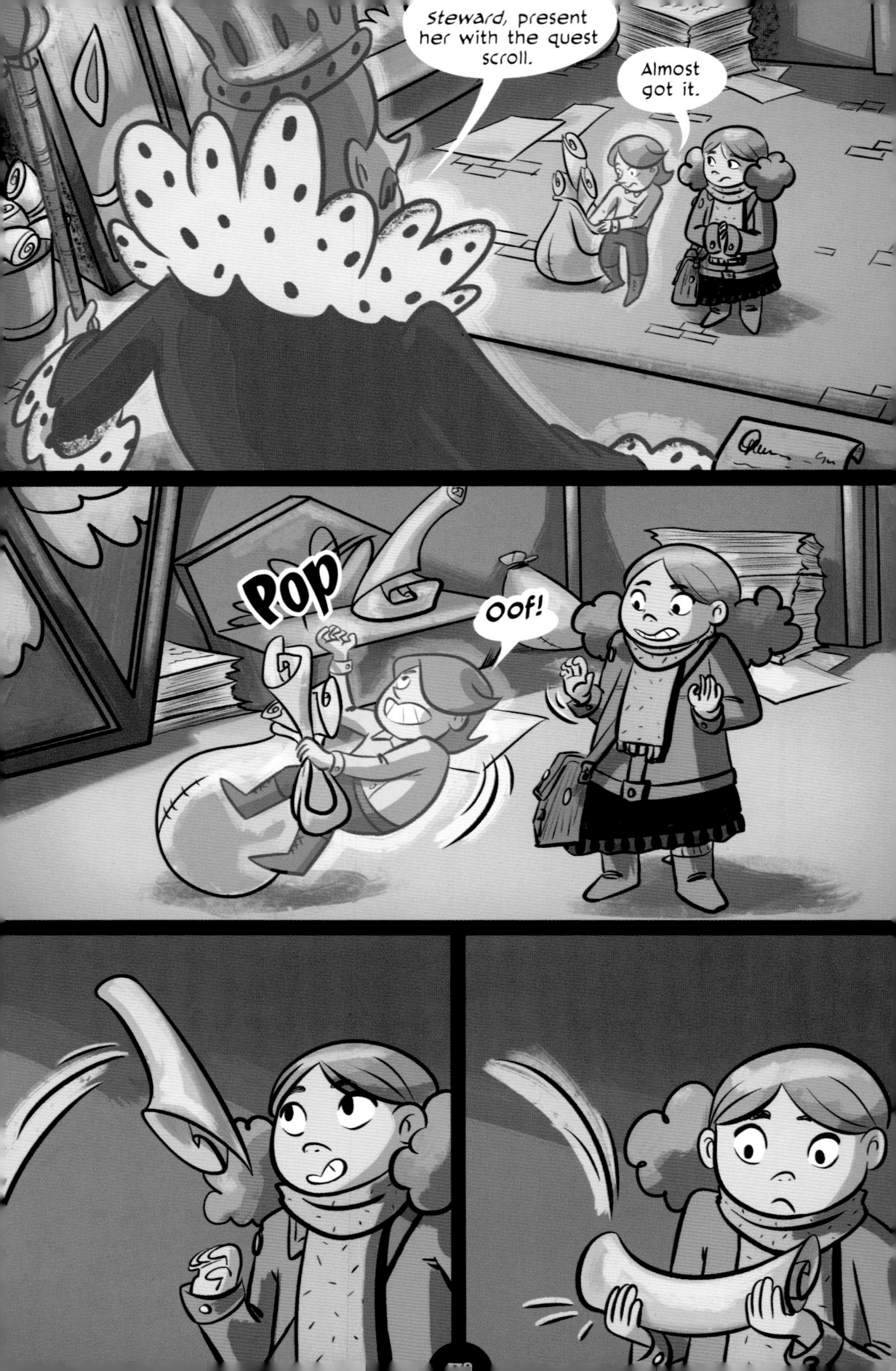
Steward, present her with the quest scroll.
Almost got it.
Pop
Oof!

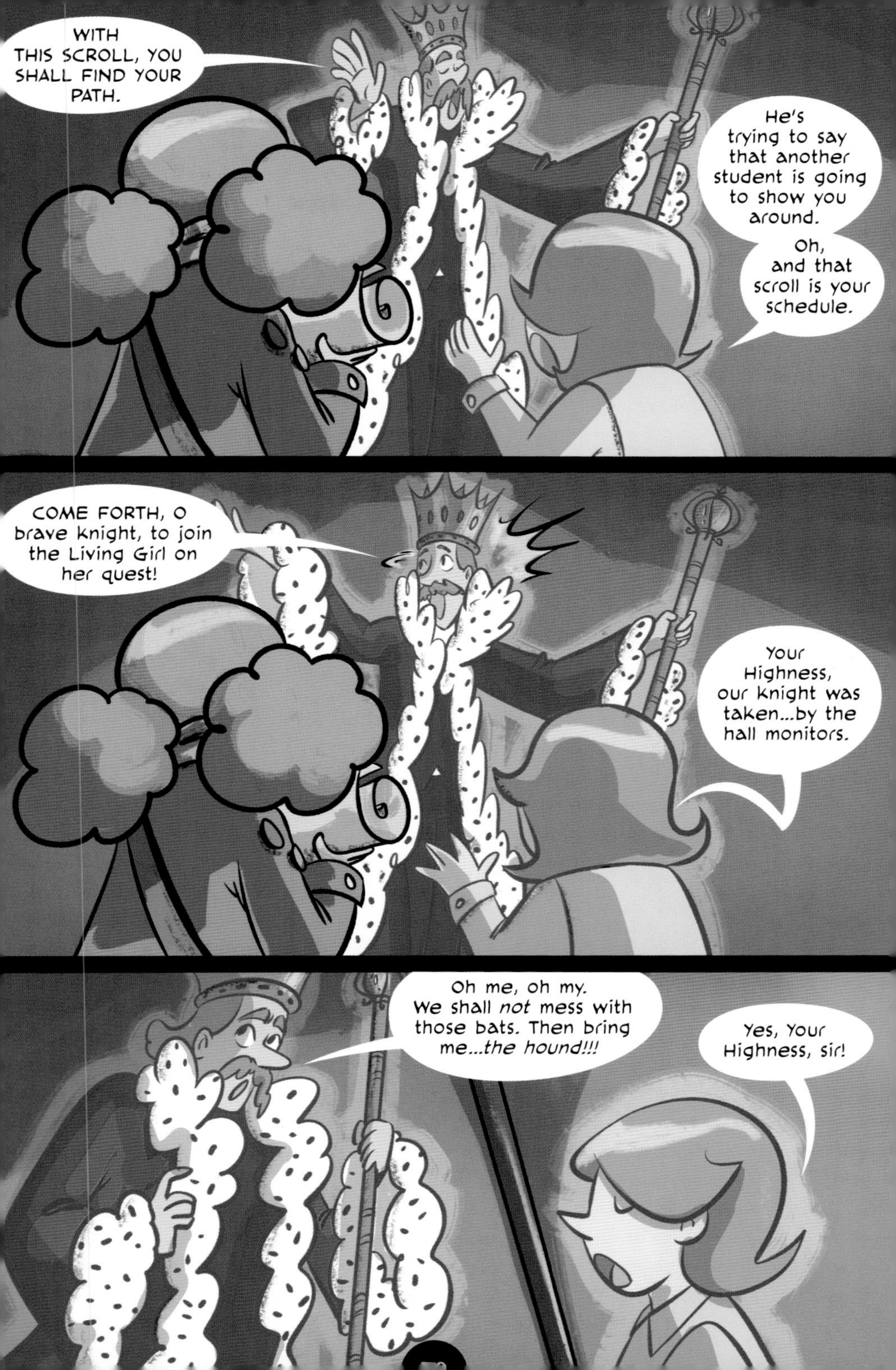
WITH THIS SCROLL, YOU SHALL FIND YOUR PATH.
He's trying to say that another student is going to show you around.
Oh, and that scroll is your schedule.
COME FORTH, O brave knight, to join the Living Girl on her quest!
Your Highness, our knight was taken...by the hall monitors.
Oh me, oh my. We shall *not* mess with those bats. Then bring me...*the hound!!!*
Yes, Your Highness, sir!

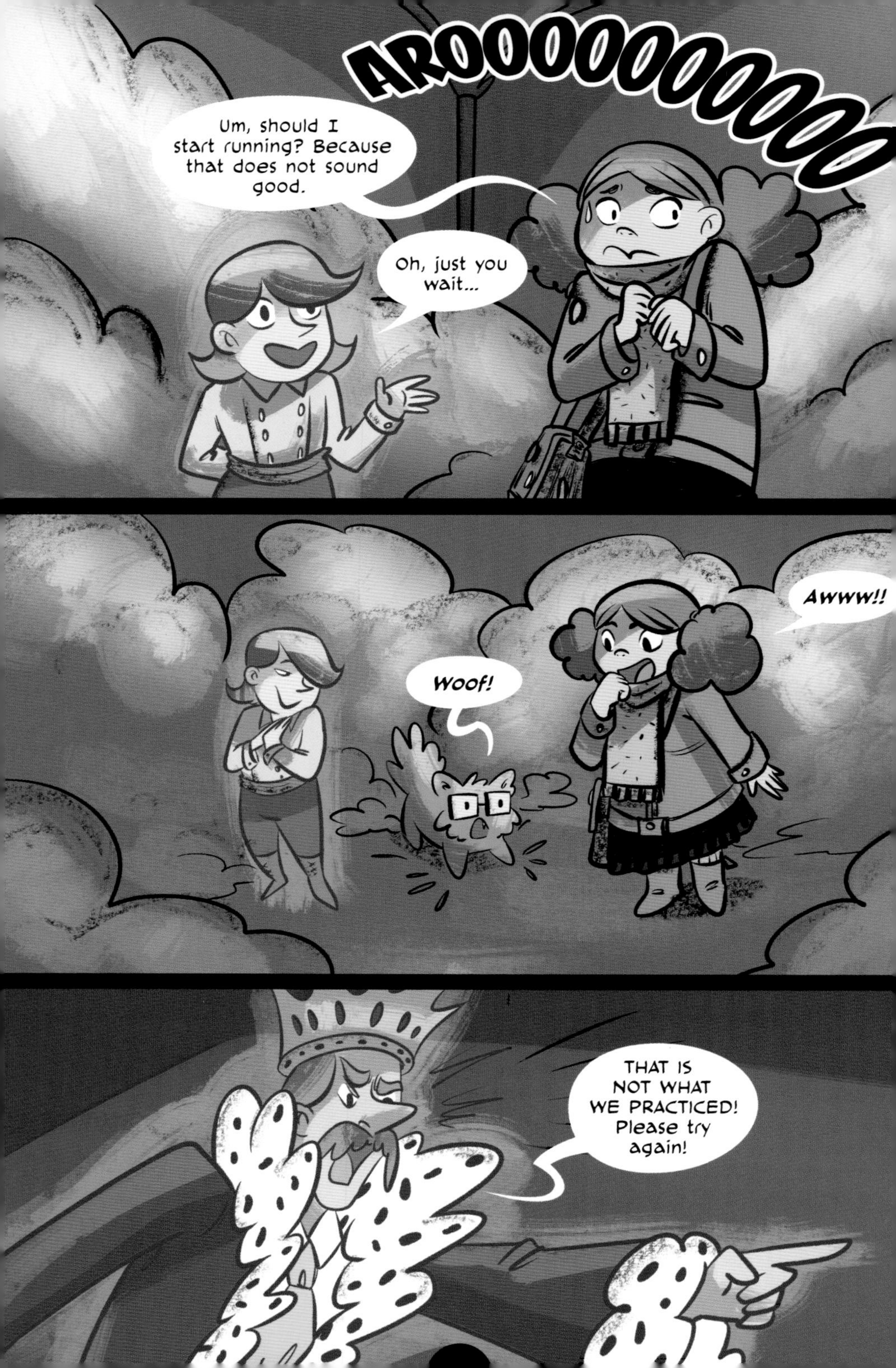
AROOOOOOOOOO
Um, should I start running? Because that does not sound good.
Oh, just you wait...
Woof!
Awww!!
THAT IS NOT WHAT WE PRACTICED! Please try again!

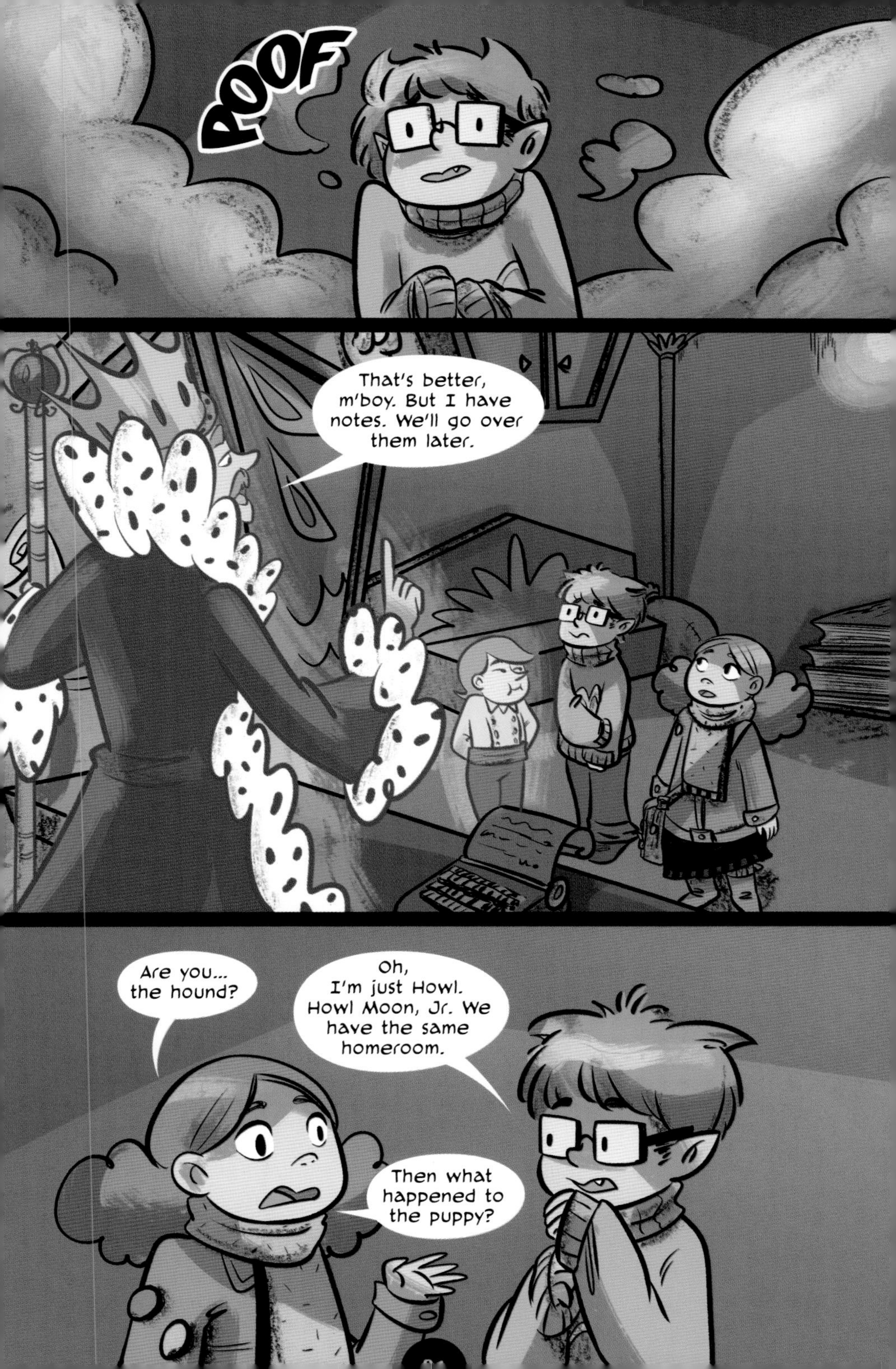
POOF
That's better, m'boy. But I have notes. We'll go over them later.
Are you... the hound?
Oh, I'm just Howl. Howl Moon, Jr. We have the same homeroom.
Then what happened to the puppy?

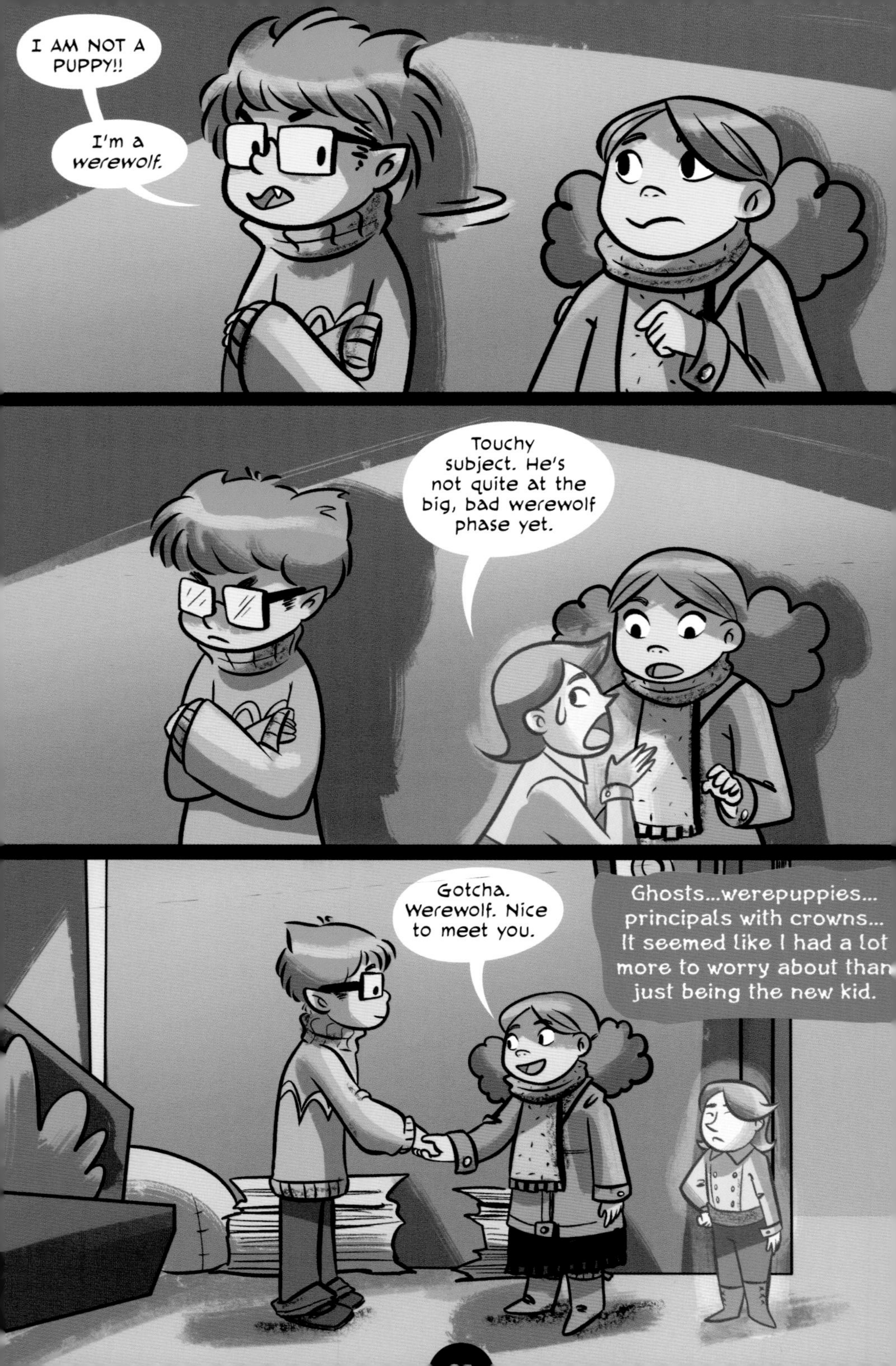
I AM NOT A PUPPY!!
I'm a *werewolf.*
Touchy subject. He's not quite at the big, bad werewolf phase yet.
Gotcha. Werewolf. Nice to meet you.
Ghosts...werepuppies... principals with crowns... It seemed like I had a lot more to worry about than just being the new kid.

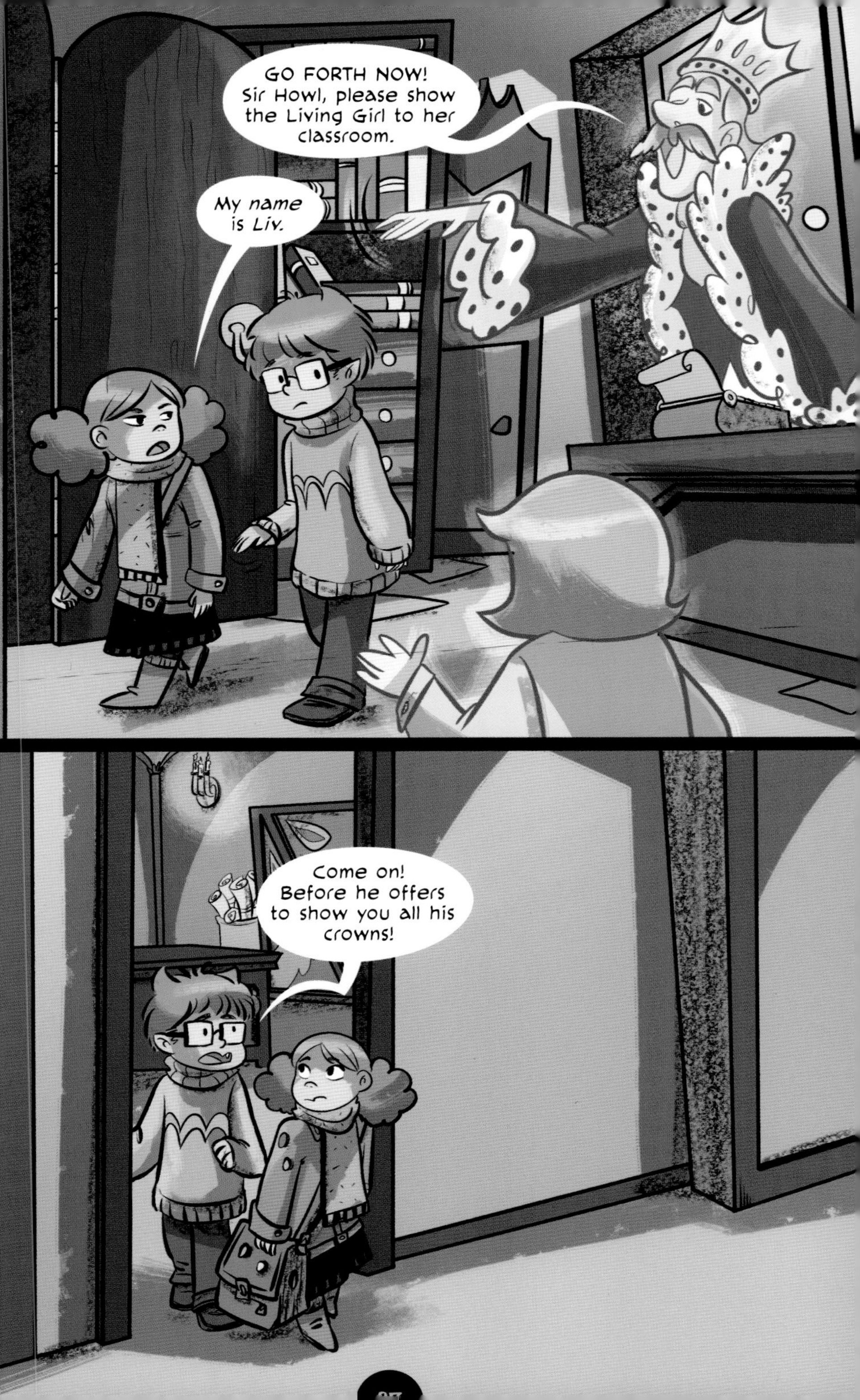
GO FORTH NOW! Sir Howl, please show the Living Girl to her classroom.
My *name* is *Liv.*
Come on! Before he offers to show you all his crowns!

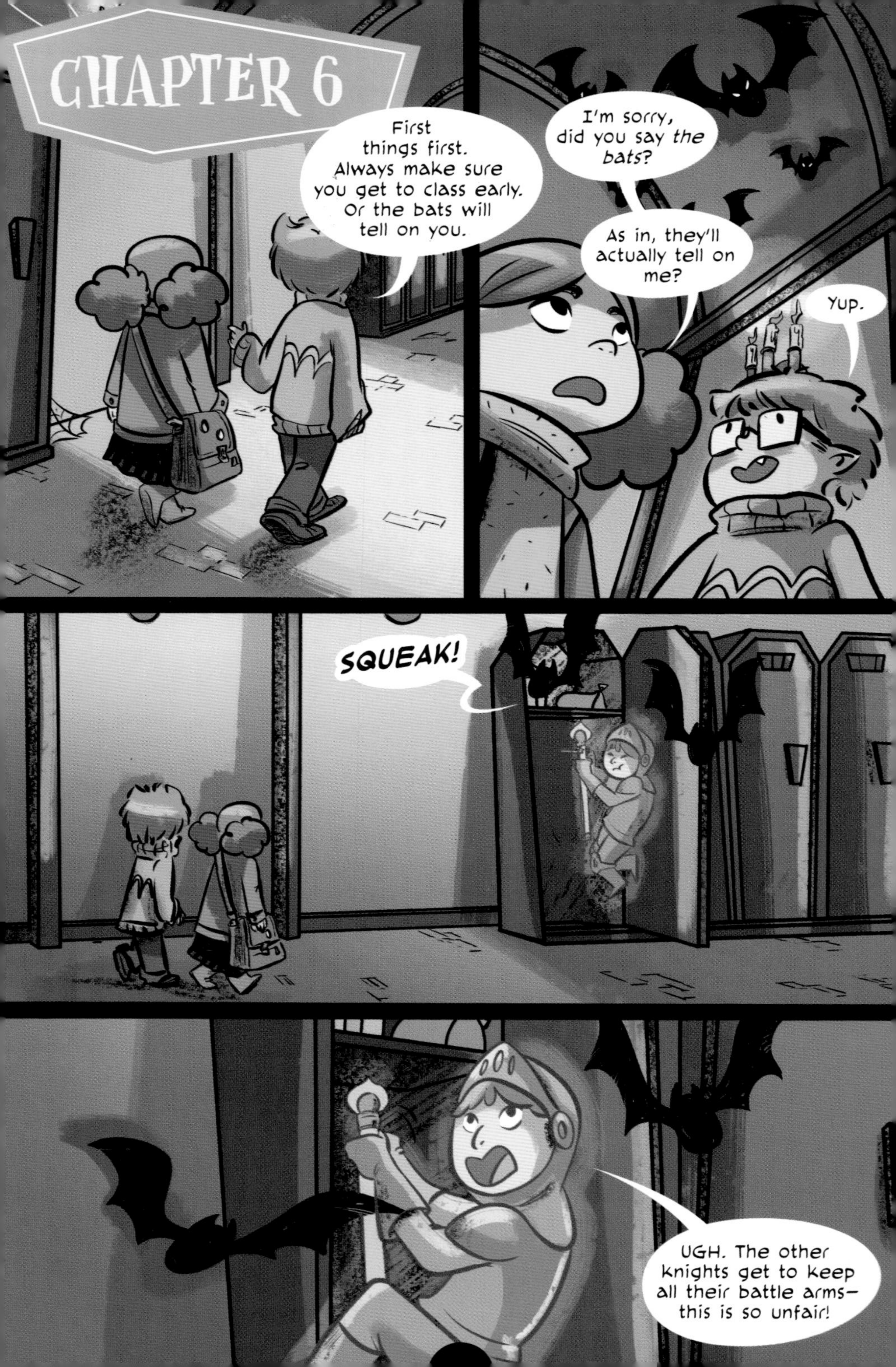
CHAPTER 6
First things first. Always make sure you get to class early. Or the bats will tell on you.
I'm sorry, did you say *the bats?*
As in, they'll actually tell on me?
Yup.
SQUEAK!
UGH. The other knights get to keep all their battle arms—this is so unfair!

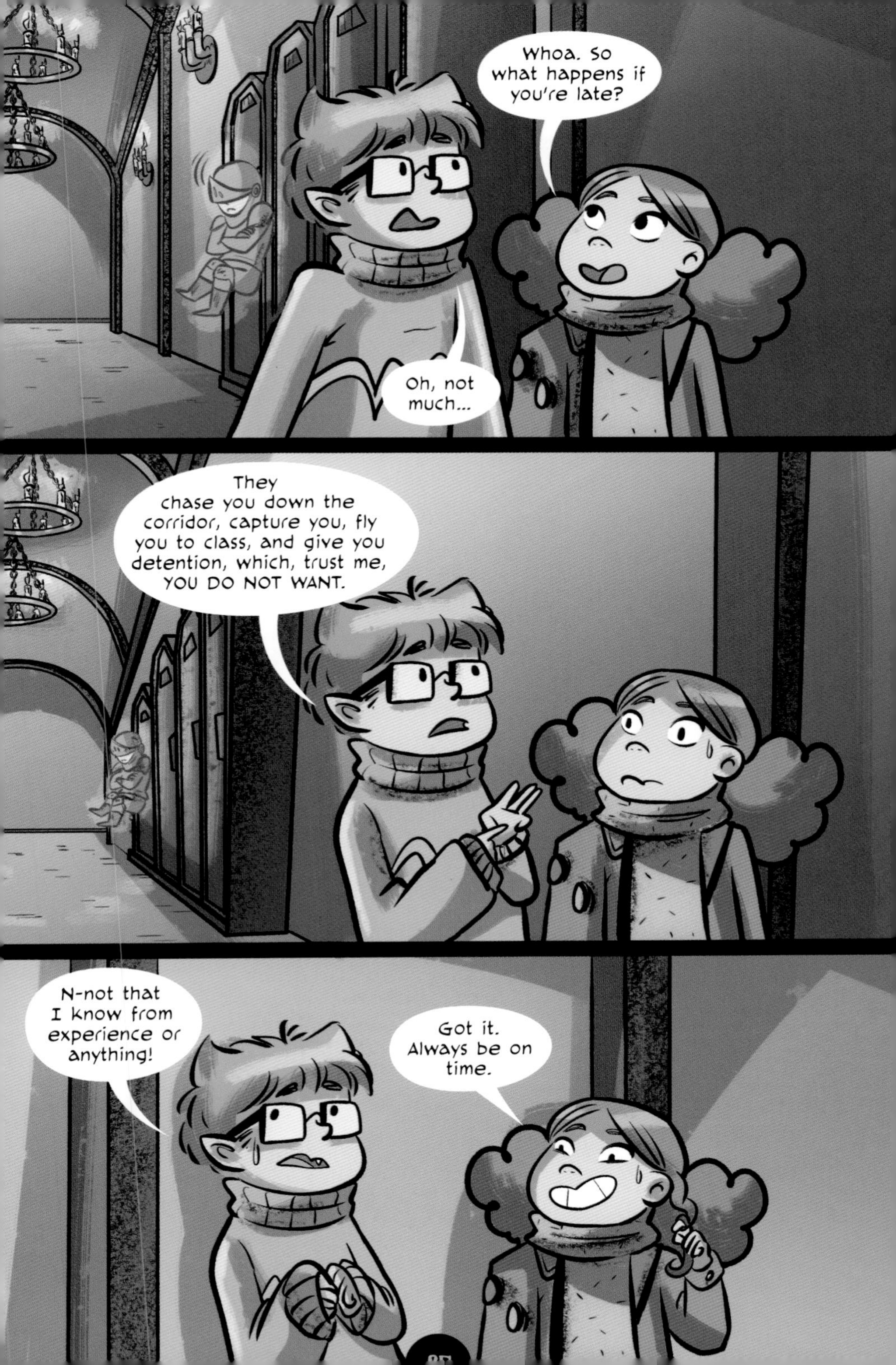

Whoa. So what happens if you're late?
Oh, not much...
They chase you down the corridor, capture you, fly you to class, and give you detention, which, trust me, YOU DO NOT WANT.
N-not that I know from experience or anything!
Got it. Always be on time.

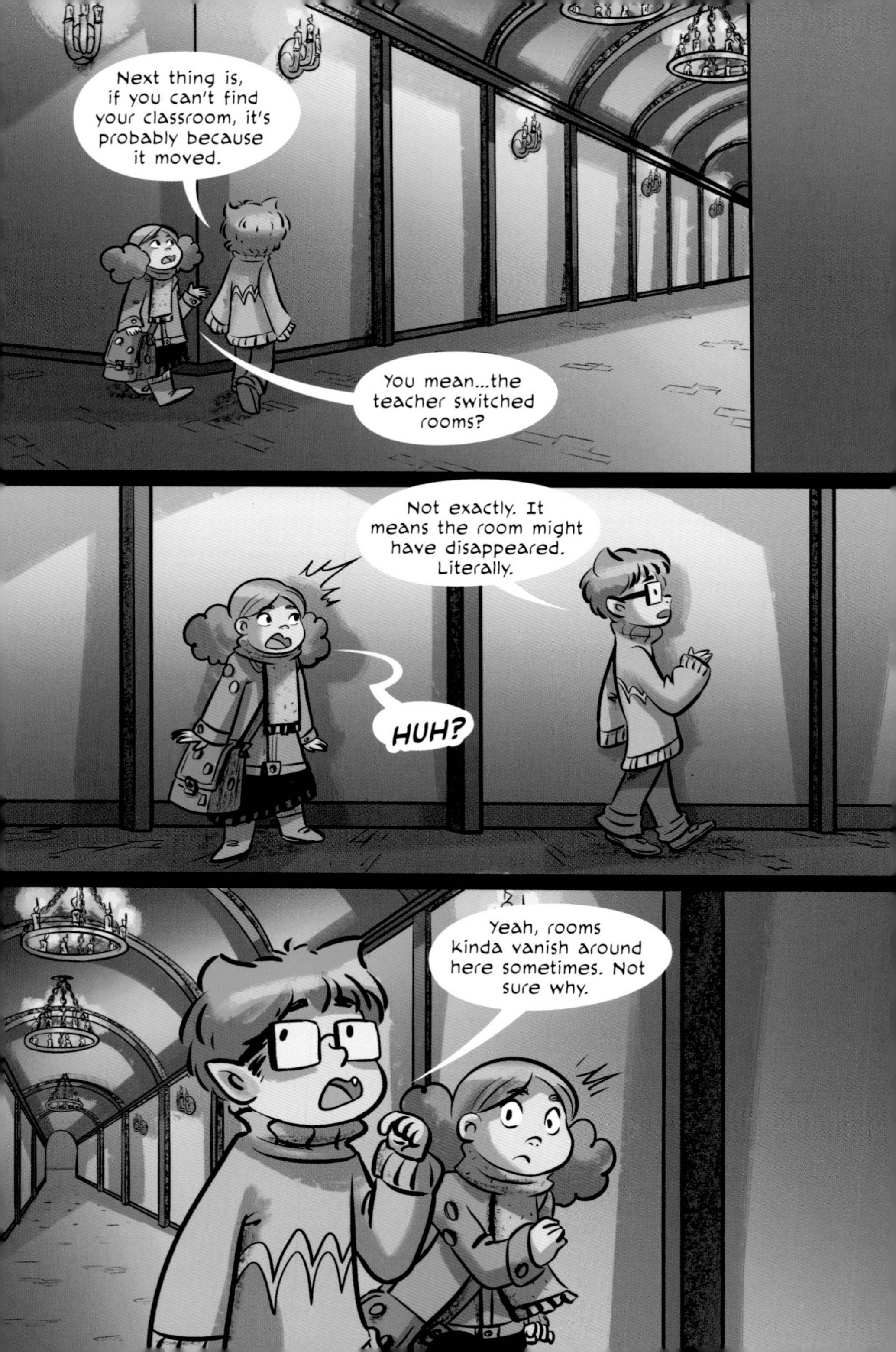

Next thing is, if you can't find your classroom, it's probably because it moved.
You mean...the teacher switched rooms?
Not exactly. It means the room might have disappeared. Literally.
HUH?
Yeah, rooms kinda vanish around here sometimes. Not sure why.

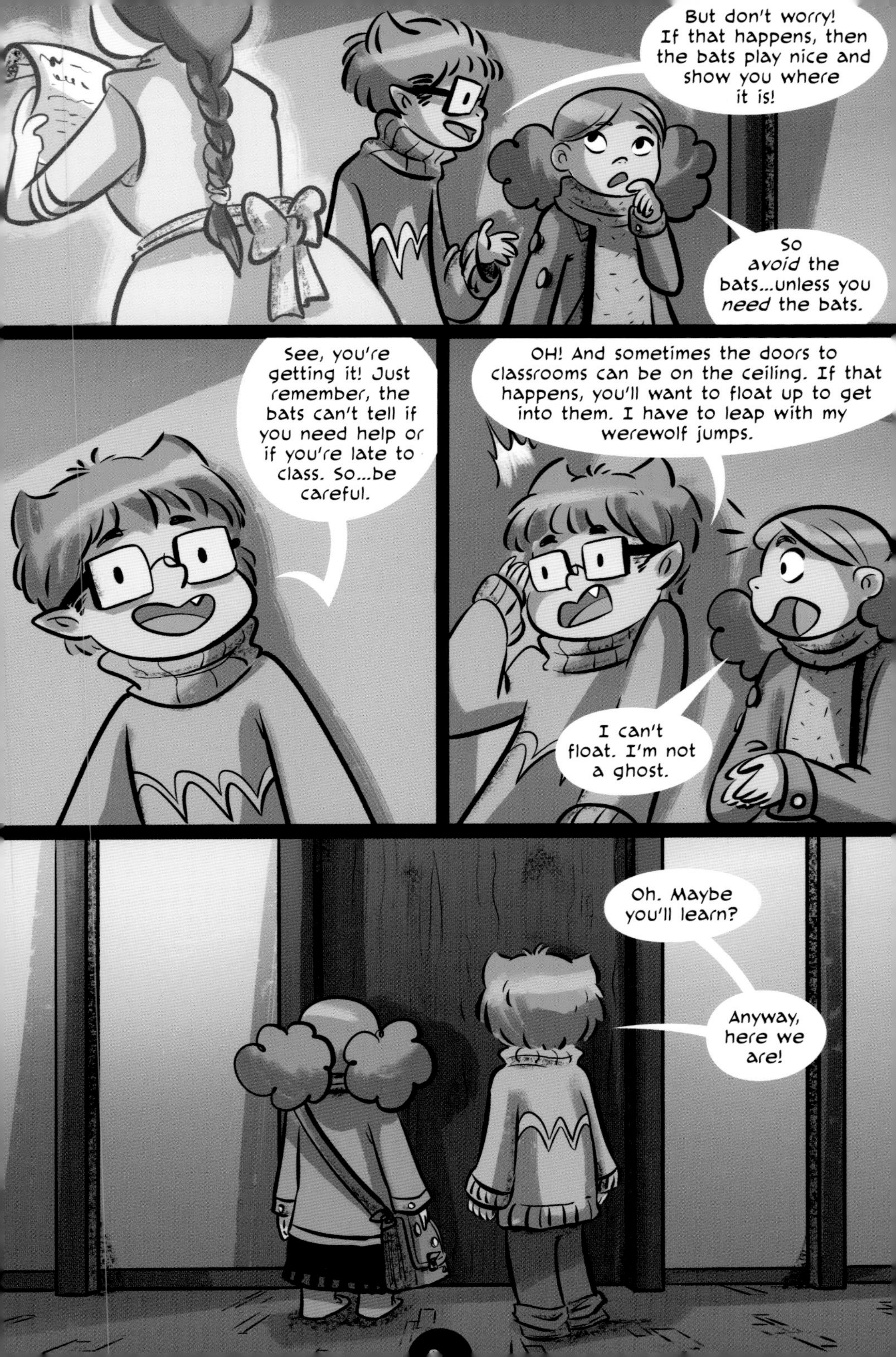
But don't worry! If that happens, then the bats play nice and show you where it is!
So *avoid* the bats...unless you *need* the bats.
See, you're getting it! Just remember, the bats can't tell if you need help or if you're late to class. So...be careful.
OH! And sometimes the doors to classrooms can be on the ceiling. If that happens, you'll want to float up to get into them. I have to leap with my werewolf jumps.
I can't float. I'm not a ghost.
Oh. Maybe you'll learn?
Anyway, here we are!

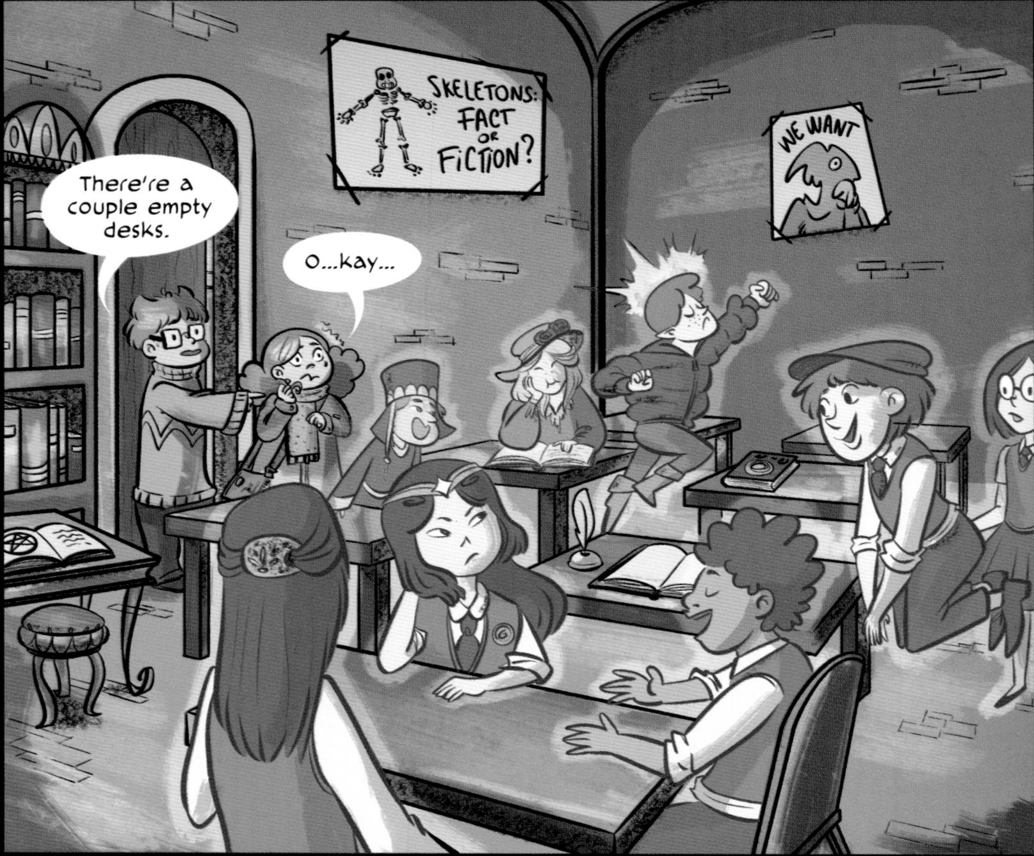
SKELETONS: FACT OR FICTION?
WE WANT
There're a couple empty desks.
O...kay...

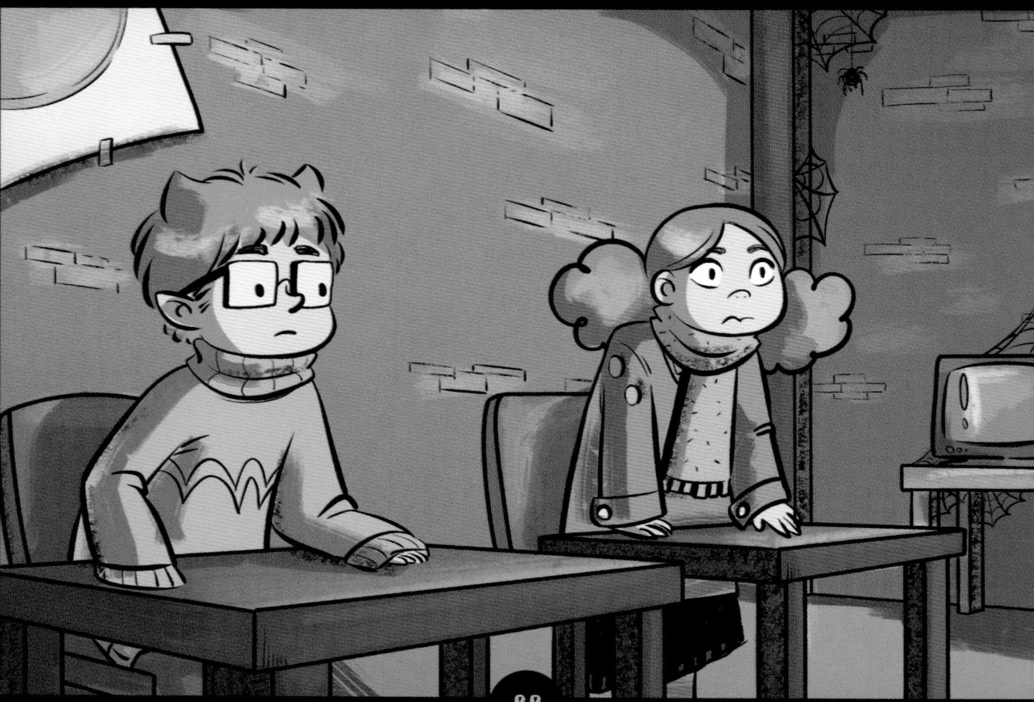

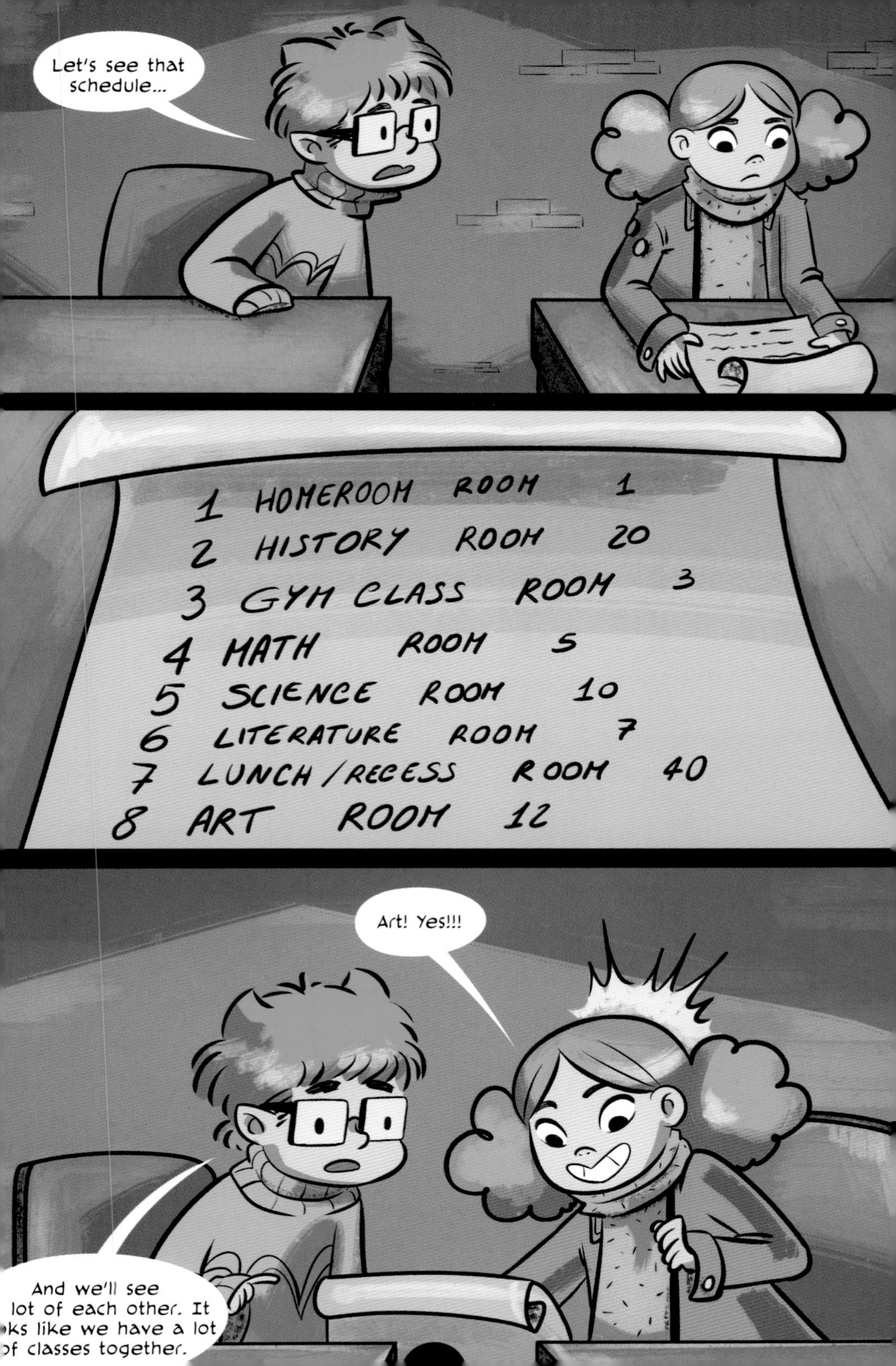
Let's see that schedule...
1 HOMEROOM ROOM 1
2 HISTORY ROOM 20
3 GYM CLASS ROOM 3
4 MATH ROOM 5
5 SCIENCE ROOM 10
6 LITERATURE ROOM 7
7 LUNCH/RECESS ROOM 40
8 ART ROOM 12
Art! Yes!!!
And we'll see lot of each other. It ks like we have a lot of classes together.

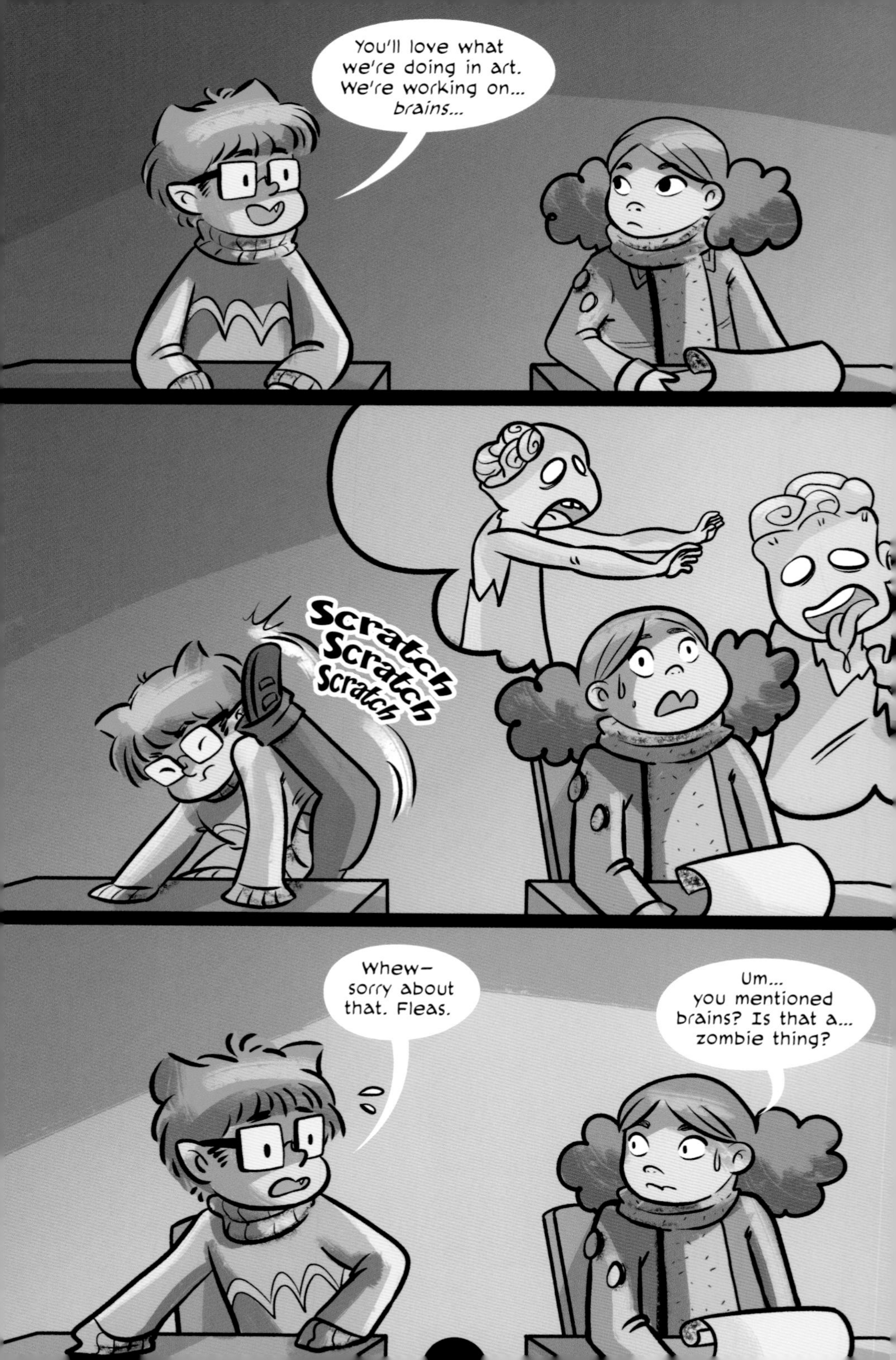
You'll love what we're doing in art. We're working on... *brains...*
Scratch
Scratch
Scratch
Whew— sorry about that. Fleas.
Um... you mentioned brains? Is that a... zombie thing?

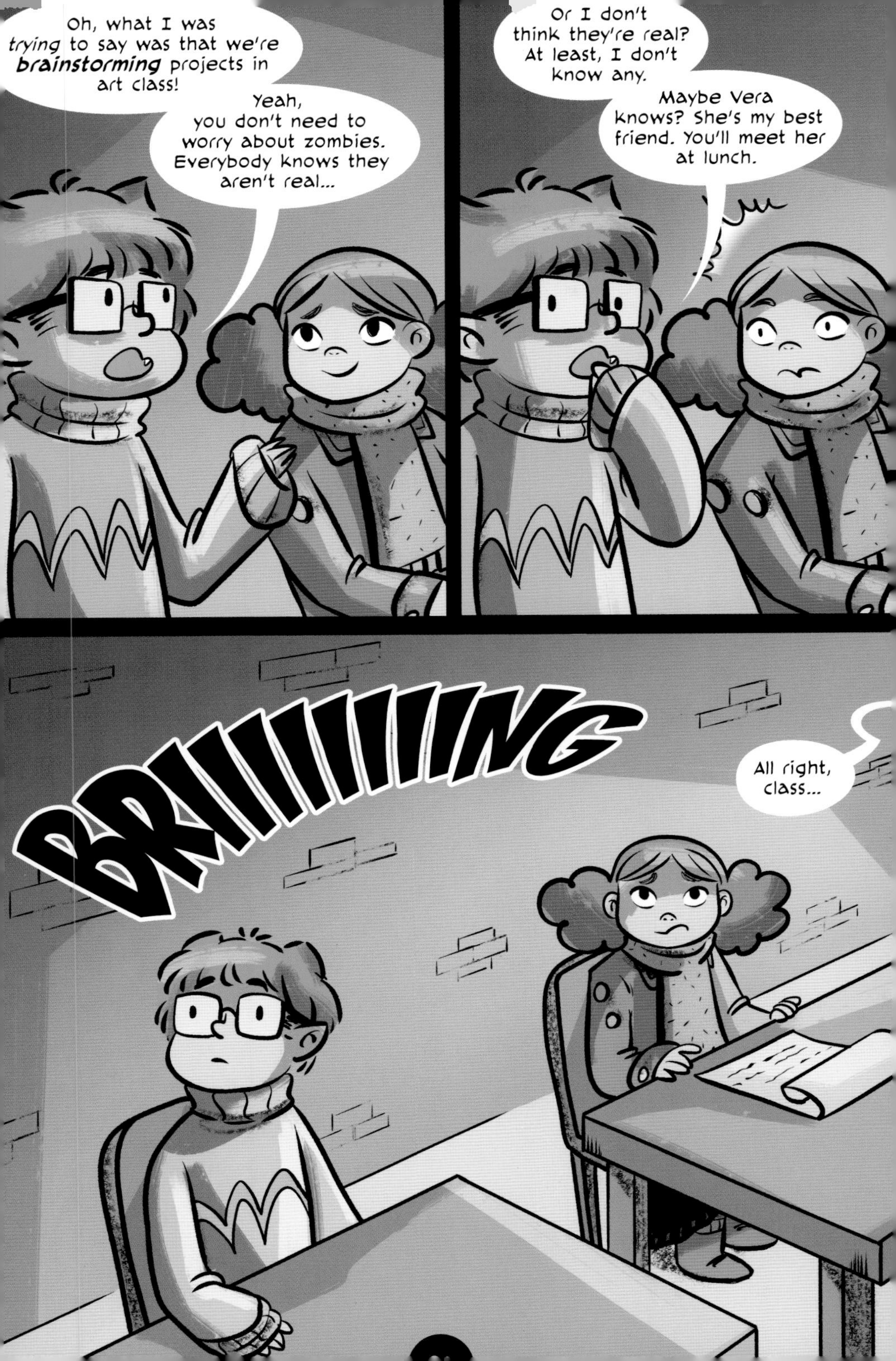
Oh, what I was *trying* to say was that we're ***brainstorming*** projects in art class!
Yeah, you don't need to worry about zombies. Everybody knows they aren't real...
Or I don't think they're real? At least, I don't know any.
Maybe Vera knows? She's my best friend. You'll meet her at lunch.
BRIIIIIIIING
All right, class...

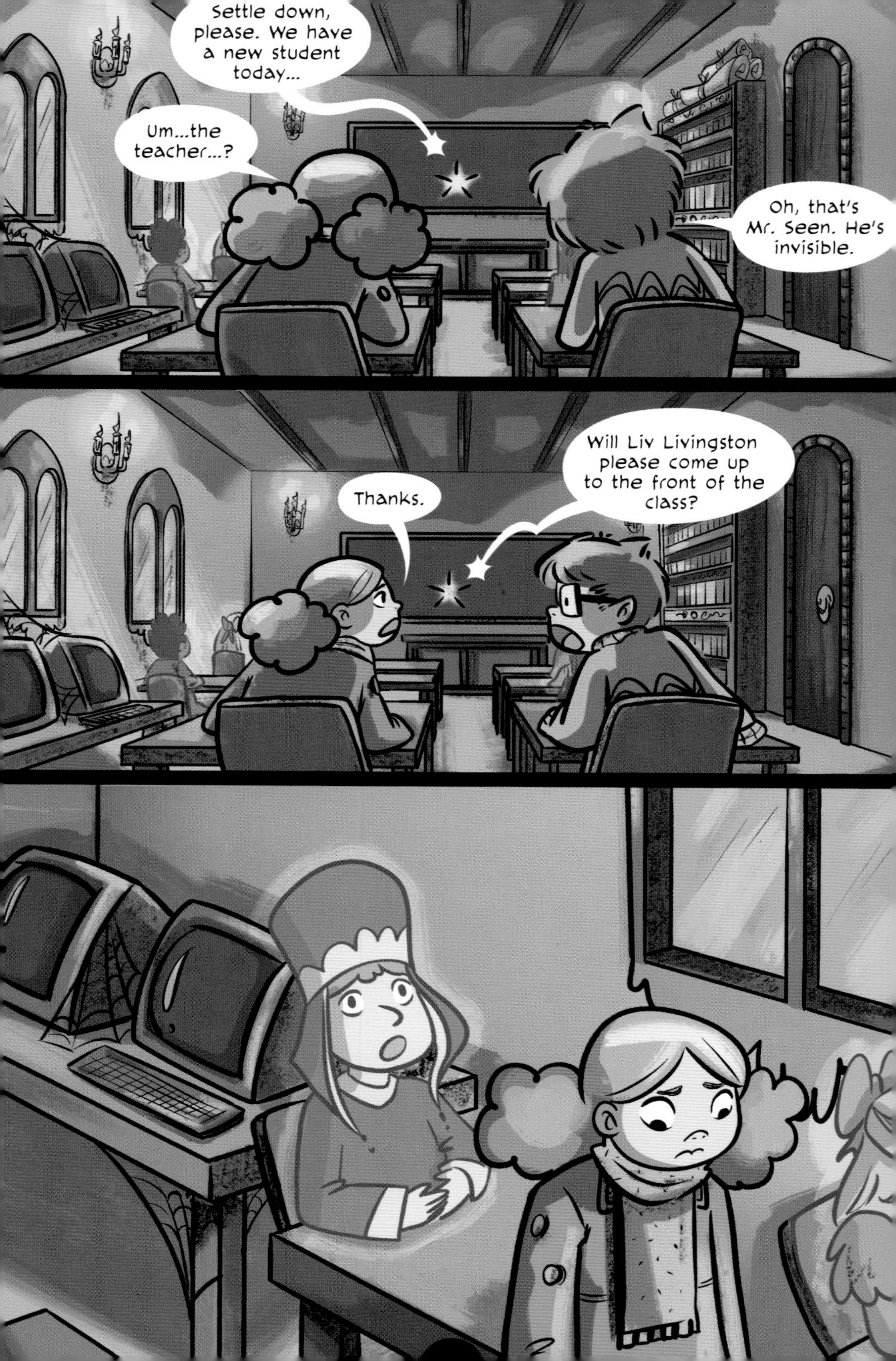
Settle down, please. We have a new student today...
Um...the teacher...?
Oh, that's Mr. Seen. He's invisible.
Thanks.
Will Liv Livingston please come up to the front of the class?

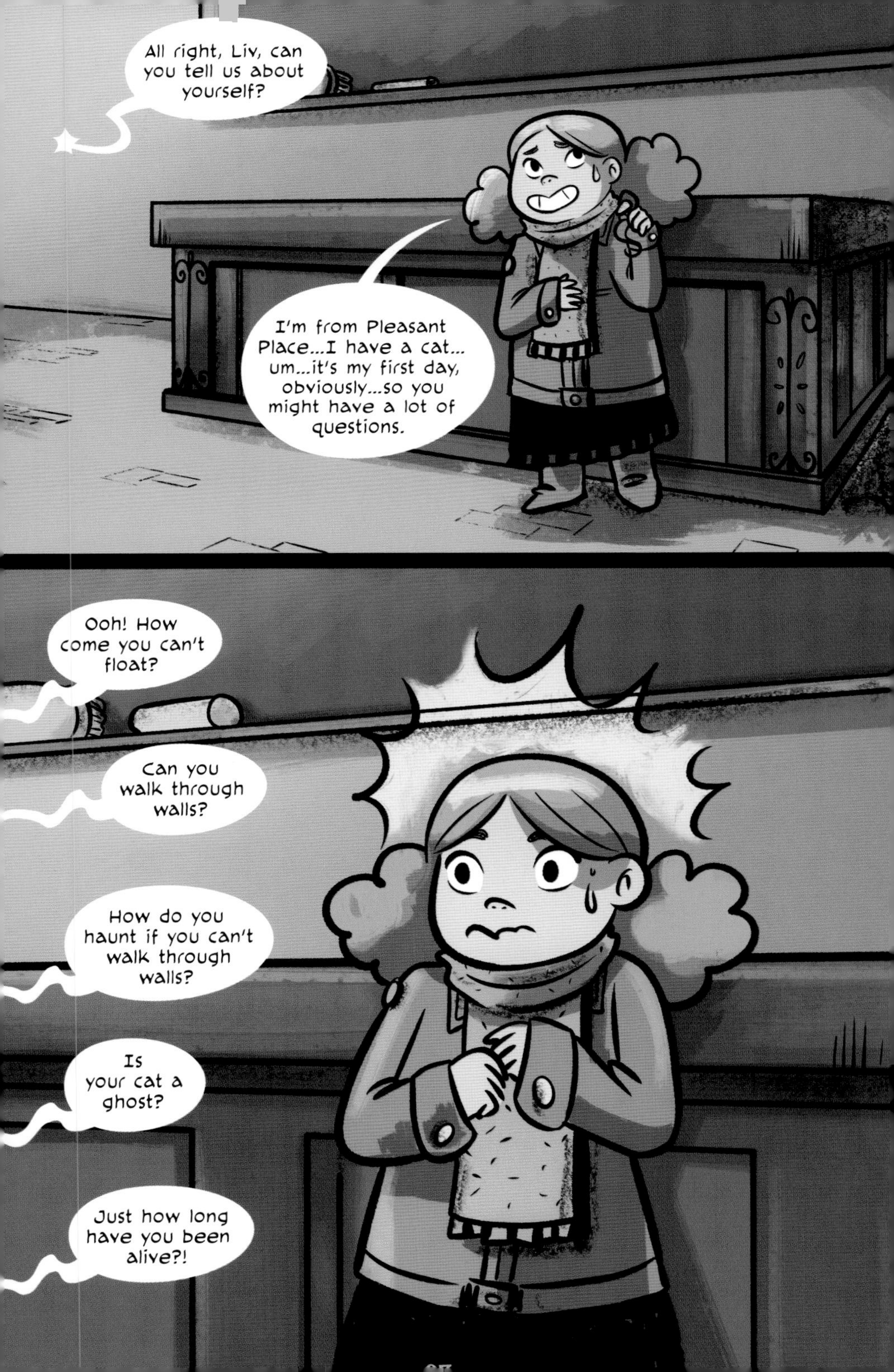
All right, Liv, can you tell us about yourself?
I'm from Pleasant Place...I have a cat... um...it's my first day, obviously...so you might have a lot of questions.
Ooh! How come you can't float?
Can you walk through walls?
How do you haunt if you can't walk through walls?
Is your cat a ghost?
Just how long have you been alive?!

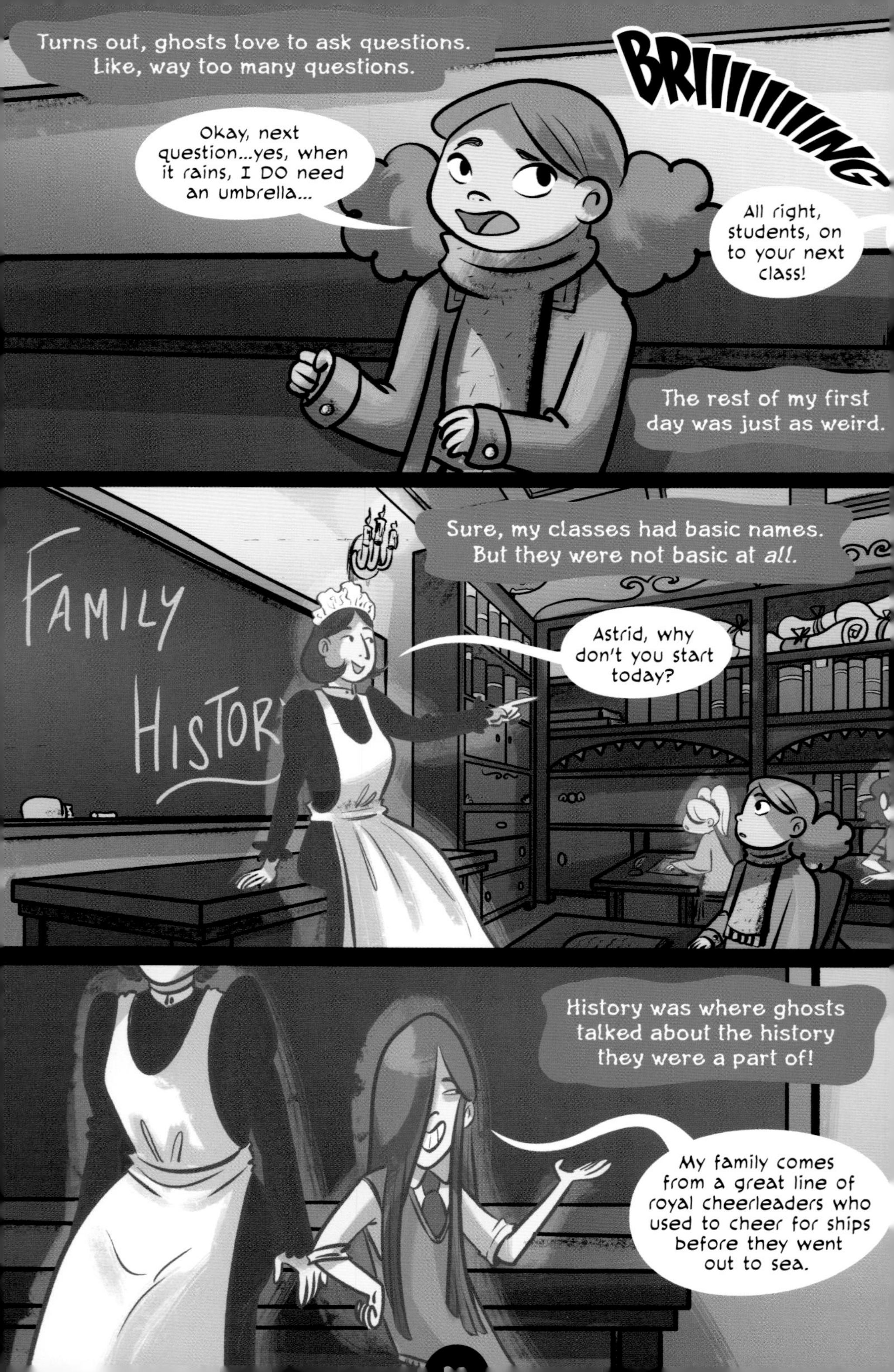
Turns out, ghosts love to ask questions. Like, way too many questions.
BRIIIIIIING
Okay, next question...yes, when it rains, I DO need an umbrella...
All right, students, on to your next class!
The rest of my first day was just as weird.
Sure, my classes had basic names. But they were not basic at *all.*
FAMILY HISTORY
Astrid, why don't you start today?
History was where ghosts talked about the history they were a part of!
My family comes from a great line of royal cheerleaders who used to cheer for ships before they went out to sea.

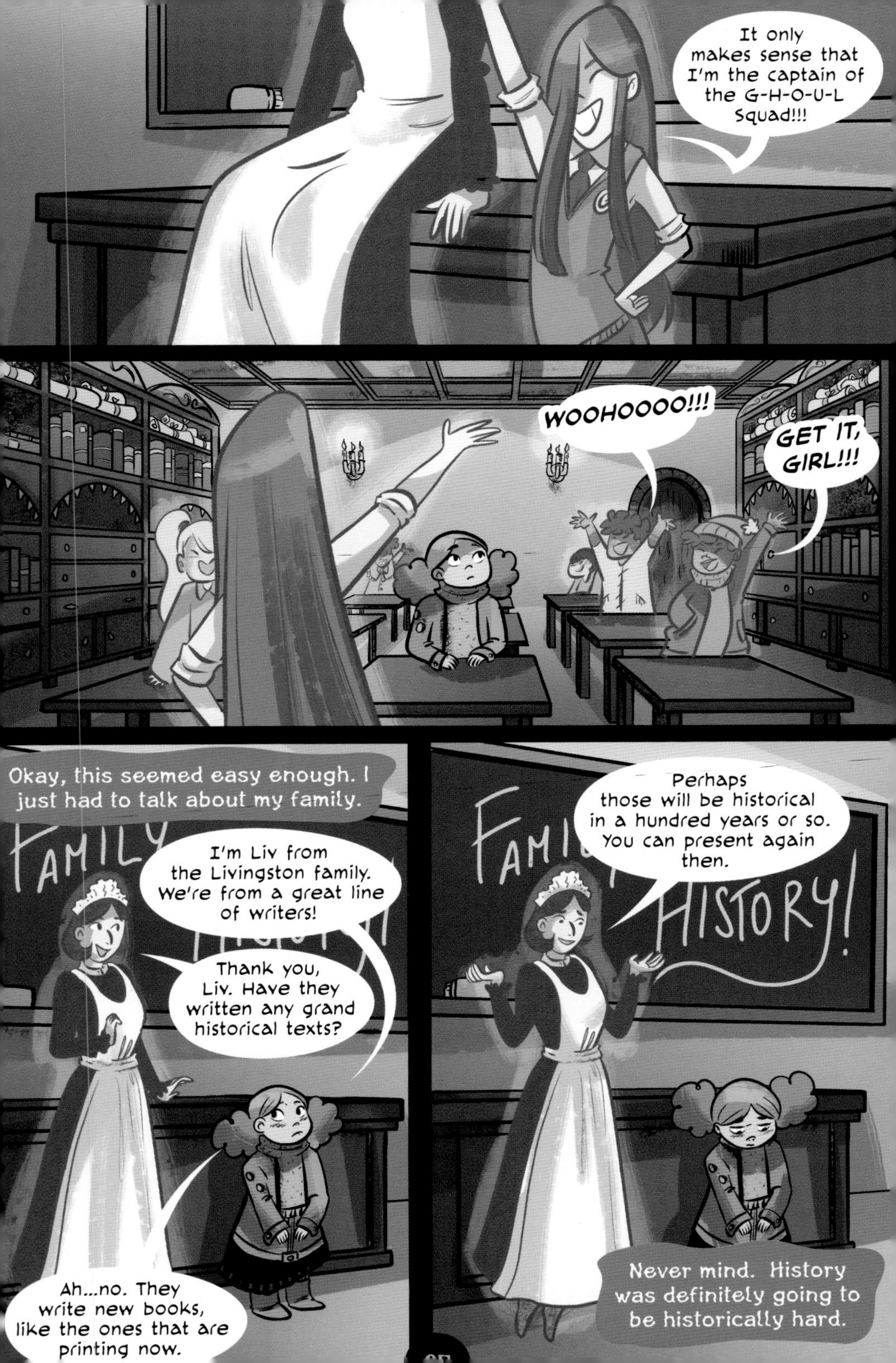

It only makes sense that I'm the captain of the G-H-O-U-L Squad!!!
WOOHOOOO!!!
GET IT, GIRL!!!
Okay, this seemed easy enough. I just had to talk about my family.
FAMILY
I'm Liv from the Livingston family. We're from a great line of writers!
Thank you, Liv. Have they written any grand historical texts?
Ah...no. They write new books, like the ones that are printing now.
FAMI
HISTORY!
Perhaps those will be historical in a hundred years or so. You can present again then.
Never mind. History was definitely going to be historically hard.

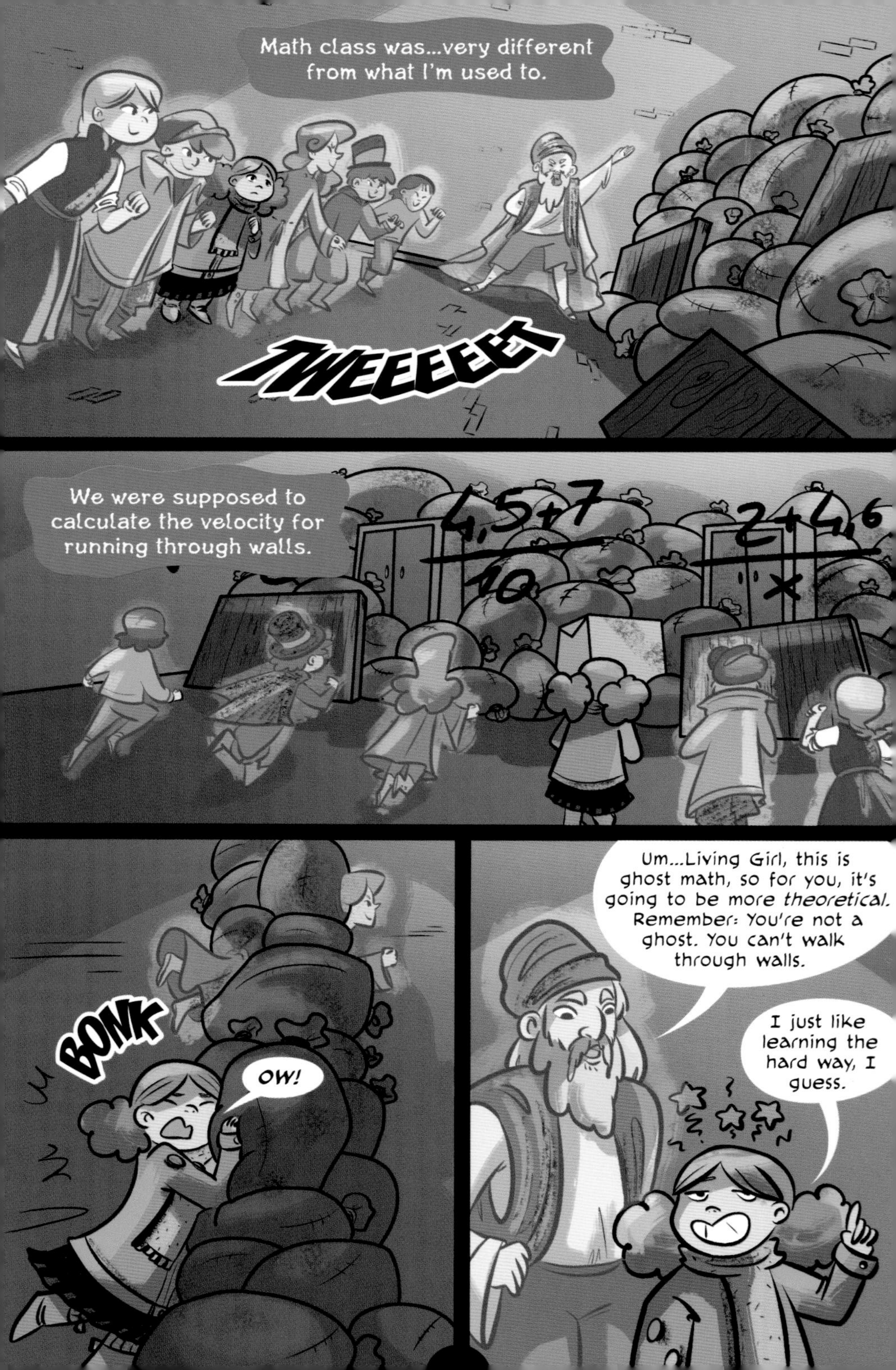
Math class was...very different from what I'm used to.
TWEEEEET
We were supposed to calculate the velocity for running through walls.
4.5+7
10
2+4.6
X
BONK
OW!
Um...Living Girl, this is ghost math, so for you, it's going to be more *theoretical*. Remember: You're not a ghost. You can't walk through walls.
I just like learning the hard way, I guess.

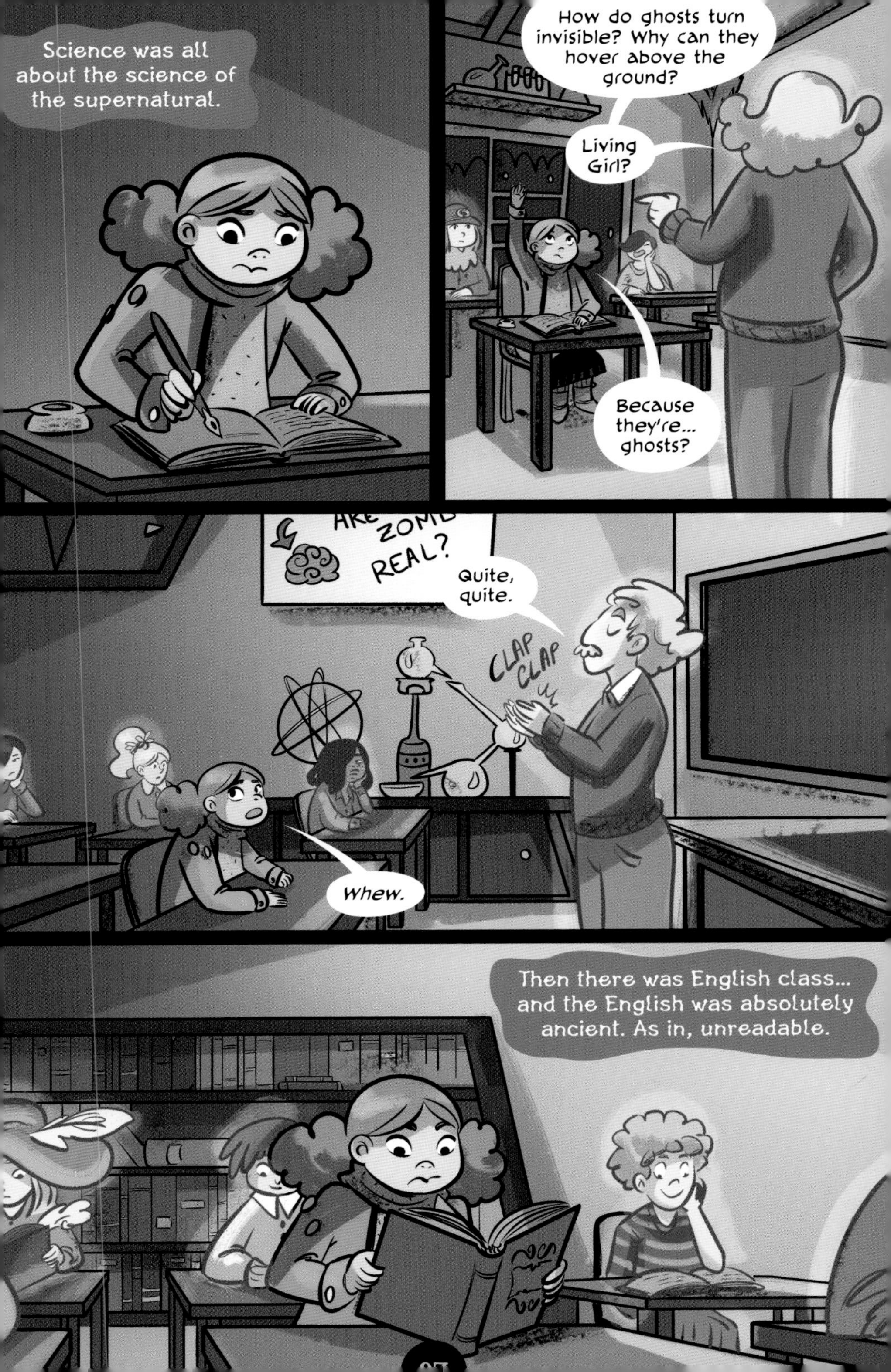

Science was all about the science of the supernatural.
How do ghosts turn invisible? Why can they hover above the ground?
Living Girl?
Because they're... ghosts?
Quite, quite.
CLAP CLAP
Whew.
Then there was English class... and the English was absolutely ancient. As in, unreadable.

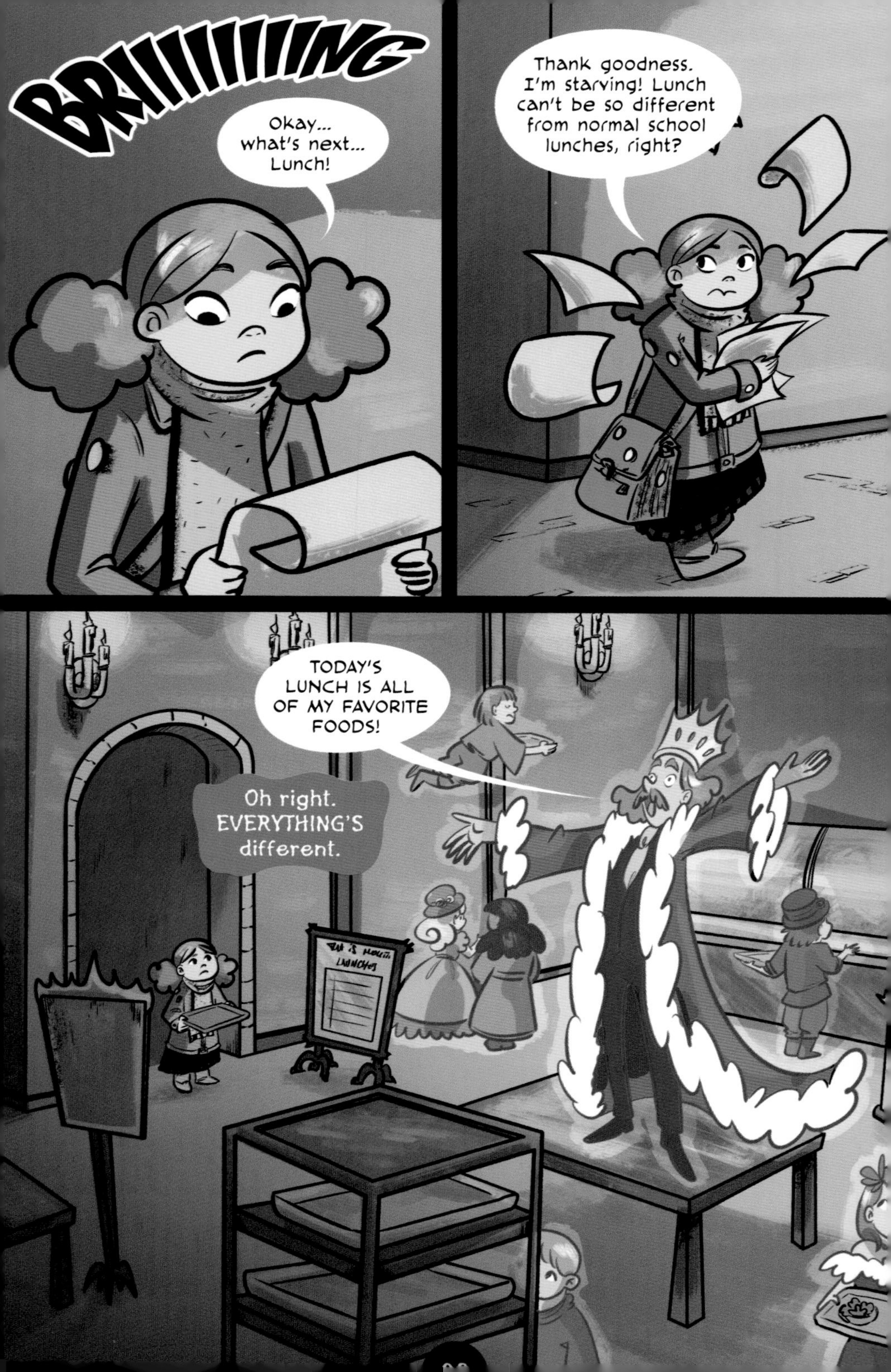
BRIIIIIIIING
Okay... what's next... Lunch!
Thank goodness. I'm starving! Lunch can't be so different from normal school lunches, right?
TODAY'S LUNCH IS ALL OF MY FAVORITE FOODS!
Oh right. EVERYTHING'S different.

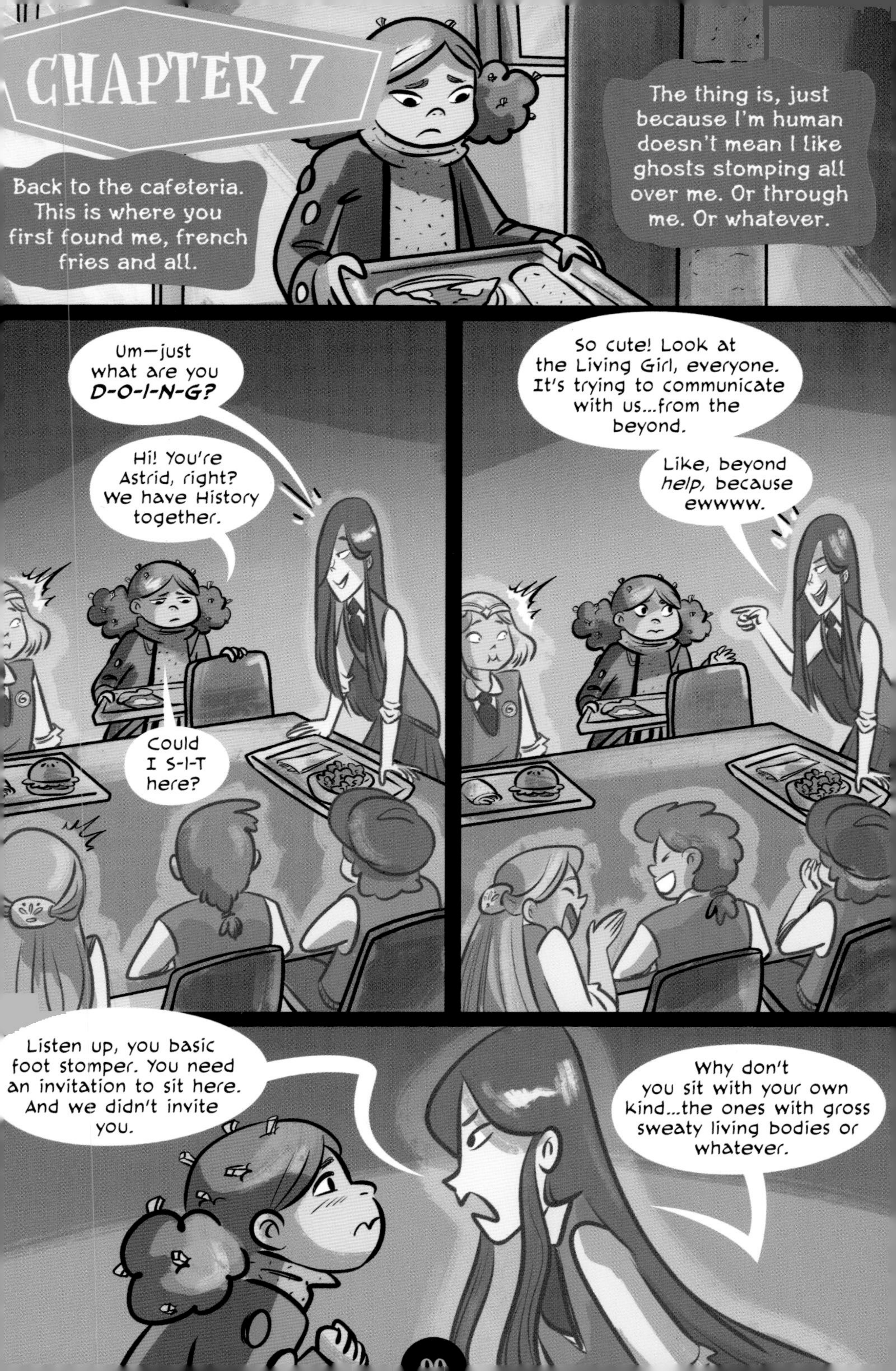
CHAPTER 7
Back to the cafeteria. This is where you first found me, french fries and all.
The thing is, just because I'm human doesn't mean I like ghosts stomping all over me. Or through me. Or whatever.
Hi! You're Astrid, right? We have History together.
Could I S-I-T here?
Um—just what are you D-O-I-N-G?
So cute! Look at the Living Girl, everyone. It's trying to communicate with us...from the beyond.
Like, beyond help, because ewwww.
Listen up, you basic foot stomper. You need an invitation to sit here. And we didn't invite you.
Why don't you sit with your own kind...the ones with gross sweaty living bodies or whatever.

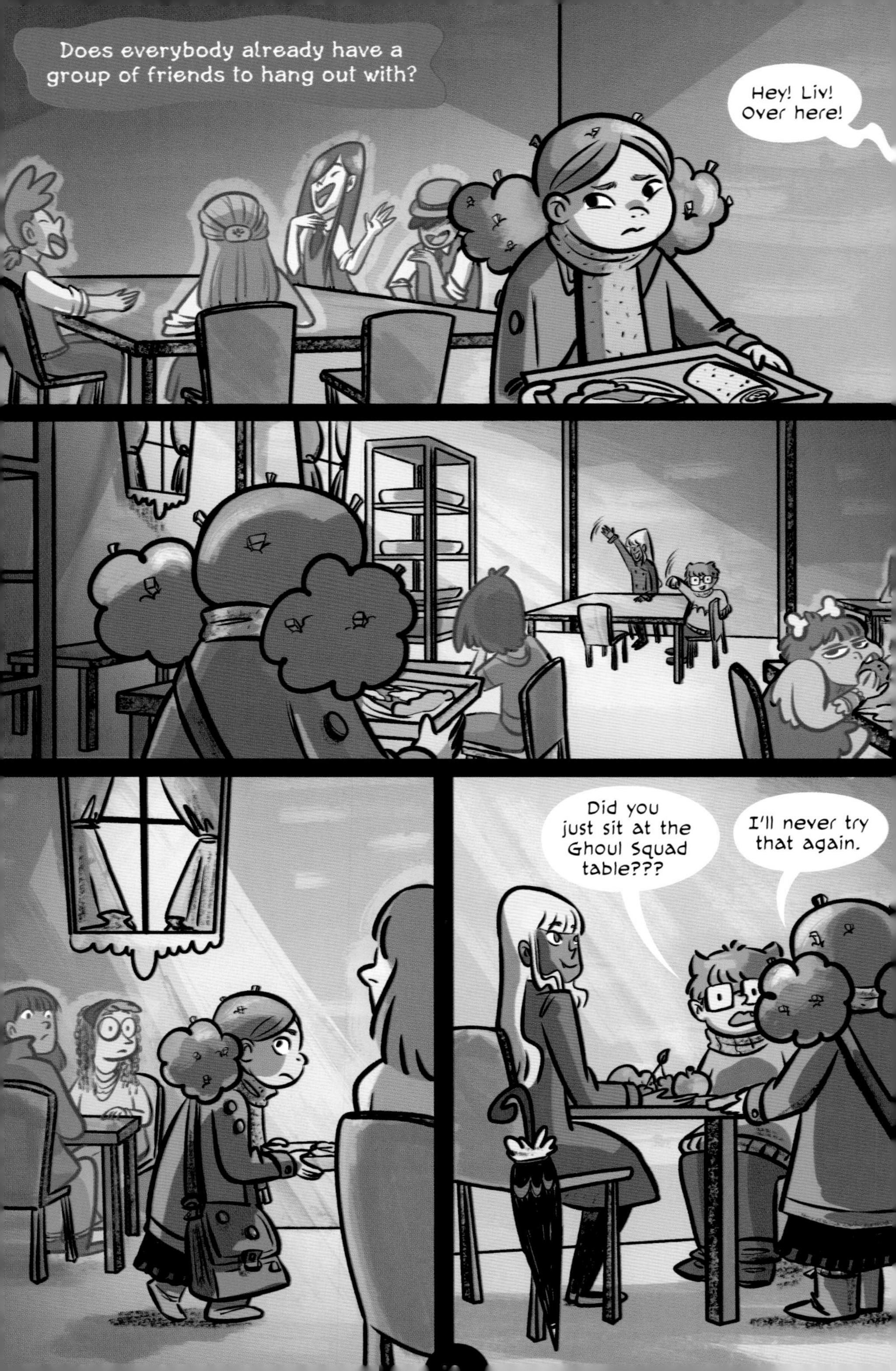
Does everybody already have a group of friends to hang out with?
Hey! Liv! Over here!
Did you just sit at the Ghoul Squad table???
I'll never try that again.

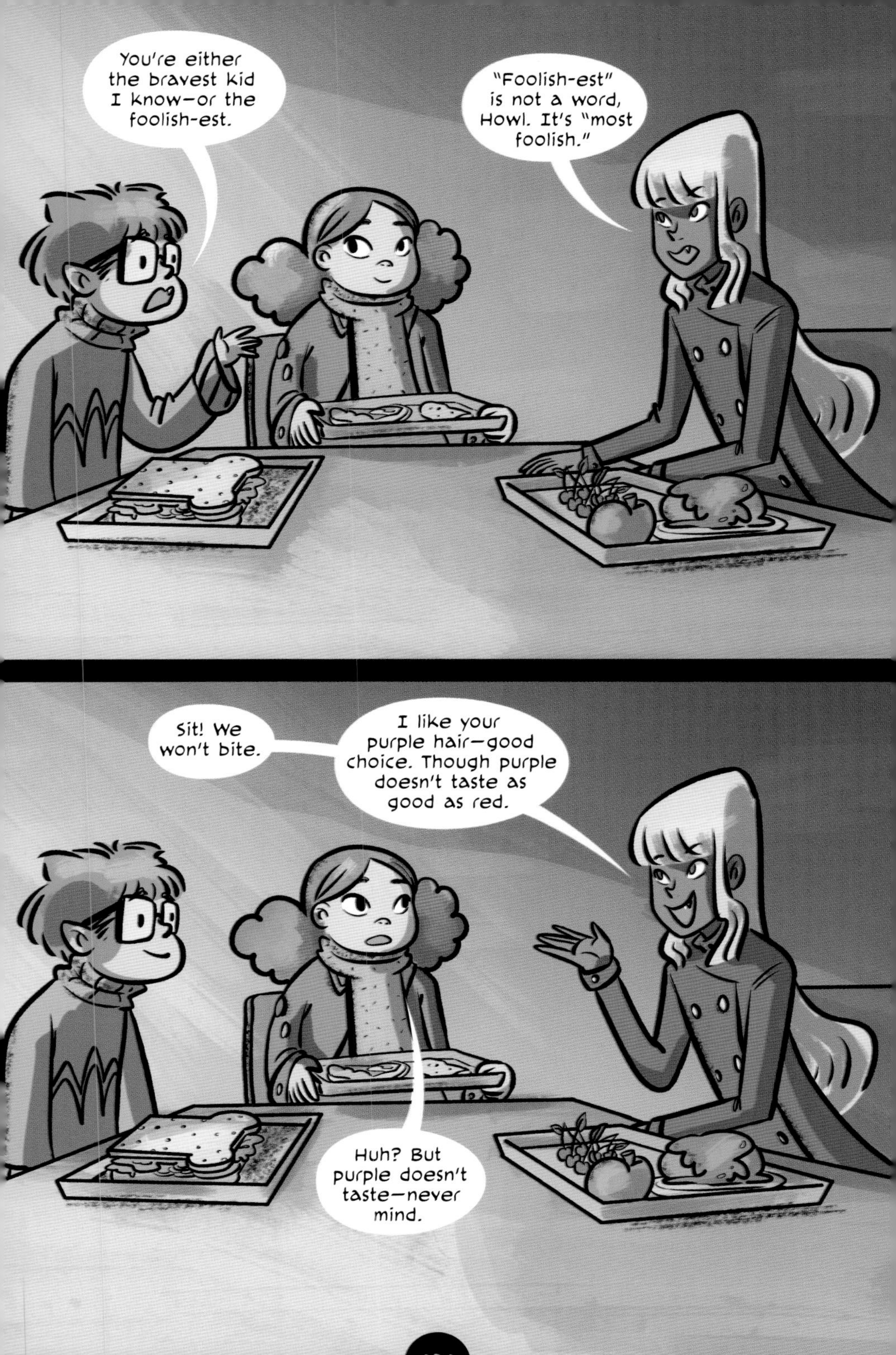
You're either the bravest kid I know—or the foolish-est.
"Foolish-est" is not a word, Howl. It's "most foolish."
Sit! We won't bite.
I like your purple hair—good choice. Though purple doesn't taste as good as red.
Huh? But purple doesn't taste—never mind.

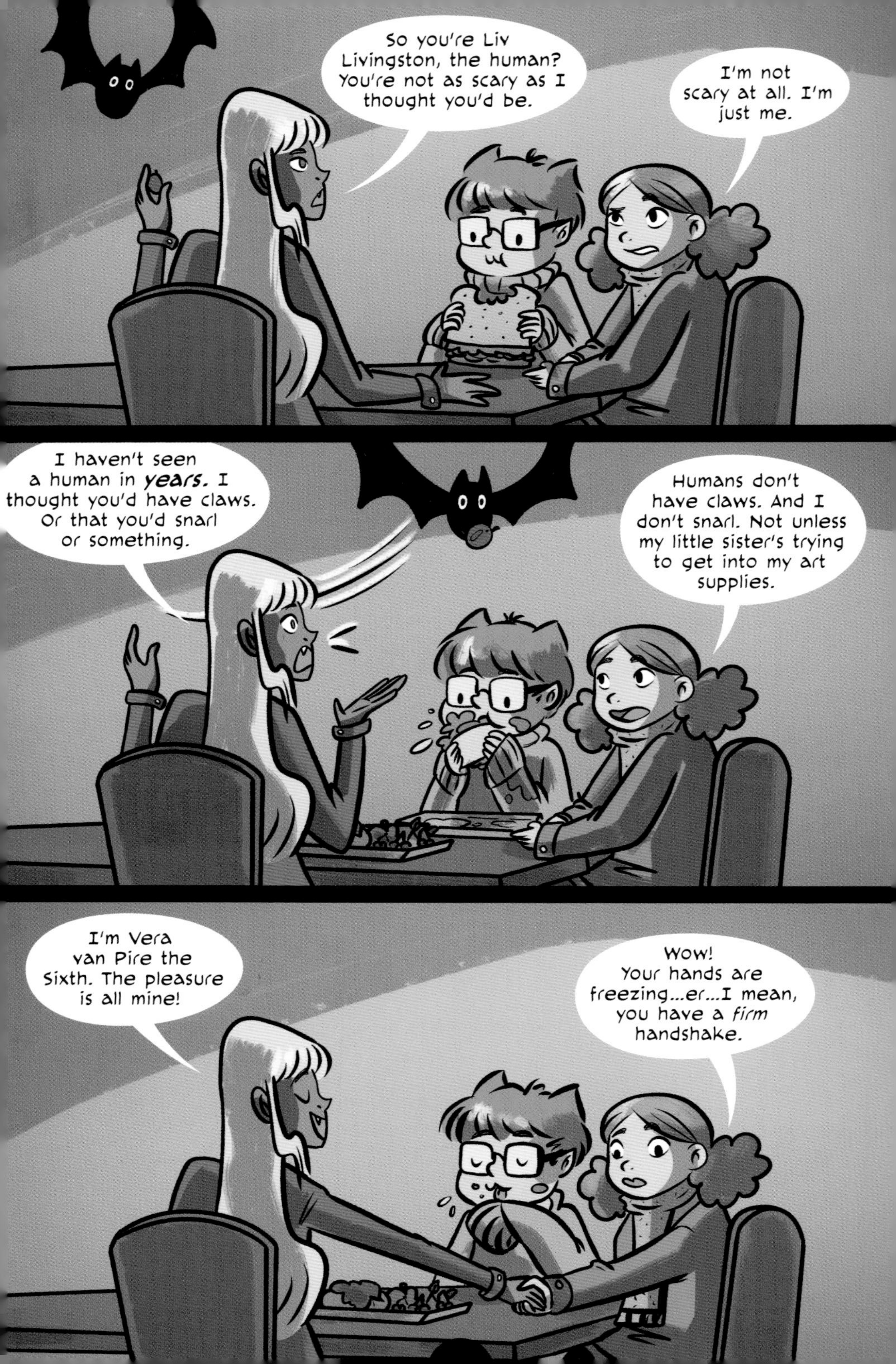
So you're Liv Livingston, the human? You're not as scary as I thought you'd be.
I'm not scary at all. I'm just me.
I haven't seen a human in *years.* I thought you'd have claws. Or that you'd snarl or something.
Humans don't have claws. And I don't snarl. Not unless my little sister's trying to get into my art supplies.
I'm Vera van Pire the Sixth. The pleasure is all mine!
Wow! Your hands are freezing...er...I mean, you have a *firm* handshake.

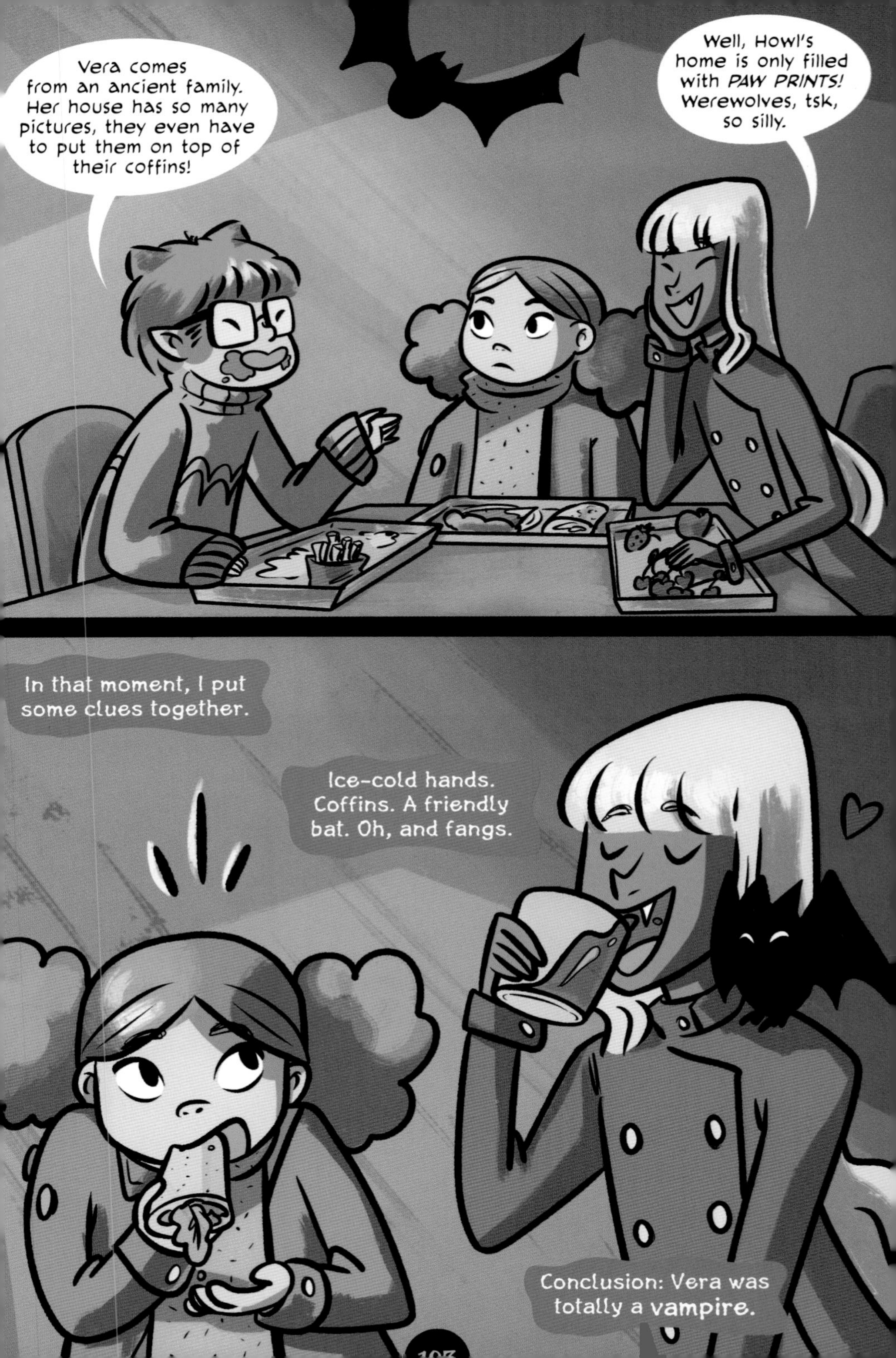
Vera comes from an ancient family. Her house has so many pictures, they even have to put them on top of their coffins!
Well, Howl's home is only filled with *PAW PRINTS!* Werewolves, tsk, so silly.
In that moment, I put some clues together.
Ice-cold hands. Coffins. A friendly bat. Oh, and fangs.
Conclusion: Vera was totally a **vampire**.

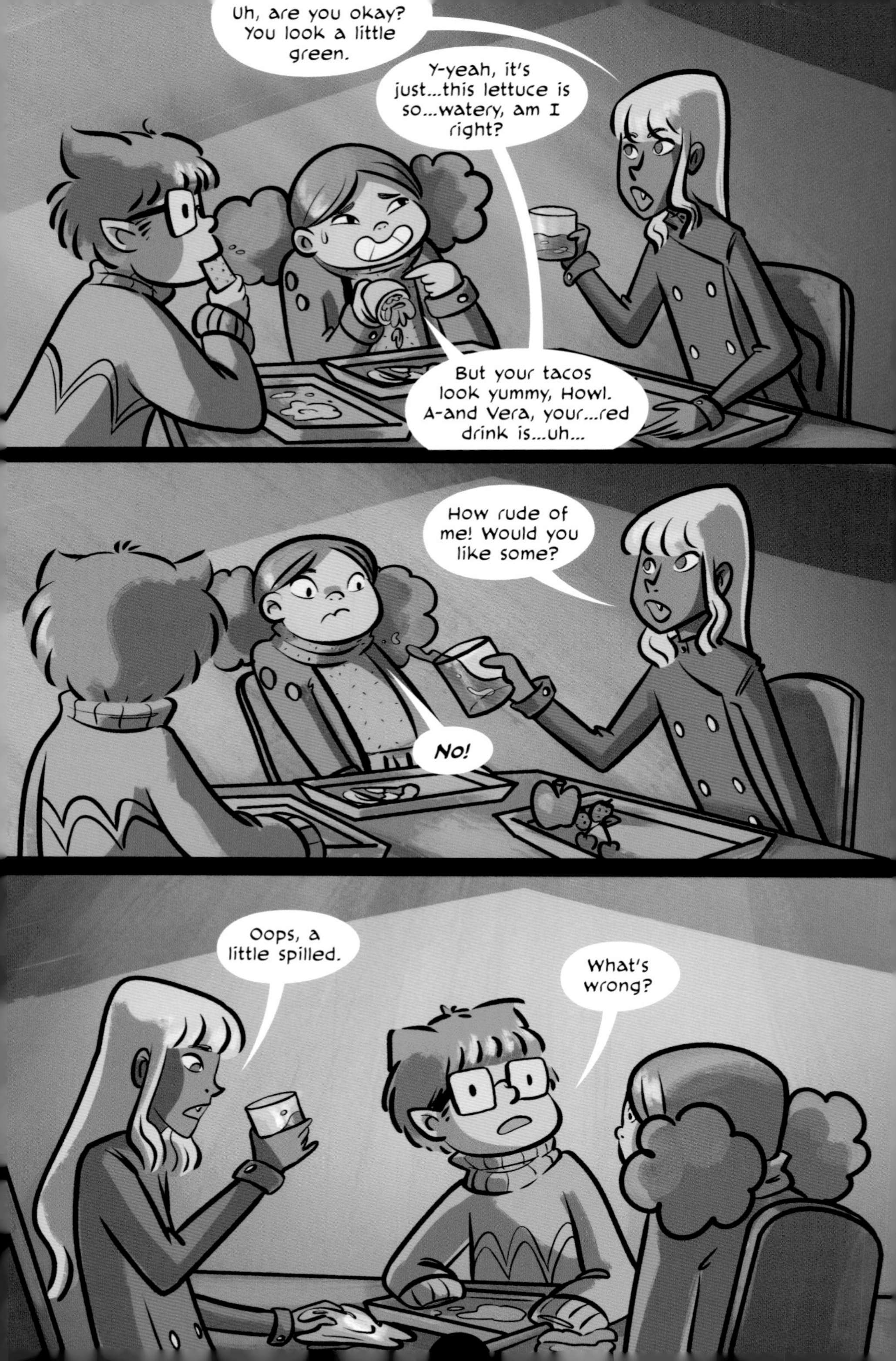
Uh, are you okay? You look a little green.
Y-yeah, it's just...this lettuce is so...watery, am I right?
But your tacos look yummy, Howl. A-and Vera, your...red drink is...uh...
How rude of me! Would you like some?
No!
Oops, a little spilled.
What's wrong?

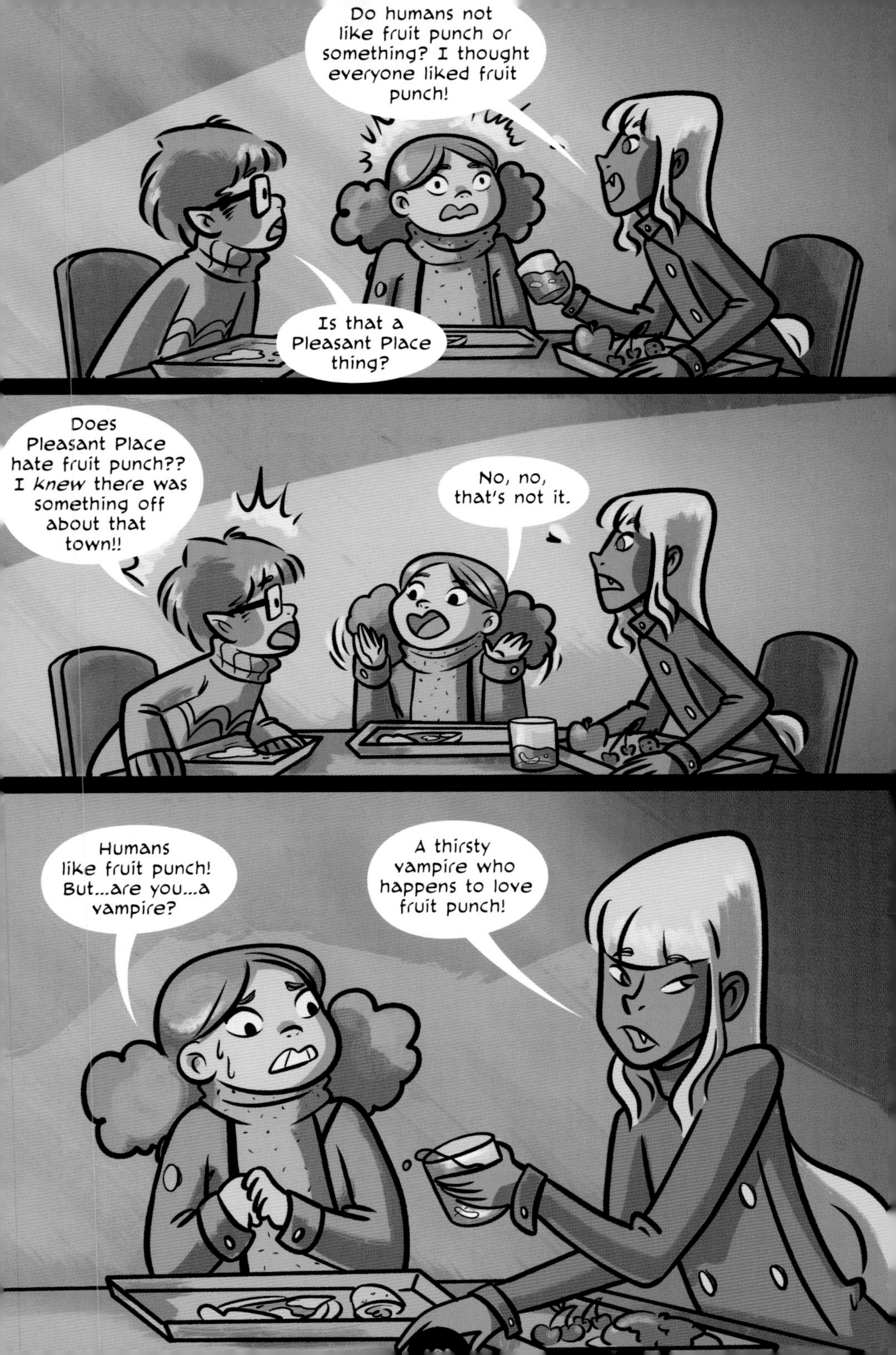
Do humans not like fruit punch or something? I thought everyone liked fruit punch!
Is that a Pleasant Place thing?
Does Pleasant Place hate fruit punch?? I *knew* there was something off about that town!!
No, no, that's not it.
Humans like fruit punch! But...are you...a vampire?
A thirsty vampire who happens to love fruit punch!

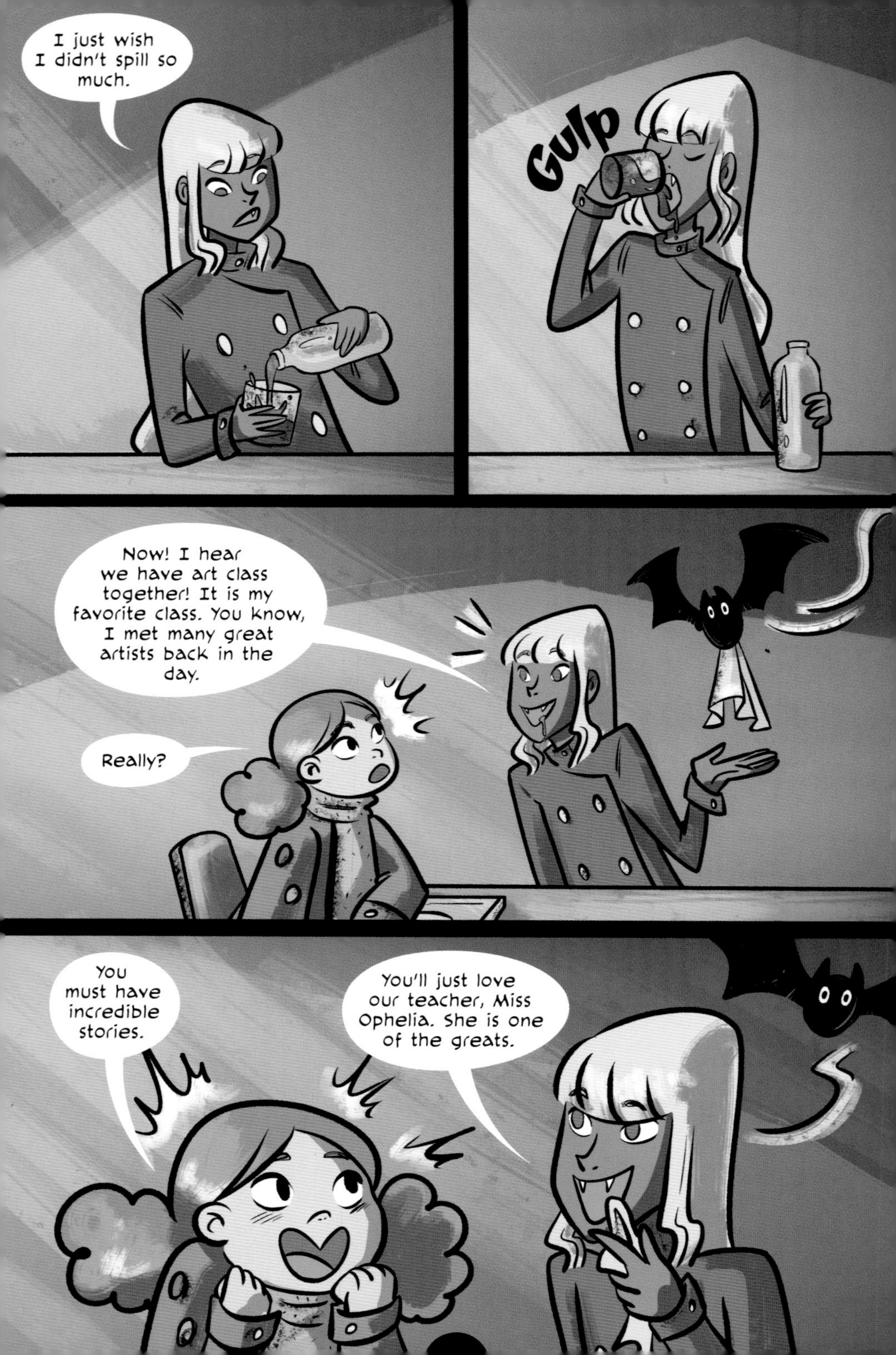
I just wish I didn't spill so much.
Gulp
Now! I hear we have art class together! It is my favorite class. You know, I met many great artists back in the day.
Really?
You must have incredible stories.
You'll just love our teacher, Miss Ophelia. She is one of the greats.

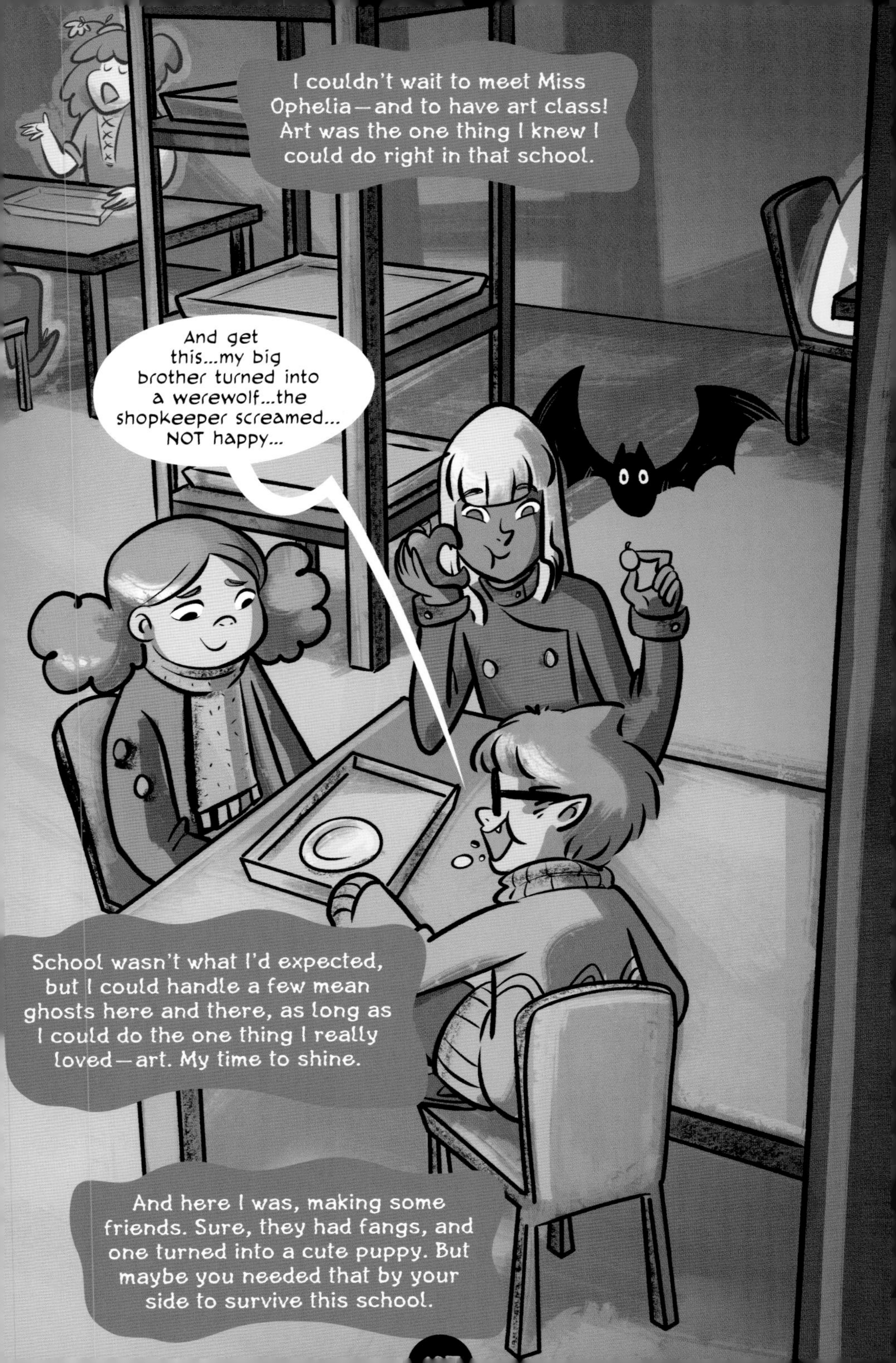
I couldn't wait to meet Miss Ophelia—and to have art class! Art was the one thing I knew I could do right in that school.
And get this...my big brother turned into a werewolf...the shopkeeper screamed... NOT happy...
School wasn't what I'd expected, but I could handle a few mean ghosts here and there, as long as I could do the one thing I really loved—art. My time to shine.
And here I was, making some friends. Sure, they had fangs, and one turned into a cute puppy. But maybe you needed that by your side to survive this school.

CHAPTER 8

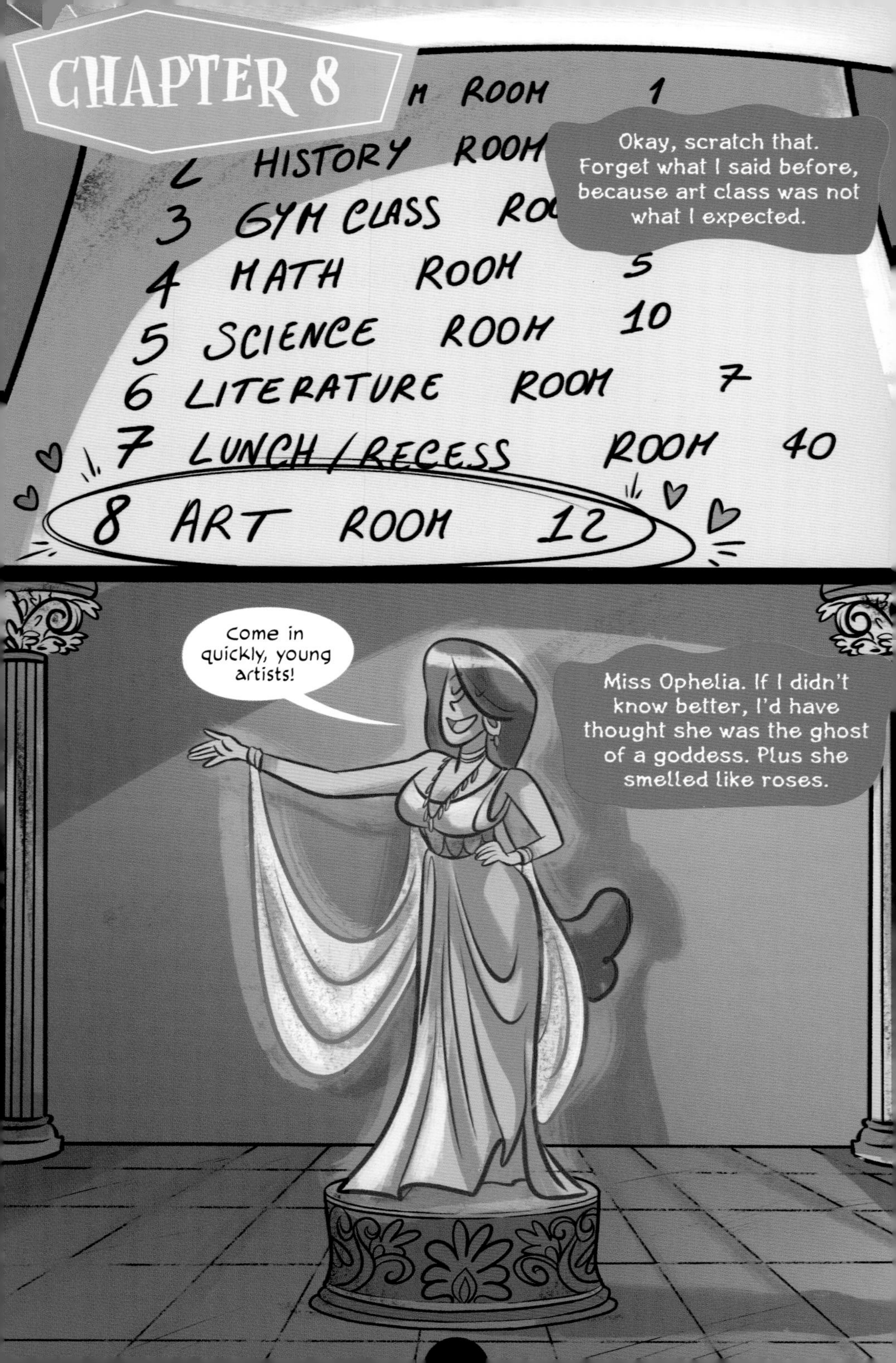

M ROOM 1
2 HISTORY ROOM
3 GYM CLASS RO
4 MATH ROOM 5
5 SCIENCE ROOM 10
6 LITERATURE ROOM 7
7 LUNCH/RECESS ROOM 40
8 ART ROOM 12
Okay, scratch that. Forget what I said before, because art class was not what I expected.
Come in quickly, young artists!
Miss Ophelia. If I didn't know better, I'd have thought she was the ghost of a goddess. Plus she smelled like roses.

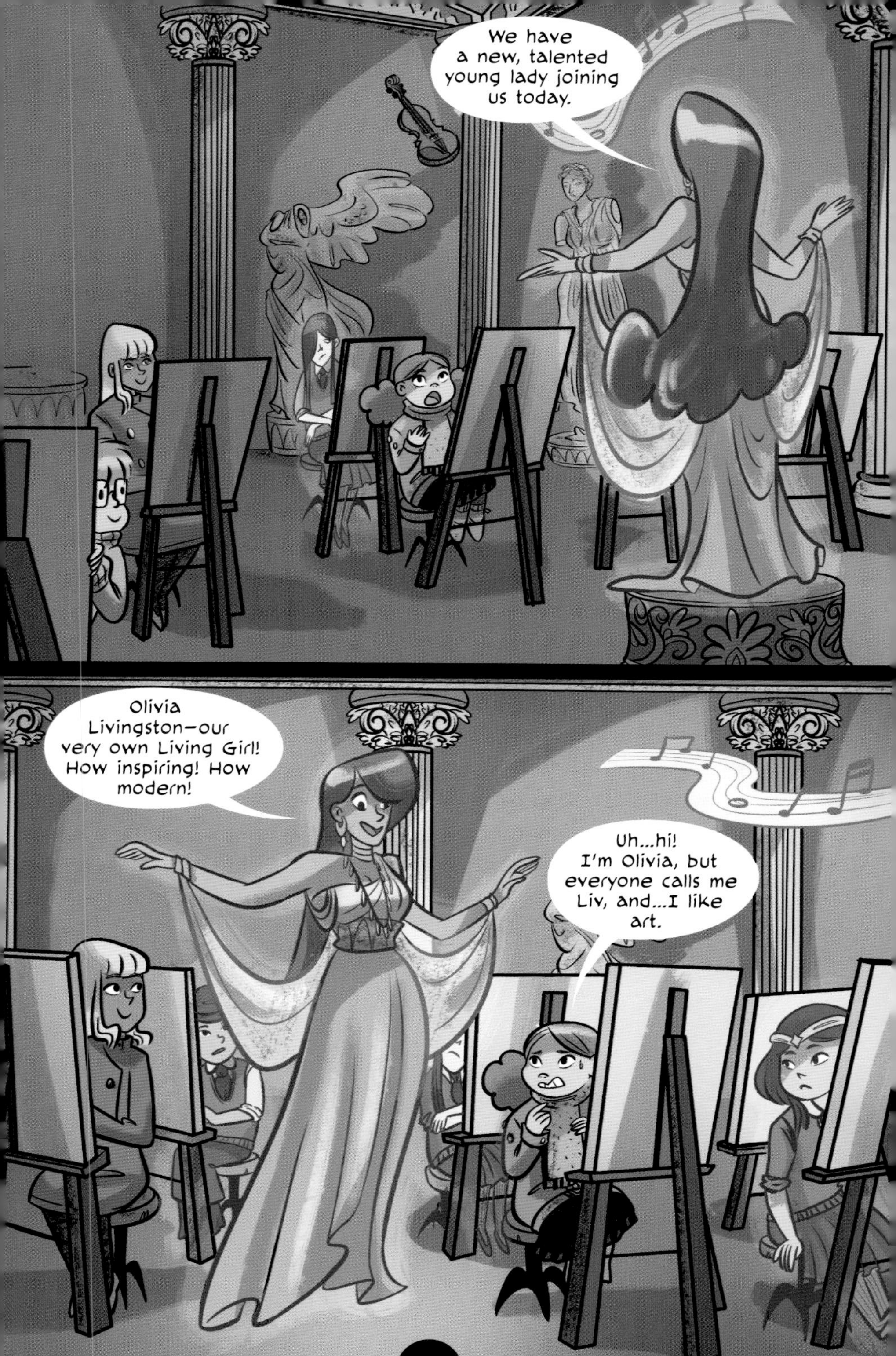
We have a new, talented young lady joining us today.
Olivia Livingston—our very own Living Girl! How inspiring! How modern!
Uh...hi! I'm Olivia, but everyone calls me Liv, and...I like art.

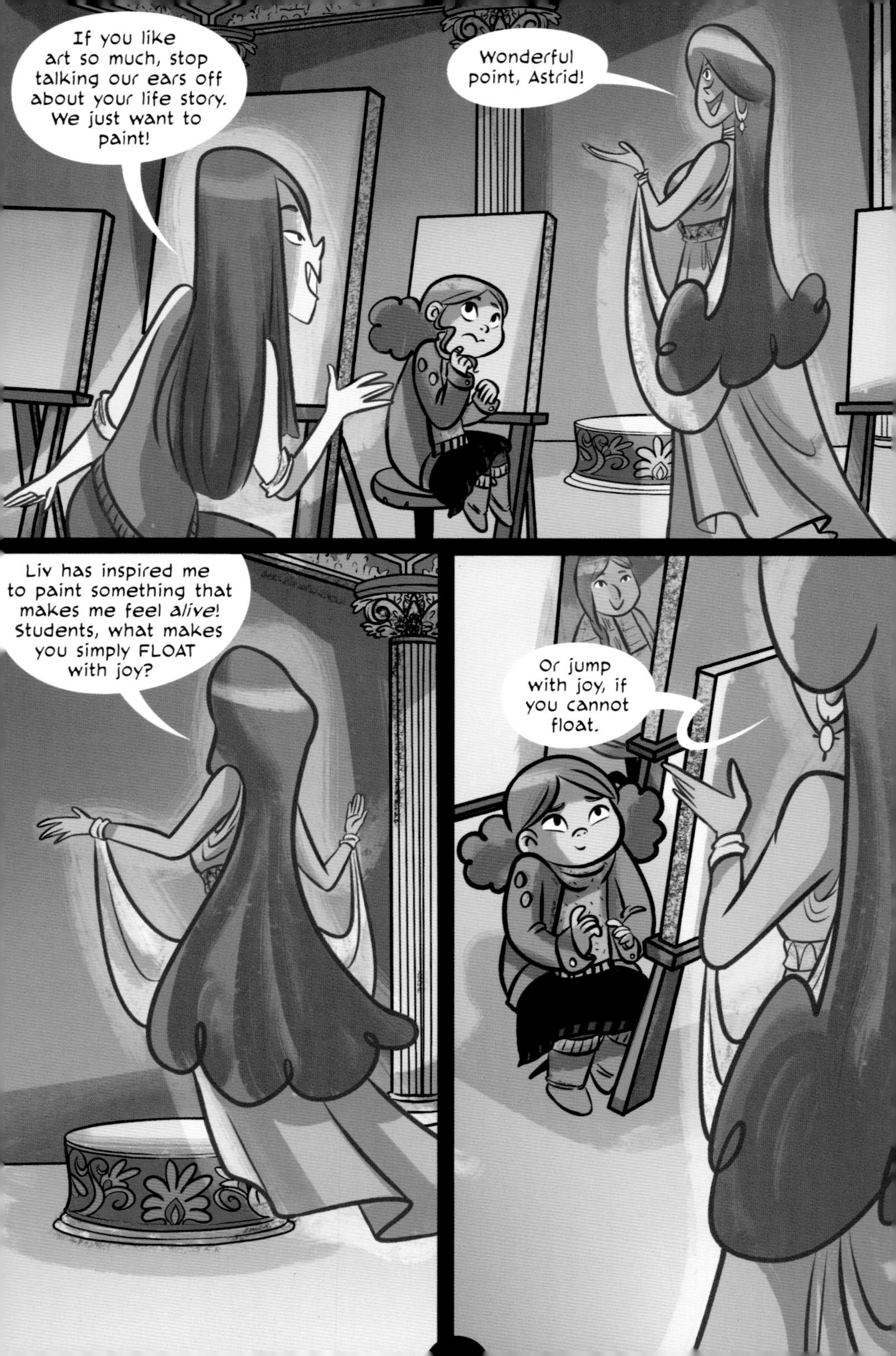
If you like art so much, stop talking our ears off about your life story. We just want to paint!
Wonderful point, Astrid!
Liv has inspired me to paint something that makes me feel *alive*! Students, what makes you simply FLOAT with joy?
Or jump with joy, if you cannot float.

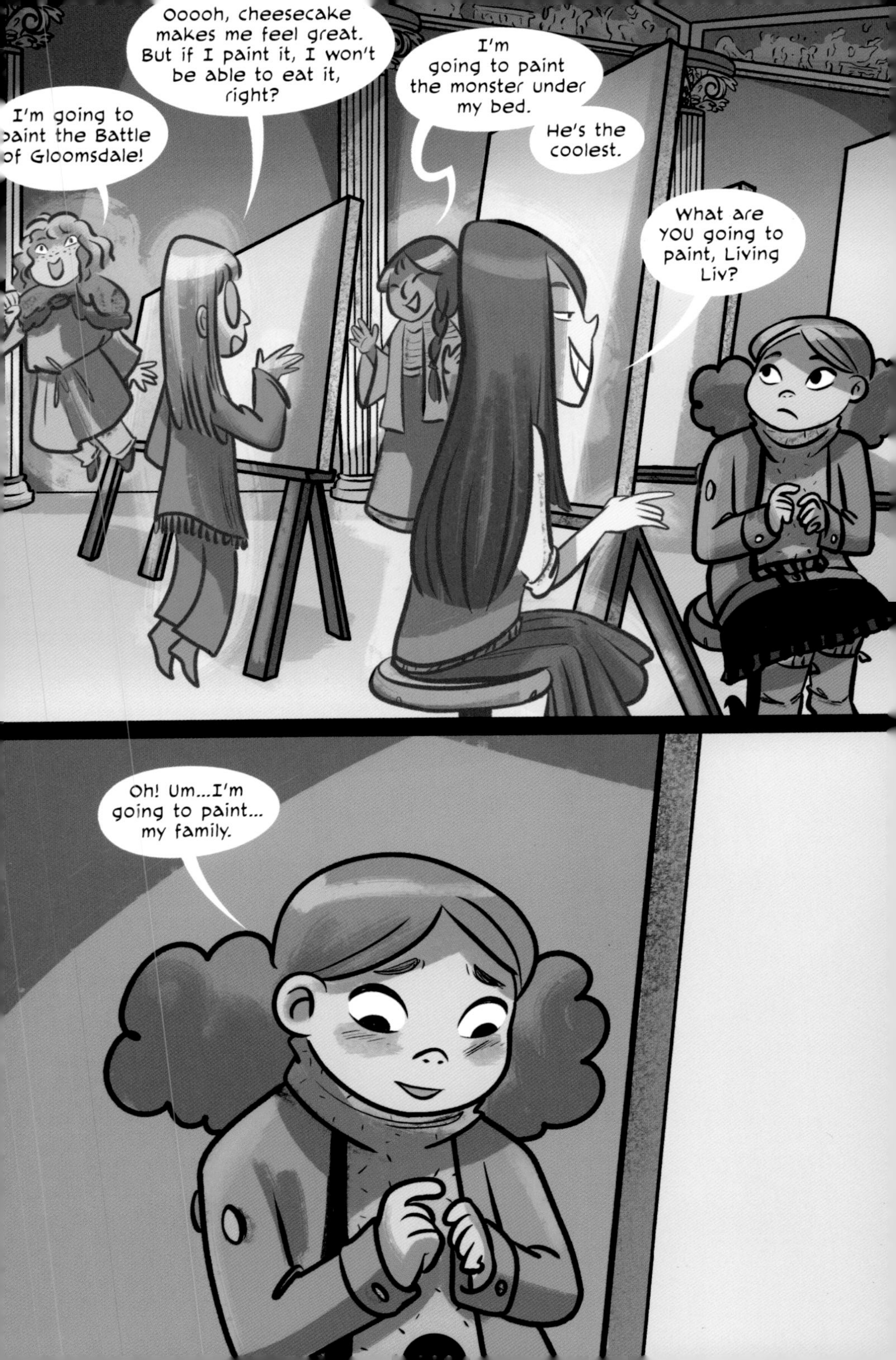
I'm going to paint the Battle of Gloomsdale!
Ooooh, cheesecake makes me feel great. But if I paint it, I won't be able to eat it, right?
I'm going to paint the monster under my bed.
He's the coolest.
What are YOU going to paint, Living Liv?
Oh! Um...I'm going to paint... my family.

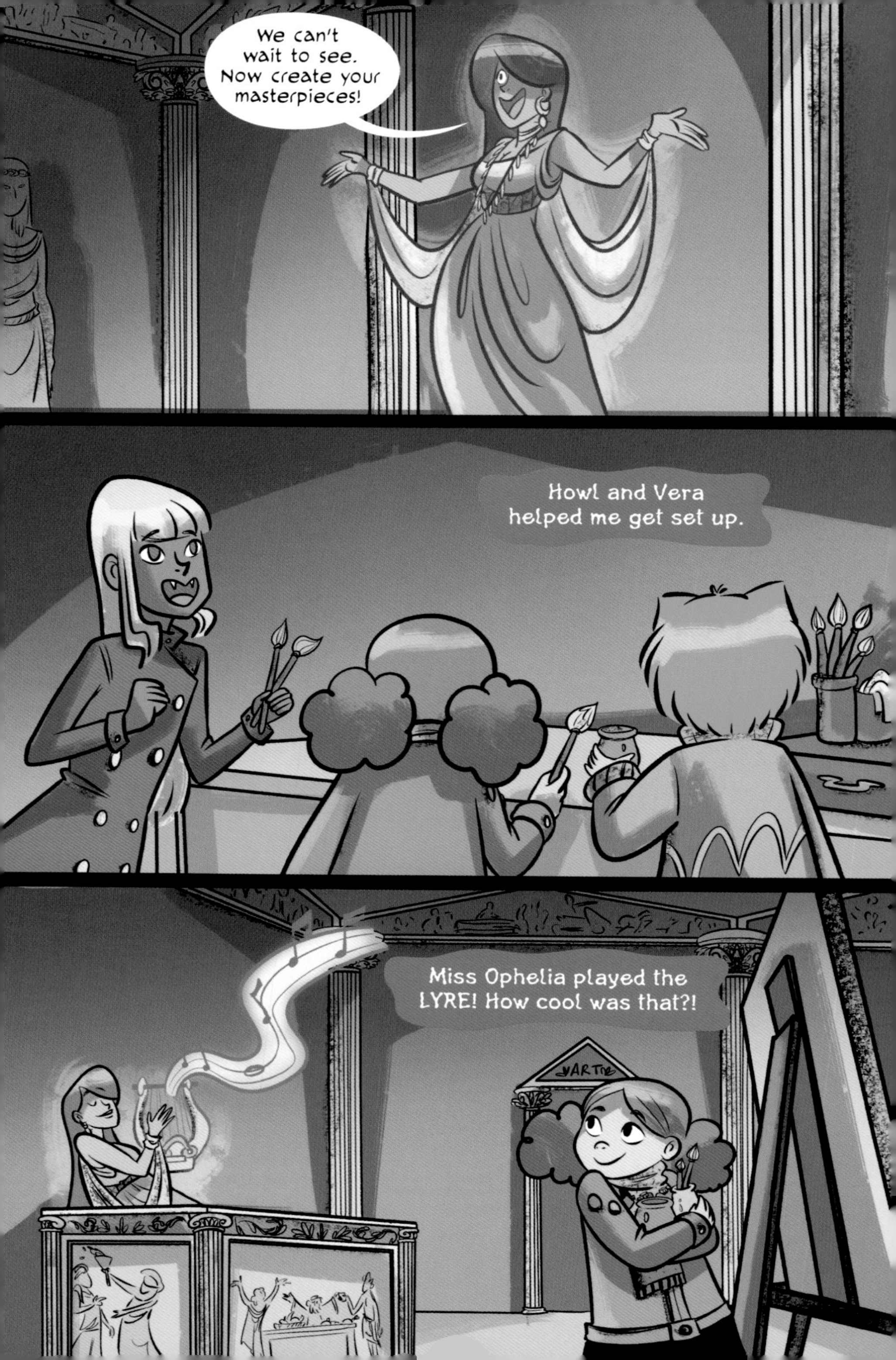
We can't wait to see. Now create your masterpieces!
Howl and Vera helped me get set up.
Miss Ophelia played the LYRE! How cool was that?!
ART

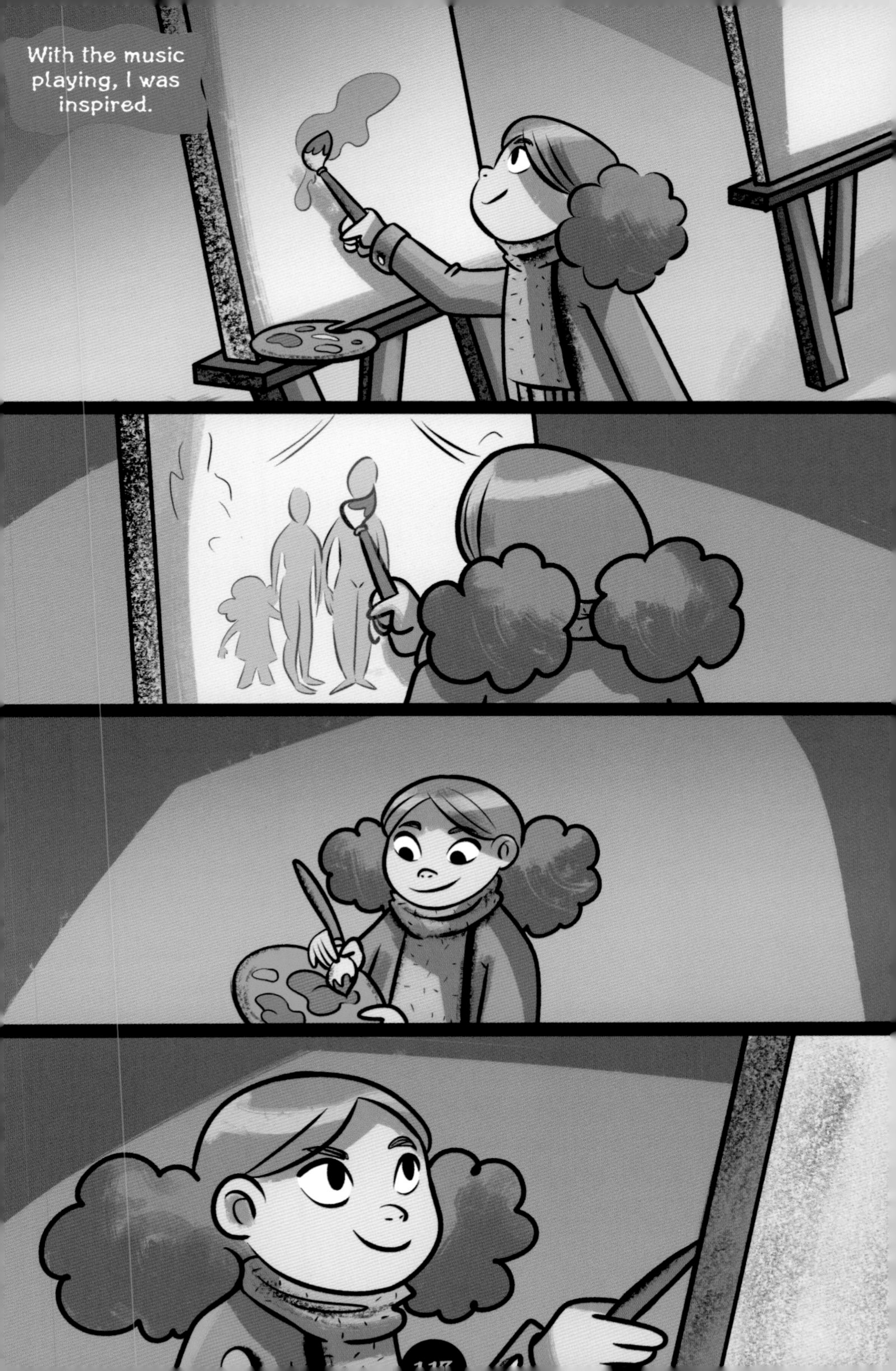
With the music playing, I was inspired.

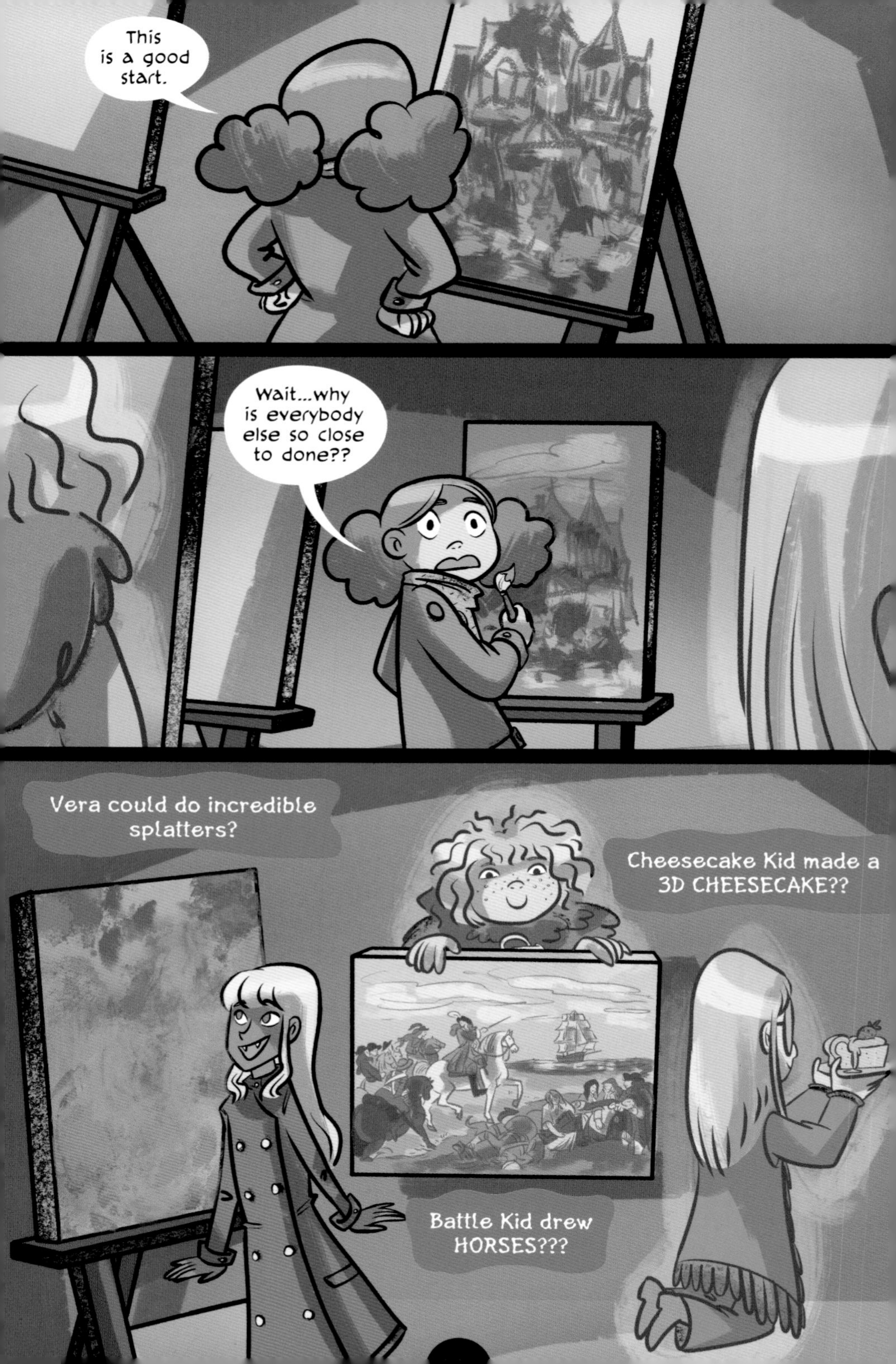
This is a good start.
Wait...why is everybody else so close to done??
Vera could do incredible splatters?
Cheesecake Kid made a 3D CHEESECAKE??
Battle Kid drew HORSES???

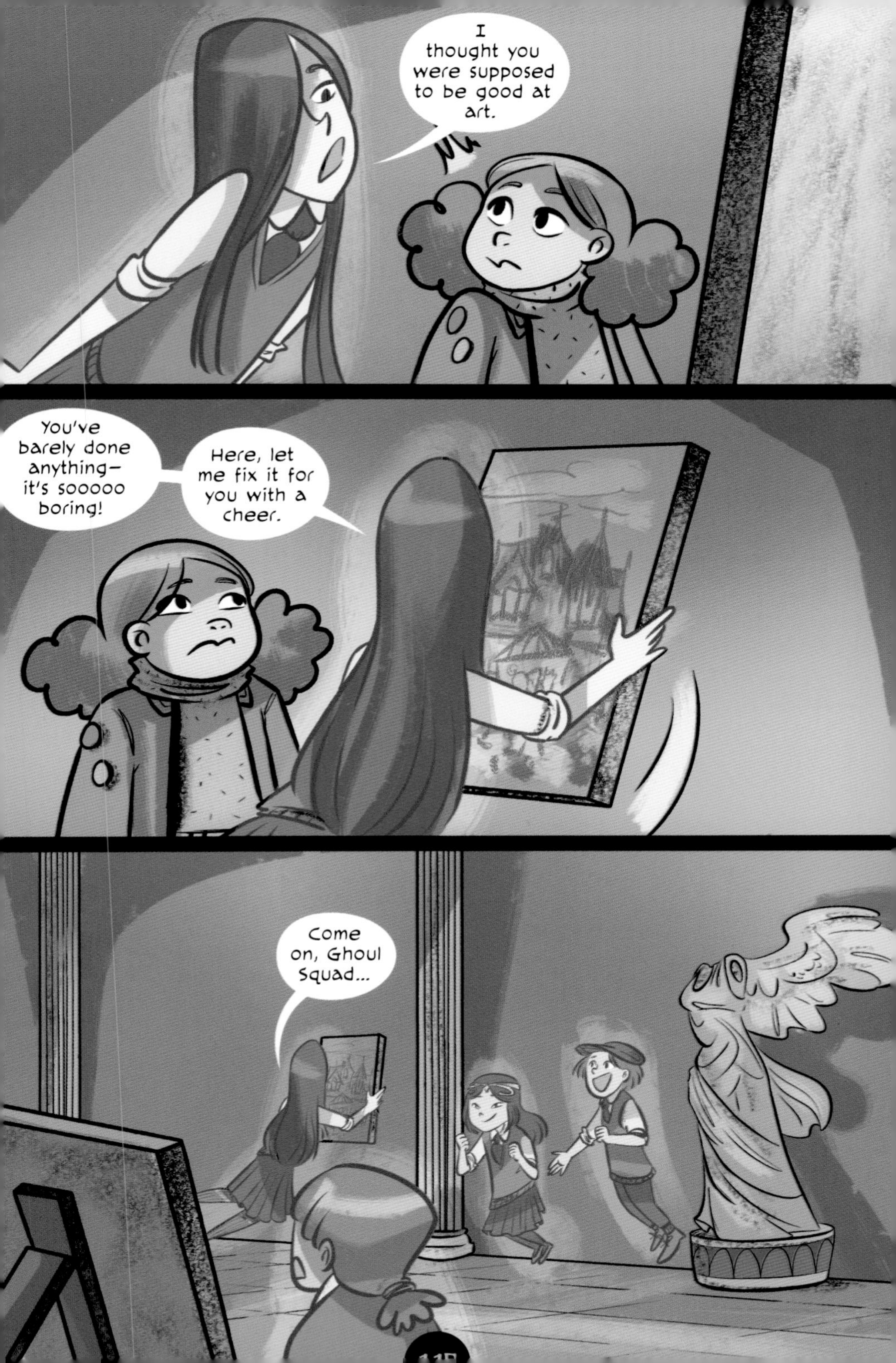
I thought you were supposed to be good at art.
You've barely done anything— it's sooooo boring!
Here, let me fix it for you with a cheer.
Come on, Ghoul Squad...

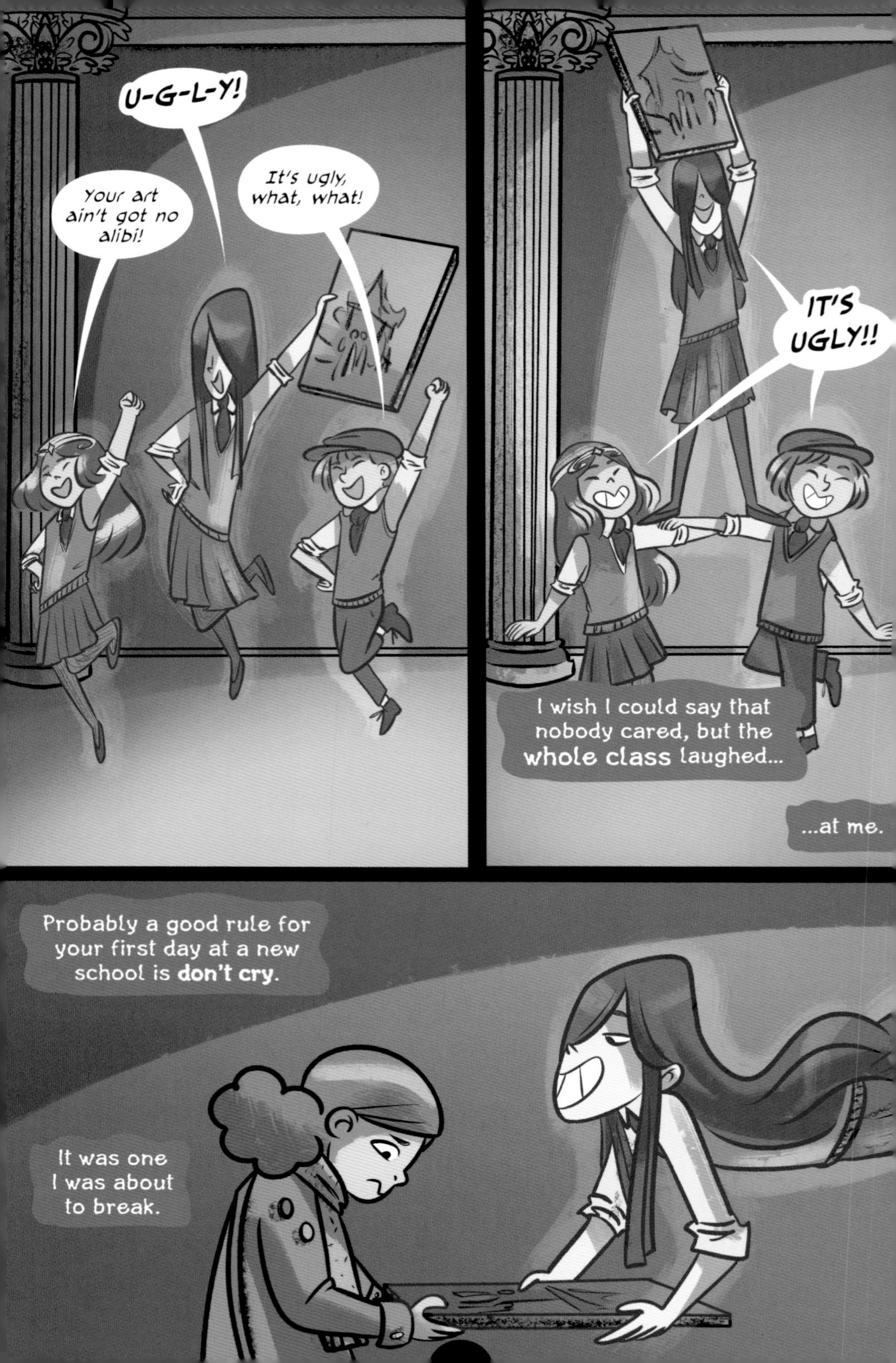
Your art ain't got no alibi!
U-G-L-Y!
It's ugly, what, what!
IT'S UGLY!!
I wish I could say that nobody cared, but the whole class laughed...
...at me.
Probably a good rule for your first day at a new school is don't cry.
It was one I was about to break.

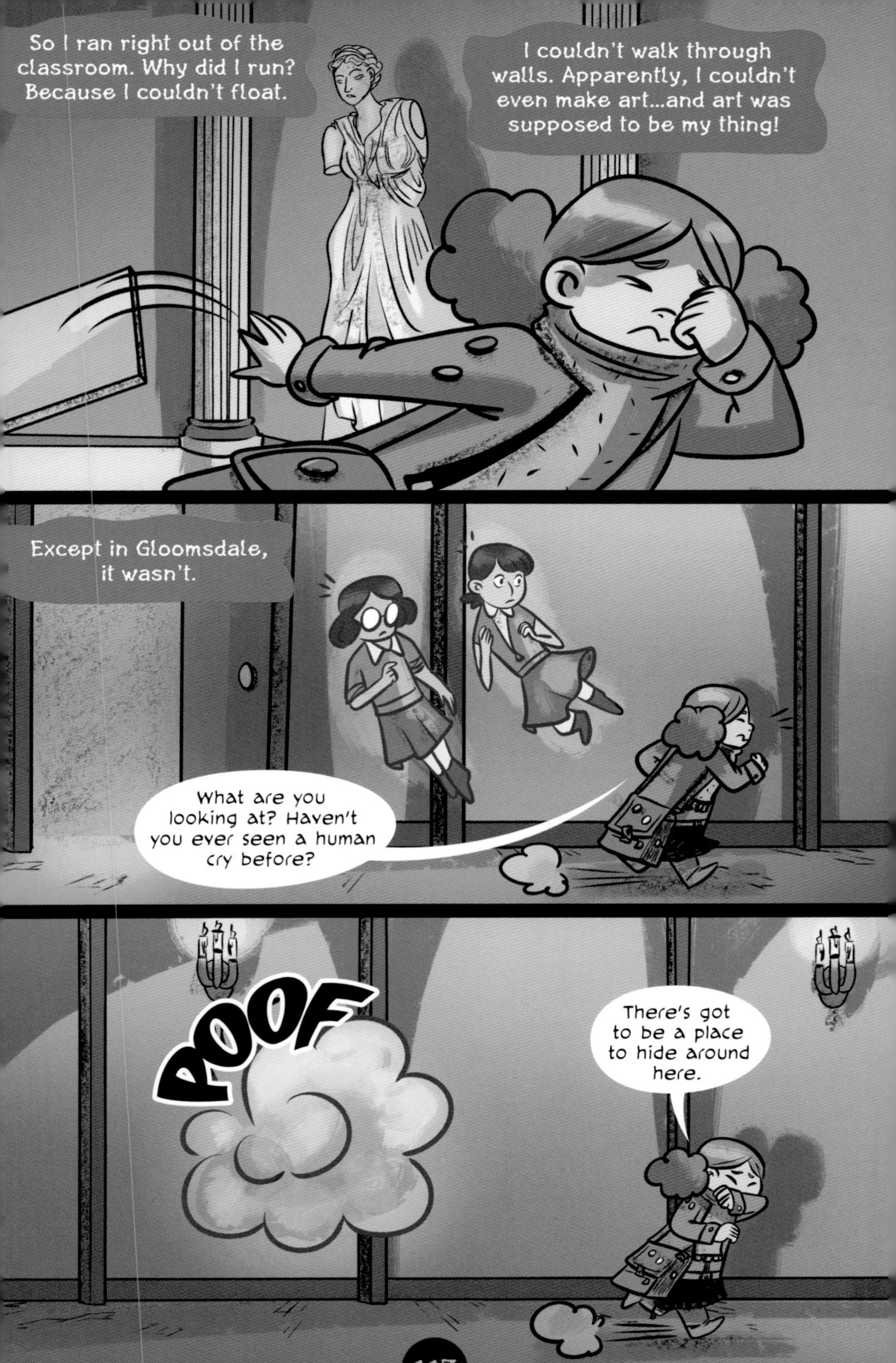
So I ran right out of the classroom. Why did I run? Because I couldn't float.
I couldn't walk through walls. Apparently, I couldn't even make art...and art was supposed to be my thing!
Except in Gloomsdale, it wasn't.
What are you looking at? Haven't you ever seen a human cry before?
POOF
There's got to be a place to hide around here.

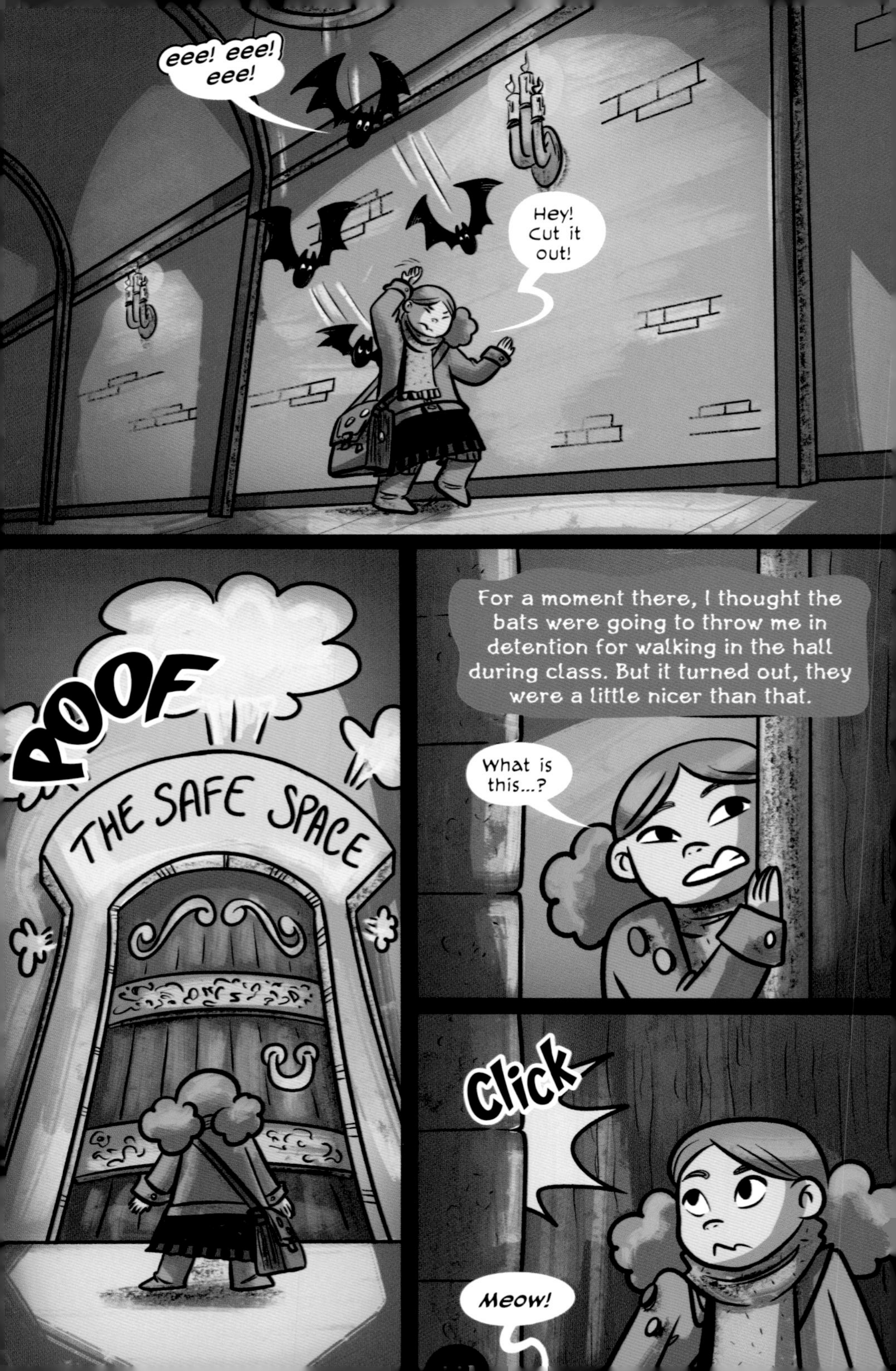
eee! eee! eee!
Hey! Cut it out!
POOF
THE SAFE SPACE
For a moment there, I thought the bats were going to throw me in detention for walking in the hall during class. But it turned out, they were a little nicer than that.
What is this...?
Click
Meow!

CHAPTER 9

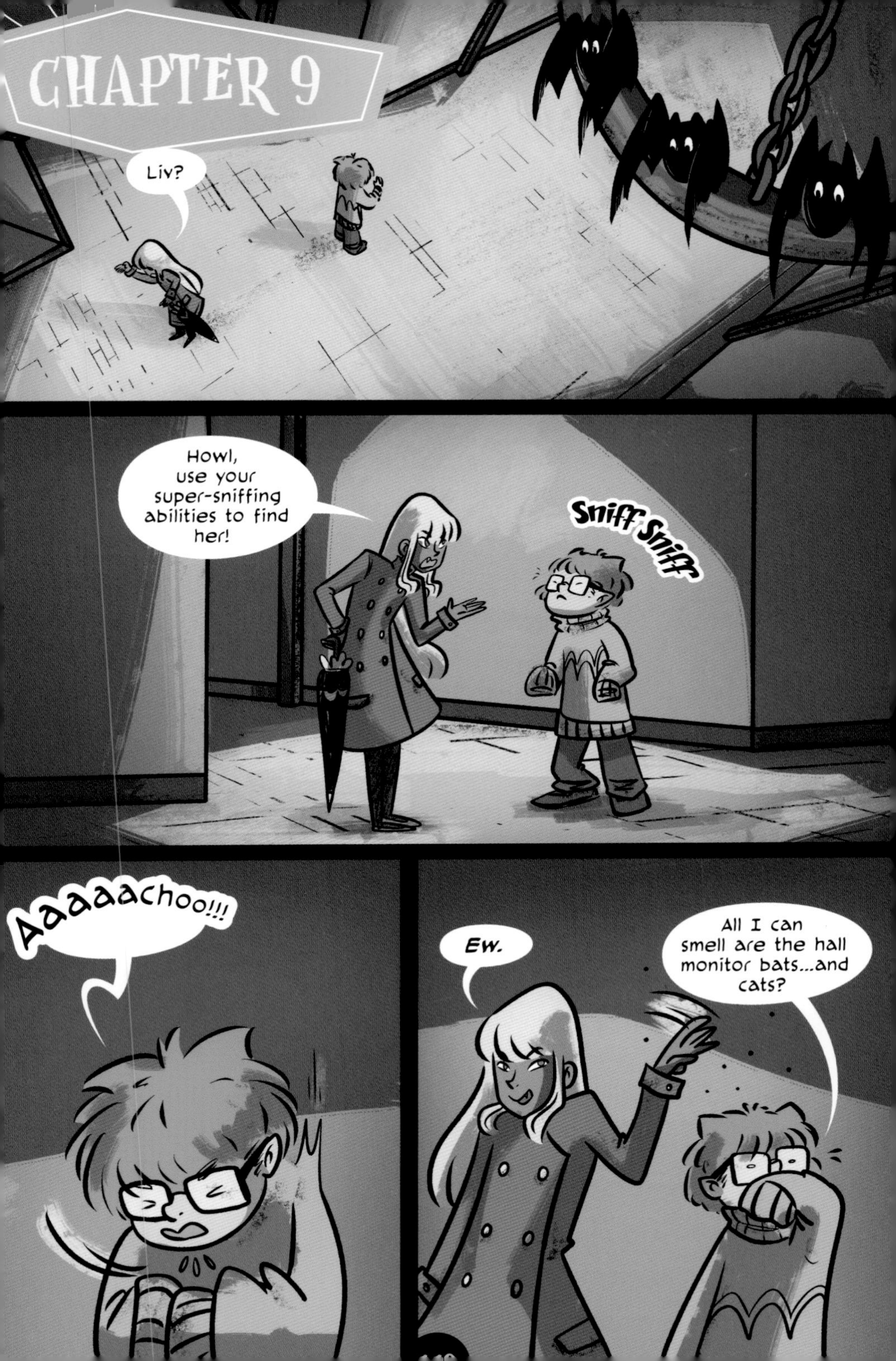

Liv?
Howl, use your super-sniffing abilities to find her!
Sniff Sniff
Aaaaachoo!!!
Ew.
All I can smell are the hall monitor bats...and cats?

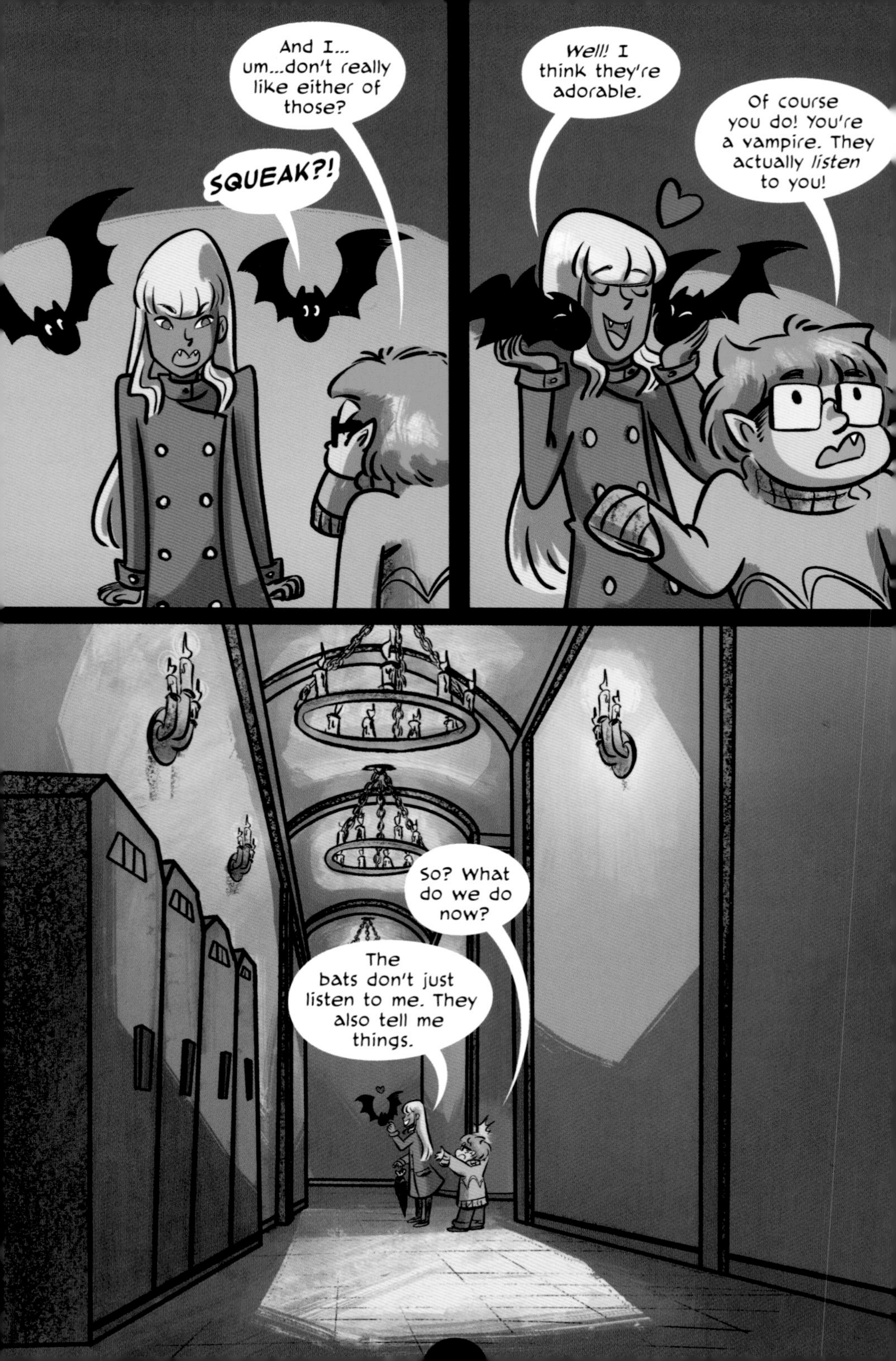

And I... um...don't really like either of those?
SQUEAK?!
Well! I think they're adorable.
Of course you do! You're a vampire. They actually listen to you!
So? What do we do now?
The bats don't just listen to me. They also tell me things.

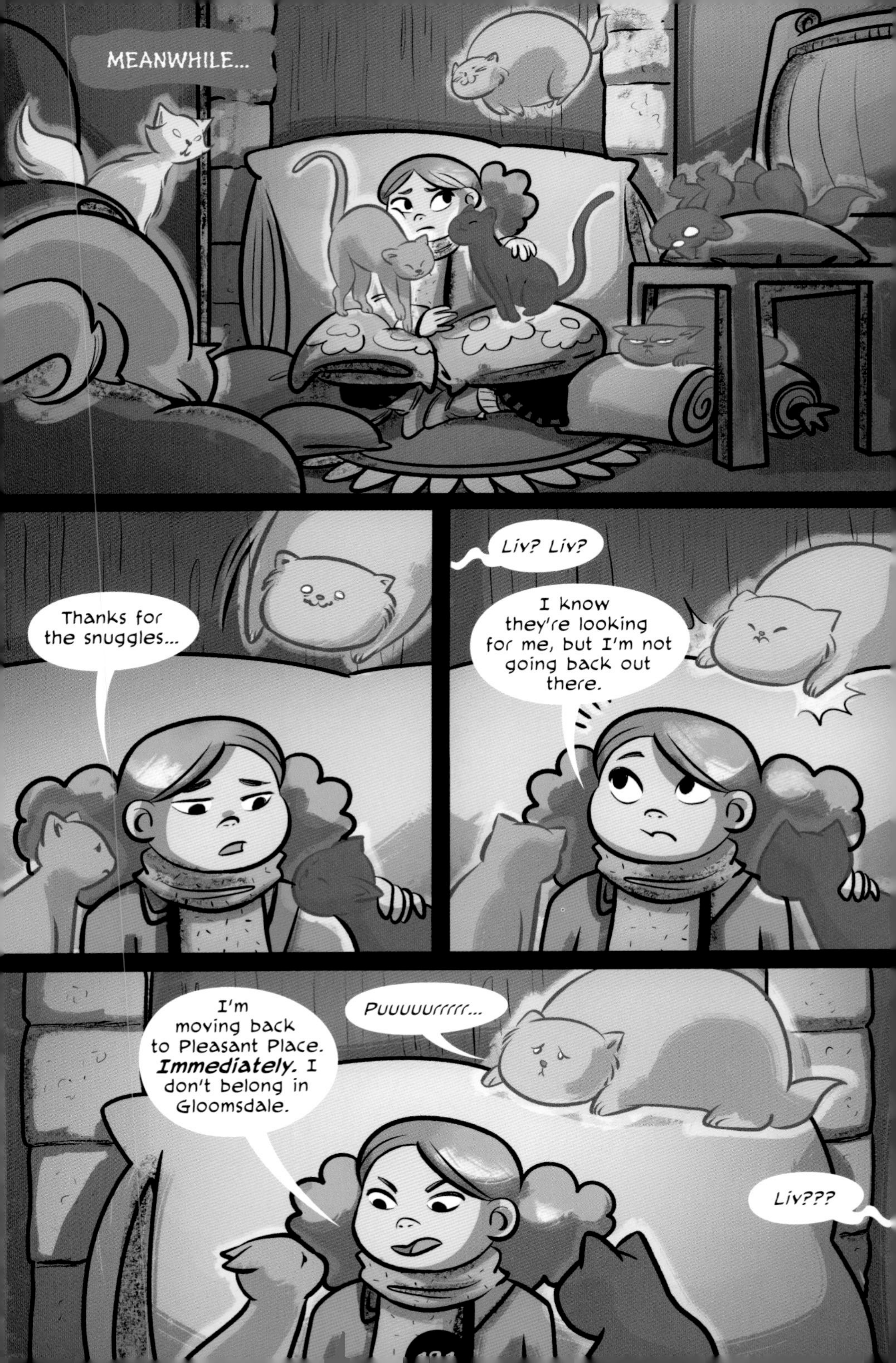
MEANWHILE...
Thanks for the snuggles...
Liv? Liv?
I know they're looking for me, but I'm not going back out there.
I'm moving back to Pleasant Place. *Immediately.* I don't belong in Gloomsdale.
Puuuuurrrrr...
Liv???

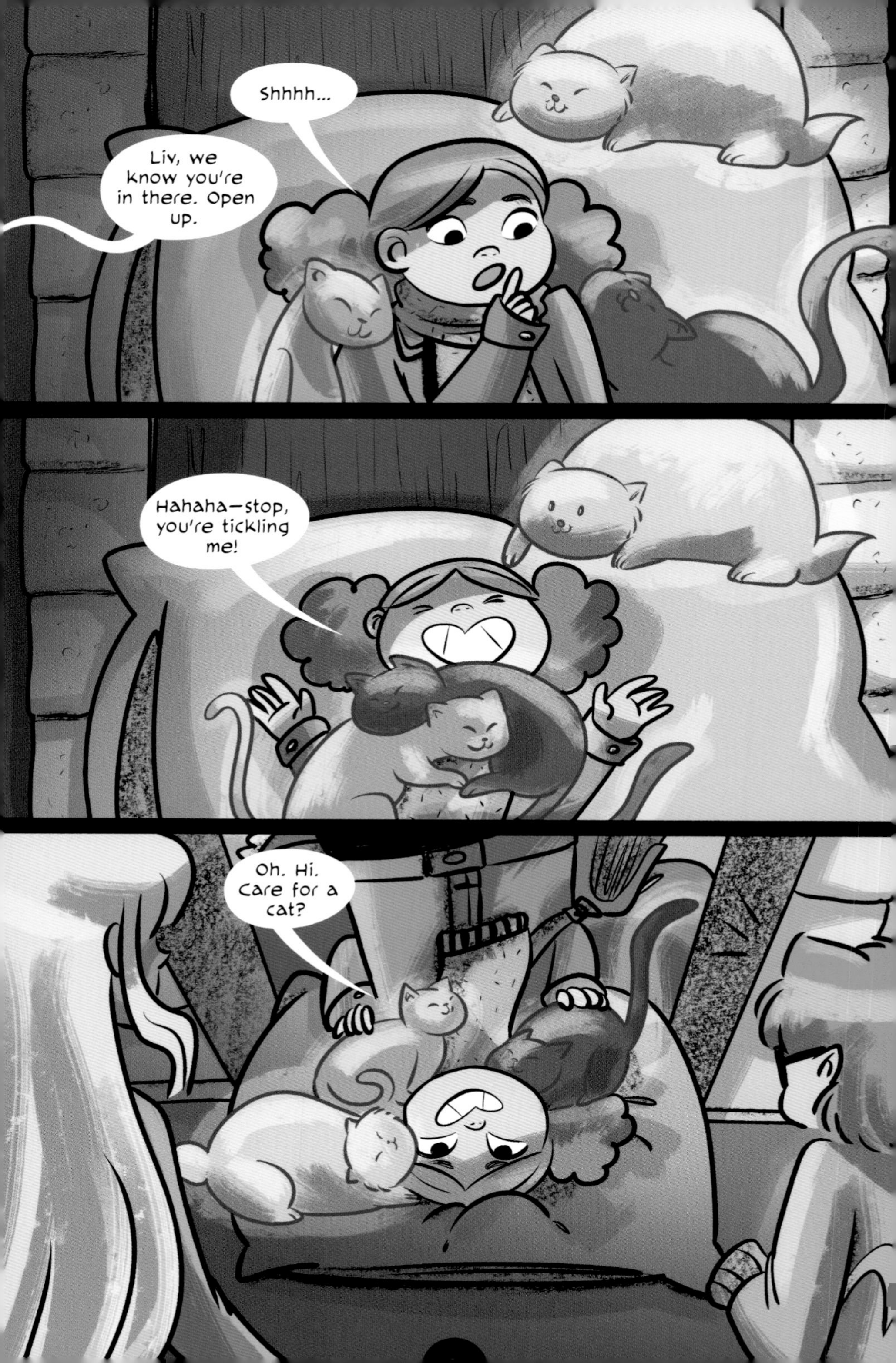
Shhhh...
Liv, we know you're in there. Open up.
Hahaha—stop, you're tickling me!
Oh. Hi. Care for a cat?

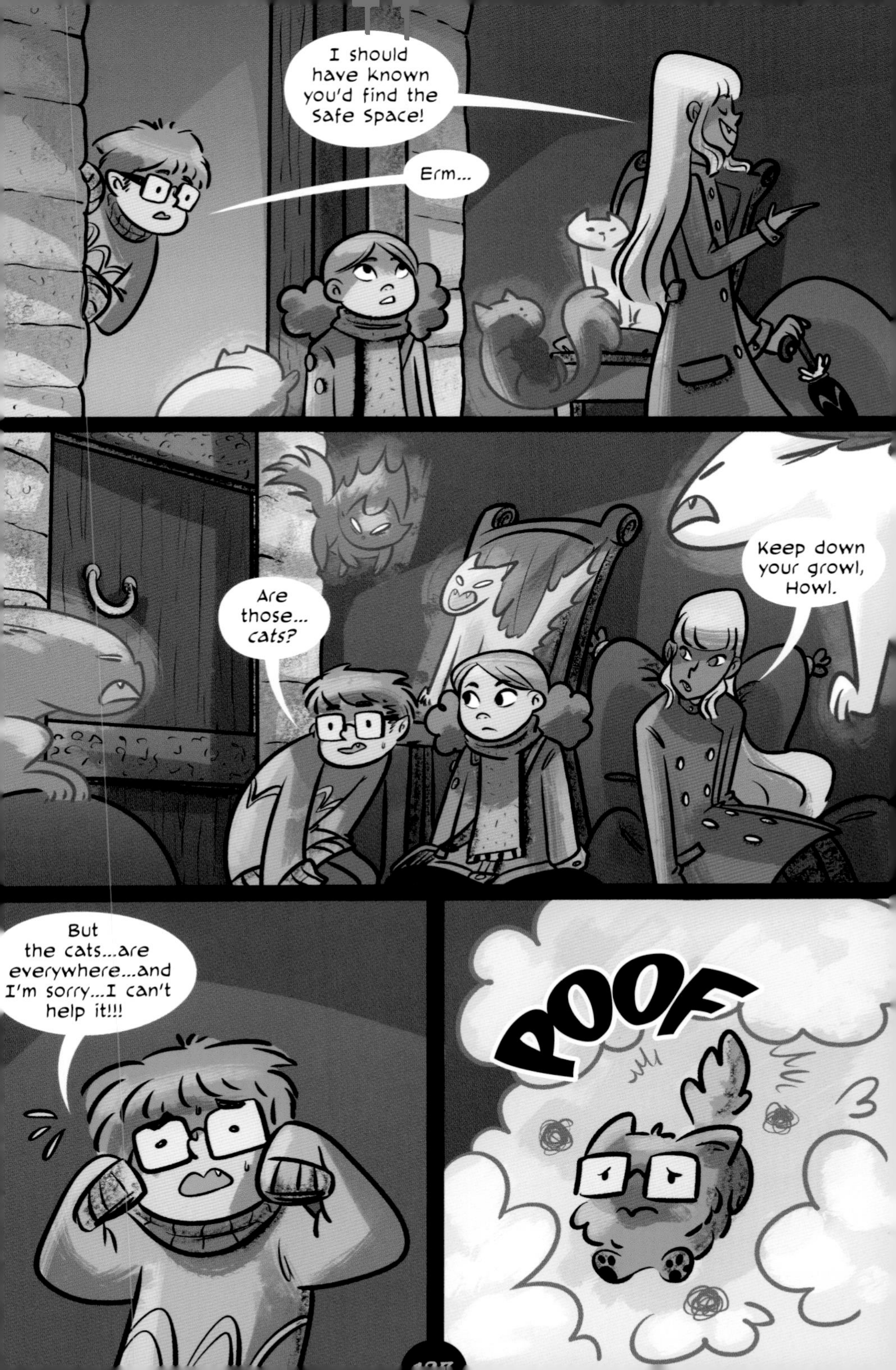

I should have known you'd find the Safe Space!
Erm...
Are those... cats?
Keep down your growl, Howl.
But the cats...are everywhere...and I'm sorry...I can't help it!!!
POOF

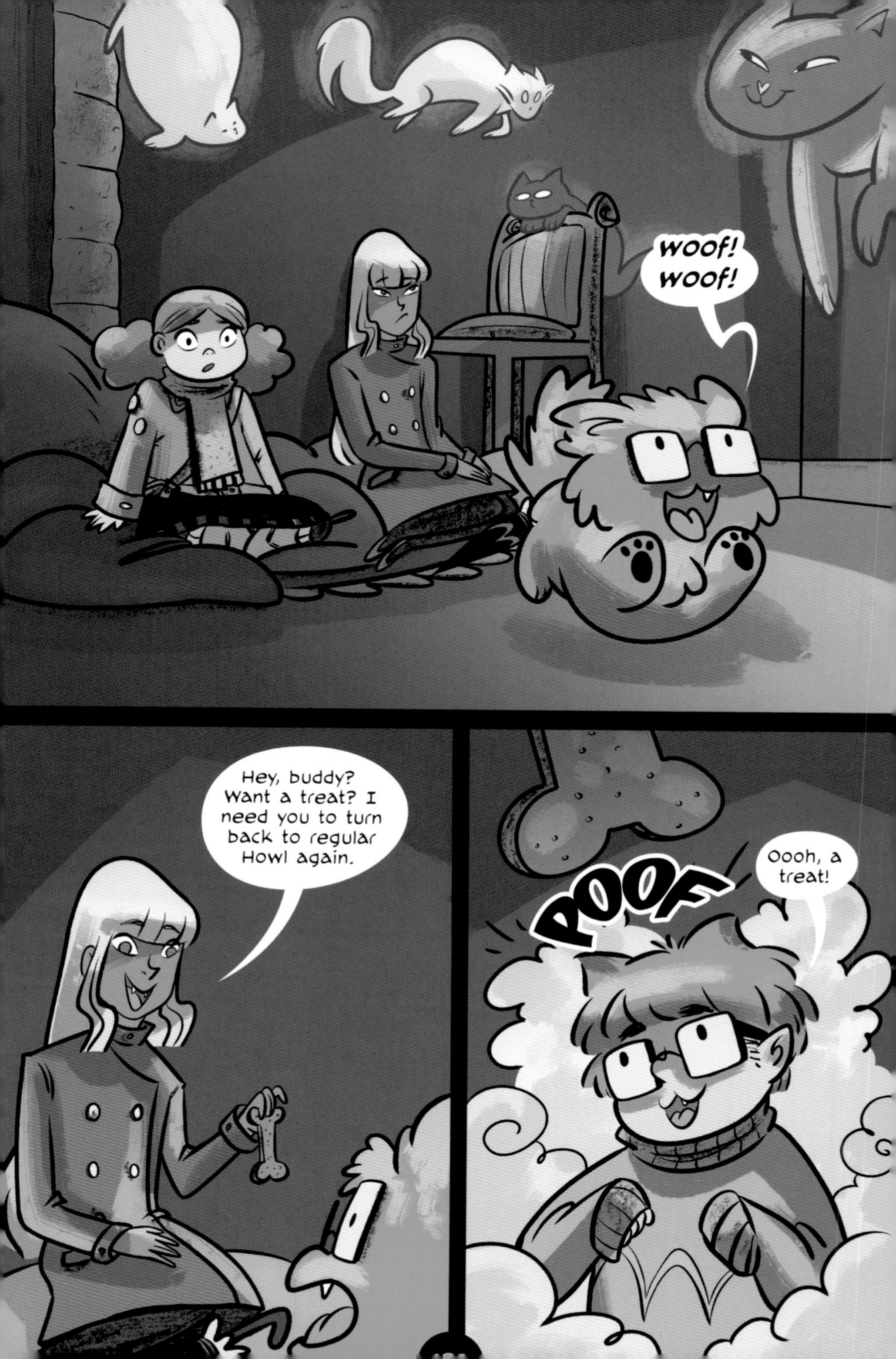
woof! woof!
Hey, buddy? Want a treat? I need you to turn back to regular Howl again.
POOF
Oooh, a treat!

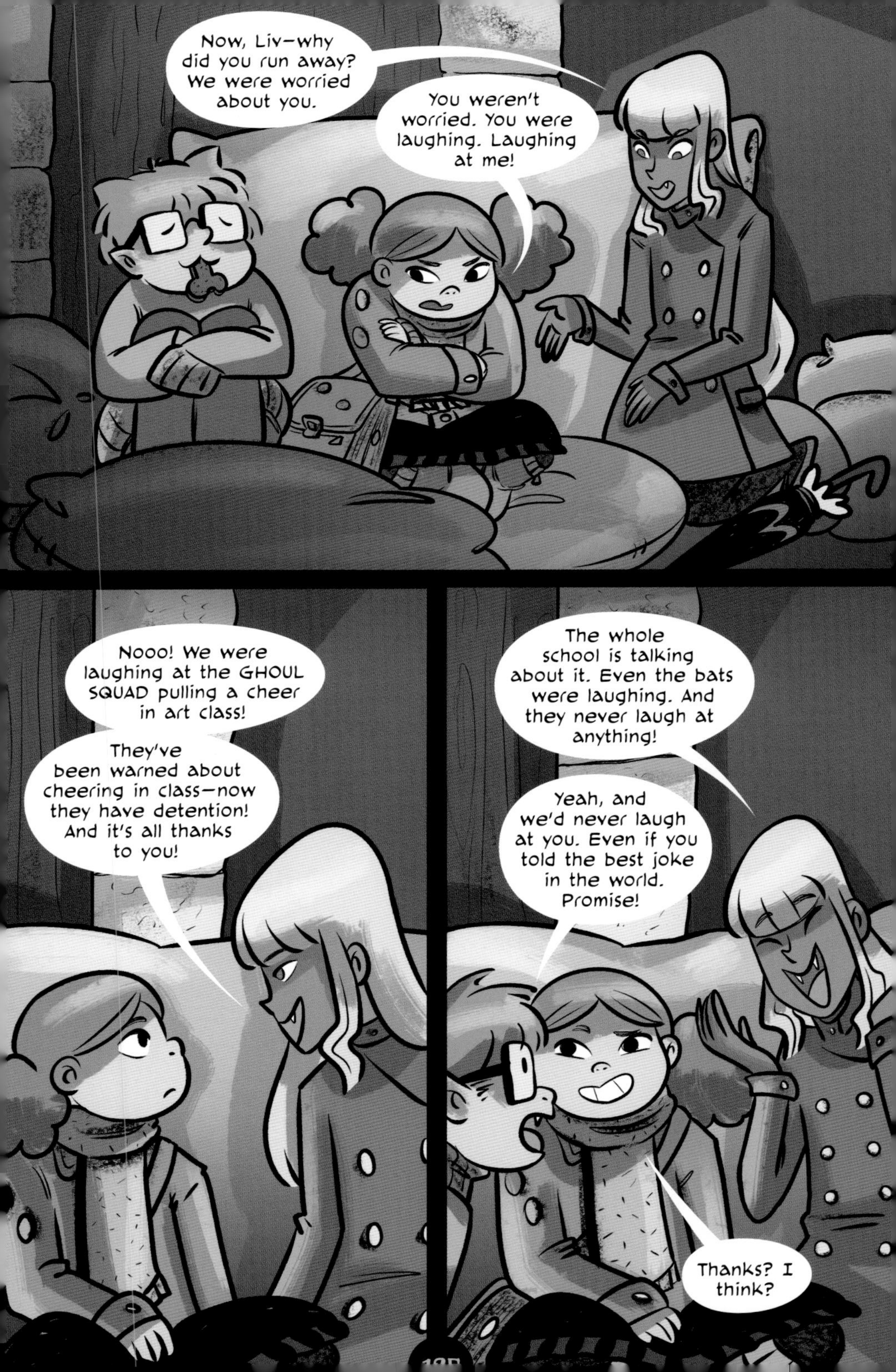
Now, Liv—why did you run away? We were worried about you.
You weren't worried. You were laughing. Laughing at me!
Nooo! We were laughing at the GHOUL SQUAD pulling a cheer in art class!
They've been warned about cheering in class—now they have detention! And it's all thanks to you!
The whole school is talking about it. Even the bats were laughing. And they never laugh at anything!
Yeah, and we'd never laugh at you. Even if you told the best joke in the world. Promise!
Thanks? I think?

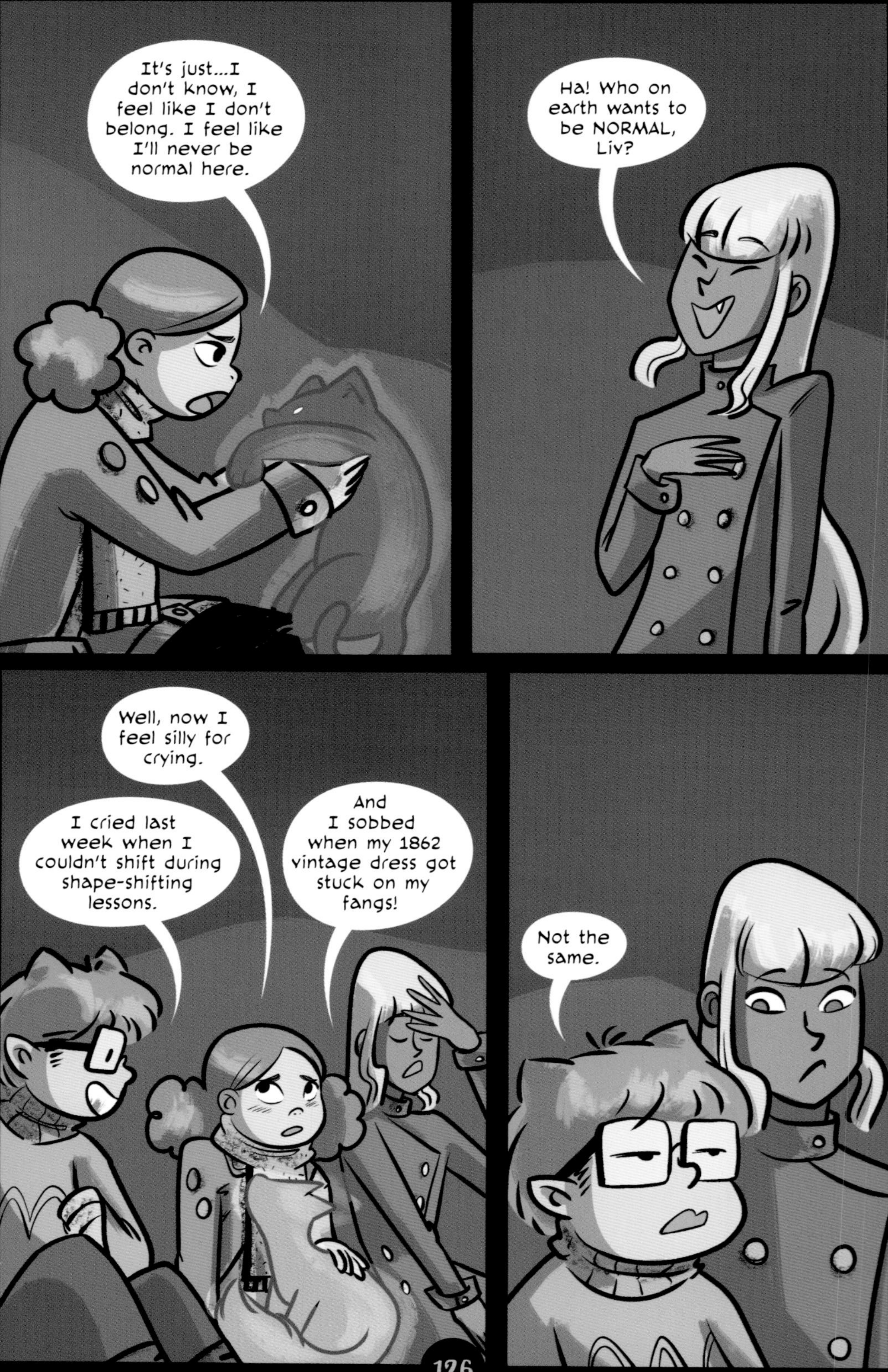
It's just...I don't know, I feel like I don't belong. I feel like I'll never be normal here.
Ha! Who on earth wants to be NORMAL, Liv?
Well, now I feel silly for crying.
I cried last week when I couldn't shift during shape-shifting lessons.
And I sobbed when my 1862 vintage dress got stuck on my fangs!
Not the same.

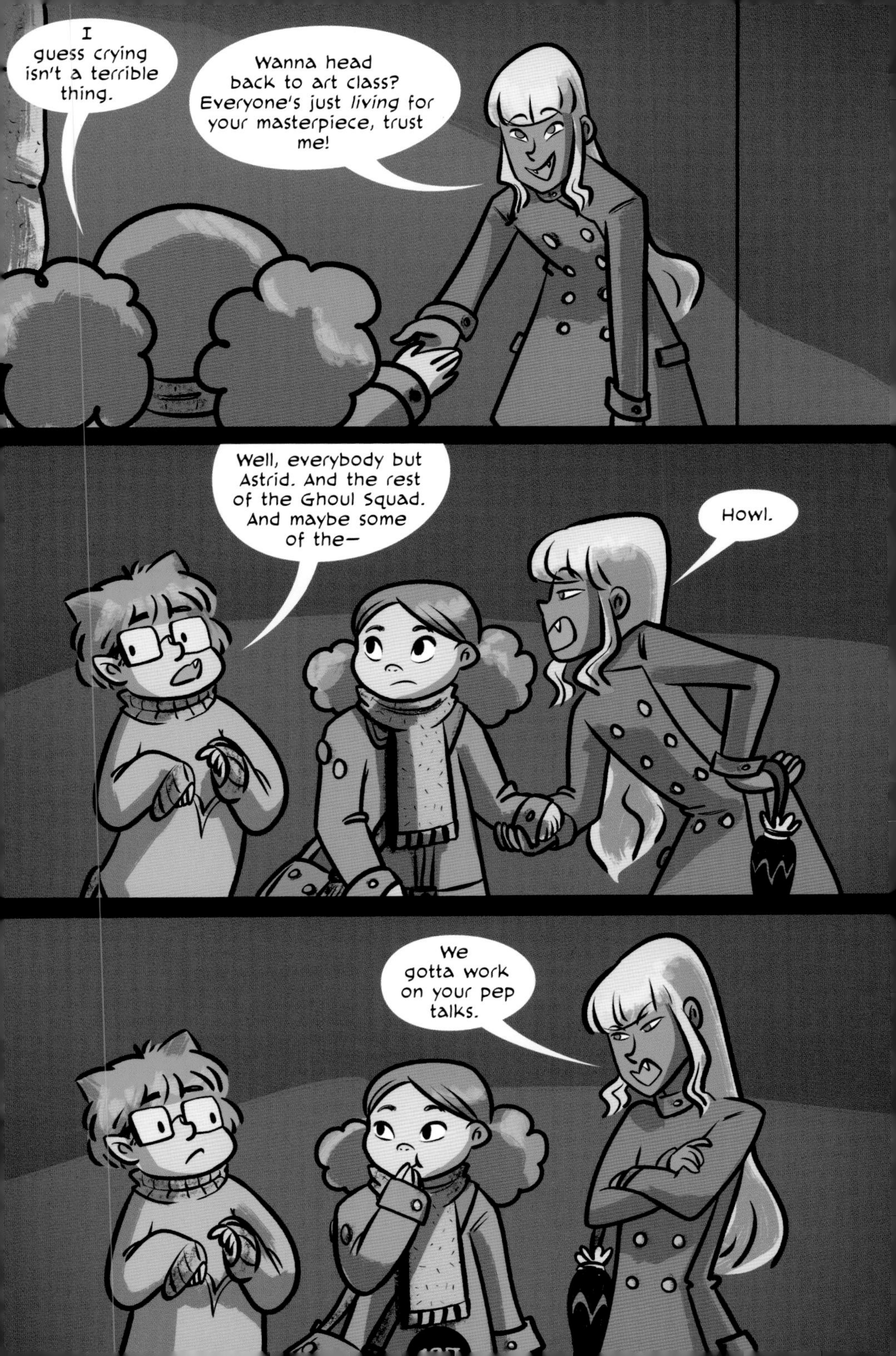
I guess crying isn't a terrible thing.
Wanna head back to art class? Everyone's just *living* for your masterpiece, trust me!
Well, everybody but Astrid. And the rest of the Ghoul Squad. And maybe some of the—
Howl.
We gotta work on your pep talks.

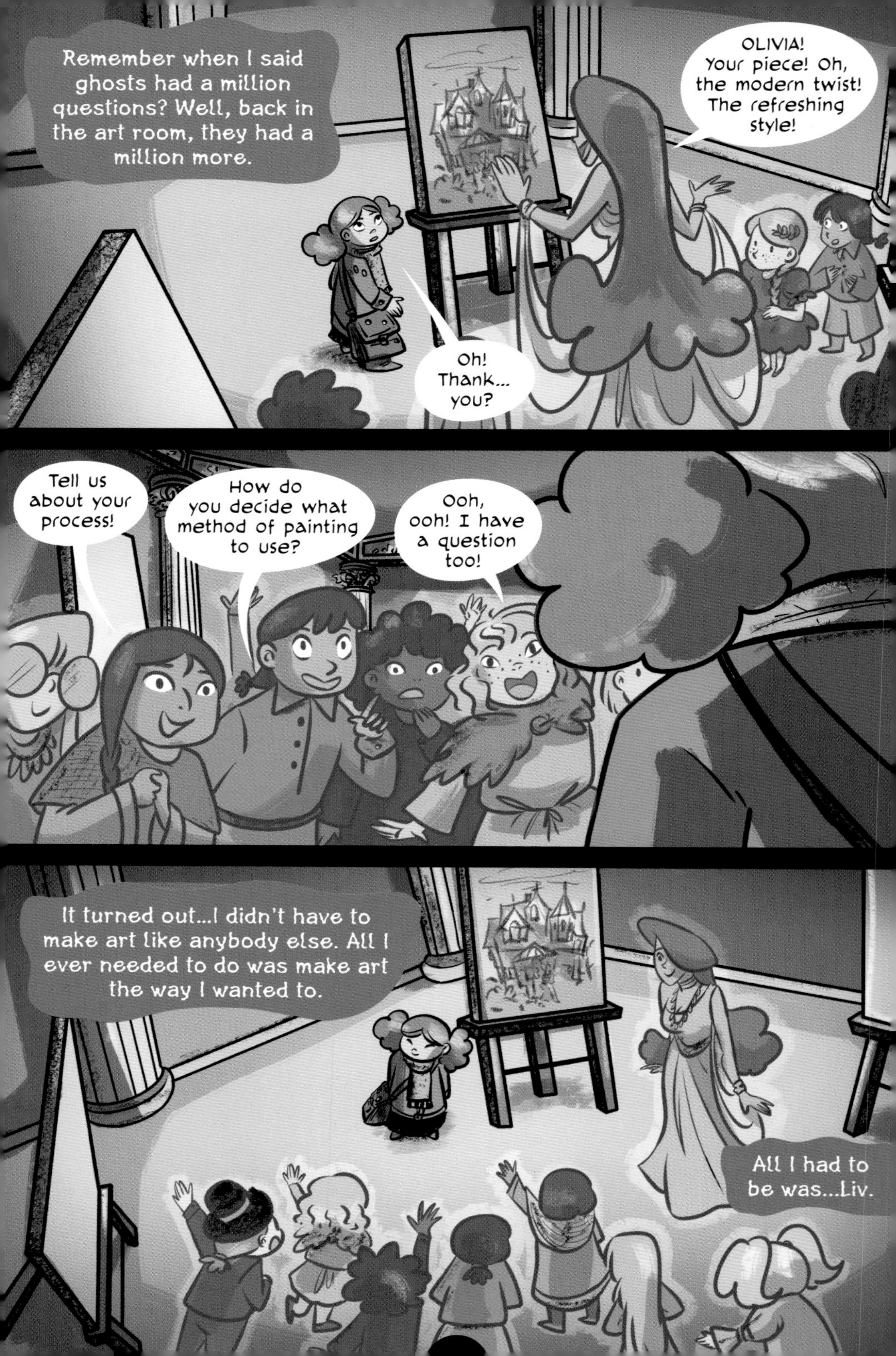
Remember when I said ghosts had a million questions? Well, back in the art room, they had a million more.
OLIVIA! Your piece! Oh, the modern twist! The refreshing style!
Oh! Thank... you?
Tell us about your process!
How do you decide what method of painting to use?
Ooh, ooh! I have a question too!
It turned out...I didn't have to make art like anybody else. All I ever needed to do was make art the way I wanted to.
All I had to be was...Liv.

CHAPTER 10

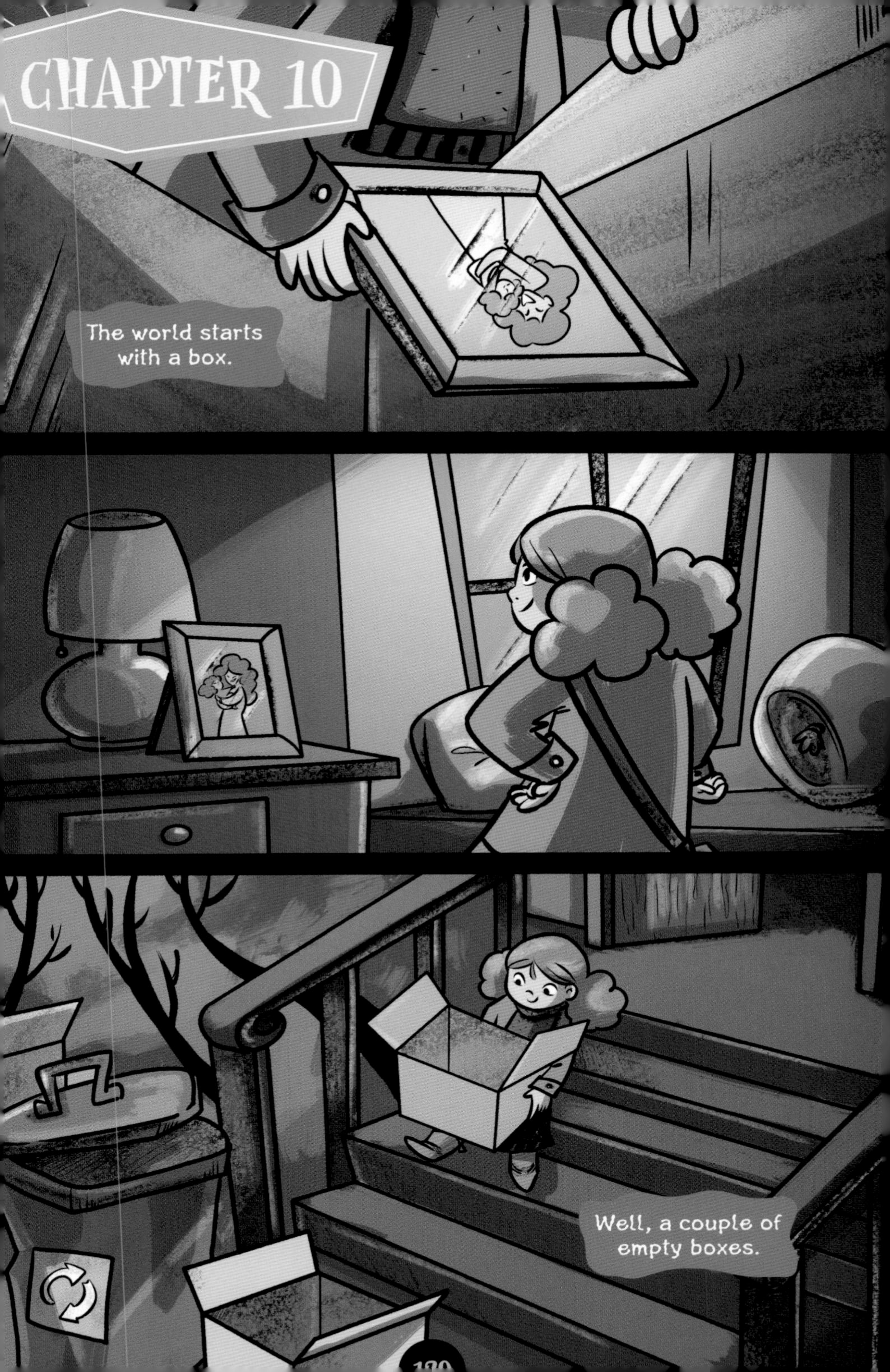
The world starts with a box.
Well, a couple of empty boxes.

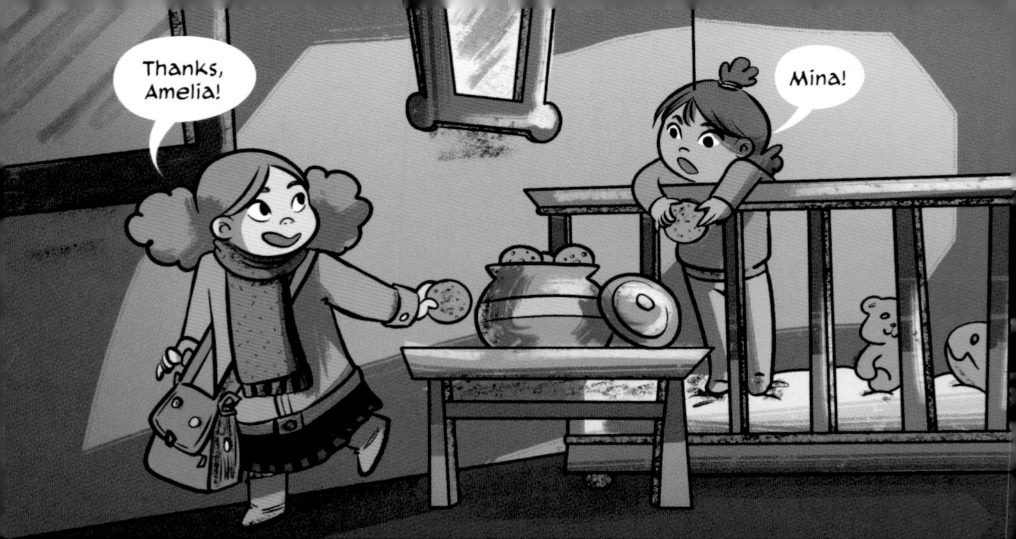
Thanks, Amelia!
Mina!
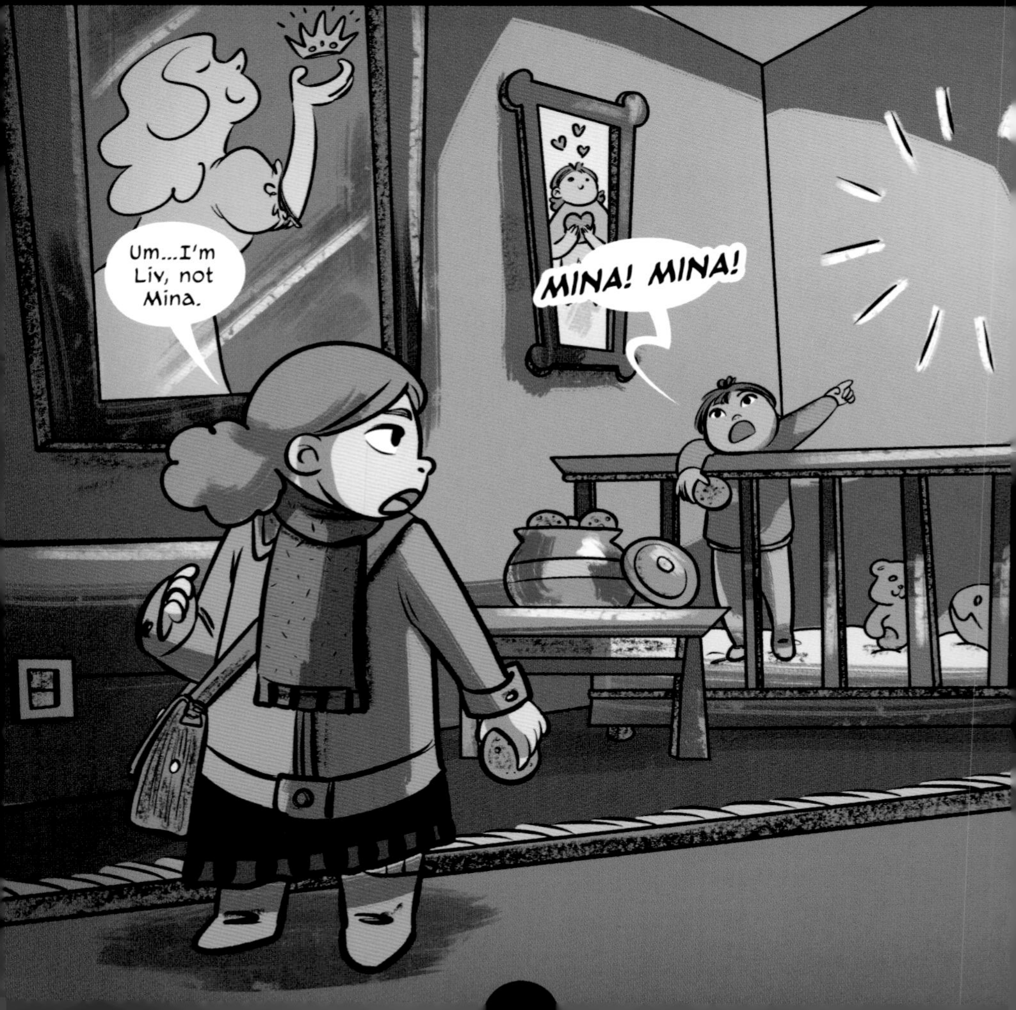
Um...I'm Liv, not Mina.
MINA! MINA!

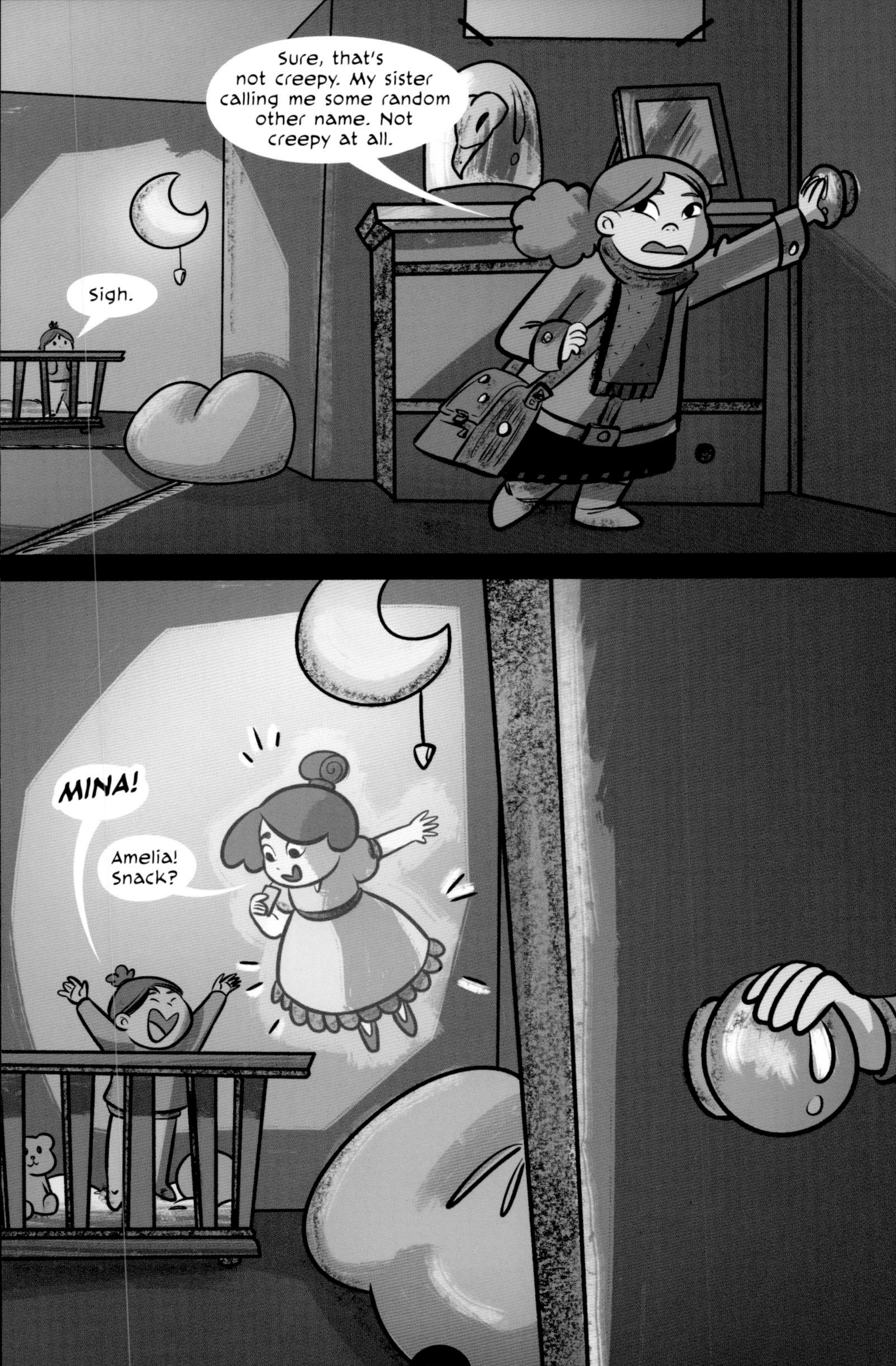
Sure, that's not creepy. My sister calling me some random other name. Not creepy at all.
Sigh.
MINA!
Amelia! Snack?

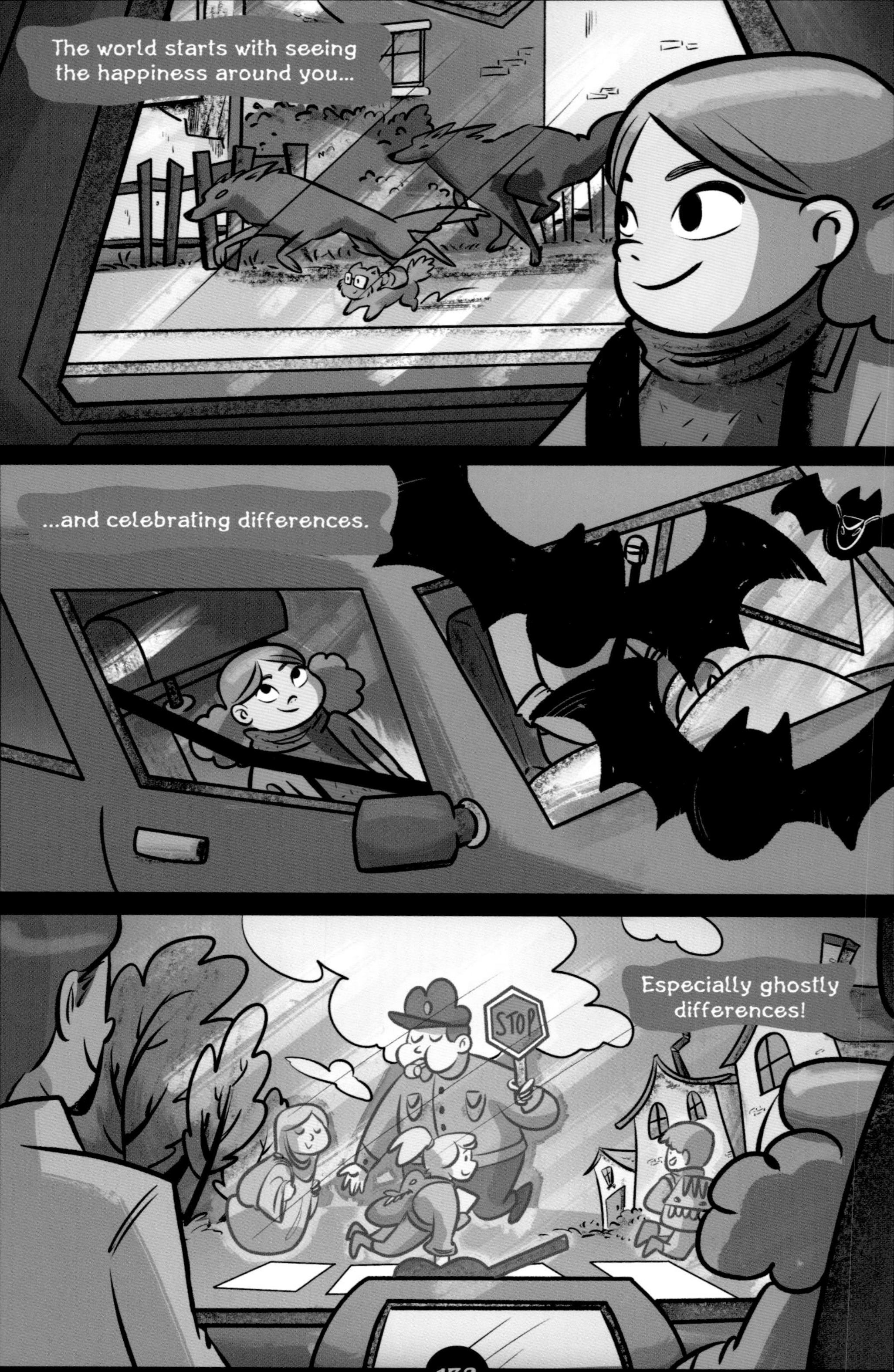
The world starts with seeing the happiness around you...
...and celebrating differences.
Especially ghostly differences!
STOP

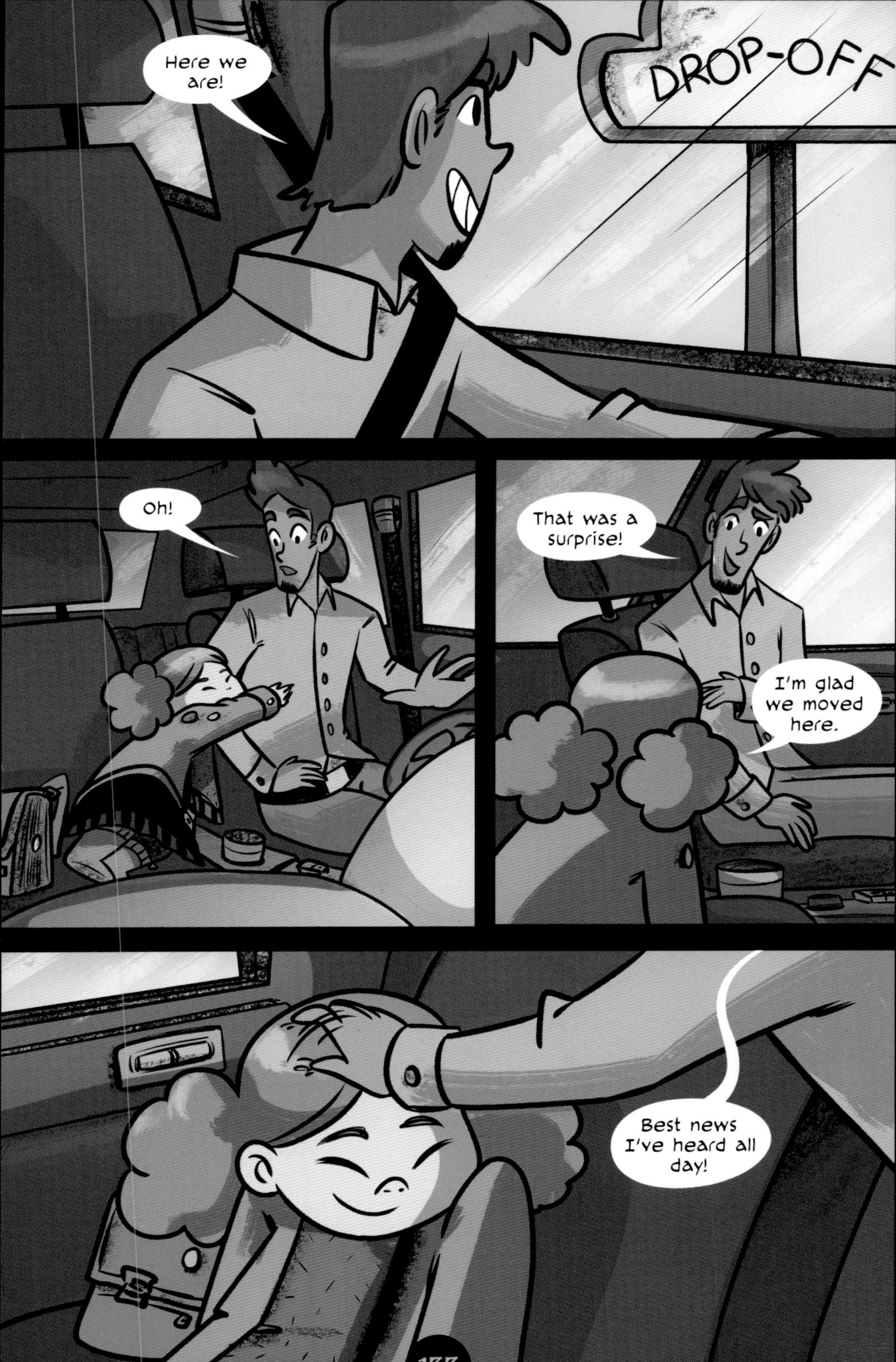

Here we are!
DROP-OFF
Oh!
That was a surprise!
I'm glad we moved here.
Best news I've heard all day!

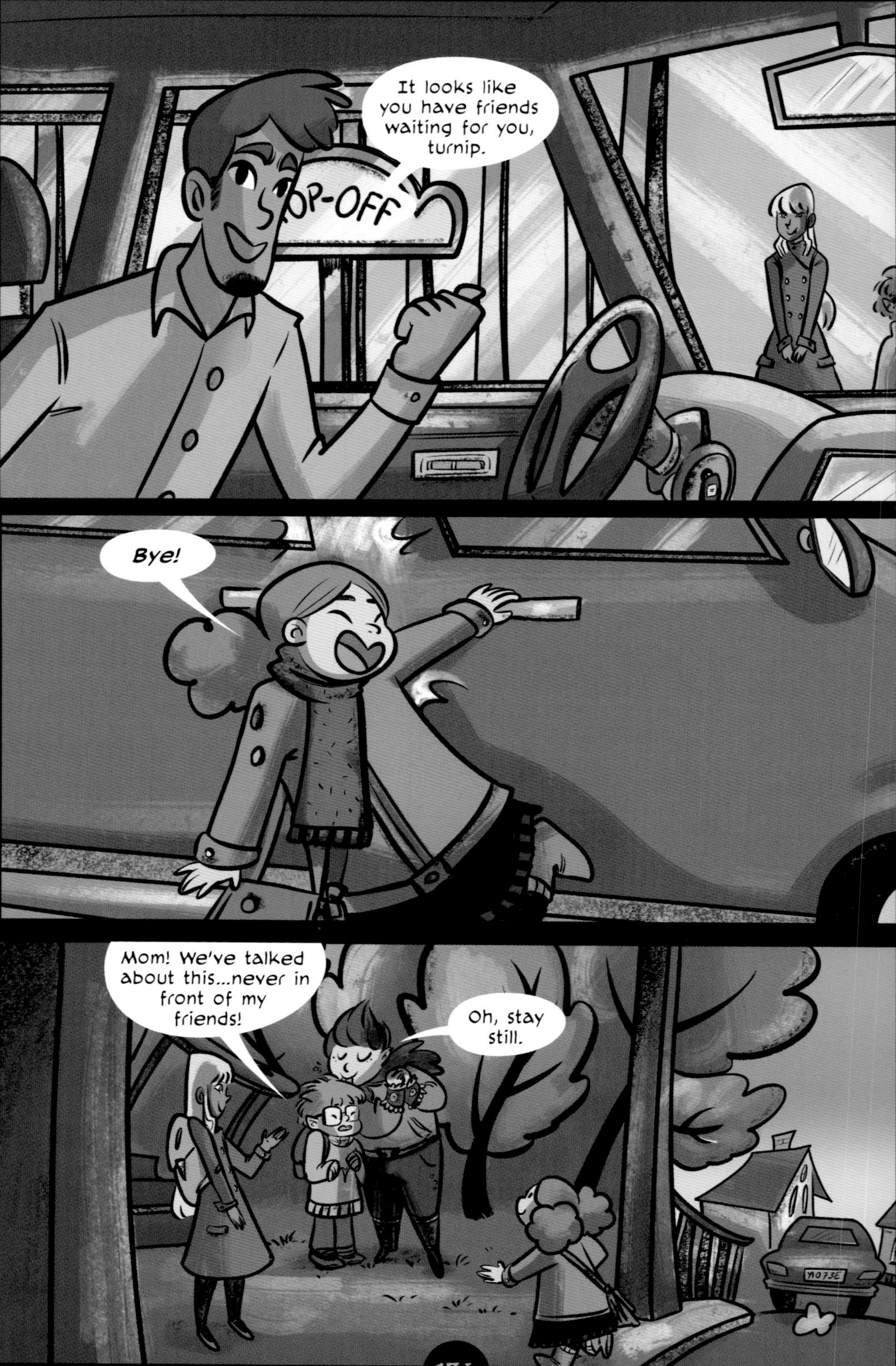

It looks like you have friends waiting for you, turnip.
OP-OFF
Bye!
Mom! We've talked about this...never in front of my friends!
Oh, stay still.

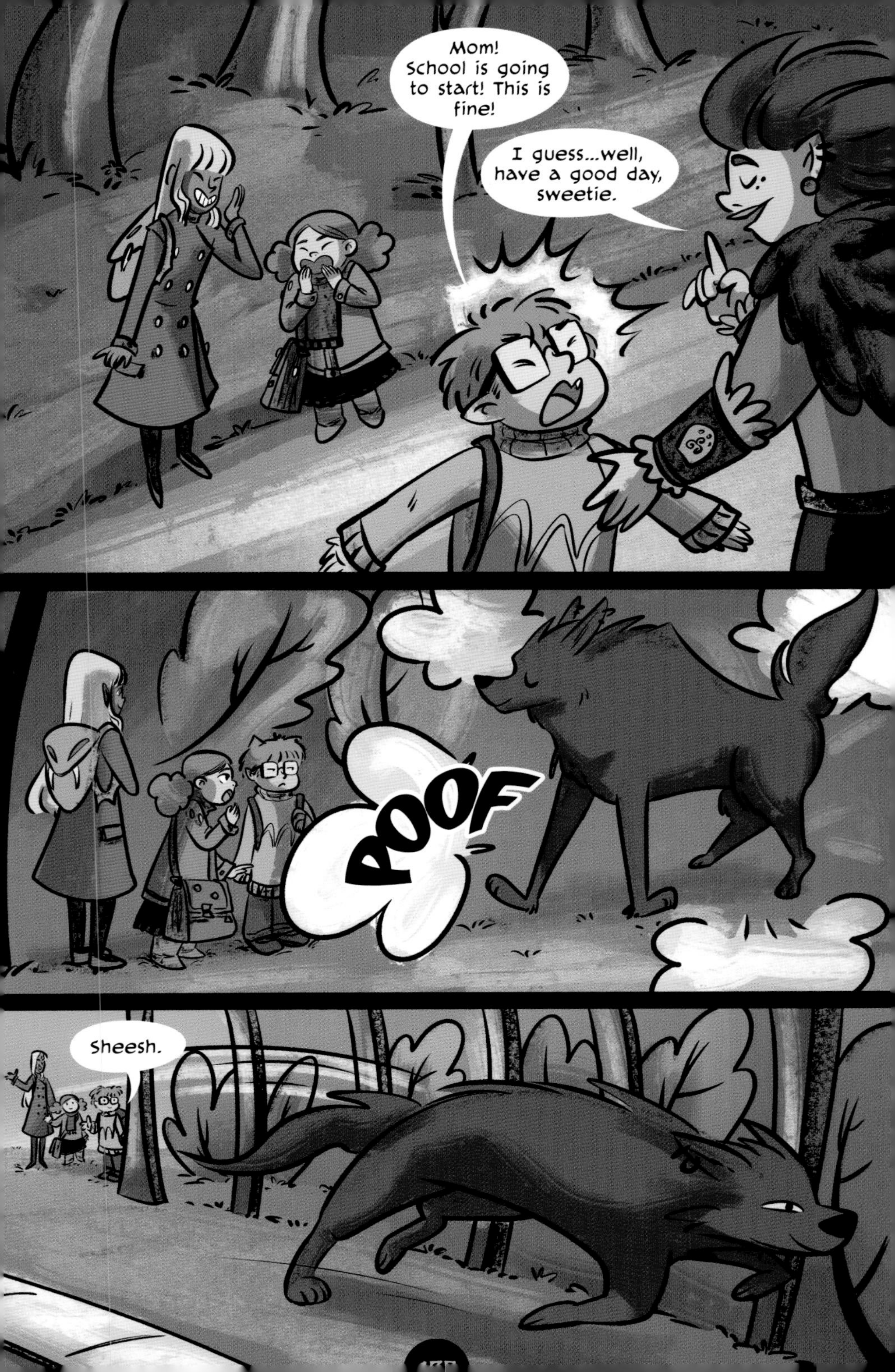

Mom! School is going to start! This is fine!
I guess...well, have a good day, sweetie.
POOF
Sheesh.

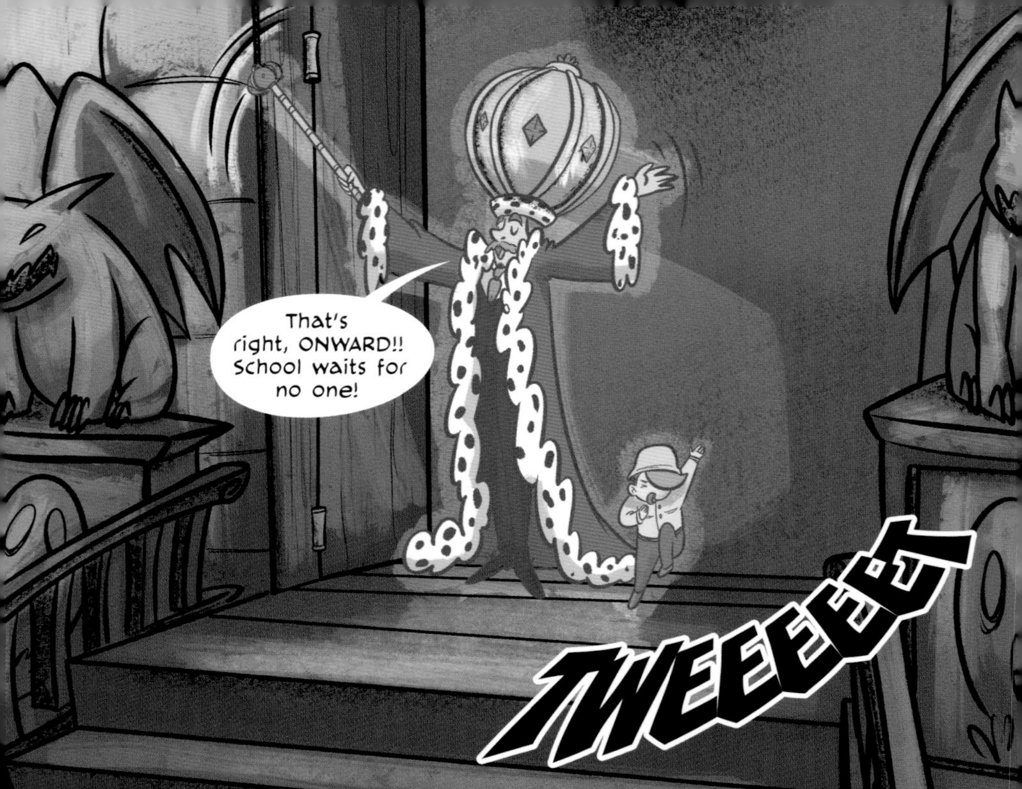
That's right, ONWARD!! School waits for no one!
TWEEEEET
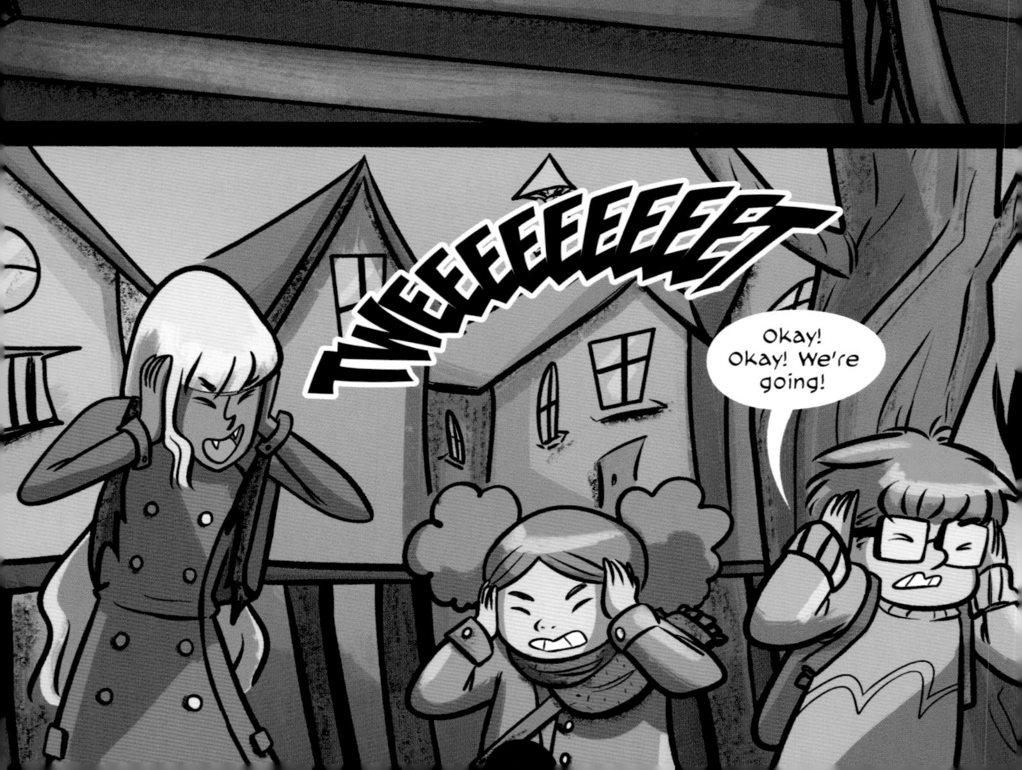
TWEEEEEEEEET
Okay! Okay! We're going!

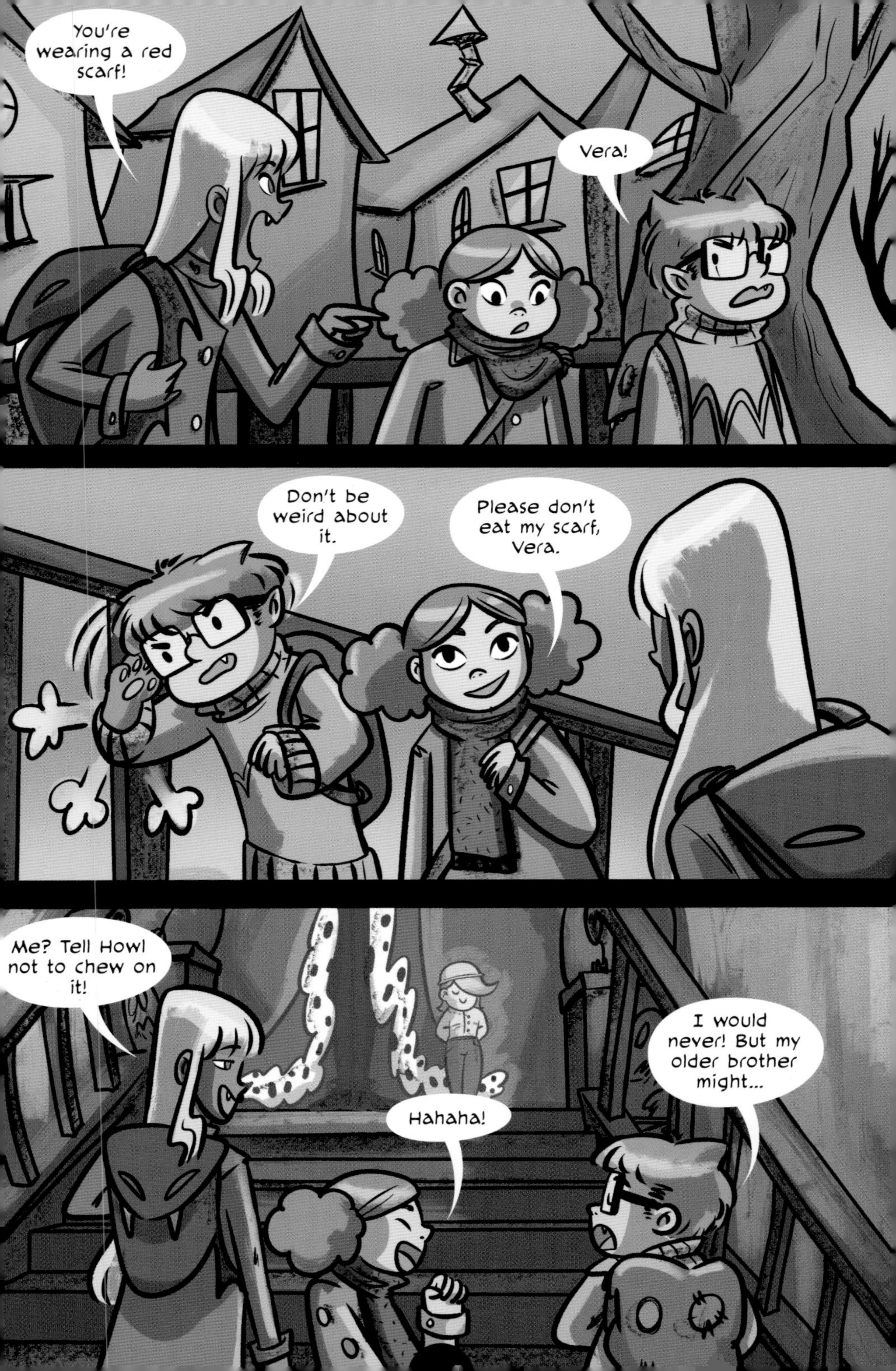
You're wearing a red scarf!
Vera!
Don't be weird about it.
Please don't eat my scarf, Vera.
Me? Tell Howl not to chew on it!
Hahaha!
I would never! But my older brother might...

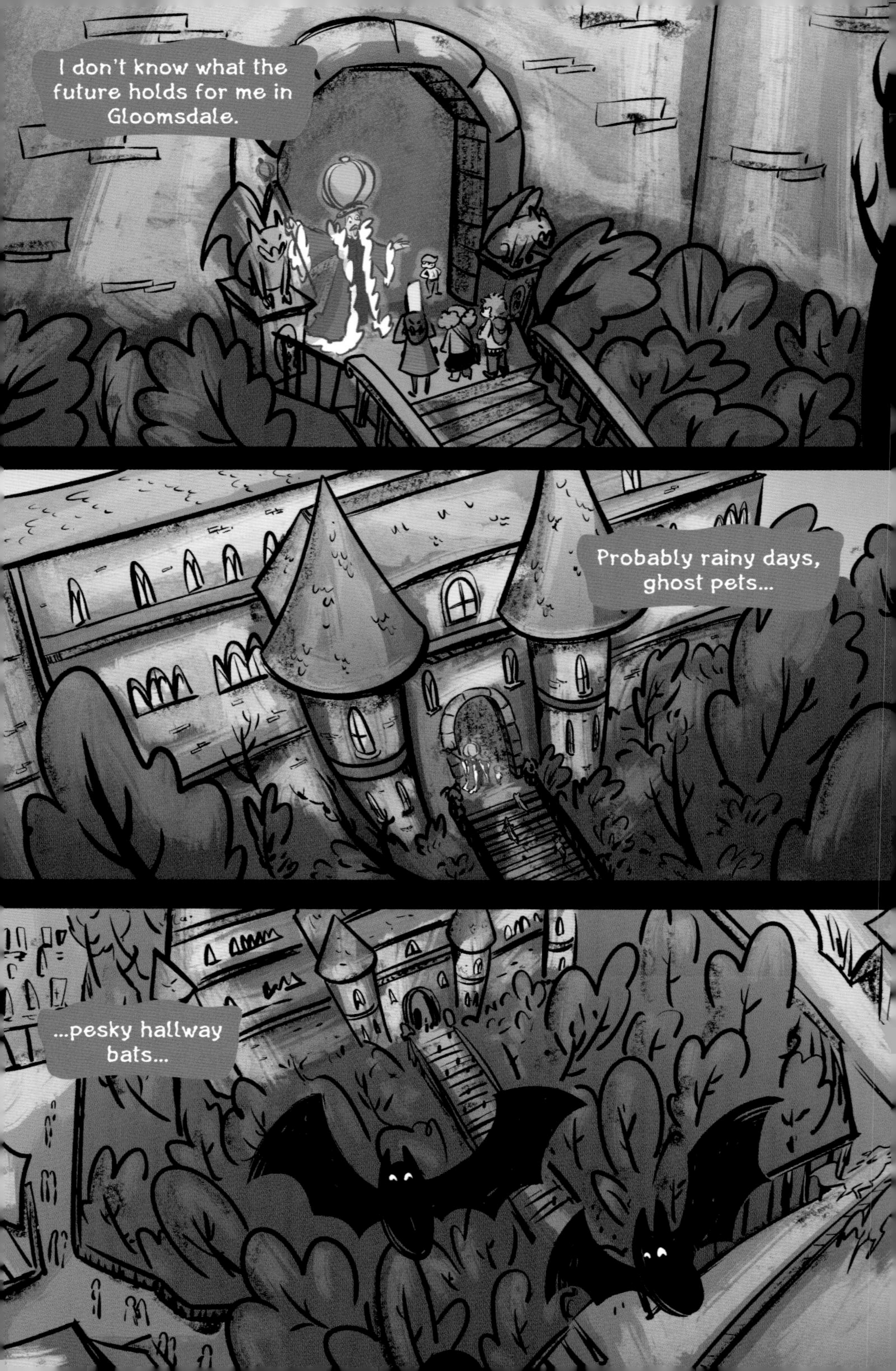
I don't know what the future holds for me in Gloomsdale.
Probably rainy days, ghost pets...
...pesky hallway bats...

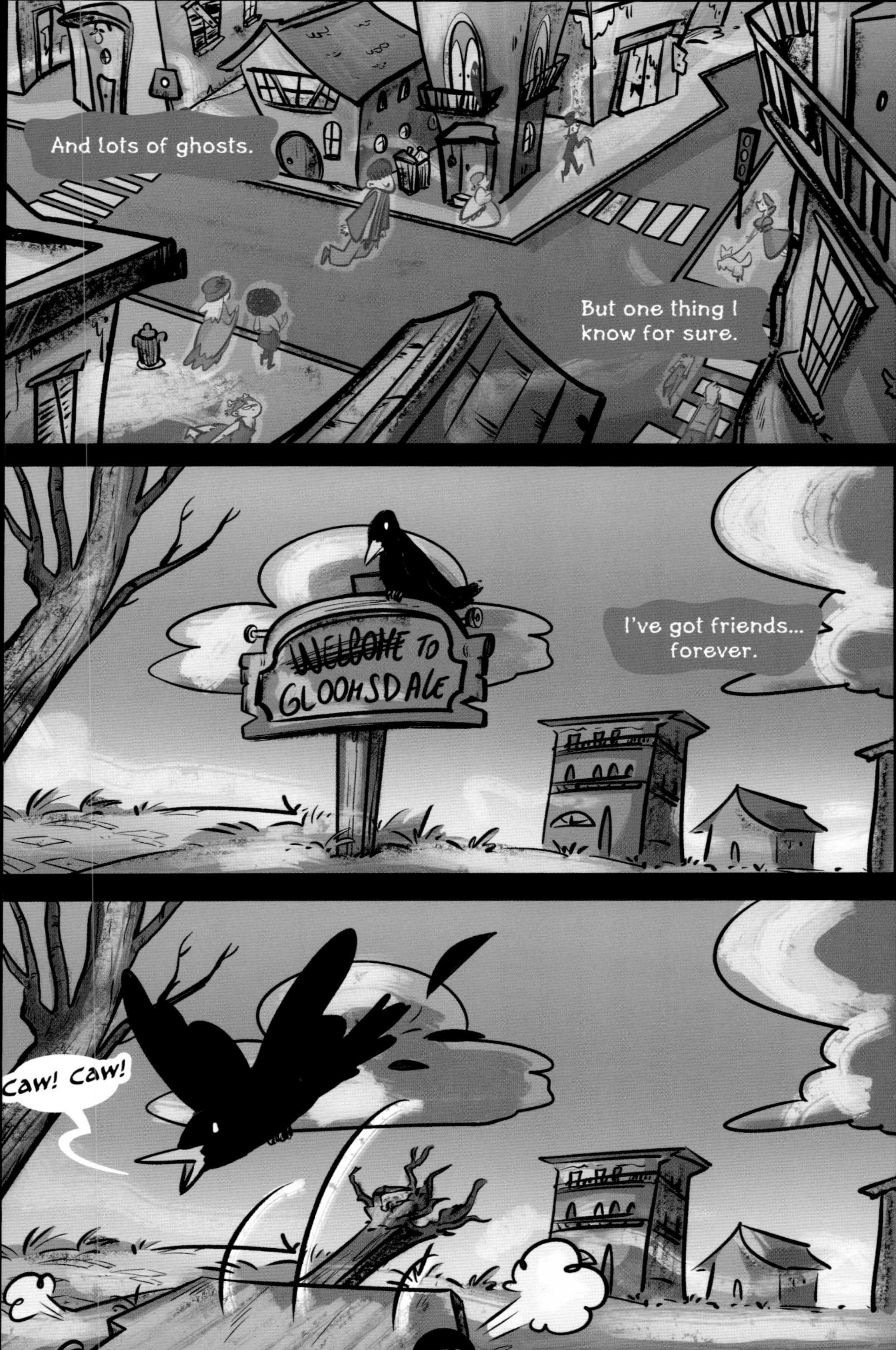
And lots of ghosts.
But one thing I know for sure.
WELCOME TO
GLOOMSDALE
I've got friends... forever.
CAW! CAW!

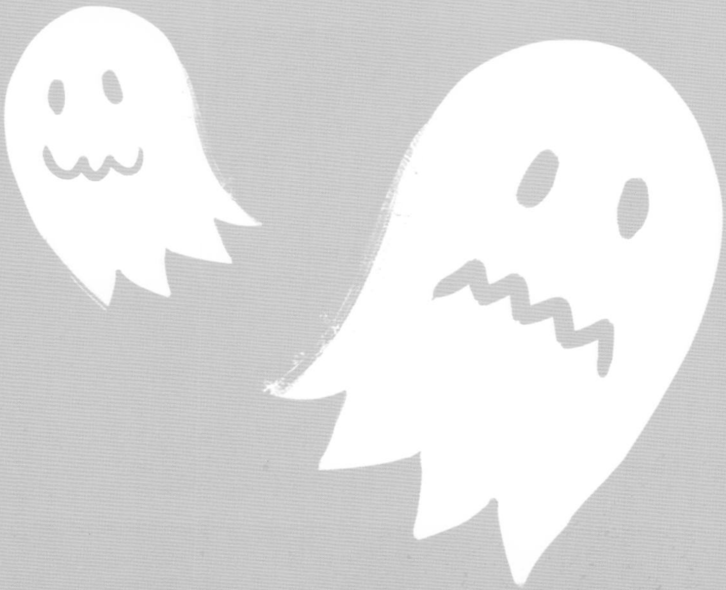

Can't get enough of

Spirited?

Check out the next adventure...

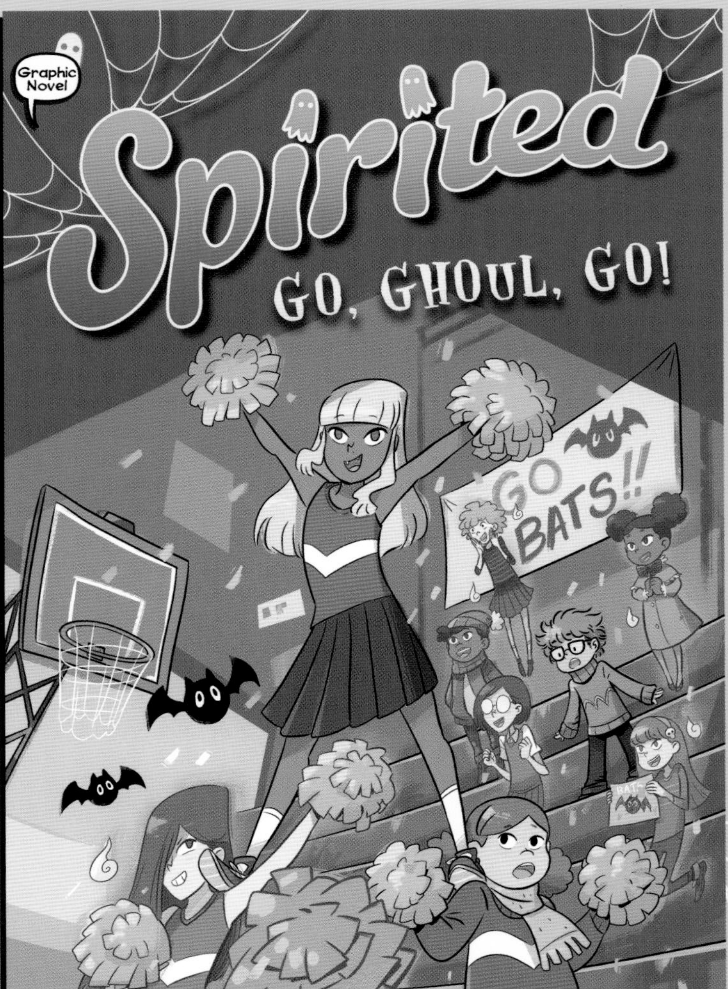

Graphic Novel
Spirited
GO, GHOUL, GO!
GO BATS!!

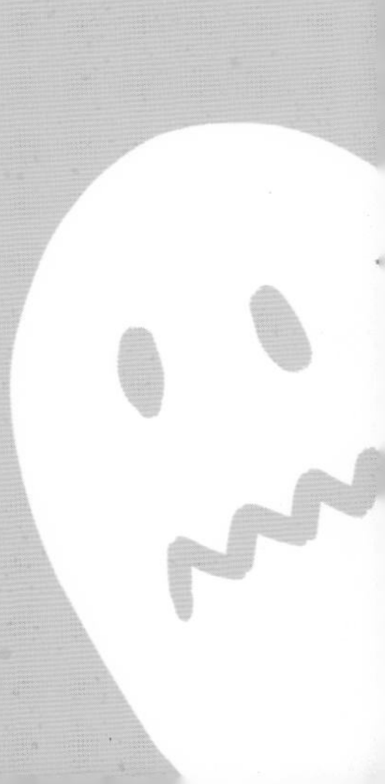